NEW TOEIC
一本攻克新制多益
聽力 ╋ 閱讀
700⁺

**完全比照
最新考題趨勢精準命題**

不容錯過的多益應考攻略，透過短期密集訓練，培養高效解題思維，
一網打盡聽力閱讀 Part 1~Part 7 所有題型！

Eduwill語學研究所——著　關亭薇——譯

音檔使用說明

STEP 1

掃描書中 QRCode

STEP 2

快速註冊或登入 EZCourse

STEP 3
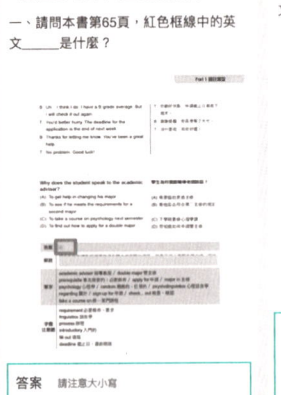
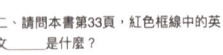

回答問題按送出

答案就在書中（需注意空格與大小寫）。

STEP 4

完成訂閱

該書右側會顯示「已訂閱」，表示已成功訂閱，即可點選播放本書音檔。

STEP 5

點選個人檔案

查看「我的訂閱紀錄」會顯示已訂閱本書，點選封面可到本書線上聆聽。

序言

考多益就選 EZ TALK！

對於不知道該朝哪個方向航行的人來說，並不存在所謂的順風
無論學習什麼，目標一定要明確。如果為了考取證照，就要設定在今年之內達成目標；如果想學好外語，就要設定能夠不依賴字幕看懂外國影集，或是在旅遊時能夠用當地語言，進行簡單的日常對話。如果在開始學習前，沒有設定明確的目標，很容易在過程中受到極小誘惑而動搖，或是受到看似不起眼的困難阻礙，最終陷入意外漫長的旅程，考多益也適用同樣道理。許多企業和國家考試經常以多益成績代替英文成績，因此如果你準備多益是為了是找份好工作，最重要的就是設定明確的目標分數。如此一來才能不受外力動搖，早早實現目標。若職業或工作內容與英文並無密切相關，一般要求的分數約莫落在 600 至 700 分。由於多益測驗中常考題型有一定的出題模式，命題趨勢變化不大，因此只要有本設計優良的教材作為後盾，就能輕鬆取得 700 分。

只需短短兩週，短期內取得 700 分以上的學習成果
多益要考到 700 分，並不需要特別厲害的英文知識。多益的對話和文章基本上都是以日常商務情境為基礎，當中使用的詞彙和句型，往往會重複出現在每次測驗中。本書內容讓您在原有的英文基礎之上，添加必要的「解題技巧」，協助您更有效率地解題，考取目標分數。藉由大數據分析過去三年的多益歷屆試題，精選考取 700 分必備的常考考題，以協助您實現目標。因此本書過濾掉太過困難的題目和複雜多餘的說明，僅收錄目標 700 分以上所需的核心內容。

目次

LC

PART 1

照片描述		22
UNIT 01	人物照片	24
UNIT 02	事物照與風景照	26
高分祕訣		28
PART TEST		30

PART 2

應答問題		36
UNIT 03	Who, What, Which 問句	38
UNIT 04	When, Where 問句	40
UNIT 05	How, Why 問句	42
UNIT 06	一般問句、表示建議或要求的問句	44
UNIT 07	附加問句、選擇疑問句	46
UNIT 08	間接問句、直述句	48
高分祕訣		50
PART TEST		52

PART 3

簡短對話		56
UNIT 09	詢問主旨或目的	58
UNIT 10	詢問說話者或地點	60
UNIT 11	詢問相關細節	62
UNIT 12	詢問建議或要求	64
UNIT 13	詢問下一步的行動	66
UNIT 14	詢問說話者的意圖	68
UNIT 15	圖表整合題	70
PART TEST		72

PART 4

簡短獨白		78
UNIT 16	通話訊息	80
UNIT 17	公告與導引	82
UNIT 18	演說與講座	84
UNIT 19	廣告與廣播	86
UNIT 20	觀光與參訪	88
PART TEST		90

RC

PART 5

句子填空		96
UNIT 01 名詞		100
UNIT 02 代名詞與限定詞		102
UNIT 03 形容詞與副詞		106
UNIT 04 介系詞與連接詞		108
UNIT 05 動詞		112
UNIT 06 動狀詞		114
UNIT 07 關係代名詞		116
UNIT 08 詞彙		120
PART TEST		128

PART 6

段落填空		134
UNIT 09 時態		136
UNIT 10 詞彙		138
UNIT 11 連接副詞		140
UNIT 12 句子插入題		142
PART TEST		144

PART 7

閱讀理解		150
UNIT 13 電子郵件與信件		152
UNIT 14 文字簡訊與線上聊天		156
UNIT 15 報導、公告、廣告		160
UNIT 16 雙篇與多篇文章		166
PART TEST		176

實戰模擬試題　　186

本書特色

LC

列出各大題的考題重點及解題策略
精選多益聽力測驗中最常出現的考題類型，並列出各題型的解題策略。特別收錄 PART 3 和 PART 4 中經常出現的解題線索，培養從聽力音檔中迅速找出答案的能力。

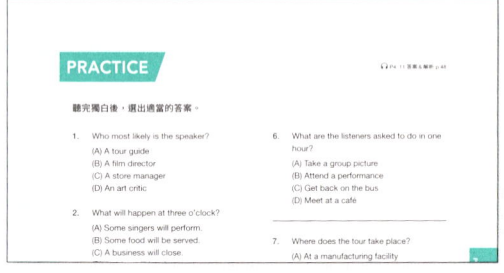

PRACTICE
全面分析近年的多益歷屆試題，精選符合聽力命題方向的關鍵考題。讓讀者能立刻將剛學到的知識應用至考題中，確實熟悉考試內容，並為實戰做好充分準備。

高分祕訣
對多益新手來說，PART 1 和 PART 2 為相對容易提高分數的大題。因此本書收錄兩大題最實用的得分祕訣，幫助讀者獲取高分。建議讀者仔細研讀，便能在最短時間內，戰勝多益測驗。

RC

靠理論鞏固基礎
全面分析最新命題方向，精選出達成目標分數 700 分以上所需的重點知識。

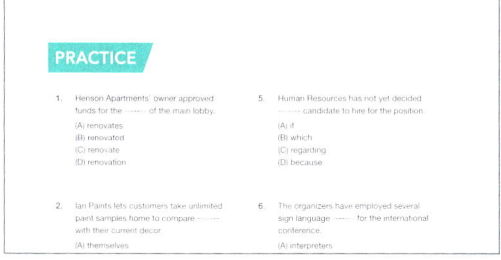

CHECK-UP & PRACTICE
透過「CHECK-UP」單元，輕鬆檢查前面學習的理論和解題策略，並於「PRACTICE」單元診斷測驗練習反映最新命題方向的仿真試題，鞏固解題實力。

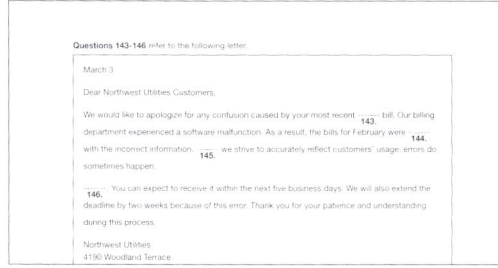

PART TEST
在各大題章節的最後，以「PART TEST」單元作結，藉此熟悉實戰臨場感。

7

兩週速成學習計畫表

聽力與閱讀分開的學習計畫表

第1週	DAY 1	DAY 2	DAY 3	DAY 4	DAY 5	DAY 6	DAY 7
聽力	UNIT 01~02 月　日	UNIT 03~05 月　日	UNIT 06~08 月　日	UNIT 09~12 月　日	UNIT 13~15 月　日	UNIT 16~18 月　日	UNIT 19~20 月　日

第2週	DAY 8	DAY 9	DAY 10	DAY 11	DAY 12	DAY 13	DAY 14
閱讀	UNIT 01~03 月　日	UNIT 04~06 月　日	UNIT 07~08 月　日	UNIT 09~12 月　日	UNIT 13~14 月　日	UNIT 15~16 月　日	實戰模擬試題 月　日

聽力與閱讀同時的學習計畫表

第1週	DAY 1	DAY 2	DAY 3	DAY 4	DAY 5	DAY 6	DAY 7
聽力 閱讀	UNIT01 UNIT01 月　日	UNIT02 UNIT02 月　日	UNIT 03-04 UNIT 03 月　日	UNIT 05-06 UNIT 04 月　日	UNIT 07 UNIT 05 月　日	UNIT 08 UNIT 06 月　日	UNIT 09-10 UNIT 07 月　日

第2週	DAY 8	DAY 9	DAY 10	DAY 11	DAY 12	DAY 13	DAY 14
聽力 閱讀	UNIT 11-12 UNIT 08 月　日	UNIT 13-14 UNIT 09-10 月　日	UNIT 15 UNIT 11-12 月　日	UNIT 16-17 UNIT 13-14 月　日	UNIT 18-19 UNIT 15 月　日	UNIT 20 UNIT 16 月　日	實戰模擬試題 月　日

四週速成學習計畫表

聽力與閱讀分開的學習計畫表

第1週	DAY 1	DAY 2	DAY 3	DAY 4	DAY 5
聽力	UNIT 01~02 月　日	UNIT 03~04 月　日	UNIT 05~06 月　日	UNIT 07~08 月　日	UNIT 09~10 月　日

第2週	DAY 6	DAY 7	DAY 8	DAY 9	DAY 10
聽力	UNIT 11~12 月　日	UNIT 13~14 月　日	UNIT 15~16 月　日	UNIT 17~18 月　日	UNIT 19~20 月　日

第3週	DAY 11	DAY 12	DAY 13	DAY 14	DAY 15
閱讀	UNIT 01~02 月　日	UNIT 03~04 月　日	UNIT 05~07 月　日	UNIT 08 月　日	UNIT 09~10 月　日

第4週	DAY 16	DAY 17	DAY 18	DAY 19	DAY 20
閱讀	UNIT 11~12 月　日	UNIT 13~14 月　日	UNIT 15 月　日	UNIT 16 月　日	實戰模擬試題 月　日

聽力與閱讀同時的學習計畫表

第1週	DAY 1	DAY 2	DAY 3	DAY 4	DAY 5
聽力 閱讀	UNIT 01~02 UNIT 01 月　日	UNIT 03 UNIT 02 月　日	UNIT 04 UNIT 03 月　日	UNIT 05 UNIT 04 月　日	UNIT 06 UNIT 05 月　日

第2週	DAY 6	DAY 7	DAY 8	DAY 9	DAY 10
聽力 閱讀	UNIT 07 UNIT 06 月　日	UNIT 08 UNIT 07 月　日	UNIT 09 UNIT 08 名詞 月　日	UNIT 10 UNIT 08 形容詞 月　日	UNIT 11 UNIT 08 副詞 月　日

第3週	DAY 11	DAY 12	DAY 13	DAY 14	DAY 15
聽力 閱讀	UNIT 12 UNIT 08 動詞 月　日	UNIT 13 UNIT 09 月　日	UNIT 14 UNIT 10 月　日	UNIT 15 UNIT 11 月　日	UNIT 16 UNIT 12 月　日

第4週	DAY 16	DAY 17	DAY 18	DAY 19	DAY 20
聽力 閱讀	UNIT 17 UNIT 13 月　日	UNIT 18 UNIT 14 月　日	UNIT 19 UNIT 15 月　日	UNIT 20 UNIT 16 月　日	實戰模擬試題 月　日

多益測驗介紹

何謂多益測驗？

TOEIC為Test of English for International Communication（國際溝通英語測驗）的簡稱，測驗目的為測試英語非母語的人士，是否具備在日常生活或商務上所需的實用英語能力。

測驗題型

題型	Part		題數		時間	分數
聽力 (LC)	Part 1	照片描述	6	100	45分	495分
	Part 2	應答問題	25			
	Part 3	簡短對話	39			
	Part 4	簡短獨白	30			
閱讀 (RC)	Part 5	句子填空	30	100	75分	495分
	Part 6	段落填空	16			
	Part 7	閱讀理解	單篇閱讀	29		
			雙篇閱讀	10		
			多篇閱讀	15		
總計	7 Parts		200題		120分	990分

命題範圍與主題

命題範圍涵蓋實際用於日常生活和工作中的主題，不會針對特定文化或職業出題。聽力測驗包含美國腔、英國腔、澳洲腔等各國發音。

一般商務	簽約、協商、業務、宣傳、行銷、商業企劃
金融財務	預算、投資、稅金、請款、會計
研發	研究、產品開發
製造	工廠管理、生產線、品管
人事	徵人、升遷、退休、員工培訓、新進員工
辦公室	會議、備忘錄、電話、傳真、電子郵件、辦公室設備與用具
活動	學術研討會、宴會、聚餐、頒獎典禮、博覽會、產品發表會
房地產	建築、房地產買賣和租賃、企業用地、水電瓦斯設備
旅遊和休閒娛樂	交通工具、機場、車站、旅遊行程、飯店與租車預訂、延期或取消、電影、展覽、表演

報名方式
如何報名多益測驗？
- 採網路報名方式，請至台灣多益測驗主辦官網（https://www.toeic.com.tw）查詢報名時間。
- 報名測驗需提供近6個月內拍攝的照片，請提前準備好照片的JPG檔案。
- 多益追加報名約在考前3週開放，需另外支付追加報名費用。建議提前確認報名時間，並於規定時間內完成報名。

應試當天攜帶物品

身分證	有效的身分證件（中華民國國民身分證正本或有效期限內之「護照」正本）。
書寫用具	2B鉛筆、橡皮擦（不可使用原子筆或簽字筆）。

測驗流程

上午場次	下午場次	測驗流程
09:30 – 09:45	14:30 ~ 14:45	說明如何填寫答案卡
09:45 – 09:50	14:45 ~ 14:50	休息時間
09:50 – 10:05	14:50 ~ 15:05	確認身分證件
10:05 – 10:10	15:05 ~ 15:10	發放試題本與確認是否有破損
10:10 – 10:55	15:10 ~ 15:55	聽力測驗（Listening Test）
10:55 – 12:10	15:55 ~ 17:10	閱讀測驗（Reading Test）

成績查詢

測驗分數	考生可於成績開放查詢期間內至多益官方測驗服務專區查詢成績。
成績單寄送	成績單將於測驗結束後的第12個工作日以平信方式寄出。期限內可申請補發，免費補發僅限一次。

各大題題型介紹

PART 1 照片描述

題型說明	看試題本上的照片，聽完四個短句後，選出最符合照片的描述。
題數	6題
照片類型	單人獨照、雙人、多人照片、事物與風景照

PART 2 應答問題

題型說明	聽完題目句與三句回應句後，選出最適當的答案。
題數	25題
題目句類型	Wh開頭問句、一般問句、表示建議或要求的問句、附加問句、選擇疑問句、間接問句、直述句

題本示意圖

各大題題型介紹

PART 3 簡短對話

題型說明	聽完雙人或三人對話後，針對相關的三道考題選出最適當的答案。
題數	39題（13組對話 x3題）
對話類型	雙人對話（11組）與三人對話（2組） 最後3組雙人對話（第62~70題）會同時附上圖表資訊。
考題類型	詢問主旨、目的、說話者、地點、相關細節、建議、要求、下一步的行動、即將發生的事、掌握意圖、圖表整合

題本示意圖

PRACTICE　　　　　　　　　　　🎧 P3_03 答案&解析 p.24

請聆聽對話，填寫空白處的句子後，選出適當的答案。

W　Hi, Mr. Davis. This is Christina Whitley from the Westbury Small Business Association.
M　Oh, yes. Hello, Ms. Whitley.
W　_____.
M　I see. I can probably still attend it.
W　I hope so. I'll e-mail you an updated registration packet. Also, your travel and registration fees will be covered by us.
M　Thank you. I'll double check whether or not I can participate in the event. If not, I will probably send my assistant manager in my place.

1. Why is the woman calling the man?
   (A) To request the payment of a bill
   (B) To inform him of a schedule change
   (C) To invite him to give a presentation
   (D) To share some management strategies

聽完對話後，選出適當的答案。

2. What are the speakers mainly discussing?
   (A) A headquarters relocation
   (B) A software upgrade
   (C) A proposed merger
   (D) A market regulation

3. What is the purpose of the woman's call?
   (A) To promote an event at a park
   (B) To introduce a cleaning service
   (C) To arrange a facility tour
   (D) To ask about volunteer opportunities

4. What is the conversation mainly about?
   (A) Organizing some merchandise
   (B) Training staff members
   (C) Changing a window display
   (D) Labeling boxes for shipping

PART 4 簡短獨白

題型說明	聽完獨白後，針對相關的三道考題選出最適當的答案。
題數	30題（10篇獨白 x3題）
獨白類型	簡訊、公告、介紹、演說、講座、廣告、廣播、觀光、導覽等，最後2篇（第95~100題）會同時附上圖表資訊。
考題類型	詢問主旨、目的、說話者、聽者、地點、相關細節、建議、要求、下一步行動、即將發生的事、掌握意圖、圖表整合

題本示意圖

PRACTICE

P4_11 答案&解析 p.48

聽完獨白後，選出適當的答案。

1. Who most likely is the speaker?
   (A) A tour guide
   (B) A film director
   (C) A store manager
   (D) An art critic

2. What will happen at three o'clock?
   (A) Some singers will perform.
   (B) Some food will be served.
   (C) A business will close.
   (D) A video will be shown.

3. What is The First Step?
   (A) A club
   (B) A book
   (C) A podcast
   (D) A play

4. Why is Hamilton Manor famous?
   (A) It has been the filming location for movies.
   (B) It was designed by a prominent architect.
   (C) It is the venue for a popular festival.
   (D) It has an extensive art collection.

5. According to the speaker, what do visitors like to do at Hamilton Manor?
   (A) Make a wish
   (B) Sample food
   (C) Go swimming
   (D) Collect flowers

6. What are the listeners asked to do in one hour?
   (A) Take a group picture
   (B) Attend a performance
   (C) Get back on the bus
   (D) Meet at a café

7. Where does the tour take place?
   (A) At a manufacturing facility
   (B) At a nature park
   (C) At a concert hall
   (D) At a shopping center

8. What did Annette Harvey do?
   (A) She built a bridge.
   (B) She filmed a commercial.
   (C) She designed a building.
   (D) She donated some money.

9. What does the speaker mean when she says, "that area is closed to visitors"?
   (A) The tour will be shorter than usual.
   (B) A partial refund will be issued.
   (C) The listeners should not worry.
   (D) Some signs should be followed.

各大題題型介紹

PART 5 句子填空

題型說明	句子中會出現一個空格，從四個選項中選出最適合填入的單字或片語。
題數	30題
考題類型	・文法題（選出正確的文法） ・詞彙題（選出符合文意的詞彙）

題本示意圖

PRACTICE

答案 & 解析 p.59

1. Most voters ------- believe that the city's main roads need to be better maintained.
   (A) firm
   (B) firmness
   (C) firmer
   (D) firmly

2. There are several event signs ------- the wall that should be taken down within this month.
   (A) on
   (B) as
   (C) within
   (D) in

3. Ms. Hensley created a ------- database in which comments from Globe Autos customers can be stored.
   (A) securing
   (B) secure
   (C) secures
   (D) securely

4. The Parmona Museum offers hands-on workshops ------- short lectures.
   (A) for instance
   (B) whether
   (C) as well as
   (D) in case

5. The summer sales event will last ------- the month of July.
   (A) inside
   (B) throughout
   (C) even so
   (D) among

6. ------- Ms. Caruso rearranged the furniture in the waiting area, the space looked much larger.
   (A) After
   (B) Following
   (C) Notwithstanding
   (D) Especially

7. Bea's Beauty will ------- release its new foam cleanser on its website.
   (A) soon
   (B) due to
   (C) while
   (D) timely

8. The property will require extensive renovations before it is ------- to be used as an office.
   (A) suiting
   (B) suitability
   (C) suitable
   (D) suitably

110

PART 6 段落填空

題型說明	文章中會出現四個空格，分別選出最適合填入的單字、片語或句子。
題數	16題（4篇文章×4題）
考題類型	・文法題（選出正確的文法） ・詞彙題（選出符合文意的詞彙） ・句子插入題（選出符合文意的句子）

題本示意圖

Questions 135-138 refer to the following e-mail.

To: All Redhawk Towers Tenants
From: Jennifer Milligan
Date: February 20
Subject: Power outage

Dear Redhawk Towers Tenants,

An interruption to the electricity supply ------- for all buildings on Jennings Street and Pine Street
                  135.
between 12th and 14th Avenue. Power will be shut off in order to perform essential maintenance
tasks. Work will take place on February 25 and 26 from 9 A.M. to noon.

Please plan ahead for the outage on ------- day. Computers should be shut down prior to the
                  136.
outage. -------. Food stored in refrigerators and freezers will be fine if the doors are kept closed.
      137.
Thank you for your ------- and patience.
           138.

Jennifer Milligan
Property Manager, Redhawk Towers

135. (A) has scheduled
(B) schedules
(C) is scheduled
(D) is scheduling

136. (A) only
(B) most
(C) all
(D) each

137. (A) Several apartment units are now available.
(B) Those left on could be damaged by an unexpected shutdown.
(C) We can confirm that safety is taken seriously.
(D) The noise will no longer be a disturbance to everyone.

138. (A) donation
(B) cooperation
(C) destination
(D) confirmation

GO ON TO THE NEXT PAGE

145

各大題題型介紹

PART 7 閱讀理解

題型說明	閱讀完文章後，針對該文章對應的2至5道題目選出適當的答案。	
文章數/題數	單篇閱讀	10篇（每篇2~4題；共29題）
	雙篇閱讀	2組（每組5題；共10題）
	多篇閱讀	3組（每組5題；共15題）
文章類型	電子郵件、信件、廣告、公告、備忘錄、報導、表格（網頁、問卷調查、請款單據）、簡訊對話紀錄等	
考題類型	詢問主旨、目的、相關細節、事實與否、推論、暗示、掌握意圖、同義詞、句子插入題	

共15篇文章（54題）

題本示意圖（單篇閱讀）

Questions 9-12 refer to the following article.

Art Corner
By Lance Colbert

When the worlds of business and art mix, it is sometimes difficult to find a balance. But local entrepreneurs Elizabeth Sanders and Timothy Marlowe are finding a way to make it work. Their new company, Art Phase, rents original paintings for commercial premises. This is great for businesses in Asheville that want a sophisticated decor but cannot afford to invest heavily in artwork.

Ms. Sanders and Mr. Marlowe got the idea while they were operating an accounting firm together. —[1]—. "We wanted to decorate our office to make a good first impression on clients," Ms. Sanders said. "However, we were just starting out, so there were a lot of other items to purchase. —[2]—. That's because trends change frequently, so paintings can look outdated after a while."

Mr. Marlowe is an amateur artist and is active in the local art community. He and Ms. Sanders founded Art Phase as a side business, and it is expected to be popular. —[3]—. Art Phase offers a wide range of paintings for rent, most of which were created by local artists. Those interested in renting artwork can have an Art Phase consultant visit their site to make recommendations based on the colors in the room and their personal style. Once selected, the artwork is delivered to the site, and it is also picked up for free at the end of the rental period. Customers can change their artwork once per quarter, and they can even receive notes from the artist about the inspiration behind the piece.

"Art Phase is a great opportunity for artists who are not yet established," explained Neil Patterson, president of the Asheville Artists Association. "They can have their art seen by many people while also earning a percentage of the rental fee. For those who can't afford a booth at Sunshine Street Market or those who do not have gallery space, this is an attractive option. —[4]—."

9. What is the purpose of the article?
   (A) To introduce an investment opportunity
   (B) To highlight the paintings of local artists
   (C) To explain a newly available service
   (D) To encourage participation in an art course

10. According to the article, what is NOT offered by Art Phase?
    (A) Pick-up and delivery
    (B) A free trial session
    (C) In-person consultations
    (D) Comments from the artist

11. What does Mr. Patterson suggest about Sunshine Street Market?
    (A) It has high fees.
    (B) It is decorated attractively.
    (C) It is near an art gallery.
    (D) It has booths of different sizes.

12. In which of the positions marked [1], [2], [3], and [4] does the following sentence best belong?
    "We were also nervous about making an upfront investment in artwork."
    (A) [1]
    (B) [2]

題本示意圖（多篇閱讀）

Questions 16-20 refer to the following invitation, brochure, and e-mail.

Chemical Engineering Conference
www.chemicalengineeringconf.com

Enjoy a weekend of informative talks and professional networking at the 5th Annual Chemical Engineering Conference beginning April 9. Our aim is to educate those working in the field about the latest trends, safety measures, and emerging technologies. For the first time, we will hold the conference at Parkview Hall, and we are pleased to have Wyatt Faber, CEO of Dalton Chemicals, as our keynote speaker.

Please see the attached brochure for the details about sponsorship.

Chemical Engineering Conference
Sponsorship Tiers

Corporate sponsorship plays an important role in the success of our conference, as it allows us to keep registration fees affordable. By becoming a sponsor, you can introduce your company to hundreds of specialists in the field, making them more familiar with your brand.

Economy — $500
- Have your company's logo featured in our printed conference program
- 10% off registration for up to 10 employees

Basic — $1,500
- Have your company's logo featured in our printed conference program and on banners in the check-in area
- 10% off registration for up to 15 employees

Premium — $2,500
- Have your company's logo featured in all areas, including on stage
- 10% off registration for all of your employees

Elite — $4,500
- Have your company's logo featured in all areas, including on stage
- 15% off registration for all of your employees
- Your employees can use our VIP lounge, which features printing and copying equipment, complimentary refreshments, phone-charging stations, and more.

E-Mail Message

To: All Holbrook Incorporated Staff <stafflist@holbrookinc.com>
From: Nancy Turner <n.turner@holbrookinc.com>
Date: March 28
Subject: Chemical Engineering Conference

Dear Staff,

The Chemical Engineering Conference is coming soon. I'm wondering who would like to attend this event, as I need to complete the registration forms. We are a sponsor for the event this year, so we are eligible for a registration discount for as many employees as we want. In addition, while you are at the event, you'll have access to the VIP lounge. Many of you will recognize this year's keynote speaker, who visited our company last year to teach a workshop on state-of-the-art chemistry tools.

Nancy Turner
Administration Director, Holbrook Incorporated

---

16. According to the invitation, what is indicated about the conference?
(A) It takes place annually at Parkview Hall.
(B) It lasts for two days.
(C) It is free to attend.
(D) It is being held for the first time.

17. What benefit of sponsorship is mentioned in the brochure?
(A) Sponsors can operate a booth at the conference.
(B) Sponsors can improve their brand recognition.
(C) Sponsors can get assistance with logo design.
(D) Sponsors can promote their business online.

18. What is the purpose of the e-mail?
(A) To explain the reasons for a decision
(B) To recruit volunteers to give a presentation
(C) To find out who is interested in attending an event
(D) To arrange transportation to a conference

19. What is stated about Mr. Faber?
(A) He led a training event at Holbrook Incorporated.
(B) He contacted Ms. Turner about sponsorship.
(C) He will join the Holbrook Incorporated staff.
(D) He has developed a new technology.

20. What level of sponsorship did Holbrook Incorporated get?
(A) Economy
(B) Basic
(C) Premium
(D) Elite

PART 1

照片描述

UNIT 01 人物照片

UNIT 02 事物照與風景照

高分祕訣

PART TEST

PART 1 照片描述

該大題考的是看試題本上的照片，聽完四個短句後，從中選出最符合照片的描述。聽力測驗共有100題，PART 1佔6題。

照片類型

照片大致可分為人物照、事物照、風景照三類。

🎧 P1_01

單人獨照

照片中僅出現一人，主要描述照片中人物的動作或狀態。

(A) She's planting some seeds.
(B) **She's using a spray bottle.**
(C) She's dusting a shelf.
(D) She's painting a pot.

(A) 她正在播種。
(B) **她正在使用噴霧瓶。**
(C) 她正在擦拭架上的灰塵。
(D) 她正在粉刷盆栽。

雙人或多人照片

照片中出現好幾個人，描述所有人的共同動作、其中一人，或某幾個人的動作。

(A) One of the men is purchasing a tire.
(B) One of the men is riding to work.
(C) **They're fixing a bicycle.**
(D) They're opening a toolbox.

(A) 其中一名男子正在買輪胎。
(B) 其中一名男子正在騎車上班。
(C) **他們在修理自行車。**
(D) 他們在打開工具箱。

事物與風景照

照片中僅出現事物或風景，並未出現人物。針對照片中事物的位置、狀態、景象描述。

(A) **Some boxes are stacked on the floor.**
(B) Some art has been hung on the wall.
(C) A ladder is leaning against a desk.
(D) There's a lamp on a rug.

(A) **地板上堆著一些箱子。**
(B) 牆上掛著一些藝術品。
(C) 梯子靠在桌上。
(D) 地毯上有一盞燈。

解題策略

🎧 P1_02

STEP 1 | 掌握照片重點
快速掌握照片中人物的主要動作和狀態、東西位置和狀態，以及人物周邊的背景。
動作：手裡拿著水果
狀態：戴著帽子

(A) She's weighing some fruit on a scale.
(B) She's holding up some fruit.
(C) She's adjusting her hat.
(D) She's chopping some vegetables.

STEP 2 | 使用刪去法選出答案
聆聽音檔時專注在動詞上，刪除動詞有誤的選項。接著確認其餘選項的描述是否與照片相符，並選出正確答案。

(A) 她正在秤一些水果的重量。
　　(✗) 沒有出現秤子
(B) 她正拿著一些水果。
　　(O) 她拿著水果
(C) 她正在調整帽子。
　　(✗) 沒有調整帽子
(D) 她正在切菜。
　　(✗) 沒在切任何東西

UNIT 01　人物照片

💡 考題重點

1. 主要以「be動詞＋ing」的形態描述照片中人物的動作或狀態，因此請特別注意聆聽動詞部分。
2. 陷阱選項中經常出現與人物動作無關的動詞，或是動作觸及的事物有誤。

🔍 常考題型與解題策略

🎧 P1_03

單人獨照

掌握照片中人物的主要動作和該動作觸及的事物、人物的姿勢和視線、穿著等狀態。

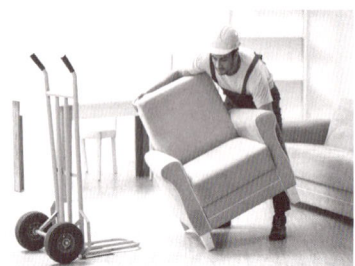

(A) A man is pushing a cart.
(B) A man is sitting on a chair.
(C) A man is lifting some furniture.
(D) A man is putting on a hard hat.

(A) 男子正在推著手推車。
(B) 男子正坐在椅子上。
(C) 男子正在抬起傢俱。
(D) 男子正在戴上安全帽。

雙人或多人照片

掌握人物的共同動作或狀態，以及特定人物的動作或狀態。針對多數人描述時，經常用 workers 或 travelers 當作主詞。

(A) They're looking at a document.
(B) They're adjusting a computer monitor.
(C) One of the people is taking off a pair of glasses.
(D) One of the people is drinking from a glass.

(A) 他們正在看文件。
(B) 他們正在調整電腦螢幕。
(C) 其中一人正在摘下眼鏡。
(D) 其中一人正喝著玻璃杯中的飲品。

人事物混合照

雖然照片中有出現人物，答案仍有可能是描述事物的選項。因此請掌握人物周遭事物的狀態和位置。

(A) The woman is drinking some water.
(B) Some plants have been arranged in a row.
(C) The woman is wiping a window.
(D) Some shelves are being assembled.

(A) 女子正在喝水。
(B) 有些植物排成一排。
(C) 女子正在擦窗戶。
(D) 有人正在組裝一些架子。

PRACTICE

請選出與照片相符的描述。

1.

(A)　(B)　(C)　(D)

2.

(A)　(B)　(C)　(D)

3.

(A)　(B)　(C)　(D)

4.

(A)　(B)　(C)　(D)

5.

(A)　(B)　(C)　(D)

6.

(A)　(B)　(C)　(D)

UNIT 02　事物照與風景照

考題重點

1. 注意聆聽表示事物位置的介系詞、介系詞片語、副詞片語。
2. 陷阱選項裡經常出現照片中未出現的人事物，請特別留意。

常考題型與解題策略

P1_05

事物照

主要為近距離拍攝家中或辦公室等室內事物的照片，因此請務必掌握照片中特別顯眼的事物位置和狀態。

(A) Some dishes have been spread around the table.
(B) A light fixture is hanging above a dining area.
(C) Chairs have been set up in a garden.
(D) Kitchen appliances are arranged for sale.

(A) 桌子周邊擺著幾個盤子。
(B) 燈具掛在用餐區上方。
(C) 花園裡擺放著一些椅子。
(D) 正在出售廚房用品。

風景照

該類型照片拍攝寬闊的建築物外觀、湖水、公園等自然景觀。選項中經常出現「There is/are +名詞」形態的描述。

(A) There's a deck overlooking a lake.
(B) Some boats are tied to a pier.
(C) Waves are crashing against the rocks.
(D) A ship is stopped at a dock.

(A) 有塊甲板俯瞰著湖面。
(B) 有些船舶繫在碼頭。
(C) 海浪沖刷著石頭。
(D) 一般船停靠在碼頭。

PRACTICE

請選出與照片相符的描述。

1.
(A) (B) (C) (D)

2.
(A) (B) (C) (D)

3.
(A) (B) (C) (D)

4.
(A) (B) (C) (D)

5.
(A) (B) (C) (D)

6.
(A) (B) (C) (D)

高分祕訣

1 請注意選項中的動詞指的是「動作」還是「狀態」。

putting on an apron (✗)
正在穿圍裙 → 指「穿上去」的動作

wearing an apron (○)
穿著圍裙 → 指「穿著」的狀態

picking up a cup (✗)
正在拿起杯子 → 指「拿起來」的動作

holding a cup (○)
拿著杯子 → 指「拿著」的狀態

2 描述人物動作時，可使用「事物」當作主詞。此類句子經常使用「現在進行式的被動語態（be+being+p.p.）」。

A window is being installed. 窗戶正在被（某人）安裝。
= They're installing a window.
　他們正在安裝窗戶。

Some potted plants are being watered.
盆栽正在被（某人）澆水。
= A woman is watering some potted plants.
　女子正在給盆栽澆水。

PRACTICE

P1_07 答案&解析 p.4

請選出與照片相符的描述。

1.

(A) (B) (C) (D)

2.

(A) (B) (C) (D)

3.

(A) (B) (C) (D)

4.

(A) (B) (C) (D)

5.

(A) (B) (C) (D)

6.

(A) (B) (C) (D)

29

PART TEST

LISTENING TEST

In the Listening test, you will be asked to demonstrate how well you understand spoken English. The entire Listening test will last approximately 45 minutes. There are four parts, and directions are given for each part. You must mark your answers on the separate answer sheet. Do not write your answers in your test book.

PART 1

Directions: For each question in this part, you will hear four statements about a picture in your test book. When you hear the statements, you must select the one statement that best describes what you see in the picture. Then find the number of the question on your answer sheet and mark your answer. The statements will not be printed in your test book and will be spoken only one time.

Statement (C), "He's making a phone call," is the best description of the picture, so you should select answer (C) and mark it on your answer sheet.

1.

2.

GO ON TO THE NEXT PAGE

3.

4.

5.

6.

PART 2

應答問題

UNIT 03 Who, What, Which 問句

UNIT 04 When, Where 問句

UNIT 05 How, Why 問句

UNIT 06 一般問句、表示建議或要求的問句

UNIT 07 附加問句、選擇疑問句

UNIT 08 間接問句、直述句

高分祕訣

PART TEST

PART 2 應答問題

聽完題目句與三句回應句後，選出最適當的答案。聽力測驗共有100題，PART 2佔25題。

題目句類型

Who 問句 以「Who（誰）」開頭的問句，可回答與人相關的內容。
Q Who's leading the new staff orientation? 誰負責新進員工的培訓？
A Mr. Barrera always does it. 一向是由Barrera先生負責。

What, Which 問句 以「What（什麼）」或「Which（哪一個）」開頭的問句，可根據疑問詞後方連接的資訊，回答相關內容。
Q What products do your company make? 你們公司生產什麼產品？
A Office supplies. 辦公室用品。

When 問句 以「When（何時）」開頭的問句，可回答與時間相關的內容。
Q When did Ms. Morgan return from her trip? Morgan女士何時旅行完回來的？
A Tuesday afternoon. 星期二下午。

Where 問句 以「Where（哪裡）」開頭的問句，可回答相關地點或出處。
Q Where are the presenters? 演講者們在哪裡？
A In the break room. 在休息室裡。

How 問句 以「How（如何／多少）」開頭的問句，可回答方法、手段、意見、數量等。
Q How should I get to the airport? 我該怎麼去機場？
A Just take a taxi. 搭計程車去。

Why 問句 以「Why（為什麼）」開頭的問句，可回答相關理由或目的。
Q Why is Mr. Stanley traveling to Atlanta? 為何Stanley先生要前往亞特蘭大？
A To inspect the new factory. 為了視察新工廠。

一般問句 以「助動詞」或「be動詞」開頭的問句，可回答肯定、否定、補充說明。有些問句會在助動詞或be動詞後方加上not。
Q Did you request a transfer overseas? 你有要求調職海外嗎？
A No, I decided to stay here instead. 沒有，我決定留在這裡。

表示建議或要求的問句 雖然題目句為問句形式，但為表示建議或要求的句子，回答的內容可表示同意或拒絕。
Q Can you pick up the dry cleaning? 你能幫我拿一下乾洗衣物嗎？
A Sure. I've got time right now. 沒問題，我現在有空。

附加問句 在直述句後方加上aren't you?或 didn't you?的問句，如同回答一般問句的方式，回覆肯定、否定、補充說明。

Q　Class registration hasn't closed, has it? 課程報名尚未截止，對嗎？
A　No, there are two days left. 沒有，還剩兩天。

選擇疑問句 使用「連接詞」或「or（或是）」，要求從兩個選項中擇一的問句。

Q　Do you prefer to take the bus or the train? 你喜歡搭公車還是火車？
A　I'd rather take the bus. 我偏好搭公車。

間接問句 一般問句當中加入Wh開頭的問句，變成間接問句，可根據題目句中的疑問詞回答相對應的內容。

Q　Do you know how I can turn on this machine? 你知道怎麼開這台機器嗎？
A　Yes, let me show you. 是，我用給你看。

直述句 陳述事實的句子，並非問句形式。由於直述句沒有固定回答模式，因此難度最高。

Q　I lost Ms. Lee's business card. 我弄丟了李女士的名片。
A　Her contact details are online. 網路上有她的聯絡方式。

解題策略

🎧 P2_01

Who proofread the quarterly report?

(A) I think Joseph did that.
(B) To inform our shareholders.
(C) Yes, before April 1st.

STEP 1｜掌握題目句重點
聽完題目句後，確認當中的疑問詞和關鍵字。

STEP 2｜使用刪去法選出答案
聆聽音檔，刪除有誤的選項。接著從剩餘選項中，確認何者為適當的答覆，從中選出答案。

(A) 我想是Joseph校對的。
　　(O) Who問句詢問校對報告的人
　　　　回答名字Joseph為適當的答覆。
(B) 為了通知我們的股東。
　　(✗)該句話適合回答詢問報告用途的問句。
(C) 對，在4月1日之前。
　　(✗)不能以Yes回答Wh問句。

37

UNIT 03　Who, What, Which 問句

1　Who 問句

考題重點

1. 題目主要詢問某項工作的負責人是誰。
2. 答句經常直接回答人名或職稱。

代表題型範例　　　P2_02

Who's transferring to the Marketing team?　誰要調到行銷部呢？
(A) Yes, I am. Thank you.　對，是我，謝謝。
(B) Great, it's like a promotion.　太好了，那就算是升遷。
(C) I heard it will be Ms. Stanley.　我聽說是Stanley女士。

常見題目句與答句

回答人名	Q　Who's in charge of the training program?　由誰負責培訓計畫？ A　Ms. Kelson is.　Kelson女士。
回答職稱或部門	Q　Who notified the interns of the time and venue changes? 誰通知實習生們時間和地點的變動？ A　The director of Human Resources.　人力資源主管。
回答公司名稱	Q　Who's going to sponsor this year's fundraiser?　誰將贊助今年的募款活動？ A　A new hotel called Paradise View.　一間叫Paradise View的新飯店。
回答不知道	Q　Who needs to review this order form?　誰需要查看此訂單的格式？ A　I'm not sure.　我不太清楚。

PRACTICE　　　P2_03 答案&解析 p.8

聽完題目後，選出適當的答覆。

1.　(A)　　(B)　　(C)　　　　2.　(A)　　(B)　　(C)

3.　(A)　　(B)　　(C)　　　　4.　(A)　　(B)　　(C)

5.　(A)　　(B)　　(C)　　　　6.　(A)　　(B)　　(C)

2 What, Which 問句

考題重點

1. 題目詢問的內容多樣，包含詢問時間、種類、意見等，因此請仔細聆聽疑問詞What和Which後方出現的名詞和動詞。
2. 題目為Which問句時，正確答案通常是出現代名詞one的選項。

代表題型範例

What is included in the rent? 房租包含什麼？

(A) Electricity and water. 電費和水費。
(B) On Atlantic Avenue. 在Atlantic大道。
(C) She lent me a bicycle. 她借我一輛腳踏車。

常見題目句與答句

■ What

時間	Q What time is the band scheduled to perform? 樂團預計幾點演出？ A The announcement said at 5. 廣播通知是5點。
種類	Q What type of file cabinet do you need? 你需要哪種文件櫃？ A A metal one. 金屬的。
意見	Q What did you think of the president's speech? 你覺得董事長的演說如何？ A She really inspired me. 她真的激勵了我。

■ Which

使用代名詞one回答	Q Which factory produces these umbrellas? 這些雨傘是哪家工廠生產的？ A The one in Louisville. 一家在Louisville的工廠。

PRACTICE

聽完題目後，選出適當的答覆。

1. (A) (B) (C)   2. (A) (B) (C)
3. (A) (B) (C)   4. (A) (B) (C)
5. (A) (B) (C)   6. (A) (B) (C)

UNIT 04　When, Where 問句

1　When 問句

考題重點

1. 題目會使用各種時態詢問特定的時間，因此請仔細聆聽疑問詞When後方be動詞或助動詞連接的時態為何（過去、現在、未來）。
2. 答句經常使用介系詞回答明確時間，或是各類與時間有關的表達。

代表題型範例　🎧 P2_06

When's the art gallery's fundraiser?　美術館的募款活動在什麼時候？
(A) Yes, a few paintings.　對，有幾幅畫。
(B) At least a thousand dollars.　至少1000美元。
(C) Next Friday at seven.　下週五7點。

常見題目句與答句

回答特定的時間：時間點、星期幾、日期	Q　When can I expect the morning mail delivery?　我什麼時候可以收到早上的郵件？ A　Around nine o'clock.　大約9點鐘。
明確回答出大約的時間點	Q　When will construction begin?　何時開始施工？ A　After the budget is approved.　待預算批准後。
非正面答覆／其他答覆	Q　When will our pasta be ready?　何時會上我們的義大利麵？ A1　I'll check with the chef.　我去跟主廚確認一下。 A2　The kitchen is very busy tonight.　今晚廚房很忙碌。

PRACTICE　🎧 P2_07　答案 & 解析 p.9

聽完題目後，選出適當的答覆。

1.　(A)　　(B)　　(C)　　　　2.　(A)　　(B)　　(C)

3.　(A)　　(B)　　(C)　　　　4.　(A)　　(B)　　(C)

5.　(A)　　(B)　　(C)　　　　6.　(A)　　(B)　　(C)

2 Where 問句

考題重點

1. 題目詢問地點、位置、出處等。
2. 雖然答句經常用介系詞回答地點或位置，但有時使用介系詞的選項為陷阱選項，請特別留意。

代表題型範例

🎧 P2_08

Where did you meet Ms. Taylor? 你在哪裡遇見Taylor女士？
(A) At 4 o'clock. 4點鐘。
(B) Yes, she was there. 對，她在那裡。
(C) In the cafeteria. 在自助餐廳裡。

常見題目句與答句

回答地點或位置	Q Where can I store my luggage? 哪裡可以寄放行李？ A At the service desk over there. 在那邊的服務台。
回答出處	Q Where's last year's quality control report? 去年的品質控管報告在哪裡？ A You can find it on the company's website. 你可以在公司的網站上找到。
回答人物	Q Where should the new filing cabinets be placed? 新的文件櫃要放在哪裡？ A Jenice has a floor plan. Jenice有平面圖。

PRACTICE

🎧 P2_09 答案&解析 p.10

聽完題目後，選出適當的答覆。

1. (A) (B) (C)   2. (A) (B) (C)
3. (A) (B) (C)   4. (A) (B) (C)
5. (A) (B) (C)   6. (A) (B) (C)

UNIT 05　How, Why 問句

1　How 問句

💡 考題重點

1. How 後方連接助動詞或 be 動詞時，其意思為「如何」，詢問的是方法、手段、意見。

2. How 後方連接形容詞或副詞時，多半會詢問時間、數量、頻率、價格等，因此聆聽時請特別留意題目前半段的內容。

📎 代表題型範例　🎧 P2_10

How can I place an order for catering? 如何訂購外燴餐飲服務？
(A) Yes, you can. 是，你可以。
(B) Just fill out this order form. 請填寫這張訂單。
(C) About 70 to 100 people. 大約 70 到 100 人。

✏️ 常見題目句與答句

方法或手段	Q　How do I set the security alarm? 如何設定安全警報？ A　First, input your five-digit code. 首先輸入你的 5 位數密碼。
意見	Q　How was the employee holiday party yesterday? 昨天的員工假期派對如何？ A　It was great. 非常棒。
數量或價格	Q　How many people visited the house for sale on Mill Street? 　　有多少人參觀了 Mill 大街上的待售房屋？ A　About 25. 25 個人左右。
時間或頻率	Q　How long will it take to get to Chicago? 去芝加哥需要多久時間？ A　Four hours by train. 坐火車 4 個小時。

PRACTICE　🎧 P2_11 答案 & 解析 p.11

聽完題目後，選出適當的答覆。

1.　(A)　(B)　(C)　　　2.　(A)　(B)　(C)

3.　(A)　(B)　(C)　　　4.　(A)　(B)　(C)

5.　(A)　(B)　(C)　　　6.　(A)　(B)　(C)

2　Why 問句

考題重點

1. 請仔細聆聽「Why + 助動詞/be動詞」後方連接的主詞和動詞為何。
2. 答句經常直接使用because/for或不定詞to V來回答，但有時也會出現省略的形式。

代表題型範例

🎧 P2_12

Why is the library closing early tonight?　為何圖書館今晚提早關門？

(A) Because it's a holiday.　因為今天是假日。
(B) A couple of librarians.　兩個圖書館管理員。
(C) This was the closest place.　這是最近的地方。

常見題目句與答句

回答原因或理由	Q	Why didn't Ms. Granger's article appear in the magazine? 為何Granger女士的文章沒有刊登在雜誌上？
	A	They're still fact-checking it.　他們還在進行事實查核。
回答目的	Q	Why is Mr. Gonzalez visiting our branch?　Gonzalez先生為何來訪我們的分公司？
	A	To meet the staff.　與工作人員見面。
用反問方式答覆	Q	Why has the train stopped so long at this station? 為什麼火車在這一站停這麼久？
	A	Didn't you hear the announcement?　你沒聽到廣播通知嗎？

PRACTICE

🎧 P2_13　答案&解析 p.12

聽完題目後，選出適當的答覆。

1. (A)　(B)　(C)　　2. (A)　(B)　(C)

3. (A)　(B)　(C)　　4. (A)　(B)　(C)

5. (A)　(B)　(C)　　6. (A)　(B)　(C)

43

UNIT 06　一般問句、表示建議或要求的問句

1　一般問句

💡 考題重點

1. 題目主要詢問事實、意見、經驗、計畫等，請務必聽清楚be動詞或助動詞的時態和題目的主詞。
2. 答句經常直接回答Yes或No，但有些答案會省略Yes和No，採取補充說明或非正面答覆的方式，請特別留意。
3. 有時會出現否定疑問句，在be動詞或助動詞後方加上not。碰到此類型題目句時，答案為肯定時回答Yes；否定則回答No。

📎 代表題型範例　　🎧 P2_14

Do you have fresh fruits on your dessert menu?　甜點菜單上有新鮮水果嗎？
(A) Thanks, but I'm not hungry.　謝謝，但我不餓。
(B) Yes, we have strawberries and peaches.　是的，有草莓和桃子。
(C) They make these locally.　他們是在當地生產的。

✏️ 常見題目句與答句

Be	Q　Are you interested in taking an online Italian class?　你有興趣參加義大利語線上課程嗎？ A　No, I'm very busy these days.　不，我最近很忙。
Do / Does / Did	Q　Did you hear the news about the vacation policy?　你有聽說關於休假政策的消息嗎？ A　I wasn't at the meeting.　我沒有參加會議。
Have	Q　Have you seen the play at the Three Moons Theater?　你有看過Three Moons劇場的話劇嗎？ A　Yes, I went last weekend.　有，我上週末去過。
Can	Q　Can I place an international call from my hotel room?　我可以在飯店房間內撥打國際長途電話嗎？ A　There will be an extra fee.　會額外收取費用。

PRACTICE　　🎧 P2_15　答案＆解析 p.13

聽完題目後，選出適當的答覆。

1. (A)　(B)　(C)　　2. (A)　(B)　(C)
3. (A)　(B)　(C)　　4. (A)　(B)　(C)
5. (A)　(B)　(C)　　6. (A)　(B)　(C)

2 表示建議或要求的問句

💡 考題重點

1. 答案經常出現直接同意、拒絕建議或要求事項。
2. 請特別留意非正面答覆的選項,包含告知不同意要求的理由,或表示已完成交代事項,皆屬正確答案。

📎 代表題型範例   🎧 P2_16

Could you recommend some good restaurants in this town? 你能推薦幾間這個鎮上不錯的餐廳嗎?
(A) Sure, I know some places you'll like. 當然,我知道一些你會喜歡的地方。
(B) There are several banks. 有幾家銀行。
(C) I recommend James for security. 我推薦James擔任保全。

✏️ 常見題目句與答句

◆ 建議

Why don't you/we ...?	Q Why don't you take next week off? 下週休個假如何? A I'd rather finish my work. 我想先完成我的工作。
Would you like ...?	Q Would you like some help filling out that application? 需要協助你填寫申請書嗎? A Yes, thank you. 好的,謝謝你。

◆ 要求

Can/Could you (please) ...?	Q Can you look up the restaurant's hours online? 你可以上網查一下餐廳的營業時間嗎? A Absolutely, I'll do that right away. 當然可以,我馬上就查。
Would you (mind) ...?	Q Would you take my work shifts this week? 你這週能幫我代班嗎? A I'm traveling to London tomorrow. 我明天要去倫敦出差。

PRACTICE   🎧 P2_17 答案&解析 p.14

聽完題目後,選出適當的答覆。

1. (A) (B) (C)   2. (A) (B) (C)

3. (A) (B) (C)   4. (A) (B) (C)

5. (A) (B) (C)   6. (A) (B) (C)

UNIT 07　附加問句、選擇疑問句

1　附加問句

考題重點

1. 附加於直述句後方的問句，目的為向對方確認事實，因此聆聽題目句時，請聽清楚前半段的直述句內容即可。
2. 請把附加問句當成一般問句，可回答肯定、否定或是補充說明。無論附加問句為肯定句或否定句，只要答案為肯定，就回答 Yes；否定則回答 No。

代表題型範例　🎧 P2_18

You are planning to visit Dr. Schmidt today, aren't you?　你打算今天去拜訪 Schmidt 醫生，不是嗎？
(A) Let's sit together.　我們一起坐吧。
(B) I have a rash on my arm.　我的手臂上長了疹子。
(C) Yes, later today.　對，今天稍晚的時候。

常見題目句與答句

be	Q	Their plane is half an hour late, <u>isn't it</u>?　他們的飛機延遲半小時，不是嗎？
	A	Yes, I just heard.　對，我剛聽說。
do / have / will	Q	You transferred to this branch recently, <u>didn't you</u>? 你最近被調到這間分公司，不是嗎？
	A	No, I've worked here for years.　不，我在這裡工作好幾年了。
其他	Q	This badge should be returned to the reception desk, <u>right</u>? 這個徽章應該還給櫃檯，對嗎？
	A	Nicholas knows the procedure.　Nicholas 知道程序。

PRACTICE　🎧 P2_19　答案&解析 p.15

聽完題目後，選出適當的答覆。

1. (A)　(B)　(C)　　2. (A)　(B)　(C)
3. (A)　(B)　(C)　　4. (A)　(B)　(C)
5. (A)　(B)　(C)　　6. (A)　(B)　(C)

2 選擇疑問句

考題重點

1. 請仔細聽清楚題目句中提及的兩個選項。
2. 答句通常會直接從兩個選項中擇一回答,但有時會出現同時選擇或拒絕兩個選項,或是提出第三種選擇等,回答方式多樣,請特別留意。

代表題型範例

P2_20

Do you want to practice the speech here or in my office?
你想在這裡練習演講,還是在我辦公室裡練習?

(A) Let's go through it here. 在這裡好了。
(B) Yes, I saw him. 對,我看到他了。
(C) He spoke about it on Tuesday. 他星期二有談到這件事。

常見題目句與答句

Would you (rather/like/prefer) ... or ...?	Q	Would you like coffee or tea? 你要咖啡還是茶?
	A	Just water, please. 請給我水就好。
Do you (want to) ... or ...?	Q	Do you want to take a morning or afternoon flight to New York? 你想搭上午還是下午的班機去紐約?
	A	Which one's less expensive? 哪個比較便宜?
Are you (going to) ... or ...? /Is it ... or ...?	Q	Are you going to buy a laptop or a desktop computer? 你打算買筆電還是桌電?
	A	Laptops are more convenient. 筆電比較方便。

PRACTICE

P2_21 答案&解析 p.16

聽完題目後,選出適當的答覆。

1. (A) (B) (C)   2. (A) (B) (C)
3. (A) (B) (C)   4. (A) (B) (C)
5. (A) (B) (C)   6. (A) (B) (C)

UNIT 08　間接問句、直述句

1　間接問句

💡 考題重點

1. 請聽清楚題目句中Wh問句的疑問詞、主詞、動詞。
2. 答句經常會根據Wh問句的疑問詞回答出正確資訊，但有時會出現回應一般問句的形式，以Yes或No開頭，表達同意或拒絕對方的要求。

📎 代表題型範例　　　🎧 P2_22

Do you know when I can get a parking permit? 你知道我何時能拿到停車證嗎？
(A) Yes, thanks. I like it, too. 好，謝謝，我也喜歡。
(B) You can pick it up tomorrow morning. 你可以明天早上來拿。
(C) There are many shops near the park. 公園附近有很多商店。

✏️ 常見題目句與答句

Do you know + who / what / when / where / how / why ...?	Q　Do you know who is going to be the keynote speaker for the conference? 你知道會由誰擔任會議的主講人嗎？ A　The same speaker as last year. 跟去年的講者一樣。
Can you tell me + who / what / when / where / how / why ...?	Q　Could you tell me why I was charged an additional fifty dollars? 你能告訴我為什麼要加收50美元嗎？ A　That's the sales tax. 那是營業稅。
Can you show me + how to ...?	Q　Can you show me how to operate this ticket machine? 你能教我如何操作這台售票機嗎？ A　Yes, just a moment, please. 好的，請稍等。

PRACTICE　　🎧 P2_23　答案&解析 p.16

聽完題目後，選出適當的答覆。

1. (A)　(B)　(C)　　2. (A)　(B)　(C)
3. (A)　(B)　(C)　　4. (A)　(B)　(C)
5. (A)　(B)　(C)　　6. (A)　(B)　(C)

2 直述句

考題重點

1. 該類句子要仔細聽懂整句話,才能掌握其內容,因此屬於Part 2中難度最高的題型。
2. 直述句可使用Yes或No開頭的句子來回答。當出現Yes或No開頭的回答時,請特別留意後方提及的內容,是否符合前方Yes或No的邏輯。

代表題型範例
P2_24

That was an amazing orchestra concert. 那場管弦樂團的演奏會真令人驚艷。

(A) **The violin soloist is talented.** 小提琴獨奏家很有才華。
(B) Sorry, I'm working that day. 抱歉,我那天要工作。
(C) How did the audition go? 試鏡進行得如何?

常見題目句與答句

提出問題點	Q	The washing machine isn't working properly. 洗衣機無法正常運轉。
	A	Let's call a repair technician. 打電話給維修人員吧。
傳達消息／ 說明狀況	Q	The staff meeting has been postponed until Thursday. 員工會議已延至週四。
	A	Why is it being moved? 為何要更動?
提出想法／ 表達情感	Q	I think my employee performance review went well. 我覺得我的考績很不錯。
	A	That's good to hear. 很高興聽到這個消息。
建議／要求	Q	We should hire one more photographer for our company. 我們公司應該再請一位攝影師。
	A	I'll start the search soon. 我會儘快開始找。

PRACTICE
P2_25 答案&解析 p.17

聽完題目後,選出適當的答覆。

1. (A) (B) (C)   2. (A) (B) (C)
3. (A) (B) (C)   4. (A) (B) (C)
5. (A) (B) (C)   6. (A) (B) (C)

高分祕訣

1 當語速很快時，When和Where的發音聽起來很相似，因此請特別留意刻意混淆視聽的選項。

Q When is the new blender going to be released? 新的攪拌機何時上市？

A In the kitchen cabinet. (✗) 在廚房的櫃子裡。
The prototype is still being tested. (○) 樣機仍在測試中。

2 題目為Why問句時，使用because/for或不定詞to V回答的選項未必是正確答案，請務必聽清楚後方連接的內容是否無誤。

Q Why does the office look so empty this afternoon? 為什麼今天下午辦公室看起來空蕩蕩的？

A Because your office is next to mine. (✗) 因為你的辦公室就在我的隔壁。
A lot of people left early. (○) 很多人提前下班了。

3 題目為一般問句或附加問句時，有些陷阱選項用Yes或No回答後，後方會刻意使用與題目句相關的單字，或發音相似的單字混淆視聽，請特別留意。

Q Will you go on the business trip with me? 你願意跟我一起出差嗎？

A No, it's in terminal A. (✗) 不，在A航廈。➡ terminal（航廈）與trip（旅行）有關聯。
Yes, I'd be glad to join you. (○) 好，我很樂意加入。

Q This contract was reviewed by our legal team, wasn't it? 這份合約已經由法務部審核過了，不是嗎？

A Yes, the view outside is so nice. (✗) 是的，外面的風景很好。➡ view（風景）與review的發音相似。
Celine just approved it this afternoon. (○) Celine今天下午剛批准通過。

4 題目句為詢問特定資訊的Wh問句時，不能使用Yes/No回答；若是How about（……怎麼樣？）開頭的問句，則能用Yes/No回答。另外，題目句為傳達消息、提出想法的直述句時，答案可以用Yes或Okay回答，表示同意或答應對方的提議。

Q How about hiring an event planner to organize the holiday party?
聘請一位活動企劃來籌備假期派對怎麼樣？

A Yes, that's a good idea. 好，這是個好主意。

Q The storage room is very full. 儲藏室已經滿了。

A Yes, there's no more space in there. 是的，裡面已經沒有空間了。

5 有些提問並非單純字面上的意思，必需理解該提問背後的意圖，或是推敲出對話的脈絡，才能選出答案。

Q Who was in the break room last? 最後一個待在休息室的人是誰？

A I noticed that it was messy, too. 我也注意到那裡很髒亂。

Q Why are they cleaning the carpets now? 為什麼他們現在要清潔地毯？

A Is the noise bothering you? 噪音有打擾到你嗎？

PRACTICE

1. (A) (B) (C)
2. (A) (B) (C)
3. (A) (B) (C)
4. (A) (B) (C)
5. (A) (B) (C)
6. (A) (B) (C)
7. (A) (B) (C)
8. (A) (B) (C)
9. (A) (B) (C)
10. (A) (B) (C)
11. (A) (B) (C)
12. (A) (B) (C)

PART TEST

PART 2

Directions: You will hear a question or statement and three responses spoken in English. They will not be printed in your test book and will be spoken only one time. Select the best response to the question or statement and mark the letter (A), (B), or (C) on your answer sheet.

7. Mark your answer on your answer sheet.
8. Mark your answer on your answer sheet.
9. Mark your answer on your answer sheet.
10. Mark your answer on your answer sheet.
11. Mark your answer on your answer sheet.
12. Mark your answer on your answer sheet.
13. Mark your answer on your answer sheet.
14. Mark your answer on your answer sheet.
15. Mark your answer on your answer sheet.
16. Mark your answer on your answer sheet.
17. Mark your answer on your answer sheet.
18. Mark your answer on your answer sheet.
19. Mark your answer on your answer sheet.
20. Mark your answer on your answer sheet.
21. Mark your answer on your answer sheet.
22. Mark your answer on your answer sheet.
23. Mark your answer on your answer sheet.
24. Mark your answer on your answer sheet.
25. Mark your answer on your answer sheet.
26. Mark your answer on your answer sheet.
27. Mark your answer on your answer sheet.
28. Mark your answer on your answer sheet.
29. Mark your answer on your answer sheet.
30. Mark your answer on your answer sheet.
31. Mark your answer on your answer sheet.

ENERGY

即便速度緩慢，只要堅持到底，便能贏得比賽。

—— 伊索寓言（Aesop）

PART 3

簡短對話

UNIT 09 詢問主旨或目的

UNIT 10 詢問說話者或地點

UNIT 11 詢問相關細節

UNIT 12 詢問建議或要求

UNIT 13 詢問下一步的行動

UNIT 14 詢問說話者的意圖

UNIT 15 圖表整合題

PART TEST

PART 3 簡短對話

聽完雙人或三人對話後，針對相關的三道考題選出最適當的答案。聽力測驗共有100題，PART 3佔39題（13組對話×3題），每回測驗有兩篇三人對話文。

考題類型

主旨或目的
詢問對話的主旨、說話者來電或來訪的目的。

說話者或地點
詢問說話者的身分，包含職業或工作地點等，或是詢問對話的地點。

相關細節
- 特定資訊：針對對話中提及的內容詢問「什麼、是誰、何時、哪裡、如何、為什麼」等詳細資訊。
- 提及內容：詢問說話者針對特定對象所提及的內容。

建議或要求事項
詢問說話者向對方提出的建議、請求或要求。

下一步的行動或即將發生的事
詢問說話者下一步的行動或往後會發生的事。

掌握說話者的意圖
針對說話者說過的話詢問其意思、背後含義，或是說出該句話的理由。

圖表整合題
指與目錄、地圖、表格等各式各樣的圖表一同出現的考題。

解題策略

STEP 1 | 掌握題目重點
請於對話播放前，事先閱讀題目，由關鍵字確認題目詢問的內容，並預測答題線索可能會出現的位置。

STEP 2 | 從對話中找出答題線索
聆聽對話的過程中，根據關鍵字找出答題線索。

STEP 3 | 選出正確答案
選擇與答題線索相同的內容、替換同義詞或是換句話說的選項作為答案。

🎧 P3_01

32. What is the purpose of the woman's visit?
    (A) To update an address
    (B) To apply for a job
    (C) To book a consultation
    (D) To make a complaint

33. What does the woman say about her neighbor?
    (A) He recommended a business.
    (B) He works as a technician.
    (C) He was disappointed with the service.
    (D) He has recently moved.

34. What does the man suggest the woman do?
    (A) Call another branch
    (B) Pay in installments
    (C) Read a pamphlet
    (D) Purchase some insurance

W Hello. I'm here about solar panels for a residential property. [32] I heard that you give a free consultation to potential customers, so I'd like to make an appointment for one of those. My name is Christine Arnold, and I live at 935 Roane Avenue.

M Thanks for coming. Let's see... Are you available this Saturday at 2 P.M.?

W Yes, that would be great, thanks. Actually, [33] my neighbor used your services last year, and he suggested that I get my panels from you. But I'm a little worried they'll be too expensive for me.

M If that's your concern, [34] you could make the payments in several installments to spread out the cost.

中譯

32. 女子來訪的目的為何？
    (A) 為了更新地址
    (B) 為了應徵工作
    (C) 為了預約諮詢
    (D) 為了投訴

33. 關於她的鄰居，女子說了什麼？
    (A) 他推薦了一間公司。
    (B) 他是一名技術人員。
    (C) 他對服務感到失望。
    (D) 他最近搬家了。

34. 男子建議女子做什麼？
    (A) 打給另一間分公司
    (B) 分期付款
    (C) 閱讀手冊
    (D) 購買一些保險

女 你好，我來這裡找住宅用的太陽能板。[32] 聽說你們會為潛在客戶提供免費諮詢，所以我想預約其中一項諮詢。我叫 Christine Arnold，住在 Roane 大道935號。

男 謝謝妳的來訪。我看看…這週六下午2點妳有空嗎？

女 有，太好了，謝謝。事實上，[33] 我鄰居去年使用過你們的服務，他建議我向你們購買太陽能板。但我有點擔心，它對我來說可能會太貴。

男 如果妳擔心這一點，[34] 可選擇分期付款以分攤費用。

UNIT 09　詢問主旨或目的

考題重點

1. 答題線索通常會出現在前半段對話中，因此請專心聆聽。
2. 有時會到對話後半段才提及主旨，因此聽完前半段對話後，仍無法確認主旨時，請先解決另外兩題，最後再回頭作答主旨題。

常見考題

主旨　What are the speakers (mainly) discussing? 說話者（主要）在談論什麼？
What is the conversation (mainly/mostly) about? 對話內容（主要）是什麼？

目的　Why is the man calling? 男子為什麼打電話來？
What is the purpose of the woman's visit/call? 女子來訪／來電的目的為何？

代表題型範例

🎧 P3_02

M　Good morning, Dove Botanical Gardens. W　Hello. I recently learned that you hold weddings at your site. I've just started planning my wedding, and I'm looking for a venue. Um, I'm wondering how much it would cost to hold the event there. M　Well, it depends on the duration of the event. I can e-mail you an information packet, if you'd like. W　That would be wonderful. I saw the photo gallery on your website, and everything looks so beautiful. And I love that it's a remote setting. M　Oh, about that... We are no longer running our shuttle service from Renwick Subway Station. So, make sure to take that into consideration.	男　早安，這裡是Dove植物園。 女　你好，我最近從網站上得知你們有在舉辦婚禮。我剛開始籌劃我的婚禮，正在尋找場地⋯⋯嗯⋯⋯我想知道在那裡舉辦一場活動需要花多少錢。 男　哦，這取決於活動的時長。如果你願意的話，我可以用電子郵件傳送資料集給你。 女　太好了。我在你們網站上看到了相冊集，一切看起來都很美麗。而且我很滿意它位在一個僻靜的地方。 男　哦，關於那部分⋯⋯ 我們已經不再提供從Renwick地鐵站出發的接駁服務，所以請務必考量這一點。
Why is the woman calling? To inquire about fees	女子為什麼打電話來？ 為了詢問費用

切勿錯過的答題線索

I'd like to book a flight from Miami to Seattle on May 17.　我想預訂5月17日從邁阿密飛往西雅圖的班機。
I'm calling to see if you have time to work on a project for my marketing firm.
我打電話是想問你有沒有時間為我的行銷公司做一個專案。
Let's talk about your job performance this year.　我們來談談你今年的工作表現吧。
Have you heard the news about our merger with Vocon Automotive?　你有聽說我們要與Vocon汽車合併的消息嗎？

PRACTICE

🎧 P3_03 答案&解析 p.24

請聆聽對話，填寫空白處的句子後，選出適當的答案。

> W　Hi, Mr. Davis. This is Christina Whitley from the Westbury Small Business Association.
> M　Oh, yes. Hello, Ms. Whitley.
> W　_____.
> M　I see. I can probably still attend it.
> W　I hope so. I'll e-mail you an updated registration packet. Also, your travel and registration fees will be covered by us.
> M　Thank you. I'll double check whether or not I can participate in the event. If not, I will probably send my assistant manager in my place.

1. Why is the woman calling the man?
   (A) To request the payment of a bill
   (B) To inform him of a schedule change
   (C) To invite him to give a presentation
   (D) To share some management strategies

聽完對話後，選出適當的答案。

2. What are the speakers mainly discussing?
   (A) A headquarters relocation
   (B) A software upgrade
   (C) A proposed merger
   (D) A market regulation

3. What is the purpose of the woman's call?
   (A) To promote an event at a park
   (B) To introduce a cleaning service
   (C) To arrange a facility tour
   (D) To ask about volunteer opportunities

4. What is the conversation mainly about?
   (A) Organizing some merchandise
   (B) Training staff members
   (C) Changing a window display
   (D) Labeling boxes for shipping

UNIT 10　詢問說話者或地點

考題重點

1. 與詢問主旨或目的的考題相同，答題線索通常會出現在前半段對話中，因此請專心聆聽前半段提及的職業、地點等關鍵字。
2. 除了詢問說話者的身分或職業外，還有可能詢問行業、工作地點、部門等各式各樣的問題。

常見考題

說話者　Who (most likely) is the man?　男子（最有可能）是誰？
Where do the speakers (most likely) work?　說話者（最有可能）在哪裡工作？
What field/industry/department do the speakers (most likely) work in?
說話者（最有可能）從事哪個領域、行業、部門的工作？

地點　Where (most likely) is the man?　男子（最有可能）在哪裡？
Where does the conversation (most likely) take place?　對話（最有可能）在哪裡進行？

代表題型範例

🎧 P3_04

W　Alex, I heard you did a great job leading the meeting with Allstar Incorporated. They really liked the new advertising campaign you proposed. You're setting up more meetings with new clients this month, right? M　Yes, but I've been thinking of doing video conferences rather than meeting face to face. W　Aren't there always problems with the video conference system? M　Well… I've just read an article about a new system that we might want to purchase. I'll send some details about it to you when I get back to my desk.	女　Alex，我聽說你在主持與Allstar公司的會議上表現相當出色。他們非常喜歡你提議的新廣告活動。這個月你準備安排更多與新客戶的會議，對嗎？ 男　是的，但是比起面對面開會，我在考慮進行視訊會議。 女　視訊會議系統不是常常出問題嗎？ 男　嗯…我剛讀了一篇文章，關於我們可能會想購買的新系統。等我回到座位上，再把詳細資訊傳給妳。
What field do the speakers most likely work in? Advertising	說話者最有可能從事哪個領域的工作？ 廣告

切勿錯過的答題線索

Welcome to Alpha Gym. How can I help you?　歡迎來到Alpha健身房，有什麼需要幫忙的嗎？
This is Jack Wilson, a freelance photographer.　我是自由攝影師Jack Wilson。
Hi, **I'm calling from** the company Greenwood. We're interested in filming a scene for a movie in the library.
你好，我是從Greenwood公司打來的。我們想在圖書館拍攝一部電影的場景。
I'm pleased with the sales of **our brand's** cakes, pies and cookies this season.
我對我們本季品牌的蛋糕、派和餅乾的銷量感到滿意。

PRACTICE

🎧 P3_05 答案&解析 p.25

請聆聽對話，填寫空白處的句子後，選出適當的答案。

W _____.
　　Are you a member here?
M Actually, this is my first visit. I recently moved to the area.
W Well, there is no charge to become a member. You just have to show proof of address, such as a utility bill or apartment lease.
M Great. Do you offer any classes for the community?
W Absolutely. We have a wide range of classes for adults. Here is the schedule for this month. But just so you know, we're closed next week because of the holiday.
M Okay. Are there public computers as well?
W Yes, just over there. You can use them anytime.

1. Where is the conversation most likely taking place?
   (A) At a library
   (B) At a real estate agency
   (C) At an electronics store
   (D) At a fitness center

聽完對話後，選出適當的答案。

2. Who most likely is the woman?
   (A) An electrician
   (B) A janitor
   (C) An interior decorator
   (D) A property manager

3. What industry does the man work in?
   (A) Publishing
   (B) Food service
   (C) Health care
   (D) Agriculture

4. Where does the man work?
   (A) At a restaurant
   (B) At a television station
   (C) At a business institute
   (D) At a movie theater

61

UNIT 11　詢問相關細節

💡 考題重點

1. 題目會使用What, Who, How, Why等疑問詞開頭的問句，詢問對話中的特定資訊或說話者提及的內容。
2. 選項通常會將對話中出現的答題線索，採用換句話說的方式，改寫成其他內容。且選項多為長度較長的句子，因此建議作答前先閱讀選項，掌握內容重點。

🔍 常見考題

特定資訊　What did/does/will the man ~? 男子做了什麼、在做什麼、將要做什麼？
　　　　　　Who/When/Where/How/Why did/does/will the woman ~?
　　　　　　女子和誰、何時、在哪裡、如何、為什麼/做了、在做、將要做什麼？

提及的內容　What does the man say about ~? 關於～男子說了什麼？

📎 代表題型範例

🎧 P3_06

W　Good morning, and welcome to Sunburg Community Center. How may I help you? M　Hello. I'm interested in finding a place to play racquetball. I just moved to this town for a new job, and someone at work recommended this place. W　Great! We have four racquetball courts, but you have to be a member to use them. M　Okay. Would it be possible to see your facilities? W　Of course. I'll ask my coworker, Amy, to show you around. Wait here just a moment, please.	女　早安，歡迎來到Sunburg社區中心。有什麼需要幫忙的嗎？ 男　你好，我想找個地方打壁球。因為新工作的關係，我剛搬到這個鎮上，工作認識的人推薦了這裡。 女　太好了！我們有四個壁球場，但你必須加入會員才能使用。 男　我知道了，我可以看一下你們的設施嗎？ 女　當然可以，我請我同事Amy帶你參觀，請在這裡稍等一下。
What did the man recently do? He moved into the area.	男子最近做了什麼？ 他搬到了這個區域。

💡 切勿錯過的答題線索

選項中會直接提及題目出現的關鍵字，或是採取換句話說的方式。
What is some **software** being used for? 軟體用來做什麼？
I recently purchased your **software** to keep track of my warehouse inventory.
我最近買了你們的軟體來追蹤我倉庫的庫存。

Why does the woman want to **make a change**? 為什麼女子想要改變？
We may need to **alter the route** so it's less difficult for our camera operators to follow the action.
我們可能要改變路線，才能讓攝影師更容易跟上動作。

PRACTICE

🎧 P3_07 答案&解析 p.27

請聆聽對話，填寫空白處的句子後，選出適當的答案。

> M Hello, I'm supposed to meet Anthony Shaw here for an interview. I'm from the *Worthington Herald*.
> W Ah, yes. He's expecting you, so he'll be out in a moment. _____.
> M Yes, he's been such a big part of the local basketball scene. A lot of people will miss him when he retires at the end of the season.
> W Right. He's very talented. Anyway, could I get you something to drink while you wait?
> M Thanks, but I'm fine.

1. Who is Anthony Shaw?
   (A) A maintenance worker
   (B) A coach
   (C) A receptionist
   (D) A journalist

聽完對話後，選出適當的答案。

2. Why is the man disappointed?
   (A) A proposal was rejected.
   (B) A meeting was canceled.
   (C) A board member has resigned.
   (D) A presentation included some errors.

3. What problem does the woman mention?
   (A) There's a misprint on the ticket.
   (B) Some bus fares have increased.
   (C) The weather is bad.
   (D) Some repairs are needed.

4. What does the man say about a brand?
   (A) It receives many positive reviews.
   (B) It has an affordable price.
   (C) It is currently out of stock.
   (D) It uses high-quality materials.

UNIT 12　詢問建議或要求

考題重點

1. 一般為題組的最後一題，答題線索通常會出現在後半段對話中。
2. 建議先看過題目，確認說話者的性別後，再仔細聆聽指定說話者提出的建議，或要求對方做的事。

常見考題

建議　What does the man suggest (doing)?　男子建議做何事？
　　　　What does the man offer to do?　男子提議要做何事？

要求　What does the man ask/tell the woman to do?　男子要求女子做什麼？
　　　　What does the woman ask for?　女子提出什麼要求？

代表題型範例

🎧 P3_08

W　Hi, I've purchased a ticket for your special exhibit of contemporary art. I'd like to take some pictures of the paintings. Is that allowed? M　Yes, um... but please make sure you turn off your flash first. W　Okay, great. I'm looking forward to this exhibit. M　I hope you enjoy it. And here's a brochure of our future events that you might be interested in. W　Thanks. I'll give that a look. M　Also, I suggest you hold onto your ticket. You can show it at the café to get a discount.	女　你好，我買了當代藝術特別展的門票。我想拍攝幾張畫作的照片，這是被允許的嗎？ 男　可以，但… 要麻煩你先關掉閃光燈。 女　好，沒問題。我很期待這次的展覽。 男　希望你會喜歡。這本手冊上有我們未來將舉辦的活動，也許你會感興趣。 女　謝謝，我來看一下。 男　另外，我建議妳保管好門票，在咖啡廳出示，就可以享有折扣優惠。
What does the man suggest doing? Keeping a ticket	男子建議做什麼？ 保留門票。

切勿錯過的答題線索

Why don't you send me a detailed description of the work?　能否把那項工作的詳細說明傳給我？
Maybe we should organize more workshops to draw people in.　也許我們應該多安排一些工作坊來吸引人們參與。
I can / I'd be happy to teach my system to the rest of the department.
我很樂意向部門其他人員教授我的系統。
Could you bring me a sandwich from the cafeteria?　能幫我從自助餐廳拿一個三明治嗎？

PRACTICE

🎧 P3_09 答案&解析 p.29

請聆聽對話，填寫空白處的句子後，選出適當的答案。

> M　Mijin, I plan to apply for the assistant manager role, but _____ ?
>
> W　I'd be happy to. You've been doing an excellent job on the sales team, and I'm really impressed with how hard you worked after being assigned to a new territory.
>
> M　Thanks a lot. I'm actually quite proud of how I was able to exceed my sales targets by so much. It helped to boost my confidence.

1. What does the man ask the woman to do?

    (A) Proofread a sales catalog
    (B) Visit a client
    (C) Give a presentation
    (D) Write an evaluation

聽完對話後，選出適當的答案。

2. What does the woman offer to do?

    (A) Work on the weekend
    (B) Order some flowers
    (C) Look for some materials
    (D) Hold a tenants' meeting

3. What does the man suggest doing?

    (A) Making promotional videos
    (B) Inviting celebrities to the store
    (C) Offering discount coupons
    (D) Holding a decorating contest

4. What does the man ask for?

    (A) A dessert recipe
    (B) A promotional brochure
    (C) A copy of an invitation
    (D) A contact list

UNIT 13　詢問下一步的行動

考題重點

1. 答題線索通常會出現在後半段對話中，使用will, be going to等句型，表達未來的計劃。
2. 題目詢問即將發生的事情時，選項多半為完整句，因此建議提前閱讀題目，確認主詞和關鍵字。

常見考題

下一步的行動
What will the man (most likely) do next?　男子接下來（最有可能）做什麼？
What does the woman say she will do?　女子說她將會做什麼？

即將發生的事
What will happen ~?　~會發生什麼？
What event will take place ~?　~將發生什麼事件？

代表題型範例

🎧 P3_10

M　The new billboard for our gym went up yesterday. I think it's going to be a great way to advertise our business.	男　我們健身房的新廣告看板昨天掛起來了，我認為這將是宣傳我們公司的好方法。
W　I saw it as I was driving to work this morning. It looks great.	女　我今天早上開車上班的路上有看到，看起來不錯。
M　Yeah, and I'm glad it's on such a busy road.	男　對，我很高興它位在交通繁忙的道路上。
W　Right. Many people will see it, so we'll probably get a lot of new members this month. We should make sure all employees know how to register new members.	女　沒錯，很多人都會看到，所以這個月我們可能會增加很多新會員。我們應該要讓全體員工都知道如何註冊新會員。
M　That's a good point. I'll e-mail everyone now with a reminder of how to do it.	男　你說的沒錯，我會發一封電子郵件給每個人，提醒他們如何操作。

What does the man say he will do?　男子說他會做什麼？
Send a message　傳送一則訊息。

切勿錯過的答題線索

I'll / I'm going to send you links to their website.　我會把他們網站的連結傳給你。
I need to look for the service records for the lawn mower.　我需要查一下割草機的維修記錄。
Let me show you around our facility.　我帶你參觀我們的設施。
There'll be a children's poster competition next month.　下個月將舉辦一場兒童海報比賽。

PRACTICE

🎧 P3_11 答案&解析 p.30

請聆聽對話，填寫空白處的句子後，選出適當的答案。

> W Hi, I tried to use the library's self-checkout machine, but there was a message saying that I owe a fine. Here is my card.
>
> M Let me see... Yes, it looks like one of your books was returned late. You'll have to pay a fine of $1.25 before checking out anything new.
>
> W Oh, that's no problem. I can pay it now. Sorry about that.
>
> M It happens. _____.
> We're selling used books to purchase new computers for the library.

1. What will take place next Saturday?

    (A) A writing workshop
    (B) A poetry reading
    (C) A computer class
    (D) A fundraising event

聽完對話後，選出適當的答案。

2. What will the woman most likely do next?

    (A) Write down an address
    (B) Confirm a schedule
    (C) Introduce a crew member
    (D) Provide a cost estimate

3. What will happen next week?

    (A) A theater will be renovated.
    (B) A play will open.
    (C) A poster will be printed.
    (D) An acting award will be presented.

4. What does the woman say she will do?

    (A) Take some measurements
    (B) Paint a room
    (C) Sign a contract
    (D) Install some lights

UNIT 14　詢問說話者的意圖

考題重點

1. 提前確認題目列出的引用句，接著專心聆聽對話中，該句話前後出現的對白。
2. 作答時不能受限於單字或句子於字典中的意思，而是要掌握說話者的意圖，根據前後文意確認整句話的含義。唯有理解整段對話的脈絡和文意，才能選出正確答案。

常見考題

意思或背後含義	What does the woman mean/imply when she says, "~"? 女子說：「～」意指／暗示什麼？
目的	Why does the man say, "~"? 男子為什麼要說：「～」？

代表題型範例

🎧 P3_12

M　Hello, Ms. Hodge? This is Tony from Fremont Furniture. I'm calling about your order of three leather sofas for your hotel's lobby. They were supposed to be delivered today, but I'm afraid there's going to be a delay.

W　We're shooting the commercial on Friday. Our site needs to look its best.

M　I'm very sorry for the inconvenience. Our supplier is having some distribution issues. I'll call you tomorrow to confirm the new delivery date.

男　你好，Hodge女士，我是Fremont傢俱公司的Tony。我打電話來詢問您為貴飯店大廳訂購三張真皮沙發的事。它們原定於今天出貨，但恐怕會延遲。

女　我們星期五要拍廣告。大廳要看起來完美無暇才行。

男　對於造成您的不便，我深感抱歉。我們的供應商遇到一些物流問題。我明天會致電給您，確認新的出貨日期。

Why does the woman say, "We're shooting the commercial on Friday"?
To show concern

為什麼女子會說：「我們星期五要拍廣告」？
為了表達擔憂。

切勿錯過的答題線索

引用句前方出現對方的建議或要求時：該引用句可能為表達同意／答應，或是反對／拒絕。

W　What if we donated our reusable water bottles for the registration gift bags?
　　我們捐贈可重複使用的水瓶，當成註冊禮怎麼樣？
M　You know, our company hasn't made a profit yet. 你知不知道，我們公司目前尚未獲利。➡ 反對提議

引用句後方出現道歉、提出解決方案、表達有共鳴或讓對方安心的話語時：該引用句極有可能為表達不滿、驚訝、擔憂等情緒。

M　They want 3,000 full color brochures printed by Friday. 他們希望在星期五之前印出3000本彩色手冊。
W　Four of our people are on vacation. 我們員工中有四個人在休假 ➡ 表達對訂單的擔憂
M　What about increasing the rate we pay for overtime, just for this job?
　　單純針對此項工作調高加班費如何？

PRACTICE

🎧 P3_13 答案&解析 p.32

請聆聽對話，填寫空白處的句子後，選出適當的答案。

> W Hi, Mr. Fox. Our team of consultants has gone over your business model, and we've come up with some ideas to expand your footwear brand.
>
> M That's great. We've been struggling to make a name for ourselves in the market, so your insights will be helpful.
>
> W All right. So, _____?
>
> M They usually market to an older clientele.
>
> W Hmm... _____.

1. Why does the man say, "They usually market to an older clientele"?
   (A) To express disappointment
   (B) To agree with a plan
   (C) To reject a suggestion
   (D) To offer assistance

聽完對話後，選出適當的答案。

2. What does the man mean when he says, "it's very cold today"?
   (A) He wants to change his seating request.
   (B) Taking public transportation was uncomfortable.
   (C) The heater should be turned up.
   (D) He may have to postpone a meeting.

3. Why does the man say, "That property was just posted a few days ago"?
   (A) To make an offer
   (B) To provide an excuse
   (C) To explain an error
   (D) To express surprise

4. What does the woman imply when she says, "that equipment gets used a lot"?
   (A) A high-quality product was purchased.
   (B) A problem is not surprising.
   (C) A training session is not needed.
   (D) An expense is reasonable.

69

UNIT 15　圖表整合題

考題重點

1. 圖表包含目錄、表格、地圖、平面圖、優惠券、其他圖片等種類多樣。請務必在對話播放前查看圖表，掌握關鍵字。
2. 請特別留意四個選項的內容是否出現在對話中。對話中提及多個選項內容時，請搭配圖表逐一比對，確認對應內容是否正確。

常見考題

Look at the graphic. What/Which/Who/When/Where ~?　請看圖表，什麼、哪一個、誰、何時、哪裡～？

代表題型範例

P3_14

W　Jason, have you had a chance to try out the new software yet? It has a lot of nice new features, but it doesn't run very fast.
M　Are the other team members experiencing the same problem?
W　Yeah. Many of my team members have said the same thing. We should report it to someone in charge.
M　**I'll call the IT department and ask them to look into this issue.**

女　Jason，你有機會試用新的軟體嗎？它有很多不錯的新功能，但運行速度不是很快。
男　其他團隊成員是否也遇到相同的問題？
女　是的，許多我的團隊成員也說過同樣的話，我們應該向負責人報告。
男　**我會打電話給技術部門，要求他們調查這個問題。**

Extension	Title
567	Accounting Manager
599	IT Manager

Look at the graphic. Which extension number will the man most likely call?
599

分機	職稱
567	會計部經理
599	技術部經理

請看圖表，男子最有可能撥打哪個分機號碼？
599

切勿錯過的答題線索

時間順序	The live music will start **at the same time as** dinner.	晚餐時間將有現場音樂表演。
位置或方向	It's a corner room that's **right next to** the food court.	這是一間轉角客房，位在美食廣場旁邊。
比較級或最高級	**The highest** category is worth investing in.	最高的項目值得投資。
外型或模式	They're the ones with the **large star in the middle** and **smaller ones around the edge**. 它們的中間有大星星，邊緣有小星星。	

PRACTICE

🎧 P3_15 答案&解析 p.33

請聆聽對話，填寫空白處的句子後，選出適當的答案。

> W   I missed the staff meeting yesterday. Is there anything I need to know about?
> M   Well, the planning for the city's Environmental Awareness Day is going well. There's going to be a cleanup project at Hartford Park in the morning. We'll also be collecting recyclable items at city hall.
> W   Great. Did we find any sponsors for the event?
> M   Yes. Finch Landscaping is donating three hundred saplings that people can plant at home. _____ .

Trees	Heights
Alder	15 meters
Hawthorne	10 meters
Gray Willow	8 meters
Holly	6 meters

1. Look at the graphic. What kind of saplings will be donated?
   (A) Alder
   (B) Hawthorne
   (C) Gray Willow
   (D) Holly

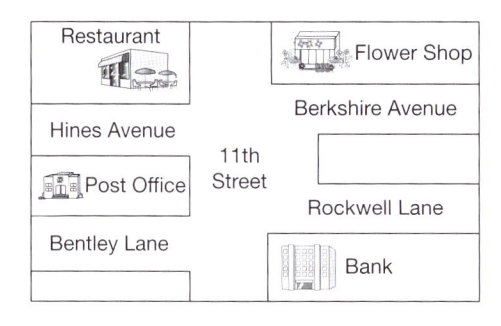

聽完對話後，選出適當的答案。

2. Look at the graphic. Which road can be closed?
   (A) Hines Avenue
   (B) Berkshire Avenue
   (C) Bentley Lane
   (D) Rockwell Lane

Flights to Berlin

Departure Time	Airline
1:35 P.M.	Kershaw Budget
3:58 P.M.	Rosco Skyteam
7:31 P.M.	Powell Airlines
8:02 P.M.	GT Airways

3. Look at the graphic. When does the woman's flight depart?
   (A) At 1:35 P.M.
   (B) At 3:58 P.M.
   (C) At 7:31 P.M.
   (D) At 8:02 P.M.

PART TEST

P3_16 答案&解析 p.35

PART 3
Directions: You will hear some conversations between two or more people. You will be asked to answer three questions about what the speakers say in each conversation. Select the best response to each question and mark the letter (A), (B), (C), or (D) on your answer sheet. The conversations will not be printed in your test book and will be spoken only one time.

32. Where does the conversation most likely take place?
    (A) At a hardware store
    (B) At a community center
    (C) At a car dealership
    (D) At a shoe store

33. What does the man suggest doing?
    (A) Hiring part-time workers
    (B) Rearranging a display
    (C) Holding a sports competition
    (D) Contacting a supplier

34. What will the man do next?
    (A) Speak to a supervisor
    (B) Send a message
    (C) Update a website
    (D) Review some figures

35. Who most likely is the man?
    (A) A landlord
    (B) A facility manager
    (C) A plumber
    (D) An electrician

36. According to Carol, what is the problem?
    (A) Some instructions were incorrect.
    (B) A coworker has been absent.
    (C) She is missing some components.
    (D) She noticed a water leak.

37. What does the man mention about a repair?
    (A) It cannot be completed right away.
    (B) It may require special parts.
    (C) It is not necessary at this time.
    (D) Its cost has recently increased.

38. Where does the man most likely work?
    (A) At a government office
    (B) At a construction firm
    (C) At a medical clinic
    (D) At an employment agency

39. According to the man, what should applicants provide?
    (A) A letter of reference
    (B) A mailing address
    (C) Proof of certification
    (D) A copy of a photo ID

40. What is scheduled for Friday?
    (A) An information session
    (B) An interview
    (C) A staff dinner
    (D) A board meeting

41. What kind of product are the speakers discussing?
    (A) A digital camera
    (B) A video game system
    (C) A printer
    (D) A smartphone

42. What event will take place this weekend?
    (A) A film screening
    (B) An annual parade
    (C) A musical performance
    (D) A business conference

43. What does the woman ask about?
    (A) How long a warranty lasts
    (B) How to get an item
    (C) How much a delivery fee is
    (D) How to return a product

44. What did the woman need help with?
    (A) Installing a window
    (B) Building a garage
    (C) Planting a garden
    (D) Removing a tree

45. Why does the woman thank the man?
    (A) He offered a discount.
    (B) He provided a recommendation.
    (C) He explained a procedure.
    (D) He arrived quickly.

46. What will the woman most likely do next?
    (A) Move her vehicle
    (B) Get a power cord
    (C) Make a payment
    (D) Select a color

47. What kind of business is the woman calling?
    (A) A hotel
    (B) An insurance company
    (C) A theater
    (D) A catering company

48. Why is the woman planning an event?
    (A) To promote a grand opening
    (B) To present some awards
    (C) To celebrate a company anniversary
    (D) To raise funds for a project

49. Why does the man say, "I was going to order everything today"?
    (A) To thank the woman for a reminder
    (B) To confirm that a request can be fulfilled
    (C) To accept a change in a deadline
    (D) To ask for a payment

50. Where do the speakers work?
    (A) At a law firm
    (B) At an employment agency
    (C) At a newspaper publisher
    (D) At a photography studio

51. What problem does the man mention?
    (A) Some equipment is missing.
    (B) Some confidential information was shared.
    (C) Employees are working too much.
    (D) A system is running slowly.

52. What does Stacey think the business should do?
    (A) Upgrade some software
    (B) Gather feedback from employees
    (C) Change the hours of operation
    (D) Provide annual bonuses

53. Who most likely is the man?
    (A) A senior accountant
    (B) A hotel manager
    (C) A building cleaner
    (D) A clothing shop owner

54. What does the woman want to do later this year?
    (A) Move to a new city
    (B) Take a trip abroad
    (C) Start her own business
    (D) Purchase a house

55. What does the man ask the woman about?
    (A) Her career goals
    (B) Her preferred start date
    (C) Her availability
    (D) Her expected salary

GO ON TO THE NEXT PAGE

56. Who most likely are the speakers?

    (A) Environmental scientists
    (B) Company investors
    (C) City council members
    (D) Construction workers

57. What is the city expected to approve?

    (A) Holding a festival
    (B) Building a pedestrian path
    (C) Expanding a parking lot
    (D) Renovating a stadium

58. What advantage of a project is mentioned?

    (A) It will save money.
    (B) It will create jobs.
    (C) It will promote health.
    (D) It will attract tourists.

59. What is the conversation mainly about?

    (A) Publishing a cookbook
    (B) Starting a podcast
    (C) Presenting at a trade show
    (D) Launching a household appliance

60. Why does the man say, "Everyone is familiar with that"?

    (A) To reject a suggestion
    (B) To confirm survey results
    (C) To praise a strategy
    (D) To acknowledge an accomplishment

61. What do the speakers agree to do?

    (A) Contact some suppliers
    (B) Visit a shop together
    (C) Record a demonstration
    (D) Browse a website

Poetry	$10
Watercolor Painting	$18
Ballet	$14
Sewing	$22

62. Look at the graphic. How much will the man most likely pay?

    (A) $10
    (B) $18
    (C) $14
    (D) $22

63. What information does the woman ask for?

    (A) A credit card number
    (B) An e-mail address
    (C) A start date
    (D) A difficulty level

64. What does the woman suggest doing?

    (A) Watching a video
    (B) Renting some equipment
    (C) Wearing special clothing
    (D) Printing a brochure

①		②
Vance Hardware	Jojo's	TG Pharmacy

③ Reppert Stadium

| Joy Café | Allen Books | Royal Cinema | Funtime Shoes |

④

	Philadelphia Weekly Forecast			
Monday	Tuesday	Wednesday	Thursday	Friday
Rainy	Rainy	Sunny	Cloudy	Sunny

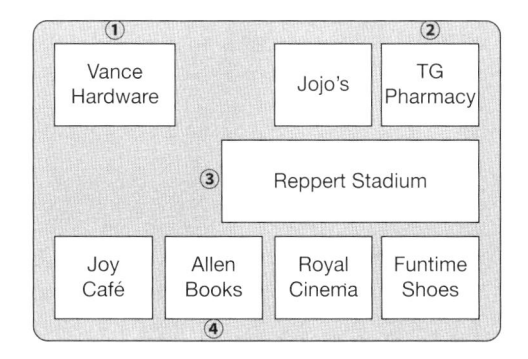

65. Why is the woman visiting the site?

    (A) To meet with investors
    (B) To perform an inspection
    (C) To hear a lecture
    (D) To have a job interview

66. What is the woman surprised about?

    (A) The transportation fee
    (B) The number of attendees
    (C) The travel time
    (D) The size of a venue

67. Look at the graphic. Where will the woman most likely get off the bus?

    (A) At stop 1
    (B) At stop 2
    (C) At stop 3
    (D) At stop 4

68. Why does the man apologize?

    (A) Some measurements must be taken again.
    (B) A work estimate was not accurate.
    (C) Some supplies have not arrived.
    (D) An employee did not provide a bill.

69. What does the man think was a good idea?

    (A) Using a different material
    (B) Changing to another company
    (C) Assessing a property's value
    (D) Requesting a rush service

70. Look at the graphic. When will the man's team most likely come back?

    (A) On Monday
    (B) On Tuesday
    (C) On Wednesday
    (D) On Thursday

PART 4

簡短獨白

UNIT 16 通話訊息

UNIT 17 公告與導引

UNIT 18 演說與講座

UNIT 19 廣告與廣播

UNIT 20 觀光與參訪

PART TEST

PART 4 簡短獨白

聽完單人的獨白後，針對相關的三道考題選出最適當的答案。聽力測驗共有100題，PART 4佔30題（10篇獨白×3題）。

獨白類型

通話訊息 來電者在答錄機留下的語音訊息、公司或政府機關事先錄好的未接來電自動語音應答。

公告與導引 與工作相關的公司內部公告及會議摘錄、公共場所播放的廣播，包含營業時間或特別活動等通知。

演說與講座 在會議、開幕式等各種活動上發表的演說或講座。

廣告與廣播 宣傳產品、服務、企業等的廣告，以及播放當地新聞、天氣預報、交通資訊等的廣播節目。

觀光與參訪 引導遊客參觀歷史遺跡等觀光景點，或實地考察工廠等各種設施。

考題類型

主旨或目的 詢問獨白的主旨或目的，包含訊息主旨、開會目的等。

說話者或地點 詢問說話者或聽者的身分，包含職業及工作地點等，或是詢問獨白出現的地點。

相關細節 針對獨白中提及的內容詢問「什麼、是誰、何時」等詳細資訊，或是詢問說話者針對特定對象提及的內容。

建議或要求事項 詢問說話者向聽者提出的建議、請求或要求。

下一步的行動或即將發生的事 詢問說話者或聽者下一步的行動或往後會發生的事。

掌握說話者的意圖 針對說話者說過的話詢問其意思及背後含義，或是說出該句話的理由。

圖表整合題 指與目錄、地圖、表格等各式各樣的圖表一同出現的考題。

解題策略

STEP 1 | 掌握題目重點
請於獨白播放前,事先閱讀題目,由關鍵字確認題目詢問的內容,並預測答題線索可能會出現的位置。

STEP 2 | 從獨白中找出答題線索
聆聽獨白的過程中,根據關鍵字找出答題線索。

STEP 3 | 選出正確答案
選擇與答題線索同樣的內容、替換同義詞或換句話說的選項作為答案。

🎧 P4_01

71. Where does the speaker most likely work?
    (A) At a bank
    (B) At a pharmacy
    (C) At a post office
    (D) At a bookstore

72. According to the speaker, what is the requirement of the job?
    (A) Management experience
    (B) Sales training
    (C) Computer skills
    (D) A business network

73. What does the speaker ask the listener to do?
    (A) Attend an interview
    (B) Upload a document
    (C) Send a reference letter
    (D) Read a contract

---

[71] Hi, this is Kate Edwards from Sapphire Bookstore. You recently applied for a sales clerk position with us. I'm sorry to say that we offered that job to someone else. However, we've just had an opening for a weekend supervisor. Your résumé said that [72] you have experience managing others. That's one of the main requirements of this role. I think you would be great for the job. So, [73] I'd like to invite you to an interview next week. Please call me back at 555-8763 if you're interested.

中譯

71. 說話者最有可能在哪裡工作?
    (A) 在銀行
    (B) 在藥局
    (C) 在郵局
    (D) 在書店

72. 根據說話者所述,該工作的資格條件為何?
    (A) 管理經驗
    (B) 銷售培訓
    (C) 電腦技能
    (D) 商務網路

73. 說話者要求聽者做什麼?
    (A) 參加面試
    (B) 上傳文件
    (C) 發送推薦信
    (D) 閱讀合約

[71] 您好,我是藍寶石書店的Kate Edwards。您最近應徵了我們書店的銷售員一職。我們很遺憾通知您,那份工作已錄取了其他人。但是,我們剛好有一個週末主管的職缺。您的履歷表上提到[72] 您有管理他人的經驗,那是擔任該職位的主要要求之一。我認為您非常適任這份工作,所以[73] 我想邀請您參加下週的面試。如果您有興趣,請撥打555-8763回電給我。

UNIT 16　通話訊息

考題重點

1. 通話訊息主要包含預約、訂單確認、徵人、業務討論、店休通知等傳遞資訊或留下諮詢事項的內容。獨白各段重點依序為：問候語與本人介紹 → 來電目的與相關細節 → 要求事項。
2. 題目經常會詢問來電目的、說話者的身分、要求事項。

代表題型範例

🎧 P4_02

問候語與本人介紹　Hi, this message is for Hank Howard. [1] This is Tonya from the Jacobson Appliance Store.

來電目的與相關細節　You stopped by yesterday and placed an order for one of our compact ovens. They're currently on sale, but [2] I believe one of our cashiers charged you incorrectly. She wasn't aware that the six-piece oven accessory set is included with all oven purchases during the promotion.

要求事項　[3] If you have time, could you please stop by our store so we can correct your receipt? If not, we can do this over the phone. Thank you for your understanding, and we apologize for the inconvenience.

您好，這是給Hank Howard的留言。[1] 我是Jacobson電器商店的Tonya。

您昨天來過賣場，訂購了我們的一款小型烤箱。它們目前正在做促銷，但[2] 我們的收銀員似乎向您收取了錯誤的費用。她並不知道優惠期間購買的所有烤箱，都會附贈烤箱配件六件組。

[3] 如果您有空的話，能否過來我們的商店，以便為您修改收據呢？如果您沒有時間，可以打電話處理。感謝您的諒解，造成您的不便，我們深感抱歉。

---

1. Where does the speaker most likely work?
   At a store
2. What is the purpose of the message?
   To correct a mistake
3. What does the speaker ask the listener to do?
   Visit the business

1. 說話者最有可能在哪裡工作？在商店。
2. 該留言的目的為何？為了修正錯誤。
3. 說話者要求聽者做什麼？造訪商店。

切勿錯過的答題線索

說話者／聽者	Hi, **this is a message for** the technology department. **This is** Satomi **from** human resources.　你好，這是給技術部的留言，我是人力資源部的Satomi。
主旨／目的	**I'm calling about** your novel, *Silver Fox*, which came out last year.　我打電話給你，是為了詢問你去年出版的小說《銀色狐狸》。
建議／要求事項	**Please** let us know which time of day you prefer.　請告訴我們您偏好哪個時段。

80

PRACTICE

🎧 P4_03 答案&解析 p.42

聽完獨白後，選出適當的答案。

1. Where does the speaker most likely work?
   (A) At a medical clinic
   (B) At a law firm
   (C) At an employment agency
   (D) At a software company

2. Why is the speaker calling?
   (A) To ask the listener for a reference
   (B) To ask the listener to give a presentation
   (C) To change an interview location
   (D) To make a job offer

3. What is the reason for a delay?
   (A) A committee must have a meeting.
   (B) A venue is fully booked.
   (C) A staff member will be unavailable.
   (D) Some supplies have not arrived.

4. What is the message mainly about?
   (A) A business trip overseas
   (B) The launch of a new product
   (C) An interview for a magazine
   (D) The relocation of a business

5. What does the speaker ask the listener to do on Thursday?
   (A) Sign a contract
   (B) Work later than usual
   (C) Bake additional items
   (D) Make a dinner reservation

6. Where will the speaker go this weekend?
   (A) To a training workshop
   (B) To a board meeting
   (C) To a music festival
   (D) To a job fair

7. What type of business is the listener calling?
   (A) An auto repair shop
   (B) A utility provider
   (C) A transportation company
   (D) An appliance store

8. What does the speaker imply when he says, "we are monitoring the situation"?
   (A) A departure schedule is uncertain.
   (B) A complaint will be filed.
   (C) Customer feedback will be assessed.
   (D) New policies have been adopted.

9. How can the listener stay updated?
   (A) By talking to a driver
   (B) By signing up for a newsletter
   (C) By sending an e-mail
   (D) By checking information online

UNIT 17　公告與導引

考題重點

1. 包含會議內容、與業務、銷售、業績或變更制度相關內容，或是公共場所的廣播通知，告知特別活動、營業時間的變動或延後。獨白各段重點依序為：公告的主旨 → 相關細節 → 要求事項或下一步的行動。
2. 題目經常會詢問主旨、聽者、地點、要求事項或下一步的行動。

代表題型範例

P4_04

公告的主旨	To begin this meeting, I have some exciting news about Charles Kent.
相關細節	[1,2] This month, he sold 35 vehicles from our lot. [2] That's the most anyone has ever sold. The previous record was 28. Great job, Charles! This month, we're going to hold a contest to keep all of the sales staff motivated. The group that has the highest sales will win a prize.
要求事項或下一步的行動	[3] I'll put you in your groups now, and then we can discuss the details.

在這場會議開始之前，我有個關於Charles Kent的振奮消息。

[1,2] 這個月他在我們的區域賣掉了35輛車，[2] 這是有史以來賣得最好的一次。先前的紀錄是28輛。做得好，Charles！這個月我們將舉辦一場比賽來激勵所有銷售人員。銷售業績最高的小組將獲得一個獎項。

[3] 我現在為你們分組，接下來我們就可以討論細節。

1. Where do the listeners most likely work?
   At a car dealership
2. What has Charles Kent recently done?
   He set a new sales record.
3. What will the speaker do next?
   Assign the listeners to groups

1. 聽者最有可能在哪裡工作？在汽車經銷商。
2. Charles Kent最近做了什麼事？他創下新的銷售紀錄。
3. 說話者接下來要做什麼事？為聽者分組。

切勿錯過的答題線索

聽者／地點	**Attention** Norton Department Store shoppers. Norton百貨的購物者請注意。
主旨／目的	**I'm happy to announce** that our new line of home office desks is selling very well. 我很高興宣佈，我們新系列的家庭辦公桌銷售極佳。
建議／要求事項	Now, **I'd like everyone to** help with a deep cleaning of the refrigerators. 現在，我希望大家幫忙把冰箱清潔乾淨。
下一步的行動	**We're going to** hold a company party next Thursday evening. 我們將於下星期四晚上舉辦公司派對。

PRACTICE

聽完獨白後，選出適當的答案。

1. Where most likely are the listeners?
   (A) At a clothing shop
   (B) At a hardware store
   (C) At an electronics store
   (D) At a bookstore

2. What does the speaker say is offered to loyalty program members?
   (A) A free item
   (B) Discount coupons
   (C) Express delivery
   (D) Advance notice of sales

3. What will begin next Monday?
   (A) Extended business hours
   (B) Some construction
   (C) An anniversary event
   (D) A clearance sale

4. What will be delivered next Friday?
   (A) Business cards
   (B) Potted plants
   (C) Light refreshments
   (D) Leather sofas

5. What is mentioned about productivity?
   (A) It has improved recently at the office.
   (B) It can be increased through regular breaks.
   (C) It directly results in higher profits.
   (D) It is the focus of the new management team.

6. According to the speaker, what is available at the reception desk?
   (A) A contract
   (B) A survey form
   (C) A catalog
   (D) An updated schedule

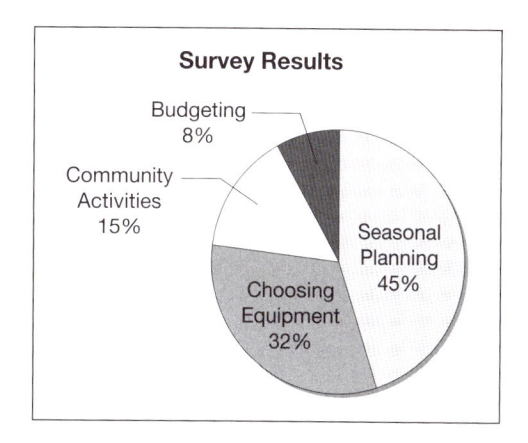

Survey Results
- Seasonal Planning 45%
- Choosing Equipment 32%
- Community Activities 15%
- Budgeting 8%

7. What kind of club are the listeners members of?
   (A) Painting
   (B) Sewing
   (C) Cycling
   (D) Gardening

8. Look at the graphic. According to the speaker, which workshop will likely be held first?
   (A) Seasonal Planning
   (B) Choosing Equipment
   (C) Community Activities
   (D) Budgeting

9. What does the speaker ask the listeners to do?
   (A) Update some contact information
   (B) Recommend venues for a workshop
   (C) Explain their survey answers
   (D) Recruit new group members

UNIT 18　演說與講座

💡 考題重點

1. 包含各種聚會或活動中的演講、研討會或學會中針對特定主題的說明、教育的內容。獨白各段重點依序為：問候語與本人介紹 → 活動或演講主題 → 相關細節 → 要求事項或下一步的行動。
2. 題目經常會詢問主旨、說話者、聽者、地點、要求事項或下一步的行動。

📎 代表題型範例

🎧 P4_06

問候語與本人介紹 Hello, everyone. My name is Janet, and I'll be leading this workshop. 演講主題 ¹ Today you'll learn how to use the latest project management software. 相關細節 There are numerous tasks needed ² when developing advertising campaigns for your clients. This program will help you manage resources, create custom images, track a brand's success, and more. 要求事項或下一步的行動 At the end, ³ I'll ask you to provide your opinions about the parts you found most helpful.	嗨，大家好！我叫Janet，我將會主持這場研討會。 ¹ 今天您將學習如何使用最新的專案管理軟體。 ² 在為您們的客戶開發廣告活動時，需要執行多項任務。該軟體將幫助您管理資源、建立客製化圖像、追蹤品牌的成功等等。 最後，³ 我會請各位針對您認為最有幫助的部分，提供相關意見。

1. What is the topic of the workshop?
   How to use some software
2. What industry do the listeners most likely work in?
   Advertising
3. What are the listeners asked to do?
   Share their feedback

1. 研討會的主題為何？如何使用軟體。
2. 聽者最有可能從事什麼行業？廣告業。
3. 聽者被要求做什麼事？
   分享他們的意見回饋。

💡 切勿錯過的答題線索

地點／主旨	**Thanks for attending** this candle making workshop. **Today we'll focus on** scented candles. 感謝您參加本次的蠟燭製作研討會，今天我們將著重於香氛蠟燭上。
說話者／聽者	**As** a software engineer, I design computer programs that help real estate agents **like you.** 作為一名軟體工程師，我設計的電腦程式能幫助像您這樣的不動產經紀人。
建議／要求事項	**Don't forget to** check your programs for the list of topics, speakers, and locations. 別忘記檢查您節目的主題清單、講者和地點。
下一步的行動	Before we begin the discussion, **let's** look at an aerial view of the railway in this short video. 在開始討論之前，我們先來看一下這段鐵道的空拍短片。

PRACTICE

聽完獨白後，選出適當的答案。

1. What event is taking place?
   (A) An art festival
   (B) A fundraising event
   (C) A music lesson
   (D) A baking contest

2. What does the organization plan to do?
   (A) Replace a roof
   (B) Train some volunteers
   (C) Change its business hours
   (D) Provide online services

3. What does the speaker encourage the listeners to do?
   (A) Watch a presentation
   (B) Purchase clothing
   (C) Enjoy refreshments
   (D) Come back again soon

4. Who is the speaker?
   (A) A government employee
   (B) A university professor
   (C) A textbook editor
   (D) A software specialist

5. According to the speaker, why were certain debate participants selected?
   (A) They have recently published books.
   (B) They come from different countries.
   (C) They are considered to be experts.
   (D) They have started their own business.

6. What does the speaker imply when she says, "this session will be recorded"?
   (A) Questions can be answered at the end.
   (B) Note-taking is not necessary.
   (C) Cell phones should be put away.
   (D) The audience should remain seated.

7. What is the topic of the seminar?
   (A) Time-saving methods
   (B) Communication skills
   (C) Retirement planning
   (D) Job hunting

8. Why does the speaker thank some of the listeners?
   (A) They registered early.
   (B) They changed seats.
   (C) They set up a room.
   (D) They submitted questions.

9. Why does the speaker mention the side entrance?
   (A) Materials for the event can be found there.
   (B) It will remain locked throughout the seminar.
   (C) Beverages are available for participants there.
   (D) It can be used in case of emergency.

UNIT 19　廣告與廣播

考題重點

1. 廣告包含宣傳產品、服務或企業等，獨白各段重點依序為：吸引注意與廣告對象 → 特色與優勢 → 打折優惠等額外資訊；廣播則包含當地新聞的播報和廣播節目，獨白各段重點依序為：節目名稱與主題 → 主要消息 → 下段廣播預告。
2. 題目經常會詢問廣告的對象、廣播主題、相關細節。

代表題型範例

🎧 P4_08

吸引注意與廣告對象　Do you have customers visit your business in person? It's important to make a good impression with a modern-looking office space. [1] That's why you should consider moving to the Doyle Business Complex.

特色與優勢　[2] We're close to Newport subway station and several bus stops, so it is easy for your employees and customers to get here, even if they don't drive.

額外資訊　We have a wide variety of unit sizes available; [3] e-mail our property manager at inquiries@doylebusiness.com to find out more. We guarantee that we'll get back to you within two business days.

是否有客戶親自拜訪您的企業呢？以現代化的辦公空間讓人留下好印象是非常重要的事。[1] 這就是為什麼您應該考慮搬到Doyle商業綜合園區。[2] 我們鄰近Newport地鐵站以及多個公車站，即使不開車，您的員工和客戶也能輕鬆來到此處。我們有多種大小的空間可供選擇，[3] 若想了解更多資訊，請傳送電子郵件到inquiries@doylebusiness.com給我們的物業經理，我們保證會在兩個工作日內回覆您。

1. What is being advertised?
   An office complex

2. What benefit of the site does the speaker highlight?
   Access to public transportation

3. According to the speaker, how can the listeners get more information?
   By sending an e-mail

1. 廣告宣傳內容為何？ 辦公綜合園區。

2. 說話者強調了該地點的哪些優勢？
   鄰近大眾運輸。

3. 據說話者所述，聽者如何獲得更多資訊？
   藉由傳送電子郵件。

切勿錯過的答題線索

廣播主題	**In today's episode, we'll be taking** a deep dive into the topic of making a career change. 在今天的節目中，我們將深入探討職業轉換的議題。
廣告對象	**Looking for** a great place to exercise? **Try** Salt Creek Fitness Center on Beach Avenue. 你正在尋找一個運動的好地方嗎？試試位在海灘大道上的Salt Creek健身中心。
打折優惠	**We are offering a special discount** to students who show their university identification cards. 我們會提供特別優惠給出示大學學生證的學生。

PRACTICE

🎧 P4_09 答案&解析 p.46

聽完獨白後，選出適當的答案。

1. What kind of business is being advertised?
   (A) An employment agency
   (B) A computer repair shop
   (C) A health-care clinic
   (D) A car rental service

2. Why is a business celebrating?
   (A) It was nominated for an award.
   (B) It will open a new branch.
   (C) It has been in business for twenty years.
   (D) It has acquired a competitor.

3. What do the listeners need to do to get a discount?
   (A) Attend an in-person event
   (B) Sign up for a newsletter
   (C) Complete a survey
   (D) Make an appointment

---

4. What is the podcast mainly about?
   (A) Career changes
   (B) Writing skills
   (C) Medical breakthroughs
   (D) Nutrition advice

5. What did Maya Dalavi recently do?
   (A) She started a website.
   (B) She taught a course.
   (C) She won a competition.
   (D) She published a magazine article.

6. What does the speaker say about podcast membership?
   (A) It can be canceled anytime.
   (B) It charges a monthly fee.
   (C) It provides additional benefits.
   (D) It helps hire new staff.

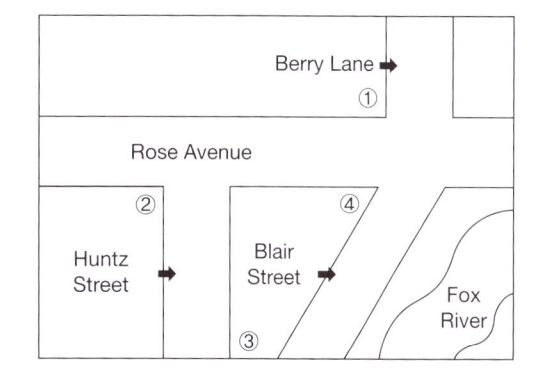

[Map showing Berry Lane (①), Rose Avenue, Huntz Street (②), Blair Street (④), location ③, and Fox River]

7. What is the broadcast mainly about?
   (A) The repair of a road
   (B) The opening of a department store
   (C) The construction of a sports facility
   (D) The route of an upcoming parade

8. What has a company donated?
   (A) Some paintings
   (B) Some seats
   (C) Some lumber
   (D) Some machinery

9. Look at the graphic. Where will the bus stop be located?
   (A) Location 1
   (B) Location 2
   (C) Location 3
   (D) Location 4

UNIT 20　觀光與參訪

考題重點

1. 包含在觀光巴士、歷史遺跡引導遊客參觀的內容，或是導遊在工廠、博物館等設施內進行的導覽。獨白各段重點依序為：問候語與本人介紹 → 觀光或參觀相關細節 → 提醒及下個行程的介紹。
2. 題目經常會提及說話者、地點、建議、要求事項或是下一步的行動。

代表題型範例

🎧 P4_10

問候語與本人介紹　[1] Welcome to Bella Beverage Company. I'm Tina, your guide for this tour.

觀光或參觀相關細節　Now, we would usually begin with a video about the company's history, but [2] I'm sorry our projector is not working. I'll send you all a link so you can watch it on our website later.

提醒及下個行程的介紹　[3] And at the end of the tour, we'll stop by the gift shop. There you can buy items with our logo such as T-shirts, tote bags, and calendars as a reminder of your visit today. As we get started, please stay with the group at all times, as machinery is currently in operation.

[1] 歡迎來到Bella飲料公司。我是負責你們本次導覽的導遊Tina。

一般照慣例我們會先播放一段關於公司歷史的影片，[2] 但很抱歉我們的投影機無法運作。我會把連結傳送給大家，你們稍後可以在我們的網站上觀看。

[3] 導覽結束後，我們將前往紀念品商店。你們可以在那裡購買印有我們公司標誌的商品，例如T恤、手提袋和日曆，作為今日來訪的紀念。現在我們即將開始導覽，因機器目前正在運轉，所以請務必隨時待在隊伍中。

---

1. Where is the tour taking place?
   At a beverage factory
2. Why does the speaker apologize to the listeners?
   Some equipment is not working.
3. What can the listeners do at the end of the tour?
   Purchase some souvenirs

1. 導覽在哪裡進行？在一家飲料工廠。
2. 說話者為什麼要向聽者道歉？有些設備無法運作。
3. 導覽結束後，聽者可以做什麼？購買一些紀念品。

切勿錯過的答題線索

地點／說話者	**Welcome to** this virtual tour of Lakeview Medical Center. **I'm** the director of the hospital, Dr. Dirk Hertz. 歡迎來到Lakeview醫療中心的虛擬導覽，我是醫院院長Dirk Hertz。
建議／要求事項	**I recommend** stopping at the top of the mountain for bird watching. 我建議可在山頂稍作停留來賞鳥。
下一步的行動	**Next, I'll** show you the latest models of our solar panels so you understand how they work. 接下來，我將展示我們最新型的太陽能板，讓您了解它們如何運作。

PRACTICE

🎧 P4_11 答案&解析 p.48

聽完獨白後，選出適當的答案。

1. Who most likely is the speaker?
   (A) A tour guide
   (B) A film director
   (C) A store manager
   (D) An art critic

2. What will happen at three o'clock?
   (A) Some singers will perform.
   (B) Some food will be served.
   (C) A business will close.
   (D) A video will be shown.

3. What is The First Step?
   (A) A club
   (B) A book
   (C) A podcast
   (D) A play

4. Why is Hamilton Manor famous?
   (A) It has been the filming location for movies.
   (B) It was designed by a prominent architect.
   (C) It is the venue for a popular festival.
   (D) It has an extensive art collection.

5. According to the speaker, what do visitors like to do at Hamilton Manor?
   (A) Make a wish
   (B) Sample food
   (C) Go swimming
   (D) Collect flowers

6. What are the listeners asked to do in one hour?
   (A) Take a group picture
   (B) Attend a performance
   (C) Get back on the bus
   (D) Meet at a café

7. Where does the tour take place?
   (A) At a manufacturing facility
   (B) At a nature park
   (C) At a concert hall
   (D) At a shopping center

8. What did Annette Harvey do?
   (A) She built a bridge.
   (B) She filmed a commercial.
   (C) She designed a building.
   (D) She donated some money.

9. What does the speaker mean when she says, "that area is closed to visitors"?
   (A) The tour will be shorter than usual.
   (B) A partial refund will be issued.
   (C) The listeners should not worry.
   (D) Some signs should be followed.

PART TEST

PART 4

Directions: You will hear some talks given by a single speaker. You will be asked to answer three questions about what the speaker says in each talk. Select the best response to each question and mark the letter (A), (B), (C), or (D) on your answer sheet. The talks will not be printed in your test book and will be spoken only one time.

71. What kind of business is being advertised?
    (A) A car rental company
    (B) A dance studio
    (C) A sporting goods store
    (D) A garden center

72. According to the advertisement, who can get a discount?
    (A) Business owners
    (B) Card holders
    (C) Charity workers
    (D) University students

73. What is the business known for?
    (A) Its helpful advice
    (B) Its large facility
    (C) Its numerous branches
    (D) Its modern website

74. Who is the speaker?
    (A) A property manager
    (B) A real estate agent
    (C) A safety inspector
    (D) A construction worker

75. What does the speaker imply when he says, "I'm sure it's full of furniture"?
    (A) An entrance may be blocked.
    (B) A storage area is probably in use.
    (C) Completing a task may be difficult.
    (D) Choosing a style will take time.

76. Why should the listener call the speaker back?
    (A) To pay a deposit
    (B) To confirm a color
    (C) To provide a reference
    (D) To select a convenient day

77. Who most likely are the listeners?
    (A) Product reviewers
    (B) Sales agents
    (C) Job candidates
    (D) Newspaper journalists

78. What aspect of the product is the speaker proud of?
    (A) It is produced domestically.
    (B) It uses very little packaging.
    (C) It is available in many countries.
    (D) It was developed by scientists.

79. What will the speaker give the listeners after the session?
    (A) A box of samples
    (B) A complimentary meal
    (C) A discount coupon
    (D) A certificate of completion

80. Who is Valentino Arruda?
    (A) A scientist
    (B) A painter
    (C) An author
    (D) A chef

81. According to the speaker, what inspires Mr. Arruda?
    (A) Listening to music
    (B) Traveling abroad
    (C) Working with experts
    (D) Spending time in nature

82. What does the speaker mean when he says, "he has a very busy schedule"?
    (A) A cancellation could not be avoided.
    (B) A talk with a guest will be brief.
    (C) The interview is a rare opportunity.
    (D) Mr. Arruda has started a new business.

83. Who is giving the talk?
    (A) A professional athlete
    (B) A financial advisor
    (C) A structural engineer
    (D) The city's mayor

84. According to the speaker, what have some people proposed?
    (A) Using recycled materials
    (B) Changing a roof design
    (C) Increasing admission fees
    (D) Expanding a parking structure

85. What will the listeners most likely do next?
    (A) Review a schedule
    (B) Watch a demonstration
    (C) Share their questions
    (D) Meet a new colleague

86. What is the broadcast mainly about?
    (A) Designing a website
    (B) Enhancing creativity
    (C) Improving communication skills
    (D) Developing healthy habits

87. What does the speaker say about Ms. Morrison's classes?
    (A) They are at full capacity.
    (B) They are aimed at beginners.
    (C) They are available online.
    (D) They are offered at no charge.

88. What does the speaker say will happen during the next show?
    (A) A contest winner will be announced.
    (B) A new host will be introduced.
    (C) Some listeners' questions will be answered.
    (D) Some event tickets will be sold.

GO ON TO THE NEXT PAGE

89. Where does the speaker most likely work?

    (A) At a photography studio
    (B) At an auto repair shop
    (C) At a stationery store
    (D) At a furniture factory

90. Why does the speaker say, "we've had a lot of cancellations"?

    (A) To explain a decision
    (B) To confirm her availability
    (C) To make a complaint
    (D) To suggest more advertising

91. What does the speaker offer to do for the staff?

    (A) Order a catered meal
    (B) Provide a day off
    (C) Let some people leave early
    (D) Hold a training event

92. Where are the listeners?

    (A) At an employee orientation
    (B) At a grand opening
    (C) At a health fair
    (D) At a fundraising dinner

93. According to the speaker, how does the product help the user?

    (A) By tracking shipments
    (B) By reducing expenses
    (C) By charging quickly
    (D) By sending an alert

94. What did the speaker learn from a survey?

    (A) That a modern design was needed
    (B) That a price was too high
    (C) That users were concerned about safety
    (D) That some instructions were confusing

1) Amusement Park
2) Stadium
3) Concert Hall
4) Antique Shop

Project Fact Sheet		
Line 1	Cost	$800,000
Line 2	Architect	Steven Gray
Line 3	Completion Date	September 1
Line 4	Size	1,200 square meters

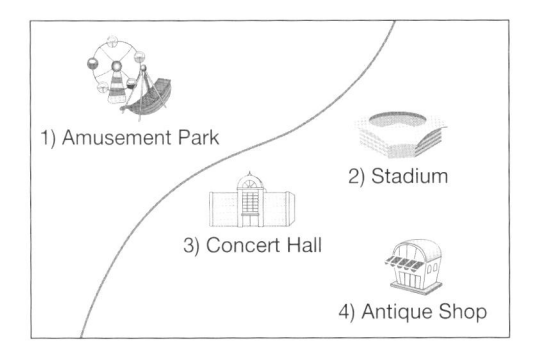

95. According to the speaker, what has caused a problem?

    (A) Heavy traffic
    (B) Severe weather
    (C) A construction delay
    (D) A computer error

96. Look at the graphic. Where does the speaker recommend going this afternoon?

    (A) Location 1
    (B) Location 2
    (C) Location 3
    (D) Location 4

97. What can the listeners do at dinner?

    (A) Request a partial refund
    (B) Express activity preferences
    (C) Take an additional tour
    (D) Choose meals for the next day

98. What kind of building is most likely being expanded?

    (A) An art gallery
    (B) A school
    (C) A fitness facility
    (D) A post office

99. What will the listeners do at the next meeting?

    (A) Volunteer for an event
    (B) View some blueprints
    (C) Meet a new employee
    (D) Provide budget reports

100. Look at the graphic. Which line has been changed?

    (A) Line 1
    (B) Line 2
    (C) Line 3
    (D) Line 4

PART 5

句子填空

UNIT 01 名詞

UNIT 02 代名詞與限定詞

UNIT 03 形容詞與副詞

UNIT 04 介系詞與連接詞

UNIT 05 動詞

UNIT 06 動狀詞

UNIT 07 關係代名詞

UNIT 08 詞彙

PART TEST

PART 5 句子填空

PART 5主要分為文法題和詞彙題。PART 5中的每道題都為一個句子，而且只有30道題，因此常被視為是閱讀部分中最簡單的大題，但是實際上卻是最難拿下滿分的大題。以往文法題的佔比較高，但在近幾年的測驗中，文法題和詞彙題的比例相差不大。其中難度較高的詞彙題，每回都會出現1至2題。這些題目無法依靠解題技巧快速答題，對於英語非母語者來說，甚至難以理解其他選項為何有誤。因此，如果你的目標分數在700分以上，最好果斷放棄解不出來的題目，最慢也要在10分鐘內完成PART 5，才能有足夠的時間應對後面的PART 6和PART 7。

文法題

作答PART 5時，建議先瀏覽選項。如果選項出現不同的詞性或形態，表示該道題屬於文法題，要先確認空格與前後單字間的關係，再選出適當的答案。

多益測驗文法題的出題範圍廣，涵蓋選出適當的詞性或形態，以及難度較高的假設語氣和倒裝句等，但幾乎不會出現難度極高的文法，因此，在此僅介紹頻繁出現的題型。

選出適當的詞性或形態

該類題型的選項由相同字根的名詞、副詞、形容詞、動詞、分詞、不定詞to V、動名詞等所構成。有時甚至不用理解文意，也能直接選出適當的詞性或形態。

Mitch Stallings set the ------- goal of increasing revenues by 40% this year.

(A) ambitiously　　　　(B) ambition
(C) most ambitiously　(D) ambitious

中譯 Mitch Stallings設立了今年營收額要增長40%的宏偉目標。

❶ 空格前方為定冠詞the、後方連接名詞goal，表示空格應填入適合修飾名詞的單字。
❷ 答案要選形容詞(D) ambitious。

近幾年有些考題除了判斷詞性或形態之外，還需確認單字的意思，才能選出答案。雖然解題時不得不去理解文意，但難度通常不高，能輕鬆答題。

The north wing of the Hawkins Library houses a ------- of rare books.

(A) collect　　　(B) collectively
(C) collector　　(D) collection

中譯 Hawkins圖書館的北館收藏大量的珍稀書籍。

❶ 空格前方為不定冠詞a、後方連接介系詞片語，表示空格應填入名詞。
❷ 選項中的名詞有(C) collector和(D) collection。根據文意，表示「收藏大量珍稀書籍」最為適當，因此答案要選(D)，意為「收藏（品）、珍藏」。

有時會出現由非ly結尾的副詞、介系詞、連接詞等組成，看起來詞性皆相異的選項。建議提前熟記非ly結尾的副詞（p.107），以及介系詞和連接詞（p.108-109），才能順利解答該類題型。

The website is ------- unavailable as it is undergoing routine maintenance.

(A) now　　　(B) beside
(C) until　　　(D) of

中譯 該網站現在無法使用，因為它正在進行例行性維護。

❶ 空格位在be動詞is和形容詞unavailable之間，應填入副詞。
❷ 因此答案要選(A) now。
　(A) 副詞；連接詞　(B) 介系詞
　(C) 連接詞；介系詞　(D) 介系詞

選出適當的代名詞

選出代名詞屬於難度相當低的考題，幾乎能在3秒內作答完畢。因此請務必迅速確認空格在句中的作用，選出答案後，跳至作答下一題。

The candidate's previous job involved customer service, so ------- has the right experience for this role.

(A) himself　　　　(B) his
(C) him　　　　　 (D) he

中譯 求職者先前的工作與客戶服務有關，因此他具備適合該職位的經歷。

❶ 空格前方為連接詞so，後方連接動詞has，表示空格應填入能當作主詞使用的單字。

❷ 因此答案要選主格代名詞(D) he。

選出適當的動詞形態

選項包含動詞的各種形態。有些考題考的是單複數的一致性、語態或時態擇一出題，也有些考題是混合兩種的複合題型。若碰到複合題型，解題方式為先判斷單複數的一致性，後確認語態或時態。

Our restaurant's seating area ------- to offer outdoor dining when the weather is favorable.

(A) renovate　　　　(B) were renovating
(C) is renovating　　(D) has been renovated

中譯 我們餐廳的座位區已經過翻修，天氣好的時候可在戶外用餐。

❶ 主詞Our restaurant's seating area為單數，為符合主動詞單複數的一致性，空格應填入動詞的單數形。

❷ (C) is renovating和 (D) has been renovated皆為單數，空格後方沒有連接受詞，因此答案要選(D) 被動語態〔be +過去分詞〕。

詞彙題

如果選項中的單字皆不相同，但詞性相同時，通常表示該道題屬於詞彙題。作答時，要先掌握整句話的脈絡，再根據文意選出最適當的答案。若重複看過兩遍後仍無法確定答案，建議果斷放棄這題，直接跳到下一題。在完成PART 7所有題目後，若還有剩餘時間，再回過頭來解決先前跳過的題目。PART 5中詞彙題所佔的比例較高，可以說該大題的得分關鍵在於詞彙量，因此建議多背一些單字。

Mr. Feldman has been participating ------- in all of VB Auto's professional development workshops.

(A) currently　　　(B) actively
(C) absolutely　　 (D) finally

中譯 Feldman先生積極參與了VB汽車公司所有的專業開發研討會。

❶ 四個選項皆為副詞，表示本題為詞彙題，因此要閱讀整句話並掌握其脈絡。

❷ 根據文意，表達「積極參與研討會」最為適當，因此答案為(B) actively。

作答詞彙題時，有時可靠空格周圍的單字找到答題線索，因此背單字時，建議不要只記下單獨的單字，應同時記住相關聯的字詞，更有助於答題。

The sales manager has successfully negotiated contracts with a ------- variety of corporate clients.

(A) long　　　(B) wide
(C) tall　　　 (D) fast

中譯 業務經理已成功與眾多的企業客戶洽談合約。

❶ 四個選項皆為形容詞，表示本題為詞彙題，因此要閱讀整句話，掌握其脈絡。

❷ a variety of通常會搭配wide一起使用，因此答案要選(B)。

子句與句子

子句由兩個或多個單字組合而成,其結構包含主詞和動詞。獨立子句可構成一個完整句子(簡單句);兩個或多個子句可組成複合句或並列句。

複合句(complex sentence)由可獨立使用的主要子句和不可獨立使用的從屬子句組合而成。從屬子句包含說明時間或理由等的副詞子句、當作主詞補語或受詞使用的名詞子句、修飾名詞的形容詞子句。並列句(compound sentence)指兩個或兩個以上可獨立使用的子句,透過對等連接詞and, but, so等結合在一起的句子。

簡單句

BT News **advertises** **heavily** **on social media**.
主詞　　　動詞　　　副詞　　介系詞片語

BT新聞在社群媒體上大量刊登廣告。

複合句

Although the building is old, **it is well maintained**.
　　　副詞子句　　　　　　主要子句(main clause)

該棟建築雖然老舊,但維持得很好。

➡ 副詞子句用來說明時間、條件、理由、對比等。此處由Although引導的子句扮演副詞的角色,表示對比。

The red light **indicates** **that the microphone is turned on**.
　　主詞　　　　動詞　　　　　　　名詞子句

紅燈亮起表示麥克風已開啟。

➡ 名詞子句在句中當作主詞、補語或受詞使用。此處由that引導的子句扮演受詞的角色。

Ms. Morris **is replacing** **Mr. Khan,** **who is retiring this month**.
　主詞　　　　動詞　　　　受詞　　　　形容詞子句

Morris女士將接替本月退休的Khan先生。

➡ 形容詞子句用來修飾名詞。此處由who引導的形容詞子句,用來修飾名詞Mr. Khan。

並列句

The survey was sent to 500 people, but **only a few responded**.
　　　可獨立使用的子句　　　　　　　　可獨立使用的子句

該份問卷調查寄送給500人,卻只有少數人回應。

➡ 用連接詞but連接兩個結構完整的句子,表示對比。

句子組成與結構

主詞＋動詞

Some participants arrived late.　有幾位參與者遲到。
　　主詞　　　　　動詞　　副詞

➡ 名詞、代名詞或其他可扮演名詞角色的字詞皆可當作主詞使用。副詞主要用於為動作或狀況提供額外資訊（包含時間、地點、方法、程度、頻率、態度等），雖然副詞並非必要成分，但缺少副詞時，有時會無法完整傳達句子的意思。

主詞＋動詞＋主詞補語

The data was incorrect.　數據不正確。
　主詞　　動詞　　主詞補語

Ms. Kim became head of the finance department last year.　金女士去年成為財務部主管。
　主詞　　　動詞　　　　　　主詞補語　　　　　　　　　　副詞

➡ 當主詞和動詞不足以表達出完整的意思時，會使用補語來補充說明。形容詞、介系詞片語、名詞、代名詞、不定詞 to V、動名詞、名詞子句等皆可當作補語使用。

主詞＋動詞＋受詞

Mr. Carter will receive a replacement this afternoon.　Carter先生將於今天下午收到替代品。
　　主詞　　　　動詞　　　　受詞　　　　　　副詞

They will begin shipping internationally next month.　他們將於下個月開始進行國際配送。
　主詞　　動詞　　受詞　　　　副詞　　　　副詞

➡ 及物動詞後方要連接受詞，名詞、代名詞、不定詞 to V、動名詞、名詞子句等皆可當作受詞使用。

主詞＋動詞＋間接受詞＋直接受詞

LY Clothing offers new customers free delivery.　LY服裝為新客戶提供免費配送服務。
　　主詞　　　動詞　　間接受詞　　　直接受詞

➡ 間接受詞可理解為「給、向…」。多益測驗中經常出現 give, send, tell, offer 等授與動詞。

主詞＋動詞＋受詞＋受詞補語

Many critics found the movie enjoyable.　許多評論家認為這部電影很有意思。
　　主詞　　　動詞　　受詞　　　受詞補語

The manager asked Ms. Yi to review the report.　經理要求Yi女士審閱這份報告。
　　主詞　　　動詞　　受詞　　　　受詞補語

➡ 受詞補語用來為受詞補充說明，形容詞、分詞、名詞、不定詞 to V、原形動詞等皆可當作受詞補語使用。

UNIT 01 名詞

答案&解析 p.55

1 冠詞、限定詞、形容詞＋名詞

■ 名詞要置於冠詞、限定詞、形容詞、分詞等修飾語的後方。
Please reply to this e-mail to verify your **attendance** / attend at the event.
請回覆此電子郵件以確認您將出席活動。

■ 如需判斷空格要填入的可數名詞為單數還是複數時，請確認空格前方是否有不定冠詞。若空格前方有不定冠詞，答案要選單數名詞；若沒有不定詞冠，答案則要選複數名詞。
The charity event was **a** big **success** / successes.
本次慈善活動大獲成功。

多益常考可數名詞	多益常考不可數名詞	形態相似的可數名詞和不可數名詞
an opening 職缺	support 支援、贊助	a permit 許可證　　permission 許可
an appointment 約定、預約	consent 同意	a process 過程　　processing 處理
results 成果	access 訪問權限	a cause 原因　　caution 注意、小心
benefits （薪資外的）津貼、福利	manufacture 製造、生產	an account 帳戶　　accounting 會計

CHECK-UP

1. Kenway Construction has begun keeping a greater supply / **supplies** of materials on hand in case additional projects become available.
2. Due to unexpected equipment issues, Retha Dentistry is not scheduling appointment / **appointments** until next week.

2 當作主詞或受詞使用的名詞

■ 名詞可當作主詞、及物動詞或介系詞的受詞使用。若難以判斷空格應該填入什麼時，建議先確認該空格在句中扮演什麼樣的角色。
Access / Accessible to the website was blocked.
網站訪問遭到阻擋。

The interior designer **provided suggestions** / suggest for remodeling the store.
室內設計師提出了重新裝修商店的建議。

The new branch will not be **in operation** / operate until September 1.
新分店要到9月1日才會營運。

CHECK-UP

3. Many event planners have expressed surprisingly / **surprise** at the rental fee for the Villa Hall.
4. Delivers / **Deliveries** from Del Logistics occasionally arrive two or three days ahead of schedule.

3 人物名詞、事物名詞、抽象名詞

■ 若空格置於名詞的位置，選項出現意思不同的名詞時，建議看完整句話後，根據文意選出適當的名詞。

人物名詞	事物名詞或抽象名詞	人物名詞	事物名詞或抽象名詞
publisher 出版人、出版社	publication 刊物、發行	accountant 會計師	account 帳號、帳戶、客戶、記述
subscriber 訂閱用戶	subscription 訂閱	depositor 存款人	deposit 訂金
producer 生產者、製造者	production 生產	contributor 捐助者	contribution 捐獻
electrician 電器技師	electricity 電力	director 管理者、經理、導演	direction 方向、指示
consultant 顧問、諮商師	consultation 諮商、協議、商談	instructor 講師	instruction 說明書、指引
applicant 申請人	application 履歷表、申請書	committee 委員會	commitment 奉獻、投入、承諾

Applications / Applicants should be sent to hr@electronix.com by February 20.
申請表應於2月20日前寄至hr@electronix.com。

Our records show that your **electricity** / electrician usage has increased significantly recently.
我們的紀錄顯示最近您的用電量顯著增加。

CHECK-UP

5. The managing director / direction strongly opposed the budget cuts that the company had proposed.
6. Customers have trusted Mantique Furniture for decades because of its committee / commitment to quality.

4 複合名詞

■ 複合名詞指的是由兩個意思不同的名詞組合成一個名詞。在多益測驗中，空格會置於複合名詞中的第一個或第二個名詞位置，要求選出適當的名詞。

tourist attraction 觀光地、旅遊景點	flight attendant 空服員
security/vacation policy 安全政策、休假規定	flight arrangements 航班安排
cancellation fee 取消手續費	earnings growth 獲利成長
expiration date 截止期限、到期日	sales figures 銷售數字
building management 大樓管理	job creation 創造就業機會
e-mail reminder 提醒通知的電子郵件	budget surplus/deficit 預算盈餘、赤字
service fee[charge] 服務費	safety regulation 安全守則
baggage allowance 行李限額	price reduction 降價

Customers were happy about the **price** / pricey reduction of the popular cereal product.
顧客對於受歡迎穀物產品的降價感到高興。

CHECK-UP

7. The tax credit would result in substantial job creation / creativity among small businesses.
8. According to selling / sales figures released by Jerome's Technologies, company profits rose 3% last quarter.

UNIT 02 代名詞與限定詞

答案&解析 p.55

1 人稱代名詞

■ 人稱代名詞指的是表示人物或事物的代名詞。根據數量、性別、所有格的不同，形態各異。

Coco Designs takes **secondhand items** and uses **them** / they to make new clothes.
Coco設計公司回收二手物品，並用它們來做新衣服。

■ 當主詞和受詞相同時，受詞的位置要使用反身代名詞。但有時候為了要強調主詞或受詞，也會使用反身代名詞，這時會置於副詞的位置，且可以省略。

Mr. Ronaldo described **himself** / him as an artist, inventor, and architect.
Ronaldo先生自稱是藝術家、發明家和建築師。

➡ 主詞Mr. Ronaldo和受詞相同，因此答案為反身代名詞。

Ms. Watson designed the pamphlets **herself** / hers with a software program.
Watson女士用軟體程式親自設計了這些小冊子。

➡ 若省略畫底線處，該句話仍是一個結構完整的句子，因此答案為反身代名詞。即使從畫底線處移除，也不會影響句子的完整度。

CHECK-UP

1. Ms. Cailot arrived to work five minutes late because **she** / her was stuck in traffic.
2. The grocery store prides **itself** / it on using only local suppliers for its produce.

2 指示代名詞和不定代名詞

■ 指示代名詞（this, these, that, those）用於特定的對象，也可用來代替前方提過的名詞。在多益測驗中，經常出現those，通常是受到分詞、介系詞片語、關係子句的修飾。

Those / Few who wish to participate in the seminar are encouraged to sign up early.
鼓勵有意參加研討會的人士儘早報名。

■ 不定代名詞（one, the other, others, another, some, any, many, none等）用來代替不特定的人事物。

Mr. Li brought two microphones: **one** for the moderator, **the other** / others / another for the presenter.
李先生帶了兩支麥克風：一支給主持人，另一支給講者。

➡ the other（提及的之外）剩下的那一個／others（不特定的）其他人事物／another（未限制範圍的）任何另一個

Mr. Kamau tried to get a ticket, but there **weren't any** / some left.
Kamau先生想買一張票，但已經沒有任何剩餘的票了。

➡ some 幾個、一些／any 可用於疑問句、否定句和條件句中，意為任何。

CHECK-UP

3. All coupons for Zack's Diner, including that / **those** issued online, will expire on December 31.
4. Participants in the conference can join any / **none** of the events which interest them.

3 限定詞

限定詞置於名詞的前方，用來表示名詞的意義或數量。

限定意思	冠詞	a(n), the
	指示限定詞	this, these, that, those
	所有限定詞	my, our, your, his, her, its, their
	疑問限定詞	what, whatever, which, whichever, whose
限定數或量	數量限定詞	every, another + 單數名詞 (a) few, many, several, both + 複數名詞 the other + 單數、複數名詞 (a) little, much + 不可數名詞 all, more, most, other + 複數名詞、不可數名詞 some, any + 單數、複數名詞、不可數名詞

Harrolds Department Store has just opened **its** / itself **first overseas branch** in Sydney.
Harrolds百貨公司剛在雪梨開設第一間海外分店。

CHECK-UP

5. The secretary orders office supplies every / when Thursday, so please e-mail him any requests you have before then.
6. JC's Camping Supplies is offering discounts on a few / any merchandise that is manufactured by Flash Sailing Co.

4 表示數量的代名詞或限定詞

■ each, every + 單數名詞 ➡ 單數動詞

Every / Many product **complies** with the brand's strict safety standards.
每件產品均符合品牌嚴格的安全標準。

■ each of + 複數名詞 ➡ 單數動詞

Each / Most of the budgets **was** approved. 各項預算皆得到批准。

■ several, many (+ of) + 複數名詞 ➡ 複數動詞

Several / Each properties on this street **are** for sale. 這條街上有幾處房地產正在出售。

■ all, more, most (+ of) + 複數名詞／不可數名詞 ➡ 複數動詞／單數動詞

All / Every items **are** 30% off this week. 本週所有商品均享七折。

CHECK-UP

7. Every / All staff currently on business trips are exempt from the mandatory monthly meeting.
8. The committee narrowed down the candidates in the logo design competition from 358 to five, and each / several of the candidates was contacted for a meeting.

PRACTICE

1. Henson Apartments' owner approved funds for the ------- of the main lobby.
   (A) renovates
   (B) renovated
   (C) renovate
   (D) renovation

2. Ian Paints lets customers take unlimited paint samples home to compare ------- with their current decor.
   (A) themselves
   (B) them
   (C) they
   (D) their

3. One of the receptionist's duties is answering ------- incoming call.
   (A) few
   (B) every
   (C) other
   (D) past

4. ------- will have access to all of Greenwich News's premium content upon remitting the initial payment.
   (A) Subscriptions
   (B) Subscribing
   (C) Subscribers
   (D) Subscribe

5. Human Resources has not yet decided ------- candidate to hire for the position.
   (A) if
   (B) which
   (C) regarding
   (D) because

6. The organizers have employed several sign language ------- for the international conference.
   (A) interpreters
   (B) interpreter
   (C) interpreting
   (D) interpret

7. A parking permit is required of ------- who wish to park in this lot.
   (A) those
   (B) itself
   (C) theirs
   (D) enough

8. A crucial ------- between the two washing machine models is that one of them has an energy-saving setting.
   (A) distinction
   (B) distinctively
   (C) distinct
   (D) distinctive

PRACTICE

9. One occupant, Victor Guerrero, said that the construction noise was not a nuisance, but ------- reported being bothered by it.
   (A) himself
   (B) whoever
   (C) others
   (D) anyone

10. Reway Manufacturing received low customer service ratings due to confusing ------- in its manuals.
    (A) instructors
    (B) instruct
    (C) instructions
    (D) instructional

11. Ms. McGuire gives ------- team members regular breaks throughout their shifts.
    (A) hers
    (B) she
    (C) her
    (D) herself

12. The board of trustees will consider expanding the business into other ventures if ------- remain high.
    (A) profited
    (B) profiting
    (C) profitable
    (D) profits

13. The ------- working on the audit must make sure their numbers are as accurate as possible.
    (A) accounted
    (B) accountants
    (C) accounts
    (D) accountable

14. Brightwood Water refunded $80 to Mr. Gilmore because ------- had been overcharged.
    (A) himself
    (B) his
    (C) him
    (D) he

15. This apartment is within walking distance of many tourist -------, making it prime real estate.
    (A) attract
    (B) attractions
    (C) attractiveness
    (D) attractively

16. ------- documents undergo an approval process for compliance with data protection laws.
    (A) Another
    (B) All
    (C) Each
    (D) This

PART 5

105

UNIT 03　形容詞與副詞

答案＆解析 p.57

1　形容詞的位置

■ 形容詞要置於名詞的前方。

Mr. Yi will step away from his duties for a **brief** / briefness time to deal with a health issue.
Yi先生將暫時離開工作崗位，以處理身體健康的問題。

■ 形容詞可當作補語使用，用於補充說明主詞或受詞。

The company **is** always **responsive** / respond to negative customer feedback.
公司總是對客戶的負面反饋做出即時回應。

The city launched a mobile app for its residents to **stay informed** / information of all municipal updates.
該城市推出一款行動應用程式，供居民隨時獲取該市的所有最新資訊。

We require bolder investments to **make** the business **profitable** / profitably.
我們需要更大膽的投資手段，才能使事業獲利。

CHECK-UP

1. Considering that Ms. Ortiz has a master's degree and five years' experience, the **initial** / initially salary offer was fairly low.
2. Following safety regulations at the construction site is mandate / **mandatory** for all visitors.

2　副詞的位置

■ 多益測驗中經常出現的副詞考題，大致可分為以下六種類型。

副詞＋及物動詞	**finally sign** the contract 最終簽訂合約	be動詞＋副詞＋分詞	be **carefully selected** 精心挑選
不及物動詞＋副詞	**increase rapidly** 急遽增加	助動詞＋副詞＋動詞	can **comfortably accommodate** 可舒適地容納
副詞＋形容詞	**unusually high** demand 異常高的需求	have＋副詞＋過去分詞	have **publicly stated** 已公開聲明

Ms. Wheeler **strongly** / strong encouraged her team members to attend the technology seminar.
Wheeler女士積極鼓勵她的團隊成員參加技術研討會。

■ 副詞可置於句末，因此當空格位在句末，且省略後不影響該句結構的完整性時，表示空格應填入副詞。

Your order will be processed **promptly** / prompt.
將迅速處理您的訂單。

CHECK-UP

3. Since graduating from university, Mr. Shaw has action / **actively** pursued a career in the film industry.
4. The filter on the air purifier should be replaced at regular intervals to ensure it is working efficient / **efficiently**.

3 需特別留意的副詞

■ 請特別留意非ly結尾的副詞，其他選項通常會出現介系詞或連接詞作為陷阱。

at least 起碼、至少	indeed 真正地、確實、實際上	still 仍舊、儘管如此、還是、然而
even 甚至	seldom 不常有、很少	alike 相似地、一樣地
now 現在、此刻	apart 分開地	soon 馬上、不久

Most of our employees have been working here for **at least** / along with five years.
我們大多數員工已經在這裡工作至少五年了。

■ 連接副詞用於連接前後句子，並修飾後方句子。連接副詞屬於副詞，因此無法連接兩個子句，請特別留意。

however 然而	otherwise 不然、否則	consequently, as a result 結果、因此
besides 而且	therefore, accordingly 因此	meanwhile 與此同時
moreover, furthermore 此外	likewise 同樣地	nevertheless 儘管、不過
instead 作為替代	above all 最重要的是	then 然後

Al's Diner serves quality food, but **above all** / even though, it is known for its reasonable prices.
Al's餐廳提供的食物品質良好，但最重要的是它以合理價格而聞名。

CHECK-UP

5. Some audience members were until / **still** trying to find their seats while the CEO made his opening remarks at the event.

6. Our latest marketing strategy has been largely unsuccessful and must **therefore** / regarding be re-evaluated and revised.

4 比較級與最高級

■ 比較級用法

The new laptop is **lighter** / light than the previous one.
新的筆記型電腦比以前那台輕。

Sonora Trucking is searching for ways to deliver packages to its customers **much** / very faster.
Sonora運貨公司正在尋找更快將包裹寄送給客戶的方法。
➡ 比較級前方可加上much, even, still, far, a lot，表示強調。

■ 最高級用法

Merose Motors is recognized as one of the **highest** / high quality automakers.
Merose汽車公司被公認為是品質最好的汽車製造商之一。

CHECK-UP

7. The new air conditioner circulates cool air much evenly / **more evenly** than the old one.

8. Strong interpersonal skills are the **most important** / as important as qualifications for the position.

UNIT 04　介系詞與連接詞

答案 & 解析 p.58

1　多益常考介系詞

■ at vs. on vs. in

時間	特定時間點 at 6 o'clock　6點整	日期、星期、特定日子 on July 20　在7月20日	年份、季節、月、上午、下午等 in 2021　在2021年
地點	特定地點或位置 at the bus stop　在公車站	距離、樓層、表面上等 on the second floor　在2樓	寬闊的區域或地點、某處的內部 in the city　在城市

■ 各類多益常考介系詞

時間點	by 在⋯之前	until 直到⋯為止	from 從⋯	since 自⋯以來
期間	during（特定活動）期間	for（用數字表現）期間	within 在⋯範圍內	throughout 從頭到尾
地點／位置	between（兩者）之間	among（三者以上）之間	within 在⋯範圍內	along 沿著
移動／方向	from 從、由	through 通過	across 穿過	
工具／方法	with 用、帶著⋯	without 沒有	by 用（方法、手段）	
對象／主題	about、on 對於⋯	regarding, concerning 關於		
讓步	despite 儘管	notwithstanding 儘管		
添加／排除	besides 除⋯之外	including 包括	excluding 除⋯之外	
其他	following 在⋯以後	like/unlike 與⋯一樣／不同	as 作為	

The supervisors must **submit** employee evaluations **by / until** the end of the month.
主管必須在月底前繳交員工考核。
➡ by表示在特定時間點之前「完成」該行為；until表示該行為「持續」至特定時間為止。

CHECK-UP

1. Our success **on / in** the third quarter is the result of an aggressive marketing campaign.
2. Starting Monday, the new cafeteria will be open daily from 8 A.M. **by / until** 8 P.M.

2　多益常考介系詞片語

理由／讓步	because of, due to, owing to, on account of 因為		in spite of 儘管
添加／排除	in addition to, on top of 除了⋯還有	except (for) 除了⋯以外	
	apart[aside] from 除了⋯還有(= in addition to)、除了⋯以外(= except for)		
其他	in front of 在⋯前面	prior to 在⋯之前	according to 根據	if not for 要不是有⋯
	instead of 作為⋯的代替	along with 與⋯一起	rather than 而不是⋯	in light of 有鑒於

CHECK-UP

3. **In front of / Prior to / Likewise** working at Hosto Corp., Jane Hamilton was employed by Popka Inc.
4. More information about the project, **on account of / in short / along with** recent photos of the park, can be found on our website.

108

3　多益常考連接詞

■ **對等連接詞**：對等連接同詞性的單字和單字、片語和片語、子句和子句。當中so只能用於連接子句。

| and 和 | but 但是 | yet 可是、然而 | or 或是 | so 因此 |

■ **相關連接詞**：由對等連接詞and、but、or等加上特定字詞組合而成的連接詞。與對等連接詞的功能相似，用於連接結構相同的句子。

either A or B　不是A就是B　　　neither A nor B　既不是A也不是B　　both A and B　A和B兩者都是
not A but B　不是A而是B　　　　not only A but (also) B, B as well as A　不但是A而且也是B

■ **從屬連接詞**：引導從屬子句，表示時間、條件、理由、讓步等意義，連接含有主詞與動詞結構完整的子句。

時間	until 直到…為止	when 當…的時候	while 當…的時候	whenever 無論何時
條件	if、provided (that) 如果是…的話		in case 假如	as if 好像、猶如
理由	since 因為	now(that) 既然		
讓步／對比	whereas 然而		wherever 無論去哪裡	
其他	so… that… 如此…以至於	given that 有鑒於	whether 是否、不管	

Rex Inc. drew 30,000 applicants, **whereas** / either only 100 people will be recruited.
Rex公司吸引了三萬名應徵者，然而僅聘用100人。

CHECK-UP

5. Human Resources keeps information about not only / both current and former employees.
6. Above / When you encounter an issue with your computer, contact Mr. Kim at extension 56.

4　介系詞 vs. 從屬連接詞

■ 介系詞後方要連接名詞（片語）；從屬連接詞後方要連接子句。請特別留意字義相近的介系詞與連接詞。

字義	介系詞	從屬連接詞
在…之前	before、prior to	before
在…之後	after、following	after
期間	during	while
在…後立刻	upon -ing	as soon as、once
沒有、除非	without	unless
由於	because of、due to, owing to、on account of	because, as, since
儘管	despite、in spite of	although、even though

The parking lot on Waverly Street was closed **during** / while the holiday.
Waverly街的停車場在假期間關閉。

CHECK-UP

7. Owing to / Because the design differed from that on the website, customers complained.
8. Beanie Coffee has opened another branch in Paris despite / although the limited success of its first branch.

109

PRACTICE

答案&解析 p.59

1. Most voters ------- believe that the city's main roads need to be better maintained.
   (A) firm
   (B) firmness
   (C) firmer
   (D) firmly

2. There are several event signs ------- the wall that should be taken down within this month.
   (A) on
   (B) as
   (C) within
   (D) in

3. Ms. Hensley created a ------- database in which comments from Globe Autos customers can be stored.
   (A) securing
   (B) secure
   (C) secures
   (D) securely

4. The Parmona Museum offers hands-on workshops ------- short lectures.
   (A) for instance
   (B) whether
   (C) as well as
   (D) in case

5. The summer sales event will last ------- the month of July.
   (A) inside
   (B) throughout
   (C) even so
   (D) among

6. ------- Ms. Caruso rearranged the furniture in the waiting area, the space looked much larger.
   (A) After
   (B) Following
   (C) Notwithstanding
   (D) Especially

7. Bea's Beauty will ------- release its new foam cleanser on its website.
   (A) soon
   (B) due to
   (C) while
   (D) timely

8. The property will require extensive renovations before it is ------- to be used as an office.
   (A) suiting
   (B) suitability
   (C) suitable
   (D) suitably

PRACTICE

9. This presentation includes ------- tips on implementing anti-fraud techniques.
   (A) helpfulness
   (B) help
   (C) helpfully
   (D) helpful

10. Board members should read the proposal prior to the meeting ------- they can be well-informed when discussing the details.
    (A) given that
    (B) so that
    (C) with
    (D) resulting

11. The director's new documentary looks ------- at the oil industry than the first one did.
    (A) most closely
    (B) more closely
    (C) closest
    (D) close

12. Martin Textiles remains ------- on the sale of cotton fiber for its profits.
    (A) depends
    (B) dependent
    (C) depend
    (D) depending

13. All confidential documents are required to be kept in locked cabinets ------- someone uses them.
    (A) without
    (B) otherwise
    (C) even
    (D) unless

14. The number of participating businesses has increased ------- since last year.
    (A) signify
    (B) significant
    (C) significantly
    (D) significance

15. We need to get consent from the city council ------- we can make plans to change this residential lot into a commercial area.
    (A) rather
    (B) although
    (C) also
    (D) before

16. ------- the employment contract, workers retain their right to form a labor union.
    (A) According to
    (B) Instead of
    (C) Provided that
    (D) Prior to

PART 5

111

UNIT 05　動詞

1　主詞與動詞的一致性

■ 如果選項列出動詞的各種形態時，請先確認動詞與主詞間的單複數是否一致。基本原則為主詞為單數，要搭配單數動詞；主詞為複數，則要搭配複數動詞。

Brax Tech's new wireless headphones <u>are</u> / is **on sale this month.**
Brax科技公司的新款無線耳機於本月進行促銷。

■ 主詞與動詞間的修飾語（分詞、形容詞子句、不定詞to V、介系詞片語），不用符合單複數的一致性，因此動詞與正前方名詞的單複數未必會一致，請特別留意。

An appliance with these labels <u>conforms</u> / conform **to all energy-efficiency regulations.**
貼有這些標籤的設備，符合所有能源效率規定。
➜ 主詞An appliance為單數名詞，搭配單數動詞conforms，符合主詞與動詞的一致性。

CHECK-UP

1. Executives at Murphy Automotive <u>expect</u> / is expecting to sell at least 100 used vehicles over the next month.
2. Thornton Textiles, a producer of cotton fabrics, have supplied / <u>supplies</u> over 50 clothing factories across the country.

2　被動語態

■ 空格後方沒有受詞時，要填入被動語態；如有連接受詞，則要填入主動語態。

The hand soap that <u>was produced</u> / produced **last month had the wrong packaging.**
上個月生產的洗手乳包裝有誤。

Hype Consultancy <u>hired</u> / has been hired **Willard Carswell as their new vice president.**
Hype 諮商公司聘請Willard Carswell擔任新的副總裁。

■ 建議熟記多益測驗中常出現的[be p.p. + 不定詞to V]。

be expected to	be asked to	be required to	be encouraged to	be scheduled to
預計會…	被要求做…	被要求做…	受鼓勵做…	預定要…
be reminded to	be intended to	be prepared to	be allowed to	be advised to
被提醒要…	打算做…	準備做…	允准做…	建議做…

The elevator is out of service, so visitors <u>are asked</u> / ask **to use the stairs instead.**
電梯已停止運轉，因此訪客被要求改走樓梯。

CHECK-UP

3. Audience members who wish to inform / <u>be informed</u> about upcoming shows should complete a form with their contact information.
4. All users <u>are required</u> / required to authenticate their account before using our cloud software.

3 時態

■ 在多益測驗中，時態題的難度較低，題目不會超出基本概念的範圍。多數時態題考的是搭配特定用法使用的時態，因此建議記下各個時態與其搭配的用法，將有助於解題。

簡單式	現在式：usually, generally, every week/month/year等 過去式：ago, yesterday, recently, lately, last week/month/year, in＋年份等 未來式：next week/month/year, tomorrow, soon, later today/this week等
完成式	現在完成式：for 一段時間、since 自⋯以來、already 已經、just 剛、yet 尚未、so far 迄今、over 歷經、in recent weeks 最近幾週、in just one year 一年之內 過去完成式：by the time ＋主詞＋過去式動詞 到⋯的時候 未來完成式：by the time ＋主詞＋現在式動詞 到⋯的時候、by 約莫在⋯ at/by the end of 在⋯結束時

The number of video streaming platforms **has increased** / increases **over the past few years**.
影音串流平台的數量在過去幾年不斷增加。

■ 當句中未使用特定用法，無法推測出對應的時態時，可根據對等連接詞，或是主要子句、副詞子句中使用的動詞，判斷出正確的時態。

The work crew **repainted** the hallway walls **and then** **cleaned** / clean the carpet thoroughly.
工人們重新粉刷走廊的牆壁，並徹底清潔地毯。

CHECK-UP

5. Newbury National Park opened / will open for hikers and campers next month.
6. The new clothing line by Bailey Sportswear is improving / has improved significantly since July.

4 主詞與動詞的一致性／語態／時態綜合題

■ 如果碰到結合主詞與動詞的一致性、語態及加上時態的綜合考題時，請先判斷主詞與動詞為單數還是複數，接著確認語態，最後再判斷時態。

B&C Landscaping **provides** / provide / is provided free consultations to new customers.
B&C景觀公司為新客戶提供免費諮詢。
⑴ 判斷單數還是複數：主詞B&C Landscaping為單數，因此可先刪去複數動詞provide。
⑵ 確認為主動或被動語態：畫底線處後方連接受詞free consultations，因此答案要選主動語態provides。

■ 如果碰到語態加上時態的綜合考題時，請先判斷時態，再確認語態。當句中未出現能判斷時態的字詞時，則先確認語態，再根據文意選出時態。

The book signing event **will be held** / is holding / was held next Thursday at 2 P.M.
簽書會將於下週四下午2點舉行。
⑴ 判斷時態：next Thursday應搭配未來式使用，因此可先刪去過去式動詞was held。
⑵ 確認為主動或被動語態：畫底線處後方未連接受詞，因此答案要選被動語態will be held。

CHECK-UP

7. The next stage of construction at the Vivitech headquarters will begin once the permits has issued / are issued / were issuing.
8. With the company under new ownership, department heads had monitored / are monitoring / will be monitored their spending more carefully than before.

113

UNIT 06　動狀詞

答案&解析 p.61

1　不定詞 to V 的位置

■ 不定詞to V具備名詞的功能，可置於主詞、補語或受詞的位置上。在多益測驗中，不定詞to V的考題經常會將空格置於補語或受詞位置。

NT&Y Technologies **is planning** <u>to merge</u> / merge with Frey in early May.
NT&Y科技公司計劃在五月初與Frey公司合併。

➡ 連接不定詞to V當作受詞的動詞：plan 計劃、hope 希望、agree 同意、promise 承諾、aim 目標、expect 預期、refuse 拒絕、fail 未能做到、would like 想要、wish 希望、offer 建議、need 需要、want 想要、decide 決定、afford 買得起、tend 傾向

■ 不定詞to V也能當作形容詞或是副詞使用，當形容詞使用時，置於名詞後方做修飾。

Atlantis Resort added a new diving pool in **an attempt** <u>to attract</u> / is attracting more visitors.
Atlantis度假村增加了一個新的潛水池，以吸引更多遊客。

<u>To ensure</u> / Have ensured quality service, all product consultations are by appointment only.
為確保優質的服務，所有產品諮詢均採預約制。

➡ 不定詞to V當作副詞使用時，若表示「為了…」的意思，可與in order to替換使用。

CHECK-UP

1. Ms. Waite would like <u>to arrange</u> / arranging a group interview for next Friday.
2. All elevators in the building will be out of service for one hour from 10 A.M. <u>perform</u> / to perform required maintenance.

2　動名詞的位置

■ 動名詞要置於介系詞的後方。

The training session is aimed **at** <u>improving</u> / improves productivity.
培訓課程的目的是提高生產力。

■ 動名詞可置於主詞、補語或受詞的位置上。

<u>Performing</u> / Performance **a thorough evaluation** is crucial before a product launch.
在推出產品之前，進行徹底的評估至關重要。
➡ 畫底線處後方連接的名詞片語a thorough evaluation，扮演受詞的角色，因此答案要選可連接受詞的動名詞。

Ms. Vela will **consider** <u>approving</u> / to approve the plans to open a branch office in Tokyo.
Vela女士將考慮批准在東京開設分公司的的計畫。

➡ 連接動名詞當作受詞的動詞：consider 考慮、include 包括、admit 承諾、avoid 避免、finish 結束、stop 停止、discontinue 中斷、suggest 提議、recommend 推薦、deny 否定、give up 放棄、postpone 延遲、delay 延期

CHECK-UP

3. The last person to leave the office must make sure the security alarm is set prior to <u>lock / locking</u> the door.
4. We suggest <u>substituting / to substitute</u> natural sweeteners for artificial ones in your favorite recipes.

3　不定詞 to V 與動名詞的慣用語

■〔be動詞＋形容詞＋不定詞to V〕慣用語

be[make] sure to 確實…	be able to 能夠…	be eligible to 有資格…
be willing to 樂意…	be advisable to 建議…	be eager to 渴望…
be proud to 自豪於…	be available to 可供使用的、可獲得的	

Vadica International **is eager** *to enter* / entering the Asian market.
Vadica國際公司迫切希望進入亞洲市場。

■ 動名詞的慣用語

look forward to -ing 期盼著…	have difficulty/trouble (in) -ing 做…遭遇困難
spend 時間或金錢 (on) -ing 花時間或金錢做…	be accustomed to -ing 習慣做…

Customers seem to have trouble *accessing* / to access their accounts from our website.
客戶似乎無法在我們的網站上登錄他們的帳戶。

CHECK-UP

5. With the backing of additional investors, the company was able increasing / *to increase* production.
6. We appreciate your support and look forward to be continuing / *continuing* to serve you.

4　分詞

■ 分詞可置於名詞前方或後方做修飾。與名詞間的關係為主動時，要使用現在分詞；與名詞間的關係為被動時，則要使用過去分詞。

Departing / Departed **passengers** must complete a security check in order to fly.
出境旅客必須完成安全檢查才能搭機。

Weardale Ski Club is **a beautiful ski resort** *located* / locating near Durham.
Weardale滑雪俱樂部是位於Durham附近的美麗滑雪度假勝地。

■ 某些過去分詞本身就是形容詞，此時過去分詞形態的形容詞不一定表示被動，請特別留意。

an informed decision 明智的決定	a detailed explanation 詳細的說明
an established company 知名的公司	a qualified applicant 合格的應徵者
an accomplished writer 優秀的作家	a distinguished scholar 傑出的學者
an experienced employee 資深的員工	a noted composer 知名的作曲家
a dedicated employee 敬業的員工	a motivated worker 積極上進的員工

CHECK-UP

7. Residents are mostly concerned about the *rising* / rise cost of public services.
8. Ms. Corbett argued that increasing company benefits could attract qualifying / *qualified* employees.

UNIT 07　關係代名詞

答案&解析 p.62

1　關係代名詞

■ 關係代名詞具備代名詞的功能，用來代替前方提過的名詞，同時兼具連接詞的功能，引導形容詞子句，連接其他子句。在形容詞子句中，關係代名詞可當作主格、受格或所有格使用，根據先行詞為人物、事物或動物，搭配不同的關係代名詞使用。

先行詞 \ 格	主格	受格	所有格
人物	who	who(m)	whose
人物、動物	which	which	whose
人物、事物、動物	that	that	-

Mr. Brown is a journalist **who** / which won the Journalist of the Year Award.
Brown先生是位榮獲年度記者獎的記者。

■ whom和which可當作介系詞的受詞使用，用法為〔介系詞+whom/which〕，此時關係代名詞後方要連接結構完整的子句。
Private messages must only be seen by the person **whom[that]** they are sent **to**.
= Private messages must only be seen by the person **to whom** / what they are sent.
私人訊息只有收件人才能查看。

CHECK-UP

1. All customers **who** / which complete a survey will be offered a discount voucher.
2. Streaming Central gives a customer three warnings about late payments, after whose / **which** the account is suspended.

2　省略關係代名詞

■ 如果省略〔關係代名詞主格+be動詞〕，先行詞後方通常是連接分詞。此時與先行詞的關係為主動時，要使用現在分詞；關係為被動時，則使用過去分詞。
The wait staff **working** / worked in the main ballroom must maintain perfect etiquette and attire.
在主宴會廳工作的服務人員必須保持完美的禮儀和服裝。
➡ 先行詞The wait staff為「工作」的人，與畫底線處的關係為主動，因此答案要選現在分詞。

■ 關係代名詞當作受格使用時，可以單獨省略。在多益測驗中，經常考的是詢問在省略關係代名詞受格的狀況下，形容詞子句中的主詞位置要填入哪一種人稱代名詞，或是動詞位置要填入什麼樣的形態。
The type of flooring we **were using** / to use / using is not available anymore.
我們曾用過的地板類型已經無法再取得了。

CHECK-UP

3. Some information containing / **contained** in the documents is outdated.
4. The CEO does everything **he** / him can to support his employees.

3 關係副詞

■ 在形容詞子句中，關係副詞具備副詞的功能，同時兼具連接詞的功能，引導形容詞子句，連接其他子句。當先行詞為時間時，使用 when；先行詞為地點時，使用 where；先行詞為理由時，使用 why；先行詞為方法時，則使用 how。

Monday is **the day**. + A weekly meeting takes place **on the day**.
= Monday is **the day on which** a weekly meeting takes place.
= Monday is **the day when** / why a weekly meeting takes place.
星期一是舉行週會的日子。

■ 根據文法規則，關係副詞後方要連接結構完整的子句；關係代名詞後方則連接不完整的子句。

Mr. Lowe received a full-time job offer from the firm <u>where</u> / which he did his summer internship.
Lowe 先生收到了他暑期實習公司提供的全職工作機會。
➡ 畫底線處後方連接結構完整的子句，因此答案要選關係副詞，兼具副詞與連接詞的功能。

Please review the employee evaluation <u>that</u> / how I have attached to this message.
請確認我附在這封郵件中的員工評估表。
➡ 畫底線處後方連接 I have attached，為缺少受詞的不完整子句，因此答案要選關係代名詞受格。

CHECK-UP

5. Dedicated fans of the brand are lined up in front of the store what / <u>where</u> the limited-edition sneakers will be released.
6. The cellphone is comprised of materials <u>that</u> / how resist damage from drops under five meters.

4 複合關係代名詞

■ 複合關係代名詞的形態為［關係代名詞 + -ever］，與關係代名詞一樣，後方要連接不完整的子句。

who(m)ever	whichever	whatever
名詞子句：無論是誰…	名詞子句：無論是哪個…	名詞子句：無論是什麼樣的…
副詞子句：無論誰做…	副詞子句：無論選哪個…	副詞子句：無論做什麼樣的…

Mr. Stevens works hard to be the best at <u>whatever</u> / any he does.
Stevens 先生無論做什麼事，都會努力做到最好。

■ 複合關係副詞的形態為［關係副詞 + -ever］，與關係副詞一樣，後方要連接結構完整的子句。

whenever	wherever	however
無論何時、每當…	無論在哪裡	不管用什麼方法、無論如何…

The manager on duty should be notified <u>whenever</u> / which a customer makes a complaint.
每當顧客投訴時，都應通知值班經理。

CHECK-UP

7. <u>Whoever</u> / However leaves the office last is expected to turn off the lights.
8. Pawan Tech developed a mobile application that offers users the latest traffic conditions whatever / <u>wherever</u> they go.

PRACTICE

答案&解析 p.63

1. Ms. Zeller invited several candidates for an interview even though they did not have the ------- qualifications for the junior researcher position.
   (A) prefer
   (B) preferred
   (C) preferably
   (D) to prefer

2. A retirement party will be held next week for Mr. Schmidt, ------- has been working for Melon Technologies for over 30 years.
   (A) all
   (B) who
   (C) this
   (D) most

3. Mr. Farrow ------- the vehicle's engine and then report any issues.
   (A) are inspecting
   (B) having inspected
   (C) inspect
   (D) will inspect

4. Our funding comes from the support of foundations as well as readers, ------- we are grateful.
   (A) when
   (B) in order to
   (C) for which
   (D) along with

5. All employees must attend next week's workshop ------- how to operate the new machinery.
   (A) understood
   (B) is understanding
   (C) understands
   (D) to understand

6. Carsen Gym will be shut down for about two months while renovations -------.
   (A) will be completing
   (B) completing
   (C) was completed
   (D) are being completed

7. The customer service department bought ------- computers because its budget was small.
   (A) used
   (B) use
   (C) user
   (D) using

8. Later this afternoon, Ms. Bullock ------- the contract terms with one of the building materials companies.
   (A) has renegotiated
   (B) renegotiated
   (C) will be renegotiating
   (D) was renegotiating

118

PRACTICE

9. You will be refunded after we receive the ------- product in the mail.
   (A) to return
   (B) returns
   (C) returned
   (D) returning

10. Mr. Grimes ------- the keynote address at the IT and security conference last Friday.
    (A) will have given
    (B) is giving
    (C) gave
    (D) was given

11. Cannon Corporation is exploring the possibility of ------- its business into Asia.
    (A) extend
    (B) extension
    (C) extensive
    (D) extending

12. Mosquito pesticide spraying operations ------- to commence before tourists come on vacation.
    (A) schedule
    (B) are scheduled
    (C) were scheduling
    (D) have scheduled

13. Customers can get a free sample of all hair-care products, ------- they prefer, in celebration of Chonie Salon's 10th anniversary.
    (A) any
    (B) whose
    (C) indeed
    (D) whichever

14. Smallville's mayor plans ------- an abandoned building into a library.
    (A) to turn
    (B) to be turned
    (C) turn
    (D) will be turned

15. The ------- product designer was awarded with the industry's top honors.
    (A) accomplish
    (B) accomplished
    (C) accomplishing
    (D) accomplishment

16. Mr. Barbour showed the electrician the light fixture ------- had been malfunctioning.
    (A) that
    (B) itself
    (C) what
    (D) whoever

UNIT 08　詞彙

常考名詞詞彙

excursion　（短期）旅行
go on an **excursion** to the Grand Canyon
去大峽谷旅行

charge　費用；責任、負責
free of **charge**　免費
the person in **charge** of the contract　合約負責人

recipient　收件人、接受者
announce the **recipient** of an award
宣布獲獎者
<相關詞> receive　收到

obstacle　障礙（物）
overcome **obstacles**　克服障礙

expertise　專業知識、專業性
demonstrate a wealth of **expertise**
展現豐富的專業知識
<相關詞> expert　專家；專業的、內行的

turnover　離職率；銷售額
high staff **turnover**　高員工離職率
an annual **turnover** of $90 million
9千萬美元的年銷售額

alignment　對齊、校直
be out of **alignment**　（排序等）不整齊
<相關詞> align　排成直線

recommendation　推薦（信）；建議
a letter of **recommendation**　推薦信
on the board's **recommendation**　在董事會的建議下
<相關詞> recommend　推薦；勸告

delegation　委任；代表團
delegation of tasks　業務委託
a member of the **delegation**　代表團的一員
<相關詞> delegate　委任（工作、任務等）；選定代表〔代理人〕

delay　延遲、耽擱
cause a **delay** in shipment　導致配送延遲
apologize for a schedule **delay**　為推遲行程道歉

certification　證書
renew one's **certification** yearly
每年更新證書
<相關詞> certify　證明

estimate　報價（單）；估計（值）
examine the **estimate** carefully
仔細檢查報價單
a rough **estimate**　大略的估計值
<相關詞> estimated　報價的；推測的

confidence　信賴；自信；祕密
have complete **confidence**　非常自信
in strict **confidence**　極其祕密地

capacity　容量、容納度；能力、地位、作用
increase the **capacity** of the stadium
增加競技場的容納人數
operate at full **capacity**　以最大值運作
in one's **capacity** as chairman of the council
以議會議長的身分

defect　缺陷
take responsibility for **defects**　對缺陷負責

request　要求、請求（書）
process a **request**　處理請求

policy　政策、方針
flexible work **policy**　彈性的工作規範

critic　評論家
draw positive reviews from **critics**
獲得評論家的肯定回覆
<相關詞> critique　批評、評論
　　　　 criticism　指責、批評

clientele　客戶
attract a young **clientele**　吸引年輕顧客
<同義詞> customer　客戶

occasion　時刻、場合；活動
for any **occasion**　在任何情況下
a memorable **occasion**　令人印象深刻的活動
<相關詞> occasionally　偶爾

120

CHECK-UP 名詞

1. The museum cannot be opened to the public until structural ------- are repaired.
   (A) definitions
   (B) defects
   (C) communications
   (D) uncertainties

2. If the dry cleaning business makes a delivery within the Philadelphia city limits, there is no extra -------.
   (A) pressure
   (B) provider
   (C) charge
   (D) area

3. Although lighter than predicted, the snow caused traffic ------- during rush hour.
   (A) delays
   (B) refunds
   (C) routes
   (D) suggestions

4. Should you file an auto insurance claim, we will examine the ------- within three business days.
   (A) expertise
   (B) account
   (C) registration
   (D) request

5. In addition to holding a degree from a prestigious university, Ms. Harris has several -------.
   (A) certifications
   (B) assignments
   (C) estimates
   (D) recipients

6. A small business loan helped Mr. Joslin overcome the ------- that were holding back his business.
   (A) attempts
   (B) obstacles
   (C) reactions
   (D) opposites

7. Library patrons completed the survey to share ------- for books that should be purchased.
   (A) recommendations
   (B) reimbursements
   (C) retrieval
   (D) resolutions

8. Tingley Travel has introduced ------- to Europe for students on summer break.
   (A) settlements
   (B) excursions
   (C) institutions
   (D) accomplishments

9. Although the store's refund ------- is clearly stated on its website, some consumers are confused about it.
   (A) policy
   (B) shelter
   (C) preference
   (D) appointment

10. The private dining room at Verity Restaurant can be reserved for any special ------- for up to 30 people.
    (A) occasion
    (B) turnover
    (C) competence
    (D) intention

常考形容詞詞彙

prior 事先的；優先的
require **prior** approval by a supervisor
需要主管的事先批准
have a **prior** claim to the business
有事業單位的優先權
[相關詞] priority 優先事項、優先權
prioritize 排列優先順序

significant 相當的；有意義的、重要的
experience **significant** growth 歷經相當大的成長
statistically **significant** 統計上有意義的
[相關詞] significantly 相當地；有意義地、重要地

frequent 屢次的、頻繁的
a **frequent** customer[visitor] 常客
[相關詞] frequency 頻率

extensive 廣泛的；大規模的
have **extensive** experience 有很多經驗
cause **extensive** damage 引起大規模損失
[相關詞] extend 延長；擴大（事業、勢力等）

utmost 最大限度的
make **utmost** efforts 盡最大的努力

individual 單獨的、個別的
speak with **individual** attendees
與每位參賽者交談

incremental 逐漸增加的、遞增的
incremental improvements 逐步進步
[相關詞] incrementally 逐漸地

supplemental 添加的、補充的
supplemental documentation 補充資料
[同義詞] extra 追加的、額外的

valid 有效的
a **valid** license 有效執照[資格證]

prestigious 有名氣的、有權威的
a highly **prestigious** award 極具權威的獎項
[相關詞] prestige 威信、名望

substantial 大量的；實在的
a **substantial** amount of money 大金額的錢財
[相關詞] substance 物質；本質、核心

attentive 注意的；關懷的、費心的
friendly and **attentive** staff 親切細心的工作人員
be **attentive** to customers' needs 注重顧客需求
[相關詞] attend 注意；出席
attention 注意、關注；關心、關懷

sizeable 相當大的
a **sizeable** income 相當多的收入

current 現在的、當前的
current prices 目前價格
the most **current** findings 最新調查結果

massive 非常多[大]的、巨大的
undergo **massive** changes 歷經巨大的變化

objective 客觀的
provide **objective** information 提供客觀資訊
[相關詞] object 物體

optimistic 樂觀的、樂天的
be cautiously **optimistic** 謹慎樂觀

exceptional （異常地）出色的；例外的
an **exceptional** work of art 卓越的藝術作品
only in **exceptional** circumstances
僅在例外情況下
[相關詞] exception 例外的人事物、例外

joint 共同的、聯合的
a **joint** effort 共同的努力
a **joint** account 一個聯合帳戶

dependable 可靠的
a **dependable** assistant 可靠的助理
[同義詞] reliable 可靠的、值得信賴的

CHECK-UP 形容詞

1. Before the new software was installed, employees spent a ------- amount of time updating customer accounts.
   (A) consecutive
   (B) direct
   (C) substantial
   (D) visible

2. The Henley Institute's public speaking class is suitable for corporate groups and ------- students.
   (A) beneficial
   (B) individual
   (C) deliberate
   (D) distant

3. A job applicant with ------- experience in management will have a good chance of being hired.
   (A) straight
   (B) extensive
   (C) compact
   (D) attentive

4. Experts are worried about the ------- impact that climate change may have on the global economy.
   (A) factual
   (B) massive
   (C) objective
   (D) original

5. The video streaming service has added a ------- number of new users in the past quarter.
   (A) current
   (B) defective
   (C) sizeable
   (D) preserved

6. Mr. Kellogg will be offered the senior accounting position if his state certification turns out to be -------.
   (A) successive
   (B) familiar
   (C) informal
   (D) valid

7. Investors were ------- about the cruise line's potential after the first trip sold out quickly.
   (A) optimistic
   (B) superior
   (C) rare
   (D) unique

8. At Rosewood Inn, guest comfort is of the ------- importance.
   (A) constant
   (B) diminished
   (C) joint
   (D) utmost

9. The new tax incentives have made a ------- difference in the number of new small businesses in town.
   (A) difficult
   (B) prepared
   (C) significant
   (D) capable

10. Following upgrades to the power plant, the city will have a more ------- supply of electricity.
    (A) dependable
    (B) patient
    (C) enthusiastic
    (D) grateful

PART 5

123

常考副詞詞彙

sincerely 真心地
sincerely hope it will succeed
真心希望它能成功
相關詞 sincere 真實的、真誠的

directly 直接地
be directly affected by related policies
直接受到相關規定的影響
相關詞 direct 直接的、直達的

newly 最近地、新地
a newly hired employee 新招聘的員工
相關詞 new 新的

primarily 主要地
be aimed primarily at young consumers
主要針對年輕消費者
相關詞 primary 主要的

currently 現在、當前
currently under construction 正在施工中
相關詞 current 現在的、當前的

soon 馬上、不久後
be expected to soon gain worldwide fame
預計很快就會享譽全球

unexpectedly 意想不到地、意外地
be unexpectedly successful 意外獲得成功
相關詞 unexpected 意想不到的、意外的

thoroughly 完全地、徹底地
clean up spills thoroughly 徹底清理灑出的東西
thoroughly confused 混亂不堪的、完全困惑的
同義詞 completely 完全地、徹底地

diligently 勤奮地、勤勞地
work diligently 勤奮工作
diligently complete the task 勤奮於完成任務

initially 起初
be used as a theater initially
起初作為劇場使用
相關詞 initial 最初的、初期的

accidentally 偶然地、意外地
prevent the door from opening accidentally
防止門自動打開
accidentally delete a file 失手刪除文件
相關詞 accidental 偶然的、突發的

comfortably 輕鬆地、無負擔地；寬裕地
win comfortably 輕鬆獲勝
be comfortably furnished （傢俱等）擺設舒適
相關詞 comfortable 舒服的、舒適的

noticeably 顯著地
noticeably higher than last quarter
明顯高於上個季度
相關詞 notice 察覺、認知、關注

far 更加、極；遠遠地
fall far behind the competition
在競爭中遠遠落後

unanimously 全體一致地
unanimously agree 全體一致同意
相關詞 unanimous 全體一致的

temporarily 暫時地、臨時地
temporarily out of stock 暫時斷貨
相關詞 temporary 暫時的、臨時的

considerably 相當地
drop considerably in value 價值明顯下降
相關詞 considerable （大小、數量、程度）相當的

immediately 立刻、馬上
immediately after the meeting 會議結束後立刻…
相關詞 immediate 立即的

recently 最近
a recently published novel 最近出版的小說
相關詞 recent 最近的

alike 相似地、相像地
try to treat all customers alike
努力平等對待每一位客人

CHECK-UP 副詞

1. Riddell Dairy Farm supplies milk ------- to local restaurants, keeping costs low.
   (A) directly
   (B) neatly
   (C) hardly
   (D) unusually

2. Our technology specialist is working ------- to restore Internet service to the office.
   (A) financially
   (B) seemingly
   (C) particularly
   (D) diligently

3. Office manager Charles Yarger ------- requested a meeting with Ms. Arlow, so she had to adjust her schedule.
   (A) commonly
   (B) indefinitely
   (C) unexpectedly
   (D) nearly

4. Founded and headquartered in Belgium, the cookware company is ------- in the process of establishing a new factory.
   (A) currently
   (B) extremely
   (C) solidly
   (D) immediately

5. The Sky Room can accommodate up to 50 guests, while the Wind Room seats between 80 and 100 people -------.
   (A) consequently
   (B) widely
   (C) comfortably
   (D) exceedingly

6. Lamora Fruit Orchard ------- confirmed that it will have a change of ownership in the upcoming quarter.
   (A) approximately
   (B) recently
   (C) heavily
   (D) randomly

7. Clotherly produces cotton T-shirts that are ------- softer than those of its competitors.
   (A) hurriedly
   (B) respectively
   (C) noticeably
   (D) closely

8. Waldeck's ------- released tablet features a high-resolution screen.
   (A) newly
   (B) absolutely
   (C) naturally
   (D) considerably

9. The sales department will be ------- moved to the fifth floor while the fourth floor is being renovated.
   (A) faintly
   (B) temporarily
   (C) sincerely
   (D) competitively

10. Because she was unfamiliar with the software, one of the trainees ------- printed 10 extra banners for Traylyn Inc.
    (A) mainly
    (B) vigorously
    (C) necessarily
    (D) accidentally

常考動詞詞彙

ensure 保證、確保
a design to **ensure** safety 保證安全的設計
ensure the quality of a new product
保證新產品的品質

feature 以…為特色、特別亮相
feature paintings by young artists
特別展示年輕藝術家的畫作

note 注意、提到
Please **note** we will be closed on Monday.
請注意我們週一沒有營業。
as **noted** earlier 正如先前提到的那樣
【相關詞】 notice 察覺、認知、關注；公告、通知

prompt 促使
prompt the mayor's resignation
促使市長辭職
【相關詞】 promptly 毫不遲延地、準時地

afford （金錢和時間上）可負擔、提供
cannot **afford** to buy new vehicles
買不起新車
【相關詞】 affordable （價格等）負擔得起的

take down 收拾掉；寫下
take down an art piece from a wall
摘下掛在牆上的美術作品
take down the minutes 撰寫會議記錄

top 超過（數量、記錄等）；高於、蓋上
top the charts for a month 一個月內佔排行榜第一名
top the previous record 超越先前的記錄
a cake **topped** with fresh fruits
上面有新鮮水果的蛋糕

bring together （人們）聚在一起
bring together business leaders and academics
企業家和學術研究者們齊聚一堂

separate 分開、分離
be **separated** from the land by a tall fence
用高聳的柵欄隔開那片土地

waive 放棄（權利、要求等）
waive a registration fee 免收註冊費

guarantee 保障、保證
guarantee an objective assessment
保證客觀評價

inquire 詢問
inquire about current interest rates 詢問當前利率

announce 發表、告知
announce an increase in prices 告知價格上漲

anticipate 預想；期待、期盼
submit a list of **anticipated** expenses for a business trip
繳交出差預估費用表
anticipate pay increases 期待加薪

coincide with 與…一致、與…同時發生
coincide with the conference 與會議時間撞期

compensate 補償
be **compensated** for any damage
任何損失都能獲得補償

cultivate 栽培（作物）；建立、結交（關係）
cultivate mainly wheat 主要種植小麥
cultivate good relations with competitors
與競爭公司建立良好的關係

withdraw 提取（金錢）；撤走、收回
withdraw money 提款
withdraw an offer 撤回提案

implement 實施、執行
implement decisions/recommendations
執行決定／建議
implement a recycling program
實施回收再利用計畫
【同義詞】 carry out 執行、實施

obscure 使模糊；遮掩
obscure the main issue 模糊主要爭論點
be **obscured** by fog 被霧遮住看不見
【近義詞】 hide 遮擋

boost 提振、提高
boost productivity 提高生產率
boost sales in Europe, its biggest market
在它最大的市場歐洲提高銷售額

CHECK-UP 動詞

1. Midco Communications and Trant Inc. have ------- a joint charity endeavor to supply Internet services to low-income households.
   (A) announced
   (B) installed
   (C) treated
   (D) calibrated

2. Please ------- that requests for time off must be approved by a supervisor one week in advance.
   (A) assess
   (B) note
   (C) secure
   (D) reschedule

3. A decrease in profits has ------- Liang Industries to increase its marketing budget.
   (A) licensed
   (B) restocked
   (C) prompted
   (D) outlined

4. The lead accountant at Kirtfield Sales reviewed the company's finances and determined that it could not ------- to renovate its building.
   (A) admit
   (B) maintain
   (C) afford
   (D) remember

5. The annual Gaming Convention ------- video game developers from across the country.
   (A) carries out
   (B) brings together
   (C) uses up
   (D) takes down

6. ------- the year's list of best-selling mystery novels is *The Door to Sandra's*.
   (A) Topping
   (B) Impressing
   (C) Generating
   (D) Seeking

7. As items often come from two or more warehouses, your order may be ------- into different packages.
   (A) mandated
   (B) separated
   (C) prioritized
   (D) demolished

8. Based on how many units were pre-ordered, the company ------- its new game console launch will be a huge success.
   (A) compiles
   (B) condenses
   (C) delegates
   (D) anticipates

9. Vance Bank reminds travelers that the bank cannot ------- the same exchange rate due to fluctuations in the currency market.
   (A) convey
   (B) guarantee
   (C) undergo
   (D) obscure

10. Reporters ------- about the stock prices and their relation to changes in executive leadership.
    (A) formulated
    (B) inquired
    (C) persuaded
    (D) occupied

PART TEST

答案&解析 p.67

READING TEST

In the Reading test, you will read a variety of texts and answer several different types of reading comprehension questions. The entire Reading test will last 75 minutes. There are three parts, and directions are given for each part. You are encouraged to answer as many questions as possible within the time allowed.

You must mark your answers on the separate answer sheet. Do not write your answers in your test book.

PART 5

Directions: A word or phrase is missing in each of the sentences below. Four answer choices are given below each sentence. Select the best answer to complete the sentence. Then mark the letter (A), (B), (C), or (D) on your answer sheet.

101. Many tutors ------- their services on community forums because it is cost-effective.

    (A) advertiser
    (B) advertise
    (C) advertisement
    (D) advertising

102. The post office does not accept international packages unless ------- contents are disclosed.

    (A) they
    (B) their
    (C) theirs
    (D) them

103. The factory supervisor was pleased with how ------- Benson Manufacturing's staff repaired the broken machinery.

    (A) electronically
    (B) increasingly
    (C) quickly
    (D) highly

104. Ms. Poole and Mr. Johnson continue to exceed ------- in their managerial positions.

    (A) expectant
    (B) expected
    (C) expect
    (D) expectations

105. The lease on the two-bedroom apartment unit must be renewed ------- October 6.

    (A) with
    (B) by
    (C) in
    (D) of

106. The meeting rooms are usually closed for ------- every weekday at approximately 8 P.M.

    (A) cleaning
    (B) disposing
    (C) speaking
    (D) painting

107. Please write in all capital letters when you ------- the customs declaration form provided by the government.

    (A) completed
    (B) completing
    (C) have completed
    (D) complete

108. Ms. Delgado explained that her ------- contract with the design firm is just a short-term contract.

    (A) steep
    (B) current
    (C) natural
    (D) occasional

109. Passengers can change their seat reservations ------- 24 hours before the flight without a charge.
    (A) since
    (B) up to
    (C) as for
    (D) in case

110. A section of Greenwich Hardware's parking lot was shut down ------- after a tree fell.
    (A) potentially
    (B) significantly
    (C) temporarily
    (D) annually

111. Vensa Airways provided travel vouchers to everyone ------- was delayed because of the flight cancellation.
    (A) what
    (B) each
    (C) who
    (D) much

112. Spectators ------- to refrain from taking unnecessary personal items into the stadium.
    (A) ask
    (B) have asked
    (C) are asked
    (D) asking

113. Sunderland Insurance's policy includes emergency calls as an ------- use of personal phones at work.
    (A) accepts
    (B) accepting
    (C) acceptable
    (D) acceptably

114. All of our garments are closely inspected ------- they are sent to AJ Fashions' stores.
    (A) regarding
    (B) below
    (C) except
    (D) before

115. The news of the merger was ------- confirmed by a source within one of the organizations.
    (A) reliably
    (B) reliable
    (C) rely
    (D) reliability

116. ------- completing her master's degree, Ms. Lewis spent two years trying to launch her own catering business.
    (A) That
    (B) According to
    (C) Prior to
    (D) Moreover

117. The bus to the theater will ------- from the pharmacy's front entrance and end on Yorkshire Street.
    (A) conduct
    (B) extend
    (C) depart
    (D) withdraw

118. To reduce the start-up costs of the business, try buying ------- office equipment.
    (A) use
    (B) used
    (C) user
    (D) uses

119. Brow Supplies has plans to develop new hard hats to improve safety at work -------.
    (A) notices
    (B) sites
    (C) goals
    (D) calendars

120. For inquiries about replacing outdated equipment, ------- Mr. Arrieta in the IT department.
    (A) determine
    (B) apply
    (C) hire
    (D) contact

GO ON TO THE NEXT PAGE

129

121. The museum will offer free behind-the-scenes tours on Saturday mornings ------- the end of August.
    (A) onto
    (B) so
    (C) because
    (D) until

122. Visitors to Clerrick National Park should report all overnight camping plans to the ranger station, located ------- the café and the children's playground.
    (A) including
    (B) into
    (C) throughout
    (D) between

123. Arden Footwear announced that it will ------- expand its line-up of hiking boots.
    (A) soon
    (B) wherever
    (C) most
    (D) so

124. The interior designer presented several ------- before the client chose light grey and yellow as the colors for her kitchen.
    (A) regions
    (B) impressions
    (C) functions
    (D) combinations

125. Under Redding Technology's new policy, salary increases are no longer -------, so employees are compensated according to their level of experience only.
    (A) negotiator
    (B) negotiates
    (C) negotiable
    (D) negotiations

126. Due to its effect on a number of industries, media outlets have ------- publicized details of the trade deal.
    (A) wide
    (B) widen
    (C) widely
    (D) width

127. ------- an item purchased on the Strike Sports website arrives damaged, it can be exchanged at no cost.
    (A) While
    (B) If
    (C) Then
    (D) That

128. RadioWave Electronics' new product demonstration received enthusiastic -------.
    (A) applause
    (B) applaud
    (C) applauding
    (D) to applaud

129. Owing to his ------- knowledge of pharmaceutical research, Max Punja will be offered the senior consultant role.
    (A) amicable
    (B) extensive
    (C) charitable
    (D) gratifying

130. Beginning immediately, all lanes of Highway 19 will be closed to non-emergency vehicles ------- severe weather conditions.
    (A) so that
    (B) as though
    (C) rather than
    (D) as a result of

ENERGY

與其改變全世界，不如先改變自己

—— 聖雄甘地（Mahatma Gandhi）

PART 6

段落填空

UNIT 09 時態

UNIT 10 詞彙

UNIT 11 連接副詞

UNIT 12 句子插入題

PART TEST

PART 6 段落填空

考題類型與命題方向

PART 6在考題類型上介於PART 5和PART 7之間。該大題有四篇文章，每篇文章有四道填空題。其中三道題為文法題或詞彙題，一道題為句子插入題，需選出符合文意的句子。要注意的是，PART 5只需閱讀一句話，便能輕鬆解題；但是在PART 6中，文法題和詞彙題除了查看空格所在的句子外，還需閱讀空格前後的句子，才能選出答案。因此，該大題的文法題經常涉及時態。在作答PART 6時，關鍵在於掌握文章整體脈絡，建議從頭開始閱讀，有助於解題。

Questions 131-134 refer to the following instructions.

答案&解析 p.71

Baldrick Accessories—Creating unique accessories featuring your name or other text is easy to do through the Baldrick Accessories website! Simply select the item you want, input your text, and choose the font, size, and color. Be sure to examine the sample image carefully before placing your order. ------- (131.), you can use the "Back" button to make any necessary changes. ------- (132.). We cannot reuse items due to the custom nature of our products. After your order is placed, you ------- (133.) the sales receipt within a few minutes. Another e-mail will be sent when your items are ------- (134.). This may take up to five days, depending on the volume of our orders.

131. (A) Consequently
(B) For example
(C) Conversely
(D) Additionally

132. (A) Subscribers to our newsletter can receive a discount.
(B) Please be aware that all sales are final.
(C) Don't forget to check back regularly for new merchandise.
(D) The delivery options will be presented to you.

133. (A) have been e-mailed
(B) were being e-mailed
(C) will be e-mailed
(D) were e-mailed

134. (A) ready
(B) brief
(C) similar
(D) exempt

解題策略

雖然作答PART 6需要閱讀完整篇文章，但其中有許多題目與PART 5類似，只需查看空格所在的句子就能選出答案。舉例來說，如果題目涉及詞性，只需確認空格所在句子的句型結構、空格前後方單字的詞性和作用，就能找出答案。但如果題目涉及時態或詞彙，且有兩個或兩個以上的選項納入考量範圍時，就不得不閱讀前後方的句子，以確認前後文意。特別是如果涉及連接句子的連接副詞，或句子插入題時，就必須透過上下文的脈絡來解題。

131. (A) Consequently
     (B) For example
     (C) Conversely
     (D) Additionally

連接副詞
作答連接副詞考題時，需要根據空格所在的句子與前方句子的關係來判斷答案。連接副詞不僅包含由單個單字構成的additionally（此外）、however（然而），還包含由多個單字組合而成的慣用表達，如in other words（換句話說）、as a result（因此）、if possible（如果可能的話），這些都經常出現在考題中。

132. (A) Subscribers to our newsletter can receive a discount.
     (B) Please be aware that all sales are final.
     (C) Don't forget to check back regularly for new merchandise.
     (D) The delivery options will be presented to you.

句子插入題
一般來說，一個段落會有一個主題，因此可以先刪去內容偏離該段落中心主旨的選項。此外，除非空格置於段落開頭處，否則大部分的空格都是以前方連接的句子作為判斷依據，確認是否能夠順暢連接。因此建議優先確認空格前方連接的句子，然後再查看後方連接的句子。

133. (A) have been e-mailed
     (B) were being e-mailed
     (C) will be e-mailed
     (D) were e-mailed

時態
如果最終選擇答案時，有多個選項涉及不同時態，建議先查看空格所在的句子中是否包含時間副詞，並確認主要子句和從屬子句的時態。如果以上皆無法確定答案，最後再根據前後文意來確認適當的時態。此外，如果文章類型為電子郵件、報導或公告等，有時可以根據該文章的撰寫日期來判斷時態。

134. **(A) ready**
     (B) brief
     (C) similar
     (D) exempt

詞彙
首先確認填入空格的選項是否能順利連接前後方的單字。如果有兩個或兩個以上的單字皆可順利連接，再根據前後文意來做判斷。

UNIT 09　時態

Questions 1-2 refer to the following web page.

Spring Flower Arrangement Course—Now Accepting Applications

Tidwell Community College ------- a new course this spring semester for the local community.
                                  1.
Award-winning florist Jennifer Goldsmith will show students how to create the perfect arrangement for special occasions as well as teach students tips on how to make their creations last longer.

Classes ------- every Tuesday and Friday evening from 7 P.M. to 10 P.M.
        2.

A final exhibition of their semester pieces will be held on June 2. For tickets, visit the community college website at www.tidwellcc.com.

---

1. (A) opening
   (B) will be opening
   (C) had opened
   (D) was opening

2. (A) are held
   (B) have been held
   (C) were held
   (D) being held

Questions 3-4 refer to the following announcement.

Big news, Classic Motors team!

We would like to congratulate Nathaniel Foreman on his promotion to Team Manager, effective August 16. Mr. Foreman ------- Classic Motors as an intern through our Russel College Internship
                                            3.
Program. He has spent the last 15 years going above and beyond for staff and making significant contributions to the company by always looking for new and innovative solutions for our finance team. We are certain that Mr. Foreman ------- in his new position. Please give him a big
                                                  4.
congratulations the next time you see him.

---

3. (A) entering
   (B) is entering
   (C) will enter
   (D) entered

4. (A) will shine
   (B) shone
   (C) shines
   (D) is shining

Questions 5-6 refer to the following advertisement.

It's Emerald Footwear's 25th anniversary!

Twenty-five years ago, Emerald Footwear opened as a small kiosk at the Plainsman Mall. Today, we have our own two-story building with a spacious display area. Our high-quality products and knowledgeable staff ------- us to become a trusted retailer. To thank our customers for their patronage over the years, we are having a special deal on September 8.
5.

Purchase one pair of shoes and get 60% off another pair. This offer ------- to any brand, with the less expensive pair receiving the discount. Please note that the deal cannot be used with any other additional coupon.
6.

5. (A) have helped
   (B) are helped
   (C) helping
   (D) were helping

6. (A) was applying
   (B) will have applied
   (C) had applied
   (D) applies

Questions 7-8 refer to the following customer review.

I just received my order of 100 napkins from Home Necessities, and I am thoroughly impressed! I often need to order table setting supplies for my catering business. However, since the company I regularly order from was out of stock, I decided to give Home Necessities a chance. The items are better constructed, and the company ------- a wider range of colors and designs. I ------- from Home Necessities exclusively from now on.
7.
8.
—Martin Quinn

7. (A) will have offered
   (B) offers
   (C) offering
   (D) was offering

8. (A) ordered
   (B) was ordering
   (C) will be ordering
   (D) had ordered

UNIT 10　詞彙

答案&解析 p.72

Question 1 refers to the following e-mail.

We would like to inform you that the Graystone Printer X302 has been discontinued, and your order has been automatically cancelled. However, many of our most recent customers have enjoyed the ------- model, the X430. Please call us at 555-2098 to place a new order or discuss refund options.

Alex's Office Supplies

1. (A) accountable
   (B) comparable
   (C) amicable
   (D) applicable

Question 2 refers to the following advertisement.

Come to Auto Masters and we will service your entire vehicle in just two hours. This includes changing the oil, ------- windshield washer fluid, rotating your tires, and more. Located next to the Fairhills Shopping Mall, we can do this while you spend time with your family. Call us at 555-2840 to book this service or one of our many others.

2. (A) remarking
   (B) rounding
   (C) reloading
   (D) refilling

Question 3 refers to the following announcement.

September marks the beginning of the new opera season for the Toronto Opera Company. Opening night is September 12 and the season runs through December 31. This year, everyone is invited to sit in on one of our ------- rehearsals every Tuesday from 2:00 P.M. to 4:00 P.M. To reserve tickets for a rehearsal, please visit the website at www.torontooc.org.

3. (A) seasonal
   (B) public
   (C) domestic
   (D) challenging

Question 4 refers to the following job posting.

Rainbow Toys is looking for a new social marketing manager. Applicants will work on making our social media platforms more accessible and creating more ------- content for our customers. For that reason, applicants should have experience in either video creation, social media platform management, or copywriting.

4. (A) lengthy
   (B) engaging
   (C) impersonal
   (D) accelerated

Question 5 refers to the following advertisement.

Booker is offering a special New Year's discount on our most popular reading plan! Sign up for the Deluxe reading plan and get ------- to over 500,000 books, plus 30% off purchases of this month's latest releases. And only Booker offers unlimited book rentals. You can take advantage of this deal today at www.booker.com/newyear.

5. (A) claim
   (B) control
   (C) access
   (D) entry

Questions 6-7 refer to the following customer review.

I have been using Manaray's furniture for years and was always satisfied with my purchases. However, after visiting a Logan's Furniture showroom, I am glad I did. The quality of furniture is on another level!

Their leather sofas are made using luxurious, soft leather. All of their designs can be customized to include a recliner as well. We also found the perfect dining room table set in mahogany wood. The table and chairs feel ------- and are sure to last a lifetime.

Please be aware that most items do not come -------. Professional assembly is available for a small additional fee. But that may not be necessary thanks to the easy-to-follow instructions included with everything.

6. (A) separate
   (B) stiff
   (C) simple
   (D) sturdy

7. (A) fixed
   (B) assembled
   (C) crumbled
   (D) pieced

UNIT 11　連接副詞

Question 1 refers to the following letter.

To Whom It May Concern,

We here at Forever Fitness would like to invite you to become a member. We have the largest array of top-of-the-line equipment in the region in a state-of-the-art, 40-acre facility. We also provide a unique feature—photo zones for those who maintain a social media presence. -------1., no photography is allowed on our regular gym floors without previous consent. Our gym offers the widest range of fitness programs of any gym, over 40 kinds. And all instructors and trainers have multiple national certifications to give you the best experience possible.

Call us at 555-2109 for a free consultation, and receive a free 1-day pass. We're sure you will come back.

Best regards,

Kelly Vasquez, Owner

1. (A) Besides
   (B) Otherwise
   (C) If not
   (D) Regardless

Question 2 refers to the following advertisement.

Get Your Business Noticed!

Do you have a great business, but nobody seems to know? We can fix that! Frankfurt Media has a team of experts ready to create the right advertising strategy for your business. We will craft the perfect TV or radio commercial and get it to your intended audience. -------2., you will have more time to focus on your business.

Go to www.frankfurtmedia.com today, and have your advertisement ready in one week!

2. (A) Nevertheless
   (B) Even so
   (C) Meanwhile
   (D) Recently

Question 3 refers to the following e-mail.

To: Mark Klein <kleinm@solarnet.com>
From: Jane Lorowitz <jlorowitz@greatconstructs.com>
Date: April 20
Subject: Schedule Change

Dear Mr. Klein,

I am writing to let you know there has been a change in the construction schedule. The current schedule has us booked until June 12. However, because of the frequent rainstorms these days, we have had to stop construction on those days. -------, we were unable to finish putting up the walls. The new estimated end date is June 20.

I would be happy to chat if you would like to discuss the schedule further.

Regards,

Jane Lorowitz

3. (A) Nonetheless
   (B) Consequently
   (C) Finally
   (D) Lastly

Question 4 refers to the following information.

After six months of renovations, Craftsbury Library is happy to announce our reopening. Some new features include a wheelchair-accessible entrance complete with a ramp and five new classrooms to hold more of our popular after-school programs. -------, we've established an occupation preparation center to help Craftsbury residents look for and secure jobs. To find out all of the new features at the library, head to our website at www.craftsburylibrary.gov.

4. (A) Hence
   (B) Accordingly
   (C) Therefore
   (D) Additionally

UNIT 12　句子插入題

答案&解析 p.74

Question 1 refers to the following e-mail.

To: All Customers
From: Keritz Audio Customer Service Team
Date: December 2
Subject: End-of-Year Closure

Keritz Audio will be closed for the end-of-the-year holiday season, effective December 23.

-------. Any orders placed after this date will be shipped in the new year. Also, please remember that delivery dates will vary depending on your exact delivery location. To view an estimated delivery schedule for your region, please check out the shipping section of our website.

We appreciate your continued support. We are looking forward to showing you the new products we have lined up for the new year.

Sincerely,

The Keritz Audio Team

---

1. (A) Please contact the courier service with your confirmation number.
   (B) Express delivery is available for an extra $5.99.
   (C) We are open from 9:00 A.M. to 5:00 P.M.
   (D) The last date you can order before the end of the year is December 22.

Question 2 refers to the following announcement.

Come visit the beautiful Catskills Waterpark for a day of fun and excitement for the whole family. Not only are we the largest waterpark in the area, we are also the most eco-friendly. We are the only waterpark in the nation to feature a completely environmentally friendly water-usage system. -------. This is done to reduce the impact on local water supplies. The park even uses hydroelectricity to power all rides and tide pools. We want families to enjoy Catskills Waterpark for generations. For tickets and information, visit us at www.catskillswaterpark.com.

---

2. (A) All water is collected from natural sources, such as rainwater and natural reservoirs.
   (B) We ask that all visitors pick up their trash when at the park.
   (C) Please refrain from using too much water during your visit.
   (D) All paper products are made from recycled paper.

Question 3 refers to the following notice.

We have recently been told that our current vendor, Global Produce Distributions, has decided to downsize their supply chain. This means we will be unable to export our citrus fruit to Northern Europe. -------. That is why we need to put a lot of effort into finding a new distributor.
    3.

One thing we pride ourselves on is our wide array of exotic fruit. See if you can find a company that needs that area supplemented. If you find any companies, please let me know.

I would like a list of possible leads by Friday afternoon to present at the weekly managers meeting.

3. (A) None of our team has ever been to Northern Europe.
   (B) Please give us a detailed list of your citrus fruit.
   (C) We need to work on increasing our supplies.
   (D) This region was a major part of our expansion plan this year.

Question 4 refers to the following information.

Charles Hartman, owner of Hartman Landscaping, has been beautifying the region for over 20 years. His team specializes in commercial and public properties.

They are well-known for their construction of the area's most popular recreational parks and spaces. -------. This 100-acre area is home to the annual George Street Music Festival.
          4.

To turn your property into a work of art, contact Hartman Landscaping today. They will help you build the perfect lawn based for your budget and requirements.

4. (A) Their office is located right next to the local post office.
   (B) They are responsible for the award-winning design of Campbell Park.
   (C) As a result, they prefer to use all native flowers and shrubs.
   (D) They are the biggest sponsors of the annual event.

PART TEST

PART 6

Directions: Read the texts that follow. A word, phrase, or sentence is missing in parts of each text. Four answer choices for each question are given below the text. Select the best answer to complete the text. Then mark the letter (A), (B), (C), or (D) on your answer sheet.

Questions 131-134 refer to the following e-mail.

To: Edward Sandoval <sandovaledward@warrenmail.com>
From: Brunswick Studios <accounts@brunswickstudios.com>
Date: February 22
Subject: Membership

Dear Mr. Sandoval,

Thank you for signing up for a one-year membership with Brunswick Studios. Our website is devoted to helping you reach new fans, write meaningful songs, and improve your performances. The content on our website ------- by musicians like you. You'll receive e-mails about special
131.
deals on products you may need, such as software programs ------- projects that require editing.
132.
To ------- the content sent to your inbox, sign into your account and select your desired options.
133.
For just $5.99 more per month, you can be upgraded to Gold Status and receive even more content. -------. So, why not give it a try risk-free?
134.

Warmest regards,

Tara Nelson
Brunswick Studios

---

131. (A) wrote
 (B) will write
 (C) is written
 (D) had been written

132. (A) into
 (B) for
 (C) our
 (D) at

133. (A) deliver
 (B) personalize
 (C) calculate
 (D) dispute

134. (A) We are pleased to have been nominated.
 (B) You can cancel anytime with no penalty.
 (C) Your feedback helps us improve our services.
 (D) The speed depends on your Internet service.

Questions 135-138 refer to the following e-mail.

To: All Redhawk Towers Tenants
From: Jennifer Milligan
Date: February 20
Subject: Power outage

Dear Redhawk Towers Tenants,

An interruption to the electricity supply ------- for all buildings on Jennings Street and Pine Street
135.
between 12th and 14th Avenue. Power will be shut off in order to perform essential maintenance tasks. Work will take place on February 25 and 26 from 9 A.M. to noon.

Please plan ahead for the outage on ------- day. Computers should be shut down prior to the
136.
outage. -------. Food stored in refrigerators and freezers will be fine if the doors are kept closed.
137.
Thank you for your ------- and patience.
138.

Jennifer Milligan
Property Manager, Redhawk Towers

---

135. (A) has scheduled
 (B) schedules
 (C) is scheduled
 (D) is scheduling

136. (A) only
 (B) most
 (C) all
 (D) each

137. (A) Several apartment units are now available.
 (B) Those left on could be damaged by an unexpected shutdown.
 (C) We can confirm that safety is taken seriously.
 (D) The noise will no longer be a disturbance to everyone.

138. (A) donation
 (B) cooperation
 (C) destination
 (D) confirmation

Questions 139-142 refer to the following blog excerpt.

Vehicles for Plumbers

If you are working as an independent plumber, it is essential that you have a vehicle. At first, you may think it's a good idea to look for the ------- option. However, it's much better to invest in a reliable vehicle from the start. -------. For example, will you have to fit into tight parking spaces or store large ------- such as power saws in it? Be sure to read the reviews for the model you are considering. -------, the vehicle you purchase will support and maybe even motivate you during your business journey.

139. (A) cheaply
    (B) as cheap as
    (C) cheapest
    (D) cheaper than

140. (A) The fuel efficiency of the vehicle is important.
    (B) Building a client base can take several months.
    (C) Plumbing jobs are steadily in demand throughout the year.
    (D) You should take some time to think about the size you need.

141. (A) electricians
    (B) uniforms
    (C) tools
    (D) pipes

142. (A) Lately
    (B) On the other hand
    (C) Otherwise
    (D) Ultimately

Questions 143-146 refer to the following letter.

March 3

Dear Northwest Utilities Customers,

We would like to apologize for any confusion caused by your most recent ------- bill. Our billing
                                                                            143.
department experienced a software malfunction. As a result, the bills for February were -------
                                                                                         144.
with the incorrect information. ------- we strive to accurately reflect customers' usage, errors do
                                 145.
sometimes happen.

-------. You can expect to receive it within the next five business days. We will also extend the
146.
deadline by two weeks because of this error. Thank you for your patience and understanding
during this process.

Northwest Utilities
4190 Woodland Terrace
Tacoma, WA 98412

143. (A) energy
     (B) energize
     (C) energetic
     (D) energizes

144. (A) given away
     (B) cashed in
     (C) brought down
     (D) sent out

145. (A) Despite
     (B) Except
     (C) Once
     (D) Although

146. (A) Please ignore the bill and wait for a new one to be issued.
     (B) Some of the electricity comes from renewable sources.
     (C) The policy is clearly outlined on our website.
     (D) We appreciate your prompt payment for the service.

PART 7

閱讀理解

UNIT 13 電子郵件與信件

UNIT 14 文字簡訊與線上聊天

UNIT 15 報導、公告、廣告

UNIT 16 雙篇與多篇文章

PART TEST

PART 7 閱讀理解

文章類型與命題方向

PART 7的文章涵蓋英語系國家，尤其是在美國日常生活中廣泛涉及的主題。該大題的難度並非取決於特定文章類型傾向簡單或困難，而是由文章篇幅長短和詞彙難易度所決定。此外，透過理解整篇文章的內容，才能選出答案的考題比例正逐漸增加，因此關鍵在於培養準確解讀文章的能力。

電子郵件、信件	要求業務支援、推薦信、訂閱定期刊物、諮詢服務、客訴
文字訊息、線上聊天	要求業務支援與報告工作進度、針對工作項目交換意見
報導	舉辦慶典活動、比賽、會議等消息；企業介紹、併購、新品上市等報導
公告	建築、設施維修工程、服務變動、宣傳服務或活動、公司內部傳閱通知
廣告	宣傳商品或服務、徵人廣告
網頁	課程、研討會說明、政策說明、產品或服務介紹、客戶評價
表格	發票、日程表、乘車證、收據

考題類型與命題方向

主旨或目的	通常只要閱讀前兩三行，就能輕鬆選出答案。但每回會出現幾道題，需要看完文章的第一段或最後一段整段，才能選出答案。 • What is **the purpose** of the article? • **Why was** the e-mail **sent**?
相關細節	PART 7最常出現的考題類型之一，題目為Wh開頭（Who, When, Where, What, How, Why）的問句，針對文中相關細節提問。 • When will the staff receive the message?
事實與否	詢問內容與文章相符或不相符的選項，屬於作答特別耗時的考題。 • What is **indicated/stated** about Adnan's Auto Garage? • What is **NOT mentioned** about the offer?
推論或暗示	PART 7最常出現的考題類型之一。需根據文章內容，推測出文中並未直接提及的相關內容，才能順利進行解題。 • What is **implied/suggested** about Loretti Co.? • Who **most likely** is Ms. Fernandez?
掌握意圖	在文字訊息和線上聊天文章中，各會出1題。考題列出的句子，其意思會隨著上下文改變，因此不能光看題目提供的內容，就貿然選擇答案，務必要掌握對話的脈絡，確認真正含義為何。 • At 8:59 A.M., what does Ms. Randolph most likely mean when she writes, "Not at all"?
找出同義詞	單篇閱讀和多篇閱讀中會出1至3題。題目列出的單字，其最常用的意思通常不會是答案，因此請根據上下文，確認單字於所在句中表達的意思，再選出相對應的同義詞。 • The word "sector" in paragraph 1, line 2, is closest in meaning to

句子插入題	僅於單篇閱讀中出2題，且為文章的最後一道題。建議先作答其他考題，待充分掌握文章脈絡後，再來解答句子插入題。請檢視題目列出的句子中是否有連接副詞、代名詞或定冠詞，將有助於解題。
	• In which of the positions marked [1], [2], [3], and [4] does the following sentence best belong?

解題策略

雖說學習本就沒有捷徑，但閱讀測驗又算是最難掌握的題型之一。許多書籍和講師都提出PART 7的解題策略，但讓我們深入思考一下，當中真的有適合自己的解題技巧或策略嗎？與其糾結於這些技巧或策略能否發揮作用，不如徹底放下所謂的閱讀技巧和攻略。對於那些原本考試分數落在700分至800分左右，或目標分數為850分以上的人來說，解題技巧和策略確實能發揮作用。但當英文能力不及那個程度時，這些技巧和策略就派不上用場了。因此在現階段，與其尋找捷徑，不如專注於走在正確的學習道路上。

閱讀測驗實際上就是閱讀加上理解。

如果只是每天看著解析本或講義上的說明，你的閱讀能力絕對不會提升。儘管在聽到說明的當下，可能會頻頻點頭，但轉身之後腦海中便什麼都不剩。這是因為沒有歷經消化的過程，無法將學到的知識內化成自己的東西。即使這個消化過程既辛苦又乏味，還是要狠下心來完成。

如果你在PART 7的答題正確率不到70%，最有效率的學習方式為確實理解每一道題目，而非練習在一定時間內匆忙做完題目。因此推薦以下兩種方式：

- 把難度較高的句子寫在筆記本上，仔細分析句型結構。透過拆解句子，理解並加以消化。
- PART 7中的答案大部分會以「換句話說（paraphrase）」的方式改寫，因此建議用螢光筆標示，或另外整理出來，熟悉文中答題線索如何被改寫成選項的內容。

解題方式採取「見林不見樹」的策略。

在多益測驗中，一篇文章至少會出兩道以上的考題，有時甚至會有一至兩道題，需要理解整篇文章內容，才能順利解答。此外，近年來多益測驗中，要求判斷事實與否（NOT True/True）的題目比例正逐漸增加，因此如果只閱讀特定幾個段落，反而難以掌握全文內容，進而更難選出題目的答案。

與其他大題相比，PART 7需要閱讀的內容較多，如果想逐一閱讀文章，可能會感到有負擔。但如果仔細觀察《ETS多益官方全真試題1000》中PART 7的文章，會發現內容難度並未到無法理解的程度。因此建議英文程度為初級的學習者，採取「見林不見樹」的解題策略，不要過於執著於找出單一題目的答題線索，而是從文章開頭開始閱讀，理解整篇文章的上下文脈絡，這樣會更容易找出答案。

如果來不及作答，建議先從多篇閱讀中簡單的題目下手。

如果扣除劃卡時間，還剩下5到10分鐘的作答時間時，建議從簡單的題目下手，千萬不要輕易放棄。許多考生常常因為所剩時間不多，而放棄作答雙篇閱讀題。然而，在雙篇閱讀題，當中五道題目中約有兩道題目，可藉由閱讀文章第一段或最後一段的兩三行來找到答案（例如詢問主旨、目的或同義詞的考題）。因此，即使所剩時間不多，也請盡可能把握時間解答這些題目。

UNIT 13　電子郵件與信件

答案 & 解析 p.78

1　掌握文章結構與脈絡

收件者　To: Bonnie Rosario <b.rosario@glendalehotel.com>
寄件者　From: Philip Hawley <philip@charackconstruction.com>
日期　　Date: April 24
主旨　　Subject: Pool Construction

Dear Ms. Rosario,

前半段　Charack Construction has received the deposit for building an outdoor pool at your hotel. A project of this scope usually takes approximately 6–8 weeks. However, we will be able to complete the work within 3 weeks, as you requested. We understand the importance of having

中段　　the facility open before the busy summer season begins. Our team can begin the work on April 28, which will initially involve clearing and preparing the ground.

後半段　Most of the details of the project have already been finalized, but you will need to choose the tile pattern. One of my employees will drop off a box of samples later today. Please look these over and let me know at our April 30 meeting which one you prefer. I will only send you tiles that we already have in stock, so there will be no issues with supply chain delays.

All the best,

寄件者　Philip Hawley
　　　　Manager, Charack Construction

❶ 告知施工所需時間
興建室外游泳池原本最長需要 8 週左右的施工時間，但是因應對方要求，預計會在 3 周內完成。

❷ 告知施工開始日
預計於 4 月 28 日開始進行清理和前期準備工作。

❸ 要求挑選磁磚
告知會寄送樣品，請對方於 4 月 30 日的會議上告知所選的磁磚樣式。

1. What is the purpose of the e-mail?
   (A) To suggest changes to a work plan
   (B) To request funds for a deposit
   (C) To introduce a construction business
   (D) To provide an update on a project

2. The phrase "drop off" in paragraph 2, line 3, is closest in meaning to
   (A) collect
   (B) deliver
   (C) reduce
   (D) doze

3. According to the e-mail, what should Ms. Rosario do before the April 30 meeting?
   (A) Confirm a size
   (B) Select some materials
   (C) Sign a contract
   (D) Review some sketches

152

2　解題步驟說明

1. What is the purpose of the e-mail?

Charack Construction has received the deposit for building an outdoor pool at your hotel. A project of this scope usually takes approximately 6–8 weeks. However, we will be able to complete the work within 3 weeks, as you requested. We understand the importance of having the facility open before the busy summer season begins. Our team can begin the work on April 28, which will initially involve clearing and preparing the ground.

> 告知施工時間，預計在3周內完成戶外游泳池工程。

> 告知施工開始日為4月28日，以及施工所需時間，表示該封電子郵件的撰寫目的，因此答案要選(D) To provide an update on a project（提供工程項目的最新進展）。

2. The phrase "drop off" in paragraph 2, line 3, is closest in meaning to

Most of the details of the project have already been finalized, but you will need to choose the tile pattern. One of my employees will drop off a box of samples later today.

> 作答「找出同義詞」的考題時，千萬不能直接選擇該單字於字典上常用的意思。請根據上下文，確認單字於所在句中表達的意思後，再從選項中選出意思最接近的單字。

> drop off所在的句子為「今日稍晚我方一名員工將送上一盒樣品」，當中「drop off」意思為「遞送東西給對方」，因此答案要選(B) deliver（遞送）。

3. According to the e-mail, what should Ms. Rosario do before the April 30 meeting?

Most of the details of the project have already been finalized, but you will need to choose the tile pattern. One of my employees will drop off a box of samples later today. Please look these over and let me know at our April 30 meeting which one you prefer.

> 提出挑選磁磚樣式的要求，並表示會送一盒樣品過去，請對方於4月30日的會議上告知所選的磁磚樣式。因此答案要選(B) Select some materials（選擇一些素材）。

PART 7

153

PRACTICE

答案&解析 p.78

Questions 1-2 refer to the following e-mail.

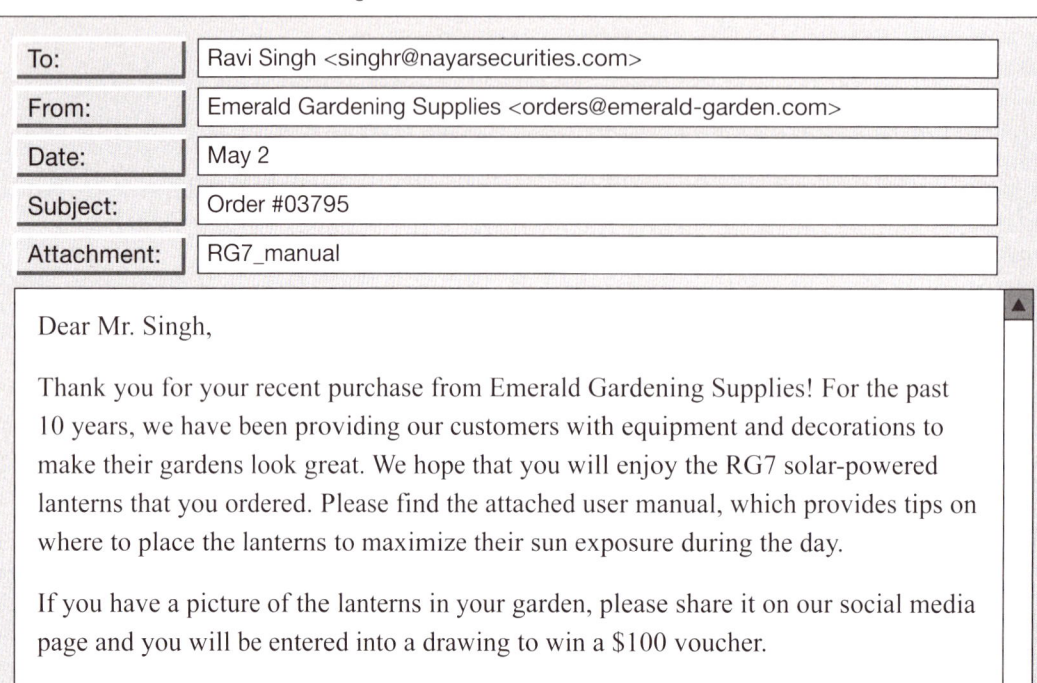

To:	Ravi Singh <singhr@nayarsecurities.com>
From:	Emerald Gardening Supplies <orders@emerald-garden.com>
Date:	May 2
Subject:	Order #03795
Attachment:	RG7_manual

Dear Mr. Singh,

Thank you for your recent purchase from Emerald Gardening Supplies! For the past 10 years, we have been providing our customers with equipment and decorations to make their gardens look great. We hope that you will enjoy the RG7 solar-powered lanterns that you ordered. Please find the attached user manual, which provides tips on where to place the lanterns to maximize their sun exposure during the day.

If you have a picture of the lanterns in your garden, please share it on our social media page and you will be entered into a drawing to win a $100 voucher.

Warmest regards,

The Emerald Gardening Supplies

1. What is indicated about the lanterns?
   (A) They should not be exposed to moisture.
   (B) They can be charged by the sun.
   (C) They are available in a variety of sizes.
   (D) They come with a ten-year warranty.

2. What is Mr. Singh asked to do?
   (A) Write a review of the product
   (B) Provide an address for sending a voucher
   (C) Show the company proof of purchase
   (D) Post an image on social media

Questions 3-6 refer to the following letter.

February 19

Melissa Hammond
HR Director
Eastbourne Solar
Malvern Building #203
Eastbourne, BN20 7AF

Dear Ms. Hammond,

It was a pleasure meeting you during the interview at your office, and I am honored that you have invited me to join the Eastbourne Solar team as a senior salesperson. Unfortunately, I am unable to accept the role, as I have decided to take a position at another company that does not require me to travel. I have a great deal of respect for your company, and I'm confident that it will continue to gain market share and expand its staff.

As promised, please find enclosed a list of the web-based e-signature tools that we talked about during the interview. I am not affiliated with any of the companies, but I believe the information will be useful to you. I plan to attend the Annual Solar Trade Exhibition later this year, so I hope to have a chance to see you there and to discuss the industry further.

Warmest regards,

Spencer Ingram
Spencer Ingram

Enclosure

3. What is the purpose of Mr. Ingram's letter?
   (A) To inquire about job duties
   (B) To introduce his company
   (C) To schedule an interview
   (D) To reject a job offer

4. What does Mr. Ingram indicate about Eastbourne Solar?
   (A) It focuses on teamwork.
   (B) It should invest more in marketing.
   (C) It has a good compensation package.
   (D) It will grow in the future.

5. What does Mr. Ingram send to Ms. Hammond?
   (A) A signed contract
   (B) A list of online tools
   (C) A proposed interview schedule
   (D) A website survey form

6. The word "attend" in paragraph 2, line 3, is closest in meaning to
   (A) go to
   (B) coincide with
   (C) come across
   (D) look after

UNIT 14　文字簡訊與線上聊天

答案&解析 p.79

1　掌握文章結構與脈絡

表達要求

Gina Quan [8:25 A.M.]
Hi, Bruno. I'm having some trouble getting to the Barraza Conference Center. I'll need to take a taxi, but I would expect that to be covered by the company.

❶ 告知聯絡目的
提出由公司負擔計程車費的要求。

相關細節

Bruno Mota [8:28 A.M.]
That's fine. Just be sure to keep your receipt. Isn't the Shelby Hotel running its shuttle service anymore?

❷-1 同意要求
同意由公司負擔費用，並提醒對方保留收據。

Gina Quan [8:29 A.M.]
Yes, but you have to book in advance. I guess they've changed their policy because last time, I took the shuttle without a reservation.

❷-2 告知飯店的政策更動
提及需事先預約才能搭乘飯店接駁車，與先前的乘車方式不同，表示政策有所更動。

確認其他事項

Bruno Mota [8:31 A.M.]
Do you need me to find a taxi service for you?

❸ 確認其他事項
詢問是否要協助對方查找計程車服務。

Gina Quan [8:32 A.M.]
Thanks, but I have a number I can call.

---

1. At 8:28 A.M., what does Mr. Mota most likely mean when he writes, "That's fine"?
   (A) He will go to a conference center in Ms. Quan's place.
   (B) He can meet Ms. Quan at a different location.
   (C) He agrees to authorize a transportation cost.
   (D) He has found the receipt for a booking.

2. What is suggested about Ms. Quan?
   (A) She is Mr. Mota's supervisor.
   (B) She would like help finding a contact number.
   (C) She lost her hotel reservation number.
   (D) She has stayed at the Shelby Hotel before.

2 解題步驟說明

1. At 8:28 A.M., what does Mr. Mota most likely mean when he writes, "That's fine"?

   Gina Quan [8:25 A.M.]
   Hi, Bruno. I'm having some trouble getting to the Barraza Conference Center. I'll need to take a taxi, but I would expect that to be covered by the company.

   Bruno Mota [8:28 A.M.]
   That's fine. Just be sure to keep your receipt. Isn't the Shelby Hotel running its shuttle service anymore?

   > Quan女士打算搭計程車,但她希望由公司支付車費。

   > Mota先生回答「That's fine」,並提醒她要保留收據。由此可知「That's fine」表示同意Quan女士的要求,因此答案要選(C) He agrees to authorize a transportation cost.（他同意簽核交通費）。

2. What is suggested about Ms. Quan?

   Bruno Mota [8:28 A.M.]
   That's fine. Just be sure to keep your receipt. Isn't the Shelby Hotel running its shuttle service anymore?

   Gina Quan [8:29 A.M.]
   Yes, but you have to book in advance. I guess they've changed their policy because last time, I took the shuttle without a reservation.

   > Mota先生詢問Shelby飯店是否不再提供接駁車服務。

   > Quan女士回答需要事先預約,並提出先前不需預約就能搭車,表示Quan女士先前住過Shelby飯店,因此答案為(D) She has stayed at the Shelby Hotel before.（她以前住過Shelby飯店）。

157

PRACTICE

Questions 1-2 refer to the following text-message chain.

Betsy Braun (1:46 P.M.)
Hi, Matthew. Have you or your team members been monitoring the Haven Street entrance?

Matthew Alvarado (1:48 P.M.)
In addition to the video monitoring, we had our usual hourly check in person about 20 minutes ago. Why do you ask?

Betsy Braun (1:49 P.M.)
I noticed that the door is unlocked. I thought it was supposed to remain locked at all times.

Matthew Alvarado (1:51 P.M.)
It is, except when deliveries are being made. Anchorage Supplies has just finished unloading everything. I've notified Eric.

Betsy Braun (1:53 P.M.)
All right, that's good to know. I'm glad someone's taking care of it.

---

1. Who most likely is Mr. Alvarado?

   (A) A security guard
   (B) A driving instructor
   (C) A video editor
   (D) A receptionist

2. At 1:51 P.M., what does Mr. Alvarado mean when he writes, "I've notified Eric"?

   (A) Eric will come to work early.
   (B) Eric will unload a truck.
   (C) Eric will lock a door.
   (D) Eric will meet with Ms. Braun.

Questions 3-6 refer to the following online chat discussion.

Kathleen Arcand [10:03 A.M.]	I'm booking the train tickets today for our meeting next week with Bancroft to sign the contract.
Gordon Walters [10:04 A.M.]	We're leaving on Tuesday, right?
Kathleen Arcand [10:07 A.M.]	Actually, since the meeting isn't until Wednesday afternoon, I thought we could go that morning and then return on Thursday morning.
Gordon Walters [10:08 A.M.]	Alright. Are we bringing brochures?
Kathleen Arcand [10:10 A.M.]	Is that necessary? They've already seen our heart monitoring equipment.
Gordon Walters [10:11 A.M.]	We can introduce some of our other items for future consideration.
Kathleen Arcand [10:13 A.M.]	Okay. I'll be sure to pack some. Also, they will take us out for dinner and a show. Macy Oliver from Bancroft is wondering what kind of show we would like to see. I've got to get back to her about that.
Peter Zhang [10:16 A.M.]	That sounds like fun.
Kathleen Arcand [10:17 A.M.]	I'm not sure what's playing. Peter, can you look into that?
Peter Zhang [10:19 A.M.]	I'll do some research to see what's on at the local theaters.
Kathleen Arcand [10:20 A.M.]	Great, but the sooner the better.
Peter Zhang [10:22 A.M.]	Of course. I'll message you within the hour.

3. In what industry do the writers most likely work?

   (A) Entertainment
   (B) Education
   (C) Publishing
   (D) Health care

4. When will a contract probably be signed?

   (A) On Tuesday
   (B) On Wednesday
   (C) On Thursday
   (D) On Friday

5. What information does Ms. Oliver want to know about?

   (A) Dietary restrictions for a meal
   (B) Meeting guests' arrival time
   (C) Preferences for a performance
   (D) Transportation costs

6. At 10:20 A.M., what does Ms. Arcand mean when she writes, "the sooner the better"?

   (A) She is concerned about missing a deadline.
   (B) She thinks some train tickets will sell out.
   (C) She wants to give a reply quickly.
   (D) She needs to leave for a meeting shortly.

159

UNIT 15　報導、公告、廣告

答案&解析 p.81

1　掌握文章結構與脈絡

標題　**Library Reopening in Beaverton**

主旨　(July 29)—The reopening of the Beaverton library will take place on September 25. —[1]—. Residents are excited about being able to use the library again, which was scheduled to reopen 18 months ago.

❶ 公告圖書館重新開放
告知 Beaverton 圖書館將於 9 月 25 日重新開放。

相關細節　Cowan Construction and Brock Builders were both selected to speed up the project process. —[2]—. However, this decision turned out to be a mistake as much time was wasted when both sides often worked on the same tasks without the other knowing it.

❷ 陳述施工中發生的問題
同時有兩間建設公司被選中，但礙於雙方溝通有問題，浪費大量的時間。因此不僅受到公眾的監督和壓力，還無法如期完工。

In addition, because the project had already gotten off to a bad start, there was increased scrutiny and pressure from the public. —[3]—. The time estimated to complete the project was not reasonable, especially compared to similar work.

The project was also supposed to include a small on-site café. —[4]—. The café option is likely to be revisited in future proposals.

❸ 提及不完善的設施
原計畫為在館內設置小型咖啡廳，預計將於日後的提案中重新考慮。

---

1. What is implied about Brock Builders?
   (A) This is its first construction project.
   (B) Its staff did not communicate well with Cowan Construction.
   (C) It will soon go out of business.
   (D) It plans to merge with Cowan Construction.

2. What does the article indicate about the library site?
   (A) Its planners had to reduce the original scope of the project.
   (B) The second phase of building is scheduled for next year.
   (C) It will be partially funded by proceeds from the café.
   (D) It is the second library branch in Beaverton.

3. In which of the positions marked [1], [2], [3], and [4] does the following sentence best belong?

   "This ultimately resulted in the creation of an impossible work schedule."

   (A) [1]
   (B) [2]
   (C) [3]
   (D) [4]

2　解題步驟說明

1. What is *implied* about **Brock Builders**?

   Cowan Construction and Brock Builders were both selected to speed up the project process. However, this decision turned out to be a mistake as much time was wasted when both sides often worked on the same tasks without the other knowing it.

   > Cowan建設公司與Brock建設公司同時被選中為圖書館施工。

   > 雙方常常在互相不知情的情況下執行同一個施工項目，浪費了大量的時間，表示兩者間的溝通有問題，因此答案為(B) Its staff did not communicate well with Cowan Construction.（員工與Cowan建設公司溝通不良）。

2. What does the article *indicate* about **the library site**?

   The project was also supposed to include a small on-site café. The café option is likely to be revisited in future proposals.

   > 專案中原本包含一間小型館內咖啡廳，但並未完工，因此答案要選(A) Its planners had to reduce the original scope of the project.（規劃者不得不縮小原本專案的範圍）。

3. In which of the positions marked [1], [2], [3], and [4] does the following sentence best belong?

   "**This** ultimately resulted in the creation of an impossible work schedule."

   In addition, because the project had already gotten off to a bad start, there was increased scrutiny and pressure from the public. —[3]—. The time estimated to complete the project was not reasonable, especially compared to similar work.

   > 作答句子插入題時，建議先閱讀題目提供的句子，再把文章從頭到尾瀏覽一遍。題目列出的句子中肯定會有連接副詞、連接詞、定冠詞或指示代名詞，閱讀時請務必掌握這些答題線索。
   > 本題句子中出現指示代名詞This，連接「導致工作行程無法完成」，請從文章中找尋內容相對應的段落。

   > 句中的This指的是「受到公眾的監督和壓力」，將句子插入[3]後，表示導致工作行程無法順利執行，前後語意通順，因此答案要選(C)。

PRACTICE

Questions 1-2 refer to the following job posting.

Corporate Recruitment Services

| HOME | **NEWLY ADDED** | JOB DATABASE | SUBMIT AN APPLICATION |

Warehouse Workers Wanted

Laird Home Furnishings is currently seeking warehouse workers for its site in Wilmar. Some on-the-job training is provided, but previous experience in a warehouse environment is preferred. Responsibilities include sorting packages according to delivery routes, loading and unloading vehicles, and keeping storage areas organized. Applicants must have a dependable way to get to the warehouse on their own, as there are no bus stops or train stations nearby.

Click here to apply.

1. What information is included in the job posting?
   (A) The expected hourly wage
   (B) The number of working hours
   (C) The schedule for training sessions
   (D) The duties of the role

2. What is a requirement of the position?
   (A) A safety certificate
   (B) Excellent computer skills
   (C) Reliable transportation to a site
   (D) Previous experience in the field

Questions 3-5 refer to the following announcement.

Share a Winning Idea and Receive Spring Sensations Vouchers!

At Spring Sensations, we are proud to offer unique products that our customers love. With your help, we can make our product line even better! We're looking for ideas for new scents for our popular body lotions and hand creams. If your scent is one of the three selected, you'll be sent $500 in Spring Sensations vouchers, and these never expire!

To enter the competition, visit the Spring Sensations social media page and leave a comment with your idea. The new scent can contain a combination of up to three dominant scents, and you should come up with a unique name for it as well. Be sure to check out our existing line at www.springsensations.com to make sure you don't suggest something that we already offer!

The contest will run from March 5 to April 20, and the winners will be announced on our website and on social media on April 25. Vouchers will be sent by e-mail on May 1.

---

3. What most likely is Spring Sensations?
   (A) A marketing firm
   (B) skincare products manufacturer
   (C) An annual festival
   (D) A retail clothing outlet

4. What is NOT a requirement of a submission?
   (A) Using a limited number of different scents
   (B) Including a name for the creation
   (C) Confirming that a combination is not already in use
   (D) Providing suggestions for packaging

5. When is the deadline for submitting entries?
   (A) March 5
   (B) April 20
   (C) April 25
   (D) May 1

Questions 6-8 refer to the following advertisement.

Maurita Analytical Inc. — Open Positions

Maurita Analytical Inc.(MAI) has been a trusted name in soil testing for agricultural sites and building projects ever since it opened its first branch in Plainview and quickly expanded to Lubbock. We provide employees with a supportive working environment, opportunities for professional growth within the organization, and competitive wages and paid vacation time.

Field Team Leader
Oversees a team of 4–5 soil technicians on sites. Prepares maps for soil collection sites and assigns tasks to team members. Mainly based in Lubbock but may require work outside the area.

Soil Technician
Visits sites in and around Lubbock to collect and label soil samples. Attention to detail is a must due to the complex steps of the collection process. Technicians work in groups, and training is provided.

Senior Laboratory Technician
Leads a team of eight technicians to conduct accurate soil testing at our laboratory in Hereford. A bachelor's degree in environmental science or a similar major is required. Some occasional travel will be necessary.

---

6. What is indicated about Maurita Analytical Inc.?

   (A) It is the only testing service in the region.
   (B) It has a good reputation.
   (C) It is still operated by its original founder.
   (D) It has discontinued its agricultural service.

7. The word "competitive" in paragraph 1, line 4, is closest in meaning to

   (A) conflicting
   (B) aggressive
   (C) reasonable
   (D) ambitious

8. What do all of the job openings have in common?

   (A) They require some travel.
   (B) They are open only to university graduates.
   (C) They pay annual bonuses.
   (D) They include managing others.

Questions 9-12 refer to the following article.

Art Corner

By Lance Colbert

When the worlds of business and art mix, it is sometimes difficult to find a balance. But local entrepreneurs Elizabeth Sanders and Timothy Marlowe are finding a way to make it work. Their new company, Art Phase, rents original paintings for commercial premises. This is great for businesses in Asheville that want a sophisticated décor but cannot afford to invest heavily in artwork.

Ms. Sanders and Mr. Marlowe got the idea while they were operating an accounting firm together. —[1]—. "We wanted to decorate our office to make a good first impression on clients," Ms. Sanders said. "However, we were just starting out, so there were a lot of other items to purchase. —[2]—. That's because trends change frequently, so paintings can look outdated after a while."

Mr. Marlowe is an amateur artist and is active in the local art community. He and Ms. Sanders founded Art Phase as a side business, and it is expected to be popular. —[3]—. Art Phase offers a wide range of paintings for rent, most of which were created by local artists. Those interested in renting artwork can have an Art Phase consultant visit their site to make recommendations based on the colors in the room and their personal style. Once selected, the artwork is delivered to the site, and it is also picked up for free at the end of the rental period. Customers can change their artwork once per quarter, and they can even receive notes from the artist about the inspiration behind the piece.

"Art Phase is a great opportunity for artists who are not yet established," explained Neil Patterson, president of the Asheville Artists Association. "They can have their art seen by many people while also earning a percentage of the rental fee. For those who can't afford a booth at Sunshine Street Market or those who do not have gallery space, this is an attractive option. —[4]—."

9. What is the purpose of the article?

    (A) To introduce an investment opportunity
    (B) To highlight the paintings of local artists
    (C) To explain a newly available service
    (D) To encourage participation in an art course

10. According to the article, what is NOT offered by Art Phase?

    (A) Pick-up and delivery
    (B) A free trial session
    (C) In-person consultations
    (D) Comments from the artist

11. What does Mr. Patterson suggest about Sunshine Street Market?

    (A) It has high fees.
    (B) It is decorated attractively.
    (C) It is near an art gallery.
    (D) It has booths of different sizes.

12. In which of the positions marked [1], [2], [3], and [4] does the following sentence best belong?

    "We were also nervous about making an upfront investment in artwork."

    (A) [1]
    (B) [2]
    (C) [3]
    (D) [4]

UNIT 16　雙篇與多篇文章

1　掌握文章結構與脈絡

目的　Thank you for placing an order with Holly Home Goods!

Order Number: 068379 ● ‥‥‥‥‥‥‥‥‥‥‥　❶ 告知聯絡目的
Delivery: To be shipped within 1–3 business days　　告知顧客的訂單編號、出貨日、寄
Ship to: 685 Aspen Lane, Irvine, CA 92614　　送地址。

相關細節

Item	Description	Pattern	Price
H190	10.5" plates, set of 6	Forest leaves	$35.99
B836	6" bowls, set of 6	Forest leaves	$25.99
M331	Coffee cups, set of 6	Blue waves	$32.99
W275	Teapots, set of 2	Forest leaves	$49.99
		Subtotal	$144.96
* Code WELCOME for 10% off the total purchase for first-time customers		Code*: WELCOME	-$14.49
		Shipping	$5.99
		TOTAL	$136.46

❷ 提供訂單明細
提供顧客下單的明細與金額。

參考事項

❸ 告知特殊事項
告知首購顧客使用代碼 WELCOME 可享九折優惠。

標題　**Holly Home Goods: Request a Return** ● ‥‥‥‥‥　❹ 提出退貨申請
於 Holly Home Goods 下單的顧客
提出退貨申請，並告知申請退貨的
理由。

相關內容
Customer: Howard Erickson
Order Number: 068379
Item(s) to be returned: M331
Reason for return request:

[ ] Item damaged　　　[✓] Other (please explain):
[ ] Wrong item sent　　Color not as expected

---

1. What is suggested about Holly Home Goods?
   (A) It is dedicated to environmental responsibility.
   (B) It allows customers to create a custom pattern.
   (C) It has products made from a variety of materials.
   (D) It offers a discount to new customers.

2. What kind of item is Mr. Erickson returning?
   (A) Plates
   (B) Bowls
   (C) Cups
   (D) Teapots

166

2 解題步驟說明

1. What is suggested about Holly Home Goods?

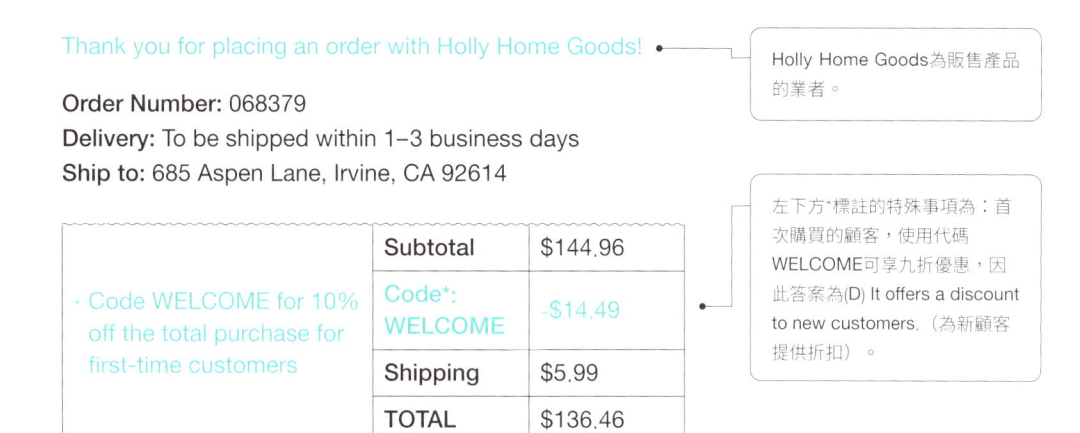

   Thank you for placing an order with Holly Home Goods!

   Order Number: 068379
   Delivery: To be shipped within 1–3 business days
   Ship to: 685 Aspen Lane, Irvine, CA 92614

	Subtotal	$144.96
· Code WELCOME for 10% off the total purchase for first-time customers	Code*: WELCOME	-$14.49
	Shipping	$5.99
	TOTAL	$136.46

   > Holly Home Goods為販售產品的業者。

   > 左下方*標註的特殊事項為：首次購買的顧客，使用代碼WELCOME可享九折優惠，因此答案為(D) It offers a discount to new customers.（為新顧客提供折扣）。

2. What kind of item is Mr. Erickson returning?

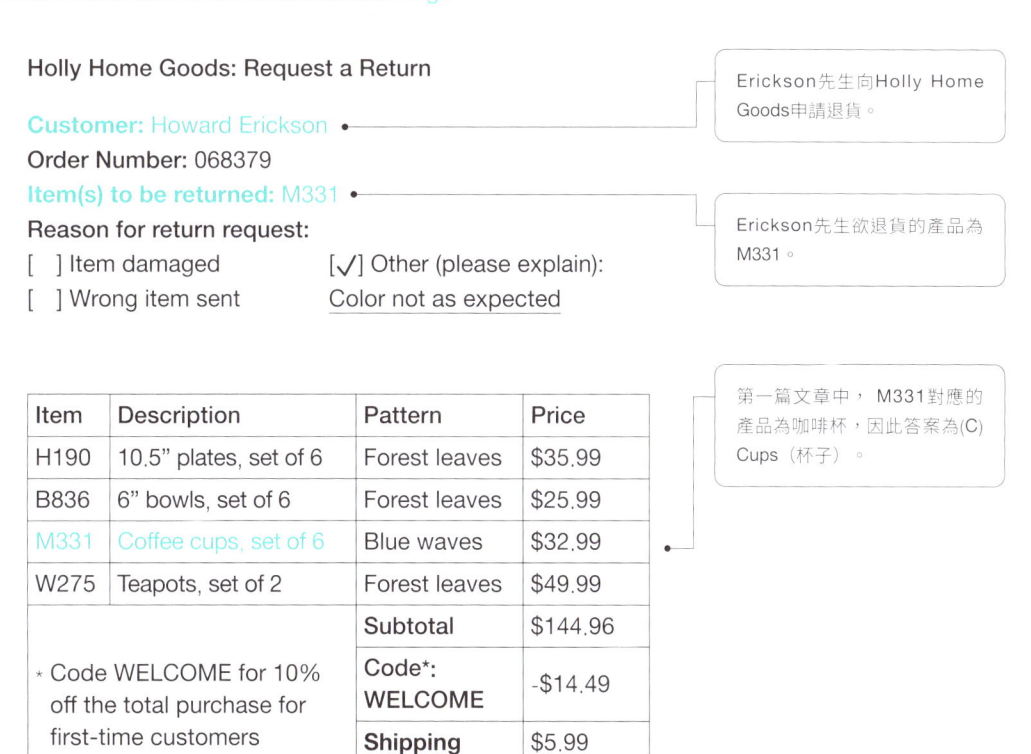

   Holly Home Goods: Request a Return

   Customer: Howard Erickson
   Order Number: 068379
   Item(s) to be returned: M331
   Reason for return request:
   [ ] Item damaged   [✓] Other (please explain):
   [ ] Wrong item sent   Color not as expected

Item	Description	Pattern	Price
H190	10.5" plates, set of 6	Forest leaves	$35.99
B836	6" bowls, set of 6	Forest leaves	$25.99
M331	Coffee cups, set of 6	Blue waves	$32.99
W275	Teapots, set of 2	Forest leaves	$49.99
* Code WELCOME for 10% off the total purchase for first-time customers	Subtotal		$144.96
	Code*: WELCOME		-$14.49
	Shipping		$5.99
	TOTAL		$136.46

   > Erickson先生向Holly Home Goods申請退貨。

   > Erickson先生欲退貨的產品為M331。

   > 第一篇文章中，M331對應的產品為咖啡杯，因此答案為(C) Cups（杯子）。

PART 7

167

PRACTICE

Questions 1-5 refer to the following article and online review.

CALGARY (13 July) — Rocky Apparel is a ski clothing company that offers a range of men's and women's jackets, ski pants, base layers, and more. Co-owners Noella Purcell and Travis Byler started with a small retail shop here in Calgary five years ago, and since then, the business has taken off. A second branch was opened in Edmonton, and demand for Rocky Apparel merchandise has grown significantly. The company has built a loyal customer base because it rigorously tests its clothing to make sure it can withstand extreme temperatures and rough treatment. The finished products are also colorful and fashionable.

Rocky Apparel previously only sold its goods in its retail shops, but last month it launched an online store that allowed it to reach customers around the world. Ms. Purcell and Mr. Byler now plan to open a third retail location at Lake Louise in November. The location was chosen because even though Lake Louise is a small village, it is in the heart of a popular skiing area, with numerous resorts surrounding it. The shop will only be open during the peak ski season, which runs from late November to late April. The co-owners are also looking into creating a partnership with ski instructors to offer discounts on ski lessons.

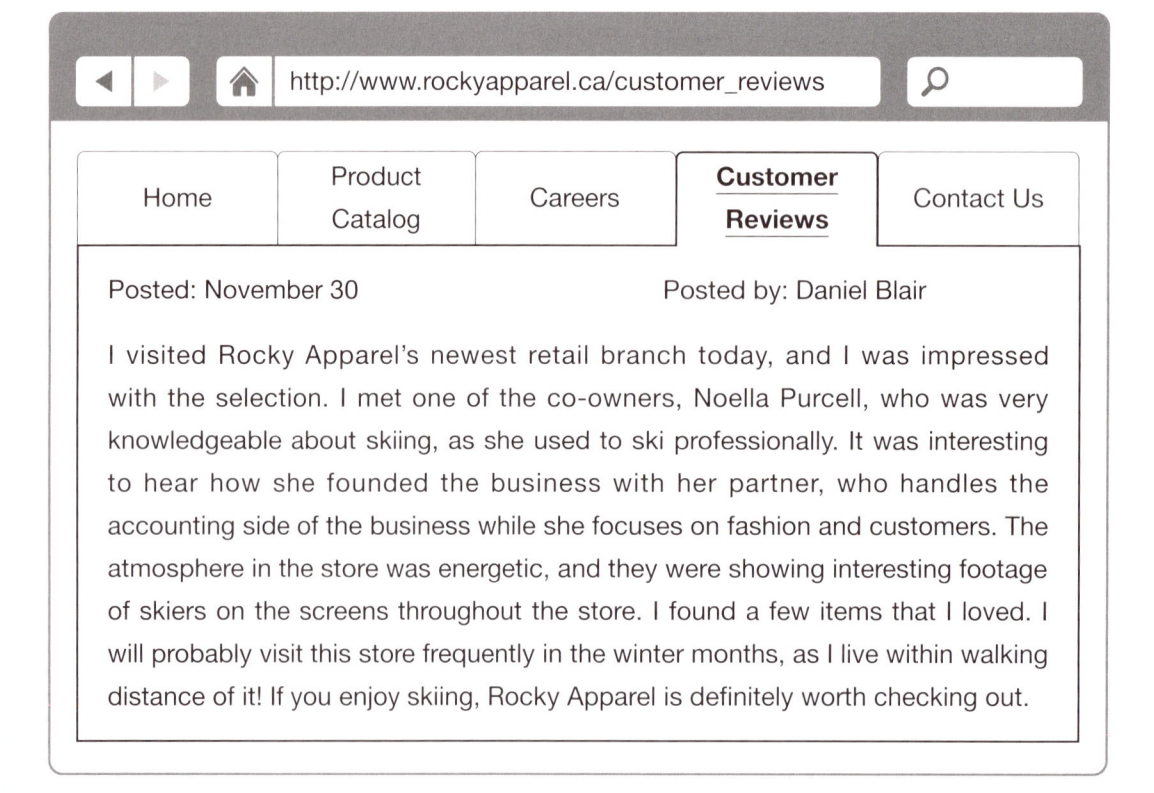

---

http://www.rockyapparel.ca/customer_reviews

| Home | Product Catalog | Careers | **Customer Reviews** | Contact Us |

Posted: November 30   Posted by: Daniel Blair

I visited Rocky Apparel's newest retail branch today, and I was impressed with the selection. I met one of the co-owners, Noella Purcell, who was very knowledgeable about skiing, as she used to ski professionally. It was interesting to hear how she founded the business with her partner, who handles the accounting side of the business while she focuses on fashion and customers. The atmosphere in the store was energetic, and they were showing interesting footage of skiers on the screens throughout the store. I found a few items that I loved. I will probably visit this store frequently in the winter months, as I live within walking distance of it! If you enjoy skiing, Rocky Apparel is definitely worth checking out.

1. What is stated about Rocky Apparel in the article?

    (A) It conducts significant testing on its products.
    (B) It has opened retail branches around the world.
    (C) It was nominated for a fashion award.
    (D) It manufactures its own fabrics.

2. What is indicated about Mr. Byler?

    (A) He is in charge of the business's bookkeeping.
    (B) He met Mr. Blair during his visit.
    (C) He used to be a professional skier.
    (D) He designs some of the clothing himself.

3. In the article, the phrase "taken off" in paragraph 1, line 7, is closest in meaning to

    (A) disappeared
    (B) departed
    (C) removed
    (D) succeeded

4. What is suggested about Mr. Blair?

    (A) He is an experienced skier.
    (B) He lives in Lake Louise.
    (C) He applied for a job at Rocky Apparel.
    (D) He worked with Ms. Purcell.

5. What is indicated about Rocky Apparel's newest shop?

    (A) Its size is the same as the second branch.
    (B) Its customers can book ski lessons there.
    (C) It is open throughout the year.
    (D) It has videos playing for customers.

Questions 6-10 refer to the following articles.

Construction Continues on New Stadium
By Courtney Wallace

DAVENPORT (January 2)—Construction of the new sports venue in northwest Davenport, Apex Stadium, is still on track, with work on the interior beginning soon. The stadium is owned by the Sigley Group, which has many buildings in its portfolio, most of which are performance venues, and is venturing into sports venues for the first time.

One of the points of the project is to bring more tourists to Davenport through large-scale sports events. The original design is for 8,000 seats, but if it can be altered to accommodate at least 10,000 seats, it would be large enough to be eligible to host the Regional Semi-Pro Tournament.

The first game scheduled at the stadium will be between the Davenport Tigers and the Waterloo Falcons on May 2.

Baseball Fans Excited about New Stadium
By Jerry Lambert

DAVENPORT (May 3)—Apex Stadium hosted a matchup between the Davenport Tigers and the Waterloo Falcons last night. The home team brought home a 3–1 win, though the Waterloo Falcons had a great showing of fans. Stephen Wilson, the head coach of the Davenport Tigers, was proud of the team's performance. "Waterloo is a tough team to beat," said Mr. Wilson. "But thanks to the hard work of Rob Sanchez and his teammates, we were able to pull off the win."

Many attendees of the game were impressed with the new building, which was designed by architect Howard Torres. The stadium will be the hosting site of the Regional Semi-Pro Tournament later this year. To view all upcoming events, visit www.apexstadium.com/events.

6. What is indicated about the Sigley Group?
   (A) It has purchased a construction firm.
   (B) It has relocated to Davenport.
   (C) It is under new management.
   (D) It only operates one stadium.

7. In the first article, the word "points" in paragraph 2, line 1, is closest in meaning to
   (A) meanings
   (B) features
   (C) locations
   (D) aims

8. What is suggested about Apex Stadium?
   (A) Its construction was funded by the city.
   (B) It expanded its original seating capacity.
   (C) Its grand opening was later than expected.
   (D) It will host a regional tournament every year.

9. What is indicated about the Waterloo Falcons team?
   (A) It has not won many games this season.
   (B) It has a smaller stadium than Apex Stadium.
   (C) Many of its fans traveled to attend a game.
   (D) There was special seating reserved for its fans.

10. Who is Rob Sanchez?
    (A) A sports reporter
    (B) An architect
    (C) A coach
    (D) An athlete

Questions 11-15 refer to the following schedule, newsletter article, and form.

Megalith Gym Franchise Owner Annual Meeting
Schedule for Saturday, October 21

7:15 A.M.	Tea, Coffee, and Donuts	Sparrow Room
8:00 A.M.	Welcome Speech Pranav Chetti, CEO	Eagle Room
8:30 A.M.	Promotion from National to Individual Sanhana Adwani, Marketing Director	Eagle Room
10:30 A.M.	Knowing Your Customer Priya Vadekar, Senior Researcher	Goldfinch Room
12:30 P.M.	Buffet lunch included with registration	Sparrow Room
1:30 P.M.	Franchise Owner Presentations: Dealing with Competition Group Class Management	Peacock Room Goldfinch Room
3:00 P.M.	New Equipment Demonstrations Ganesh Munshif, Purchasing Director	Peacock Room

Support for Franchise Owners

By William Lowery

Small business owners operating a Megalith Gym franchise attended the company's annual meeting in Dallas last weekend. Over three hundred people from across the U.S. attended the two-day event. Marketing Director Sanhana Adwani outlined what the parent company is doing to promote the chain of fitness centers and how branches can be promoted individually on a small budget. Several franchise owners were selected to give presentations at the event. Attendees also got a sneak peek at the Marietta, a motorized treadmill, and the Netzer, an upright rowing machine, which will be sent to the gyms later in the year.

Megalith Gym Franchise Owner Annual Meeting Feedback Form

Thank you for taking the time to share your opinions with us. Please rate the presentations you attended on a scale of 1 (poor) to 5 (excellent).

Presentations	Rating
Knowing Your Customer	5
Dealing with Competition	n/a
Group Class Management	5
Keeping Customers Motivated	5
Key Steps to Success	n/a
The Megalith Mission	5

Comments: I chose to book my overnight accommodations at the venue so I did not have an issue, but some people I spoke with said they arrived late because they were unfamiliar with the city and had to get to the site in heavy traffic. I felt very rushed between sessions, so I would suggest having each session end a bit earlier.

Name: Peggy Kearns

---

11. Where did attendees hear opening remarks?

    (A) In the Eagle Room
    (B) In the Goldfinch Room
    (C) In the Peacock Room
    (D) In the Sparrow Room

12. What is one purpose of the article?

    (A) To explain Ms. Adwani's new role
    (B) To provide details about upcoming courses
    (C) To encourage people to join a franchise
    (D) To highlight activities at a company meeting

13. When most likely were attendees able to see the Marietta and the Netzer?

    (A) At 8:00 A.M.
    (B) At 10:30 A.M.
    (C) At 1:30 P.M.
    (D) At 3:00 P.M.

14. What is true about Ms. Kearns?

    (A) She went to the event last year.
    (B) She attended a talk in the afternoon.
    (C) She arrived at the event late.
    (D) She lives in the city where the meeting was held.

15. What did Ms. Kearns dislike about the meeting?

    (A) The venue lacked important amenities.
    (B) There was not enough time between sessions.
    (C) It was difficult to hear the speakers.
    (D) Some sessions were held at the same time.

Questions 16-20 refer to the following invitation, brochure, and e-mail.

Chemical Engineering Conference

www.chemicalengineeringconf.com

Enjoy a weekend of informative talks and professional networking at the 5th Annual Chemical Engineering Conference beginning April 9. Our aim is to educate those working in the field about the latest trends, safety measures, and emerging technologies. For the first time, we will hold the conference at Parkview Hall, and we are pleased to have Wyatt Faber, CEO of Dalton Chemicals, as our keynote speaker.

Please see the attached brochure for the details about sponsorship.

Chemical Engineering Conference
Sponsorship Tiers

Corporate sponsorship plays an important role in the success of our conference, as it allows us to keep registration fees affordable. By becoming a sponsor, you can introduce your company to hundreds of specialists in the field, making them more familiar with your brand.

Economy—$500
- Have your company's logo featured in our printed conference program
- 10% off registration for up to 10 employees

Basic—$1,500
- Have your company's logo featured in our printed conference program and on banners in the check-in area
- 10% off registration for up to 15 employees

Premium—$2,500
- Have your company's logo featured in all areas, including on stage
- 10% off registration for all of your employees

Elite—$4,500
- Have your company's logo featured in all areas, including on stage
- 15% off registration for all of your employees
- Your employees can use our VIP lounge, which features printing and copying equipment, complimentary refreshments, phone-charging stations, and more.

E-Mail Message

To: All Holbrook Incorporated Staff <stafflist@holbrookinc.com>
From: Nancy Turner <n.turner@holbrookinc.com>
Date: March 28
Subject: Chemical Engineering Conference

Dear Staff,

The Chemical Engineering Conference is coming soon. I'm wondering who would like to attend this event, as I need to complete the registration forms. We are a sponsor for the event this year, so we are eligible for a registration discount for as many employees as we want. In addition, while you are at the event, you'll have access to the VIP lounge. Many of you will recognize this year's keynote speaker, who visited our company last year to teach a workshop on state-of-the-art chemistry tools.

Nancy Turner
Administration Director, Holbrook Incorporated

---

16. According to the invitation, what is indicated about the conference?

    (A) It takes place annually at Parkview Hall.
    (B) It lasts for two days.
    (C) It is free to attend.
    (D) It is being held for the first time.

17. What benefit of sponsorship is mentioned in the brochure?

    (A) Sponsors can operate a booth at the conference.
    (B) Sponsors can improve their brand recognition.
    (C) Sponsors can get assistance with logo design.
    (D) Sponsors can promote their business online.

18. What is the purpose of the e-mail?

    (A) To explain the reasons for a decision
    (B) To recruit volunteers to give a presentation
    (C) To find out who is interested in attending an event
    (D) To arrange transportation to a conference

19. What is stated about Mr. Faber?

    (A) He led a training event at Holbrook Incorporated.
    (B) He contacted Ms. Turner about sponsorship.
    (C) He will join the Holbrook Incorporated staff.
    (D) He has developed a new technology.

20. What level of sponsorship did Holbrook Incorporated get?

    (A) Economy
    (B) Basic
    (C) Premium
    (D) Elite

PART TEST

PART 7

Directions: In this part, you will read a selection of texts, such as magazine and newspaper articles, e-mails, and instant messages. Each text or set of texts is followed by several questions. Select the best answer for each question and mark the letter (A), (B), (C), or (D) on your answer sheet.

Questions 147-148 refer to the following instructions.

How to Set Up Your New Lanette Video Doorbell

Keep this manual for your records after installation.

1. Download the Lanette smartphone application from www.lanettetech.com and create a new account.

2. Within the app, tap "Device Setup" and select "Doorbells."

3. Scan the bar code on the back of the device. After you do so, an approval e-mail with the product number will be sent to you. Write the product ID from the e-mail here: 730950R .

4. Input your address to specify your location. Please note that this step is optional, but if you skip this step, certain features of the doorbell will not function.

5. Within the app, tap "Confirm." Your device will automatically connect to your Wi-Fi, but you will need to input the Wi-Fi password.

6. Test the device by holding down the red button on the front for three seconds. Once the green light starts flashing, your device is ready to use. Write the test date here: _____ .

Should you have any questions or concerns, please contact our customer service team at 1-800-555-4950.

147. Why should the user provide a location?
   (A) To determine which office will handle inquiries
   (B) To be provided with a shipping estimate
   (C) To be sent replacement parts
   (D) To ensure that all features can work

148. What is suggested about the instructions' user?
   (A) The user scanned a code.
   (B) The user sent a confirmation e-mail.
   (C) The user failed to receive a product number.
   (D) The user conducted a test.

Questions 149-151 refer to the following invitation.

A Celebration of Graphic Design as an Art Form

Findlay Banquet Hall
827 Ardmore Road

Friday, July 1
7:00 P.M.–9:30 P.M.

The Findlay Society of Graphic Design (FSGD) is holding its annual banquet! We invite you to attend this exciting event, which will feature a video about the activities we've held this year, information on upcoming plans, and a keynote speech about navigating the freelance world. We'll also be presenting several awards to recognize the people who have worked so hard to make our club great this year. This is an opportunity to enjoy a delicious four-course meal while socializing with fellow FSGD participants. Live music will be provided by the Rio String Quartet during the meal. There is no cost to attend the event, as it is paid by our dues.

If you plan to attend the event, please contact Patrick Slater at pslater@fsgd.org no later than June 16. When you do so, be sure to indicate how many people are in your party.

We hope to see you there!

149. For whom is the invitation most likely intended?

(A) Private donors
(B) Elected officials
(C) Computer programmers
(D) Club members

150. The word "recognize" in paragraph 1, line 4, is closest in meaning to

(A) recall
(B) realize
(C) identify
(D) acknowledge

151. What is suggested about the event?

(A) Its admission fee should be paid by June 16.
(B) Its invitation recipients can bring their guests.
(C) Its venue will be finalized soon.
(D) Its activities will be filmed.

Questions 152-154 refer to the following article.

Upgrades Approved for Valley Park

(13 February)—Mayor Christopher Wilcher has confirmed that Union City is moving forward with a project to make upgrades to Valley Park. The work is being partially funded by Union City's annual Parks and Recreation budget. The city also received a generous donation from Gary Austin, a local entrepreneur. —[1]—. Additionally, local community groups have held fundraisers to contribute to the project. For example, UC Friends hosted a used book sale.

The holes in the baseball field in the northwest section of the park will be filled in, with new grass planted where needed. —[2]—. Flower beds near the parking lot will be removed in order to make room for a covered picnic shelter that can hold up to 10 tables. Though the construction of a second parking lot was proposed, planners have decided to expand the existing lot instead. —[3]—.

Most people are looking forward to taking advantage of the improvements. —[4]—. "In my opinion, we have more pressing matters, such as the poor condition of our roads," said resident Elizabeth Arnold.

152. What is NOT mentioned as a source of funding for the upgrades?

(A) A resident's donation
(B) A bookstore
(C) An annual budget
(D) Community organizations

153. What will be a new feature of Valley Park?

(A) A sports field
(B) A picnic area
(C) A flower bed
(D) A second parking lot

154. In which of the positions marked [1], [2], [3], and [4] does the following sentence best belong?

"Nonetheless, some people think that local officials should focus on other areas."

(A) [1]
(B) [2]
(C) [3]
(D) [4]

Questions 155-158 refer to the following online chat discussion.

Naomi Rutledge [10:03 A.M.]	Good morning, team. I'd like to check in with you about the Concord Apartment Building.
Jared Padilla [10:04 A.M.]	A reporter from *Northwest Lifestyle* magazine has agreed to write an article about the upcoming grand opening, and she'd like some photographs to accompany it. Should I contact the photographer, Jonathan Webb, to arrange to take more pictures?
Naomi Rutledge [10:05 A.M.]	We already have more than enough. I'll forward you a link to our photo collection so you can choose whatever seems appropriate.
Rupert Burke [10:06 A.M.]	I'm glad we're getting additional publicity. We had aimed to get to 80% of the units reserved by this point, but we're not even at 70% yet.
Naomi Rutledge [10:07 A.M.]	The magazine article will help, and I'll keep pursuing other options.
Rupert Burke [10:09 A.M.]	We've never managed such a large building before, so it's important to get this right.
Naomi Rutledge [10:10 A.M.]	I agree. But keep in mind that there was some lost time when Katie Sullivan left the team.
Varuni Goyal [10:11 A.M.]	That's true. When Naomi stepped in, she had to get herself familiar with the work.
Naomi Rutledge [10:12 A.M.]	I feel like I'm up to speed now, so we can move forward quickly.

155. Who most likely is Ms. Rutledge?

    (A) An interior designer
    (B) A construction contractor
    (C) A property manager
    (D) A magazine journalist

156. At 10:05 A.M., what does Ms. Rutledge mean when she writes, "We already have more than enough"?

    (A) She is confident that there is time to finish some work.
    (B) She is considering adding storage space.
    (C) She does not want more work from Mr. Webb.
    (D) She thinks they can afford Mr. Webb's services.

157. What problem is mentioned in the chat?

    (A) A bill has not been paid.
    (B) A team goal was not reached.
    (C) A building has failed an inspection.
    (D) A budget was lower than expected.

158. What is suggested about Ms. Rutledge?

    (A) She has not worked on the project since the beginning.
    (B) She plans to hire Ms. Sullivan for additional help.
    (C) She would like to visit a site soon.
    (D) She is concerned about the team members' lack of experience.

GO ON TO THE NEXT PAGE

Questions 159-163 refer to the following online article and reader comment.

http://www.theoakwoodtribune.com/mysterytrain

The Oakwood Tribune, August 15, "Mystery Train"

The train begins its journey, moving along the track with a *clickety-clack*. The passengers are in their seats, enjoying some refreshments. Suddenly, actors enter the car, and a dramatic mystery unfolds. The audience members must pick up on the clues to solve the mystery. With period costumes, intriguing characters, and a different plot to enjoy every month, Mystery Train offers exciting live performances on a unique "stage"—an old-fashioned steam train!

Mystery Train has been in operation for the past 10 years, starting with a local theater group that was looking for a way to raise money. Adrian Urbano, who plays the lead role in the current run of performances, has been featured in most of the Mystery Train's shows from the beginning. "I love how engaged the audience members become with our performance," Mr. Urbano says. "It's fascinating to see their delight when the case is solved."

Mystery Train performances are offered every Thursday, Friday, Saturday, and Sunday evening as well as Saturday and Sunday afternoons. The shows run for two-and-a-half hours, with the exception of the Sunday afternoon show, which runs for 90 minutes, making it a popular option for families. Tickets can be purchased at www.mysterytrainboxoffice.com.

http://www.theoakwoodtribune.com/mysterytrain/comments

I attended the most recent Mystery Train performance, and it was amazing! I enjoyed watching the main character. Not only was he very talented, but I also have a personal connection to him, as we graduated from high school together. I remember that he loved drama classes even at that time. As the various scripts for the Mystery Train shows have been written by members of the Oakwood Writing Society (OWS), I'd love to see some of those people featured in a future edition. I know that you frequently do these sorts of stories, as I have subscribed to your publication for many years.

Gloria Ramirez

159. What is implied about the Mystery Train performances?

(A) Their storylines change regularly.
(B) Their audience members move around.
(C) They include well-known actors.
(D) They take place four times per week.

160. What is true about the Sunday afternoon shows?

(A) They are offered exclusively to families.
(B) They are the least expensive shows.
(C) They are the most popular performance.
(D) They are shorter than the other shows.

161. What is suggested about Mr. Urbano?

(A) He attended school with Ms. Ramirez.
(B) He plans to begin offering acting classes.
(C) He designs authentic costumes for the shows.
(D) He is the founder of a theater group.

162. What is Ms. Ramirez interested in doing?

(A) Submitting her work to the newspaper
(B) Reading an article about some writers of OWS
(C) Reviewing a show script in advance
(D) Joining a local writing group

163. What does the reader comment suggest about Ms. Ramirez?

(A) She frequently participates in local activities and events.
(B) She spent most of her childhood in Oakwood.
(C) She has attended several Mystery Train performances.
(D) She has been an *Oakwood Tribune* subscriber for a long time.

GO ON TO THE NEXT PAGE

Questions 164-168 refer to the following online message board, e-mail, and web page.

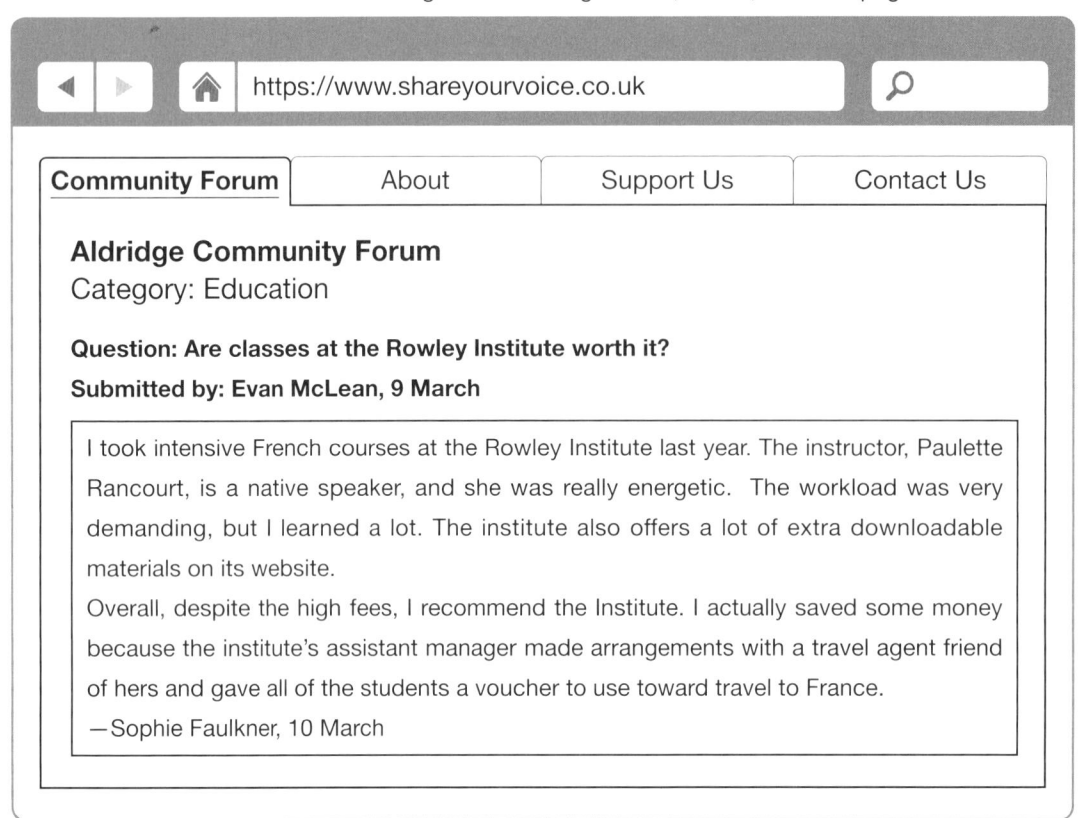

https://www.shareyourvoice.co.uk

Community Forum | About | Support Us | Contact Us

Aldridge Community Forum
Category: Education

Question: Are classes at the Rowley Institute worth it?
Submitted by: Evan McLean, 9 March

I took intensive French courses at the Rowley Institute last year. The instructor, Paulette Rancourt, is a native speaker, and she was really energetic. The workload was very demanding, but I learned a lot. The institute also offers a lot of extra downloadable materials on its website.

Overall, despite the high fees, I recommend the Institute. I actually saved some money because the institute's assistant manager made arrangements with a travel agent friend of hers and gave all of the students a voucher to use toward travel to France.

—Sophie Faulkner, 10 March

E-Mail Message

To: All staff <staff@rowleyinstitute.co.uk>
From: Lara Hurst <l.hurst@rowleyinstitute.co.uk>
Date: May 30
Subject: Manchester

Dear All,

Today will be my last day at the Rowley Institute. I am moving to Manchester to be closer to my family, but I will truly miss you all. As assistant manager, I had the opportunity to get to know all of you on both a personal and a professional level. I am impressed with your commitment to our students' success. I would particularly like to thank Dominic Archer for hiring me and giving me the opportunity to improve my management skills.

It has been a pleasure working here, and I do hope that we can stay in touch.

All the best,

Lara Hurst

182

Aldridge Local Business Awards
Category: Support for Local Education

Gold Award: Jack Talbot, Aldridge Community Center

Silver Award: Dominic Archer, Rowley Institute

Bronze Award: Holly Khan, Rowley Institute

Honorable Mention: Ava Conway, Crafton Trade School

The award winners were nominated by Aldridge residents and then selected by a judging panel of city officials and small business owners. The winners will be interviewed by a reporter from *Community Cares* magazine, and their contributions will be outlined on the Aldridge government website. Nominations for next year will be accepted after July 10.

---

164. What does Ms. Faulkner mention about the Rowley Institute?

    (A) The amount of homework is reasonable.
    (B) It provides additional materials online.
    (C) All of the instructors are native speakers.
    (D) There is an option for remote classes.

165. What is suggested about Ms. Faulkner?

    (A) Her instructor is a published author.
    (B) Her classes were paid for by her company.
    (C) She received a voucher from Ms. Hurst.
    (D) She plans to move to France.

166. What is the purpose of the e-mail?

    (A) To congratulate the staff on an achievement
    (B) To say farewell to colleagues
    (C) To ask for recommendations in Manchester
    (D) To nominate an employee as a replacement

167. What award was given to the person who hired Ms. Hurst?

    (A) Gold Award
    (B) Silver Award
    (C) Bronze Award
    (D) Honourable Mention

168. What is suggested on the web page?

    (A) The winners can advertise for free in *Community Cares* magazine.
    (B) Mr. Talbot has previously won a business award.
    (C) The awards will be distributed on July 10.
    (D) Mr. Archer and Ms. Khan work for the same employer.

實戰模擬試題

實戰模擬試題 聽力與閱讀篇

LISTENING TEST

In the Listening test, you will be asked to demonstrate how well you understand spoken English. The entire Listening test will last approximately 45 minutes. There are four parts, and directions are given for each part. You must mark your answers on the separate answer sheet. Do not write your answers in your test book.

PART 1

Directions: For each question in this part, you will hear four statements about a picture in your test book. When you hear the statements, you must select the one statement that best describes what you see in the picture. Then find the number of the question on your answer sheet and mark your answer. The statements will not be printed in your test book and will be spoken only one time.

Statement (C), "He's making a phone call," is the best description of the picture, so you should select answer (C) and mark it on your answer sheet.

1.

2.

3.

4.

5.

6.

PART 2

Directions: You will hear a question or statement and three responses spoken in English. They will not be printed in your test book and will be spoken only one time. Select the best response to the question or statement and mark the letter (A), (B), or (C) on your answer sheet.

7. Mark your answer on your answer sheet.
8. Mark your answer on your answer sheet.
9. Mark your answer on your answer sheet.
10. Mark your answer on your answer sheet.
11. Mark your answer on your answer sheet.
12. Mark your answer on your answer sheet.
13. Mark your answer on your answer sheet.
14. Mark your answer on your answer sheet.
15. Mark your answer on your answer sheet.
16. Mark your answer on your answer sheet.
17. Mark your answer on your answer sheet.
18. Mark your answer on your answer sheet.
19. Mark your answer on your answer sheet.
20. Mark your answer on your answer sheet.
21. Mark your answer on your answer sheet.
22. Mark your answer on your answer sheet.
23. Mark your answer on your answer sheet.
24. Mark your answer on your answer sheet.
25. Mark your answer on your answer sheet.
26. Mark your answer on your answer sheet.
27. Mark your answer on your answer sheet.
28. Mark your answer on your answer sheet.
29. Mark your answer on your answer sheet.
30. Mark your answer on your answer sheet.
31. Mark your answer on your answer sheet.

PART 3

Directions: You will hear some conversations between two or more people. You will be asked to answer three questions about what the speakers say in each conversation. Select the best response to each question and mark the letter (A), (B), (C), or (D) on your answer sheet. The conversations will not be printed in your test book and will be spoken only one time.

32. What kind of event is the man planning?
    (A) An anniversary celebration
    (B) A grand opening
    (C) A charity fundraiser
    (D) A retirement party

33. What does the woman say is difficult to estimate?
    (A) The delivery fee
    (B) The available colors
    (C) The labor costs
    (D) The travel time

34. What will the woman send the man?
    (A) Some samples
    (B) Some photographs
    (C) An invoice
    (D) A brochure

35. Which industry do the speakers most likely work in?
    (A) Real estate
    (B) Education
    (C) Manufacturing
    (D) Healthcare

36. According to the woman, what caused a problem?
    (A) Bad weather conditions
    (B) A missed deadline
    (C) Some damaged equipment
    (D) An error in an advertisement

37. What does the man suggest doing?
    (A) Increasing a budget
    (B) Holding another event
    (C) Hiring more workers
    (D) Reading some reviews

38. What most likely is the woman's job?
    (A) Magazine reporter
    (B) Tour guide
    (C) Museum curator
    (D) Bus driver

39. Why is the man calling?
    (A) To provide a reminder
    (B) To offer a promotion
    (C) To cancel an event
    (D) To schedule an interview

40. What will the man do next?
    (A) Update a website
    (B) Send a timetable
    (C) Check a participant list
    (D) Explain a policy

41. Who most likely are the speakers?
    (A) Bank employees
    (B) Interior designers
    (C) Delivery drivers
    (D) Safety inspectors

42. What do the speakers have to decide?
    (A) Which software to try
    (B) Where to advertise a product
    (C) How soon to open a new branch
    (D) How to recruit new employees

43. What does the man warn the woman about?
    (A) Using outdated equipment
    (B) Completing a project late
    (C) Wasting a lot of time
    (D) Exceeding a budget

44. Where most likely are the speakers?
    (A) At a library
    (B) At a fitness club
    (C) At a business school
    (D) At an art center

45. What does the man want to do?
    (A) Hire a presenter
    (B) Apply for a job
    (C) Give a demonstration
    (D) Negotiate a sale

46. How did the man learn about Teresa Connelly?
    (A) From searching online
    (B) From reading a newspaper article
    (C) From receiving a flyer
    (D) From talking to a coworker

47. What problem does the woman mention?
    (A) She lost the original report.
    (B) She cannot access a room.
    (C) Some products have been discontinued.
    (D) Some flooring is badly damaged.

48. Why does the man need some precise measurements?
    (A) The cost of a material is high.
    (B) A document will be inspected closely.
    (C) It will help him save time.
    (D) It is required by the city.

49. What will the woman most likely do next?
    (A) Unpack some tools
    (B) Place an express order
    (C) Contact a supervisor
    (D) Write down an estimate

50. Who most likely is the woman?
    (A) A post office employee
    (B) A financial advisor
    (C) A travel agent
    (D) A factory worker

51. Why does the woman suggest downloading a mobile application?
    (A) To get access to discounts
    (B) To check hours of operation
    (C) To promote some products
    (D) To print labels at home

52. Where does the man plan to go next?
    (A) To a mobile phone store
    (B) To a bus terminal
    (C) To a supermarket
    (D) To an outlet mall

53. Where do the speakers most likely work?
    (A) At a financial institution
    (B) At a chemistry laboratory
    (C) At a furniture manufacturer
    (D) At an art supply store

54. Why does the man say, "the Valdez Hotel is holding its grand opening at the end of the month?"
    (A) To reject a suggestion
    (B) To agree with a decision
    (C) To offer reassurance
    (D) To highlight some competition

55. What does the man say about Kyle and Ben?
    (A) They have contacted Fenton Industries.
    (B) They have a specialized skill.
    (C) They are the newest employees.
    (D) They are repairing a machine.

56. What is the purpose of the meeting?
    (A) To prepare for an industry event
    (B) To select job candidates
    (C) To approve a budget
    (D) To discuss product sales

57. What did the company do in August?
    (A) It lowered its prices.
    (B) It changed its management.
    (C) It launched a new website.
    (D) It expanded its color selection.

58. What do the speakers plan to do?
    (A) Merge with a competitor
    (B) Create some videos
    (C) Hold a contest
    (D) Print some brochures

59. What will most likely happen on April 3?
    (A) A security system will be changed.
    (B) An industry conference will be held.
    (C) Some visitors will come to the business.
    (D) Some award winners will be announced.

60. Why does the man say, "you've spent a lot of time in India"?
    (A) To explain a delay
    (B) To ask for help
    (C) To make a complaint
    (D) To express surprise

61. What will the woman do next?
    (A) Participate in an interview
    (B) Contact a travel agent
    (C) Confirm her attendance
    (D) Send a memo

Room 1　Sculptures	Room 3　Oil Paintings
Room 2　Watercolor Paintings	Entrance ｜ Room 4　Photographs

62. What event are the speakers preparing for?
    (A) A volunteer training
    (B) An art auction
    (C) A painting demonstration
    (D) A film screening

63. Look at the graphic. Which room does the woman suggest using for an event?
    (A) Room 1
    (B) Room 2
    (C) Room 3
    (D) Room 4

64. According to the woman, what does the site manager want to provide?
    (A) Musical entertainment
    (B) Some refreshments
    (C) Free parking
    (D) Group photographs

Silver Jewelry

Necklace	Bracelet
$120	$80
Earrings	Ring
$65	$40

65. Where are the speakers?

    (A) In an employee lounge
    (B) In a train station
    (C) In a restaurant
    (D) In a conference room

66. Why will the man travel to Cleveland?

    (A) To attend a ceremony
    (B) To inspect a building
    (C) To give a presentation
    (D) To accept an award

67. Look at the graphic. How much will the man probably spend?

    (A) $120
    (B) $80
    (C) $65
    (D) $40

Vacuum Model	Cordless	Removable Air Filter	Dusting Brush
Botello	✓		
Activa	✓		✓
Mammoth		✓	✓
Goodwin	✓	✓	

68. What did the woman do last month?

    (A) She purchased a vacuum cleaner.
    (B) She transferred to another branch.
    (C) She was offered a promotion.
    (D) She received a certificate.

69. Look at the graphic. Which model has the features requested by the customer?

    (A) Botello
    (B) Activa
    (C) Mammoth
    (D) Goodwin

70. What is the man pleased about?

    (A) An annual bonus
    (B) A staff discount
    (C) A paid holiday
    (D) A change in business hours

PART 4

Directions: You will hear some talks given by a single speaker. You will be asked to answer three questions about what the speaker says in each talk. Select the best response to each question and mark the letter (A), (B), (C), or (D) on your answer sheet. The talks will not be printed in your test book and will be spoken only one time.

71. Who is the speaker?
    (A) A factory manager
    (B) A construction worker
    (C) A theater owner
    (D) A computer technician

72. What is the facility famous for?
    (A) Its fundraising efforts
    (B) Its knowledgeable staff
    (C) Its unique architecture
    (D) Its modern equipment

73. According to the speaker, how can the listeners get a coupon?
    (A) By providing some feedback
    (B) By downloading some software
    (C) By signing up for a newsletter
    (D) By e-mailing the speaker

74. What are the listeners most likely interested in?
    (A) Painting
    (B) Poetry
    (C) Language learning
    (D) Cooking

75. What did the speaker do recently?
    (A) He studied abroad.
    (B) He launched a website.
    (C) He published a book.
    (D) He hosted a podcast.

76. What have some listeners asked about?
    (A) Getting individual advice
    (B) Taking food home
    (C) Reviewing class materials
    (D) Purchasing supplies

77. What does the speaker say will happen on Tuesday?
    (A) A crew will be announced.
    (B) A parking lot will be paved.
    (C) A project will be completed.
    (D) A bridge will close.

78. What does the speaker remind the listener to do?
    (A) Carpool to a site
    (B) Display a parking pass
    (C) Sign up for a training session
    (D) Wear warm clothing

79. What will be provided to the listener?
    (A) Safety gear
    (B) A work schedule
    (C) Coworkers' contact information
    (D) A user manual

80. What is the speaker demonstrating?
    (A) Ways to operate a salon
    (B) Ways to attract new customers
    (C) How to use a smartphone application
    (D) How to restart a security system

81. Who most likely are the listeners?
    (A) Physicians
    (B) Computer programmers
    (C) Pharmacists
    (D) Hair stylists

82. What feature does the speaker mention?
    (A) Automatic alerts
    (B) Hands-free operation
    (C) Easy uploading
    (D) Daily reminders

83. Where do the listeners most likely work?

    (A) At a bank
    (B) At a grocery store
    (C) At a museum
    (D) At a library

84. What are the listeners expected to do?

    (A) Attend a training session
    (B) Arrive to work earlier than usual
    (C) Watch for people needing assistance
    (D) Post some instructions near a machine

85. What does the speaker say will happen in October?

    (A) A new job position will be available.
    (B) A fundraiser will be held.
    (C) A building project will be completed.
    (D) A report will be made public.

86. What is being advertised?

    (A) An online course
    (B) A real estate firm
    (C) A building-inspection service
    (D) A garden design service

87. Why does the speaker say, "We have a large photo gallery"?

    (A) To justify a slow website
    (B) To provide reassurance
    (C) To explain a decision
    (D) To criticize a competitor

88. What does the speaker say the business is proud of?

    (A) Its support of local businesses
    (B) Its affordable prices
    (C) Its fast response times
    (D) Its high customer service ratings

89. Where is the speech being given?

    (A) At a training workshop
    (B) At a staff dinner
    (C) At a music competition
    (D) At a press conference

90. What does the speaker imply when he says, "I'm sure Diana would like a few lunches out"?

    (A) He can recommend a restaurant.
    (B) He wants to welcome a new employee.
    (C) He has a suggestion for a gift.
    (D) He is looking for volunteers for a task.

91. What does the speaker say about Ahmed Sharma?

    (A) He shared an innovative idea.
    (B) He will be leaving the company.
    (C) He has a lot of experience.
    (D) He will give a talk shortly.

92. What is the focus of the talk?

    (A) Improving recycling services
    (B) Cleaning up a park
    (C) Building an exercise trail
    (D) Planting more trees

93. What does the speaker imply when she says, "we have a very long list"?

    (A) Some work assignments may be changed.
    (B) A deadline will need to be extended.
    (C) The listeners will have a lot of support.
    (D) A meeting may be longer than scheduled.

94. What will the speaker hand out?

    (A) A map
    (B) A business card
    (C) A proposed schedule
    (D) A cost estimate

Lexington Dance Troupe Show

1 → 11 May | 8:00 P.M.
2 → Seat: H35
3 → Price: $15.50
4 → Ticket Number: 2367

Igor's Quest - Setup Process

Step 1. Unfold playing board
Step 2. Place resource tokens on board
Step 3. Sort cards by color
Step 4. Choose player characters

95. Why is the performance being held?
    (A) To raise funds for a community project
    (B) To celebrate a theater's anniversary
    (C) To encourage people to join a group
    (D) To promote a national tour

96. What will happen after the show?
    (A) Some photos will be taken.
    (B) Tickets will be available for sale.
    (C) Some questions will be answered.
    (D) Posters will be signed.

97. Look at the graphic. Which line should the listeners check for the prize drawing?
    (A) Line 1
    (B) Line 2
    (C) Line 3
    (D) Line 4

98. According to the speaker, what kind of product does Dorsey make?
    (A) Sound equipment
    (B) Office furniture
    (C) Tablet computers
    (D) Software programs

99. What does the speaker like about Igor's Quest?
    (A) The characters
    (B) The instructions
    (C) The artwork
    (D) The number of players

100. Look at the graphic. Which step does the speaker think could be improved?
    (A) Step 1
    (B) Step 2
    (C) Step 3
    (D) Step 4

This is the end of the Listening test.

READING TEST

In the Reading test, you will read a variety of texts and answer several different types of reading comprehension questions. The entire Reading test will last 75 minutes. There are three parts, and directions are given for each part. You are encouraged to answer as many questions as possible within the time allowed.

You must mark your answers on the separate answer sheet. Do not write your answers in your test book.

PART 5

Directions: A word or phrase is missing in each of the sentences below. Four answer choices are given below each sentence. Select the best answer to complete the sentence. Then mark the letter (A), (B), (C), or (D) on your answer sheet.

101. The sales clerk can reprint a ------- if the customer needs it.
    (A) receipt
    (B) receive
    (C) receivable
    (D) receipts

102. Come to Fairfield Park ------- the annual community picnic this Saturday.
    (A) for
    (B) until
    (C) unless
    (D) but

103. By using the bank's smartphone application, customers can ------- check their account balances.
    (A) easy
    (B) easiest
    (C) easily
    (D) easier

104. Gym members can improve their fitness levels by following a regular exercise -------.
    (A) transaction
    (B) sequel
    (C) response
    (D) program

105. A spokesperson for Sweet-Time Bakery has confirmed that it ------- a site for a new retail branch next year.
    (A) will select
    (B) to select
    (C) are selecting
    (D) select

106. The annual dance competition includes 20 groups ------- cities across the country.
    (A) from
    (B) except
    (C) as
    (D) regarding

107. ------- check all products for manufacturing defects prior to packaging them.
    (A) There
    (B) Their
    (C) Them
    (D) They

108. Upon request, the hotel's housekeeping department can replace sheets, -------, and other bedding items.
    (A) curtains
    (B) carpets
    (C) lighting
    (D) pillowcases

109. The Chung Business Institute's spring schedule will be posted ------- 9 A.M. tomorrow on the website.
    (A) after
    (B) between
    (C) recently
    (D) final

110. Best-selling author George Vasquez is currently ------- in Toronto, Canada.
    (A) committed
    (B) written
    (C) moved
    (D) based

111. Successful applicants must have experience as a bookkeeper or in a related -------.
    (A) occupied
    (B) occupant
    (C) occupation
    (D) occupying

112. Carlyle Logistics is admired for achieving ------- growth without sacrificing the quality of its services.
    (A) enthusiastic
    (B) rapid
    (C) frank
    (D) native

113. The Grand Ballroom can ------- accommodate up to 300 guests.
    (A) comfort
    (B) comfortably
    (C) comforted
    (D) comfortable

114. All Tazma Co. employees should obtain ------- from the finance department before purchasing expensive equipment.
    (A) approval
    (B) entry
    (C) regard
    (D) interest

115. PJ Shopping Center hopes to boost business through ------- business hours.
    (A) extension
    (B) extends
    (C) extended
    (D) extend

116. No one should enter or exit the conference room while the job candidate ------- interviewed by the committee.
    (A) is being
    (B) to be
    (C) to have been
    (D) has been

117. The crew leader emphasized that every technical ------- of the project must be double-checked.
    (A) specify
    (B) specification
    (C) specific
    (D) specifically

118. Employees at Jacamo Incorporated should submit all vacation requests ------- to their department heads.
    (A) directly
    (B) entirely
    (C) hardly
    (D) fairly

119. The Cayla Museum maintains a relaxing atmosphere by ------- the number of visitors allowed inside at any given time.
    (A) limiting
    (B) limited
    (C) limitation
    (D) limits

120. PowerVox has found a fresh and ------- solution to the problem of waste disposal costs.
    (A) loyal
    (B) innovative
    (C) casual
    (D) appointed

121. The committee members will tell us ------- job applicant they believe is most suitable for the role.
    (A) if
    (B) whenever
    (C) who
    (D) which

122. ------- Ericson Construction's wages are higher than average, the firm is having difficulty with recruitment.
    (A) Because
    (B) As if
    (C) Whether
    (D) Although

123. Garrison Publishing keeps ------- manuscripts on file for five years in case the market for them improves.
    (A) rejects
    (B) rejected
    (C) rejecting
    (D) rejection

124. Employees who are working from home can access company documents ------- and download the files they need.
    (A) remotely
    (B) absolutely
    (C) seriously
    (D) predictably

125. The HR manager dispatched the employee handbook to new hires so they could read it a few days ------- orientation.
    (A) ahead of
    (B) possibly
    (C) along with
    (D) highly

126. ------- designing invoices themselves, many new business owners prefer to use a template.
    (A) Rather than
    (B) In light of
    (C) Among
    (D) Into

127. Customers can send their packages overseas for ------- lower rates if the items go by ship instead of by air.
    (A) considers
    (B) considerate
    (C) considerably
    (D) consideration

128. When the discount code was accidentally leaked online, orders ------- for the new tablet computer.
    (A) got along
    (B) carried out
    (C) settled up
    (D) poured in

129. Local residents are experiencing fewer traffic delays ------- the busy tourist season has ended.
    (A) so that
    (B) now that
    (C) as though
    (D) because of

130. Users will be locked out of the system after an incorrect password ------- three times.
    (A) have been entered
    (B) has been entered
    (C) was entering
    (D) are entered

PART 6

Directions: Read the texts that follow. A word, phrase, or sentence is missing in parts of each text. Four answer choices for each question are given below the text. Select the best answer to complete the text. Then mark the letter (A), (B), (C), or (D) on your answer sheet.

Questions 131-134 refer to the following advertisement.

Special deal at Romano Cinema!

Romano Cinema is helping you start the new year with a great deal on admission. From January 2 ------- January 19, tickets for all screenings are buy one, get one free. All ------- are offering this
　　　131.　　　　　　　　　　　　　　　　　　　　　　　　　　　　　　　　　**132.**
deal, and you can take advantage of it as many times as you'd like. Please note that all complimentary tickets will be for the same show as the ------- tickets. We also have a range of
　　　　　　　　　　　　　　　　　　　　　　　　　　　　　133.
delicious snacks to enjoy during the film. ------- .
　　　　　　　　　　　　　　　　　　　　　134.

131. (A) onto
(B) toward
(C) within
(D) through

132. (A) statuses
(B) locations
(C) directors
(D) exhibits

133. (A) purchases
(B) purchased
(C) purchaser
(D) purchasing

134. (A) Award nominations will be announced soon.
(B) Contact us to apply for this role.
(C) Stop by the concession stand to purchase them.
(D) The films' running times may vary.

Questions 135-138 refer to the following article.

Kenwyn Beach Resort has scheduled its grand opening for next month. The site ------- spacious suites for guests, three on-site restaurants, indoor and outdoor pools, and more.
_{135.}

The section of the beach that is now home to the resort was left empty for decades. It was previously owned by Capital Properties, which struggled to find funding for development. -------.
_{136.}
V&G Investments procured the property to build a resort, which was named Kenwyn Beach Resort.

Architect Oscar Strope designed the entire facility to take advantage of the beautiful setting and -------. Based on other resorts in the area, Kenwyn Beach Resort is likely to be quite -------.
_{137.} _{138.}

135. (A) will include
 (B) was included
 (C) being included
 (D) has been included

136. (A) Other sites are still available for sale.
 (B) Finally, the company decided to sell it.
 (C) The tourist season runs throughout the summer.
 (D) The owner has a lot of experience in the field.

137. (A) scenery
 (B) scenic
 (C) scenically
 (D) scenario

138. (A) definite
 (B) general
 (C) heavy
 (D) popular

Questions 139-142 refer to the following e-mail.

To: Marketing Staff <marketing@camdensales.com>
From: Richard Hayes <rhayes@camdensales.com>
Date: June 18
Subject: website
Attachment: New color scheme

Dear Marketing Staff,

Please find attached the document that ------- the options for the new color scheme for our website. The updated ------- will project a more modern image for Camden Sales. -------.
                                  139.   **140.**   **141.**

I ask that you look over the choices carefully. By the end of Thursday, you should e-mail me your thoughts on which color scheme would be best. -------, your opinions will not be taken into consideration.
                                                                                         142.

Thank you,

Richard Hayes

---

139. (A) outlining
     (B) outline
     (C) outlines
     (D) had been outlined

140. (A) schedule
     (B) label
     (C) policy
     (D) design

141. (A) In addition, it will attract a greater number of younger customers.
     (B) Most people think the software is easy to use.
     (C) Fortunately, sales improved significantly last month.
     (D) I will recommend you for future projects that are similar.

142. (A) To that end
     (B) Otherwise
     (C) In contrast
     (D) Similarly

Questions 143-146 refer to the following article.

Footwear manufacturer League Footwear confirmed today that it has ------- EG Sports. "EG Sports, which is known for its trendy athletic shoes, has demonstrated ------- market success over the years, and we are proud to bring it into the League Footwear family," said Nathan Dale, a League Footwear representative.

"We know that our customers rely ------- our high-quality materials to ensure both comfort and performance," Mr. Dale explained. "All EG Sports products sold through our company will be held to the same high standards. ------- ."

143. (A) advised
 (B) acquired
 (C) consented
 (D) sustained

144. (A) impress
 (B) impression
 (C) impressive
 (D) impressed

145. (A) about
 (B) to
 (C) on
 (D) by

146. (A) So, customers can shop with confidence.
 (B) There is a range of sizes to choose from.
 (C) More information about the competition can be found online.
 (D) Therefore, each retail store will have different hours.

PART 7

Directions: In this part, you will read a selection of texts, such as magazine and newspaper articles, e-mails, and instant messages. Each text or set of texts is followed by several questions. Select the best answer for each question and mark the letter (A), (B), (C), or (D) on your answer sheet.

Questions 147-148 refer to the following e-mail.

To:	Simon Ethridge <sethridge@kessladata.com>
From:	Christy Lansing <clansing@kessladata.com>
Date:	July 28
Subject:	Letter

Dear Mr. Ethridge,

I am writing to confirm that I have received your letter dated July 26.

I have informed all teams that your last day of work will be August 11. The IT department will handle your company-owned equipment, so please call them on extension 25 prior to your final day to make the necessary arrangements. We appreciate your contributions to Kessla Data.

All the best,

Christy Lansing

147. Why did Ms. Lansing send the e-mail?
(A) To confirm a business closure
(B) To update a banking record
(C) To acknowledge a resignation
(D) To offer a job promotion

148. What should Mr. Ethridge do by August 11?
(A) Complete a form
(B) Meet with Ms. Lansing
(C) Contact the IT team
(D) Remove his personal items

Questions 149-150 refer to the following notice.

NOTICE

On Tuesday, August 22, a work crew from Despard Water Co. will begin replacing a sewer line in the area. Florence Street will be closed temporarily while the work is being carried out, meaning that the entrance to the parking lot here at Livonia Tower will be inaccessible during that time. Residents who plan to drive their vehicle between 8 A.M. on August 22 and 4 P.M. on August 23 should park on one of the nearby streets before the work begins. We apologize for any inconvenience this may cause.

149. For whom is the notice intended?
  (A) City officials
  (B) Building tenants
  (C) Construction workers
  (D) Property developers

150. According to the notice, what will happen at 4:00 P.M. on August 23?
  (A) A parking lot entrance will close.
  (B) A street will be paved.
  (C) A road will be reopened.
  (D) A crew will assess a project.

Questions 151-152 refer to the following e-mail.

TO:	Rebekah Ingram <ringram@rivendalesales.com>
FROM:	Montoya Fashions <customerservice@montoyafashions.com>
DATE:	November 18
SUBJECT:	Return request

Dear Ms. Ingram,

We have received your returned item as listed below:

    Description: Fieldcrest cashmere sweater, dark gray, medium
    Item : #748592
    Purchase price: $125.00

We are processing your refund, which will be refunded to the credit card you used for the purchase within five working days. Please note that if you earned any Montoya Fashions rewards points, these will be deducted from your account within 30 days.

Also, don't miss our new line of party dresses, now on sale for $49.99, just in time for the holiday season! Click here to browse the catalog.

Sincerely,

The Montoya Fashions Customer Service Team

151. What is one purpose of the e-mail?
 (A) To promote some new products
 (B) To confirm that a payment has been made
 (C) To explain how to sign into an account
 (D) To request credit card information

152. What is suggested about Montoya Fashions?
 (A) It accepts returns within 30 days.
 (B) It offers a loyalty program.
 (C) It only gives store credit for returns.
 (D) It sells home furnishing products.

Questions 153-154 refer to the following text-message chain.

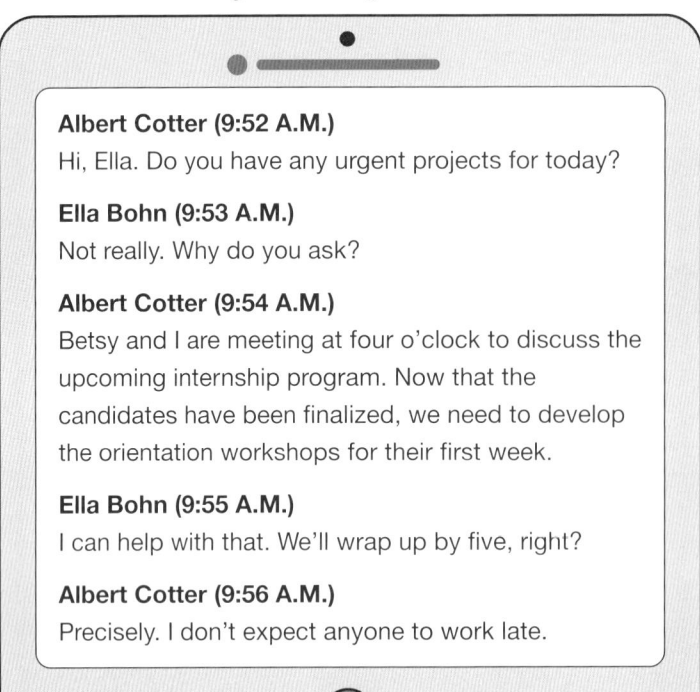

Albert Cotter (9:52 A.M.)
Hi, Ella. Do you have any urgent projects for today?

Ella Bohn (9:53 A.M.)
Not really. Why do you ask?

Albert Cotter (9:54 A.M.)
Betsy and I are meeting at four o'clock to discuss the upcoming internship program. Now that the candidates have been finalized, we need to develop the orientation workshops for their first week.

Ella Bohn (9:55 A.M.)
I can help with that. We'll wrap up by five, right?

Albert Cotter (9:56 A.M.)
Precisely. I don't expect anyone to work late.

153. Why will Mr. Cotter attend a meeting today?
    (A) To review applications for an internship
    (B) To create a training program
    (C) To conduct group interviews
    (D) To write a job description

154. At 9:56 A.M., what does Mr. Cotter most likely mean when he writes, "Precisely"?
    (A) The meeting will end by 5:00 P.M.
    (B) There will be five attendees at the meeting.
    (C) Five documents need to be prepared.
    (D) Some workers are meeting for the fifth time.

Questions 155-157 refer to the following article.

Carson's Bike Shop Still Rolling

PHILADELPHIA (October 30)—Carson's Bike Shop, a bike repair shop and retailer of bicycle parts, is celebrating its 25th anniversary. The business was founded by Carson Reese, who taught himself how to repair bicycles because cycling was his hobby. He brought in his brother, David Reese, to handle the accounting side of things, and the business steadily grew.

The business offered repair services for low prices and made most of its money through the sale of bicycle parts and cycling accessories. This approach helped the shop build up a loyal customer base over time. As demand grew, more bicycle mechanics were hired and new services were added. Five years ago, it opened a second branch in Willow Grove, and its third branch, which is in Trenton, opened last spring. Carson's Bike Shop continues to contribute to the cycling community by arranging bicycle races in Philadelphia and making donations to sports-related charities.

155. What is the article mainly about?
   (A) The success of a new invention
   (B) Trends in the cycling industry
   (C) The relocation of a shop
   (D) The history of a business

156. The word "approach" in paragraph 2, line 4, is closest in meaning to
   (A) movement
   (B) access
   (C) arrival
   (D) strategy

157. What is true about Carson's Bike Shop?
   (A) It designs bicycle accessories.
   (B) It organizes athletic competitions.
   (C) It has recently been sold.
   (D) It started in Willow Grove.

Questions 158-160 refer to the following e-mail.

E-Mail

TO:	Shirley Amundson <s_amundson@suffolkltd.com>
FROM:	Romulus Cruise Lines <booking@romuluscruiselines.com>
DATE:	July 11
SUBJECT:	Naples Cruise

Dear Ms. Amundson,

Thank you for booking a cruise with Romulus Cruise Lines departing from Naples, Italy, on September 20 and returning on September 27.

Your luxury cabin has a flat-screen television with on-demand films, a writing desk, a king-sized bed, and a private balcony. The ship features several dining areas, lounges for musical entertainment, and a large auditorium. On the top deck, you can find a swimming pool, hot tubs, and a miniature golf course.

You can park on site at the port's lot for a fee, but please note that the lot is not affiliated with Romulus Cruise Lines. You can use our free shuttle between Naples International Airport and the port. Simply show your cruise ticket confirmation e-mail.

As you prepare for your journey, keep in mind that there are some things that you are not allowed to bring on board. To view a list of these, please visit www.romuluscruiselines.com/boarding.

Have a wonderful trip!

Michael Silva
Romulus Cruise Lines

---

158. What is one purpose of the e-mail?

(A) To request feedback from a customer
(B) To describe some on-board amenities
(C) To announce a change in a departure date
(D) To offer a cruise cabin upgrade

159. What is available to Romulus Cruise Lines passengers?

(A) Discounts on flights to Naples
(B) Free parking at the port
(C) A complimentary shuttle service
(D) Vouchers for local dining

160. According to Mr. Silva, what can Ms. Amundson find on a website?

(A) Coupons for future bookings
(B) Information about restricted items
(C) Photos from previous journeys
(D) Testimonials from passengers

Questions 161-163 refer to the following letter.

8 May

Wendy Sanford
660 Rosewood Court
Brockport, NY 14420

Dear Ms. Sanford,

We would like to inform you that your home insurance policy will expire soon. Please see the details below. —[1]—. It is important for your property to be insured at all times. You should have a new policy in place before the expiration of your current policy. —[2]—.

Policy Type: Basic Home and Contents
Policy Number: 374109
Expiration Date: June 4

Our fees are $160 for a Basic Home Only policy, $180 for a Premium Home Only policy, $205 for a Basic Home and Contents Policy, and $225 for a Premium Home and Contents policy. These rates have not changed since the purchase of your current policy last year. —[3]—.

To renew your policy, simply visit www.trustedinsuranceinc.com/renew, input your policy number, and follow the on-screen instructions. This will take less than 10 minutes. —[4]—.

Regards,

Manuel Shapiro
Manuel Shapiro
Customer Service Agent, Trusted Insurance Inc.

---

161. Why was the letter written?

(A) To confirm the customer's contact details
(B) To check the value of a home
(C) To request an overdue payment
(D) To describe the state of a policy

162. How much did Ms. Sanford most likely pay last year?

(A) $160
(B) $180
(C) $205
(D) $225

163. In which of the following positions marked [1], [2], [3], and [4] does the following sentence best belong?

"Otherwise, your home and finances could be at risk."

(A) [1]
(B) [2]
(C) [3]
(D) [4]

Questions 164-167 refer to the following online chat discussion.

Helen Snyder [9:24 A.M.]	Hi, Lee and Aubrey. Have the presenters for the year-end awards banquet been decided? I want to make sure the planning is on track.
Lee Roth [9:25 A.M.]	Yes, Adele Ruiz and Craig Jacobson will be the presenters this year.
Helen Snyder [9:26 A.M.]	Great! Will we have them seated near the stage for the dinner portion of the event?
Lee Roth [9:27 A.M.]	Yes, the presenters will be seated at the front. We are most likely using Glendale Hall again, but I'm just waiting for Tina Vance at Daubert Hotel to provide a quote.
Aubrey Lujan [9:29 A.M.]	There is actually one more. Bonnie Nelson will also take the stage.
Lee Roth [9:30 A.M.]	Oh, right. I forgot about that. Things are moving so quickly.
Helen Snyder [9:31 A.M.]	Bonnie Nelson? I thought only executive staff members were giving out the awards.
Aubrey Lujan [9:32 A.M.]	The board members have been so closely involved in choosing the winners this year, so we thought that they should be represented as well.
Helen Snyder [9:33 A.M.]	That makes sense. Lee, please contact all of the presenters to ask when they are free for a conference call.

164. Who will present some awards?

    (A) Ms. Snyder
    (B) Mr. Roth
    (C) Mr. Jacobson
    (D) Ms. Vance

165. At 9:29 A.M., what does Ms. Lujan most likely mean when she writes, "There is actually one more"?

    (A) A new award category was created.
    (B) An event will include a third presenter.
    (C) Another venue is still available.
    (D) Mr. Roth has been assigned a new task.

166. Who most likely is Ms. Nelson?

    (A) An award nominee
    (B) A corporate executive
    (C) A board member
    (D) A department head

167. What does Ms. Snyder ask Mr. Roth to do?

    (A) Find out the presenters' availability
    (B) Finalize a venue soon
    (C) Print the list of award winners
    (D) Forward a copy of an invitation

Questions 168-171 refer to the following job announcement.

Programmers Wanted

Lynn Energy Advisors
Houston, Texas

Lynn Energy Advisors has several open positions for programmers to develop a smartphone application for tracking and reporting energy usage.

Lynn Energy Advisors has been voted the Most Trusted Advisory Firm in the industry for three consecutive years. Previous experience is not required, making this the ideal role for recent graduates. —[1]—. Candidates should be familiar with a range of software development tools and have a firm understanding of data protection procedures. The job involves creating and filing reports daily, so the ability to complete tasks while demonstrating care for even the smallest detail is a must. —[2]—. You will work on a small team of five people.

To apply, send a cover letter and résumé to hr@lynnenergyadvisors.com. —[3]—. We prefer to have the start date as soon as possible. —[4]—. For a full job description, visit www.lynnenergyadvisors.com.

---

168. What is suggested about Lynn Energy Advisors?

    (A) It has a good reputation.
    (B) It is under new ownership.
    (C) It will relocate to Houston.
    (D) It offers competitive wages.

169. What is indicated about the positions?

    (A) They are intended for entry-level programmers.
    (B) They offer many opportunities for promotion.
    (C) They require a background check of the applicant.
    (D) They involve maintaining energy production.

170. What is stated as a requirement of the job?

    (A) Managing a small team
    (B) Paying attention to detail
    (C) Responding to software questions
    (D) Checking colleagues' reports

171. In which of the following positions marked [1], [2], [3], and [4] does the following sentence best belong?

    "However, we are willing to wait for the right candidates."

    (A) [1]
    (B) [2]
    (C) [3]
    (D) [4]

Questions 172-175 refer to the following announcement.

City of Orland Proposal Request

Summary

The city of Orland is accepting submissions from manufacturers for digital parking meters to be used throughout the city center. These should be supplied by August 18.

Purpose

The city's outdated coin-operated meters no longer meet the community's needs and will be replaced with digital parking meters. In addition to making the payment process more convenient, as various credit cards and phone-based payment apps are accepted, the meters will also cut costs regarding city personnel having to check and empty meters. Costs are also lower for drivers because the meters can sense when a vehicle has vacated the spot and charge only for the time used, not more. Cities that have installed digital meters have benefitted from a greater number of positive reviews from out-of-town visitors. This is due to the meters being easier to use thanks to their simple and intuitive user interface.

Specifics

The manufacturer should provide 1,800 digital parking meters suitable for outdoor use. They must be capable of round-the-clock monitoring and uploading real-time data feeds to the transportation office. The meters' touchscreens should display text clearly no matter the lighting conditions.

To submit a proposal, send your bid to Jason Bahr at j.bahr@orland.gov no later than February 3. Visit www.orland.gov/project0894 to find the list of documents needed during submission.

172. What is a purpose of the announcement?
    (A) To introduce public parking fines
    (B) To describe a city's need for parking
    (C) To explain a change in parking fees
    (D) To encourage businesses to submit bids

173. What is NOT indicated as a benefit of the parking meters?
    (A) Drivers can find parking spots more easily.
    (B) A variety of payment methods can be used.
    (C) There will be a reduction in staffing costs.
    (D) Meter users will not be overcharged.

174. What has happened in other cities that started using digital meters?
    (A) They received more favorable reviews from tourists.
    (B) They reduced traffic congestion in the city center.
    (C) They raised more money for transportation projects.
    (D) They increased the number of major manufacturers in the area.

175. What is stated about the proposed meters?
    (A) They must be the same size as the current meters.
    (B) They should have a battery backup system.
    (C) They must send information to a certain location.
    (D) They should be manufactured domestically.

Questions 176-180 refer to the following web page and e-mail.

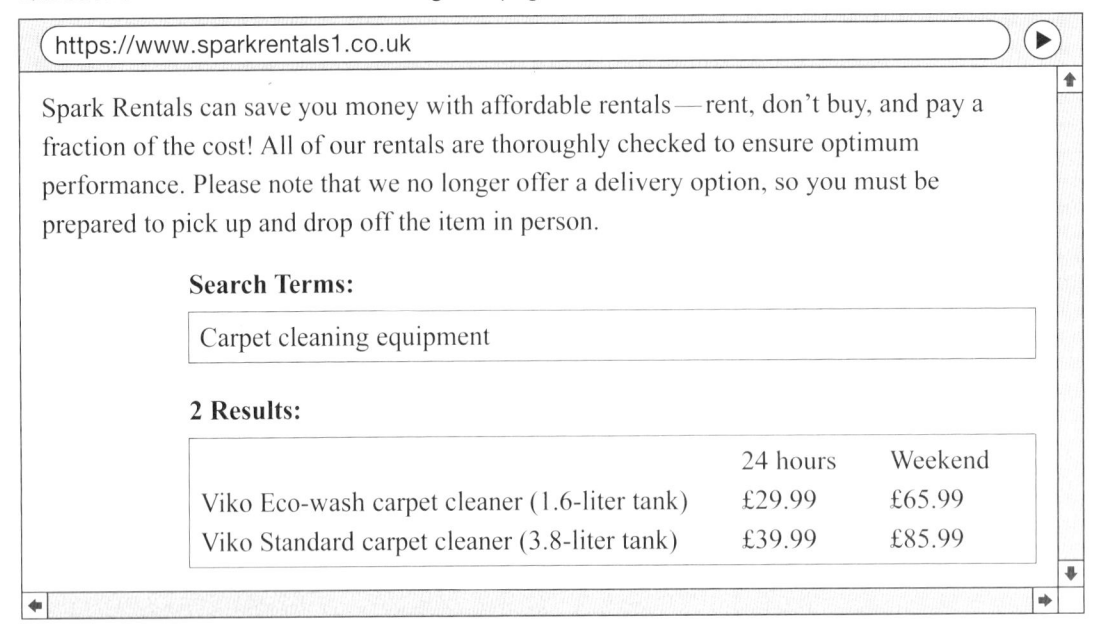

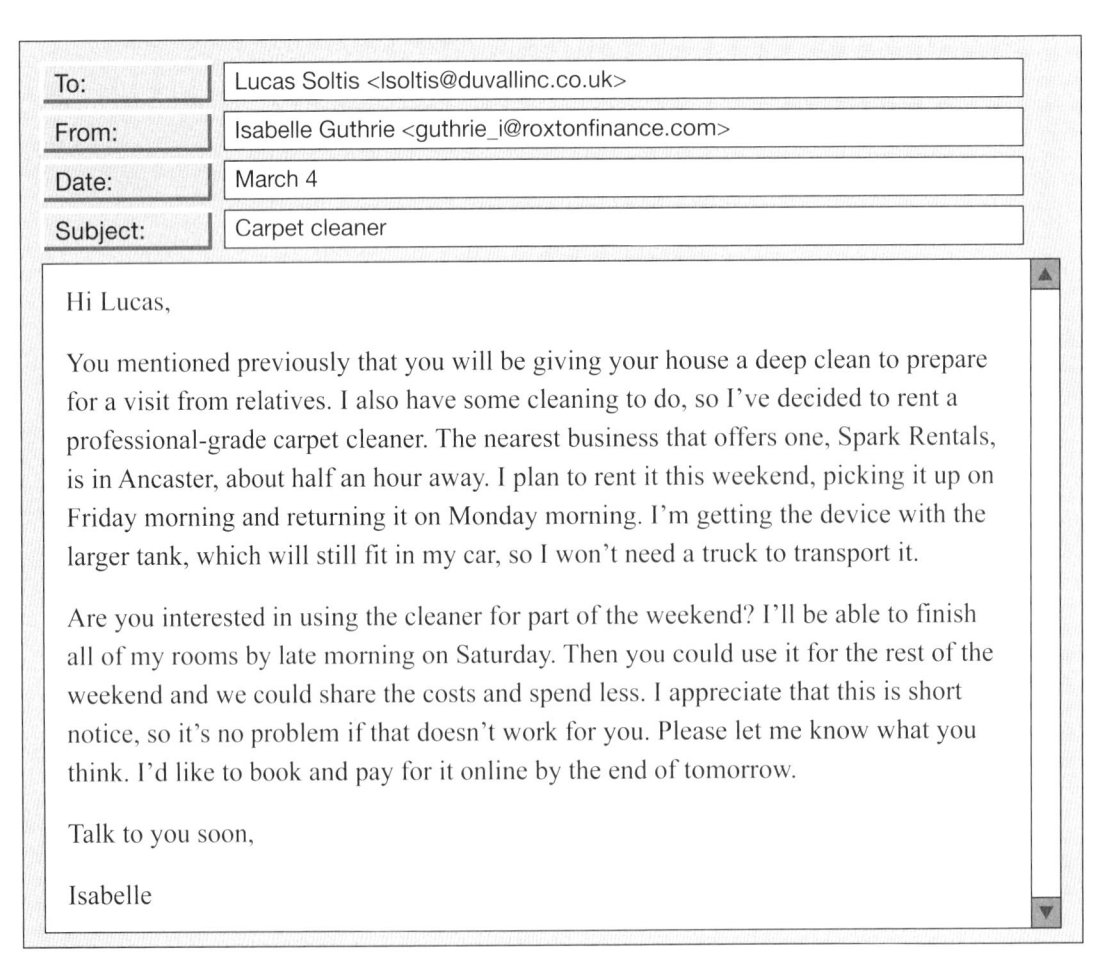

---

https://www.sparkrentals1.co.uk

Spark Rentals can save you money with affordable rentals—rent, don't buy, and pay a fraction of the cost! All of our rentals are thoroughly checked to ensure optimum performance. Please note that we no longer offer a delivery option, so you must be prepared to pick up and drop off the item in person.

Search Terms:

Carpet cleaning equipment

2 Results:

	24 hours	Weekend
Viko Eco-wash carpet cleaner (1.6-liter tank)	£29.99	£65.99
Viko Standard carpet cleaner (3.8-liter tank)	£39.99	£85.99

To:	Lucas Soltis <lsoltis@duvallinc.co.uk>
From:	Isabelle Guthrie <guthrie_i@roxtonfinance.com>
Date:	March 4
Subject:	Carpet cleaner

Hi Lucas,

You mentioned previously that you will be giving your house a deep clean to prepare for a visit from relatives. I also have some cleaning to do, so I've decided to rent a professional-grade carpet cleaner. The nearest business that offers one, Spark Rentals, is in Ancaster, about half an hour away. I plan to rent it this weekend, picking it up on Friday morning and returning it on Monday morning. I'm getting the device with the larger tank, which will still fit in my car, so I won't need a truck to transport it.

Are you interested in using the cleaner for part of the weekend? I'll be able to finish all of my rooms by late morning on Saturday. Then you could use it for the rest of the weekend and we could share the costs and spend less. I appreciate that this is short notice, so it's no problem if that doesn't work for you. Please let me know what you think. I'd like to book and pay for it online by the end of tomorrow.

Talk to you soon,

Isabelle

176. What does the web page suggest about Spark Rentals?

(A) It used to deliver equipment to customers.
(B) It provides a discount to businesses.
(C) It can acquire new equipment by special request.
(D) It sells some of its equipment after use.

177. What is the purpose of Ms. Guthrie's e-mail?

(A) To change the date of a project
(B) To recommend some cleaning products
(C) To suggest a money-saving opportunity
(D) To invite Mr. Soltis for a visit

178. In the e-mail, the word "appreciate" in paragraph 2, line 3, is closest in meaning to

(A) assess
(B) understand
(C) thank
(D) enjoy

179. What is suggested about Ms. Guthrie in the e-mail?

(A) She will go to Ancaster on a weekday.
(B) She cleans her carpets annually.
(C) She owns a truck.
(D) She has used Spark Rentals before.

180. How much will Ms. Guthrie most likely pay on the Spark Rentals website?

(A) £29.99
(B) £39.99
(C) £65.99
(D) £85.99

Questions 181-185 refer to the following article and job posting.

Beamont Laboratories to Expand Research and Development

BRISBANE (3 August)—Beamont Laboratories, a company that specializes in creating cosmetic products for international brands, is expanding its R&D staff to cater to clients seeking haircare products. Beamont Laboratories, headquartered in Brisbane and founded 18 years ago, has been a leader in innovation as well as environmental responsibility. This has led to steady growth, especially over the past five years. The expansion will be at the Canberra-based laboratory. There are also smaller sites in Melbourne and Newcastle.

The new team will be led by Gemma Gabriel, who has been with the business since the beginning, starting as a junior researcher and working her way up. She was in charge of the development of the popular product Ordell, a shampoo specially designed for those with sensitive skin. Ms. Gabriel will oversee the hiring process from start to finish.

Beamont Laboratories Job Opening
Title: Senior Cosmetic Scientist
Posted: 10 August
Application Deadline: 15 September

Become an integral part of our expanding R&D team.

KEY DUTIES:
- Designing product development schedules for various projects
- Developing, analyzing, and testing samples
- Keeping informed of advancements in laboratory techniques
- Sourcing all relevant equipment and materials for laboratory use
- Producing accurate cost estimates for future production

A degree in chemistry or similar is required (master's level preferred). Interviews will be held from 20 October to 1 November. The start date is 22 November.

181. What is indicated about Ms. Gabriel?
    (A) She plans to relocate to Brisbane for work.
    (B) She was promoted to her position five years ago.
    (C) She has worked for Beamont Laboratories for 18 years.
    (D) She will retire from Beamont Laboratories soon.

182. What is mentioned about Ordell?
    (A) It is the company's best-seller.
    (B) It is made from natural ingredients.
    (C) It can be used as a skin lotion.
    (D) It is a type of haircare product.

183. Where will the new senior cosmetic scientist most likely work?
    (A) In Brisbane
    (B) In Canberra
    (C) In Newcastle
    (D) In Melbourne

184. When will the successful candidate probably be selected?
    (A) In August
    (B) In September
    (C) In October
    (D) In November

185. What is one job responsibility of the position?
    (A) Procuring necessary supplies
    (B) Teaching techniques to team members
    (C) Inspecting production facilities
    (D) Meeting with prospective customers

Questions 186-190 refer to the following e-mails and schedule.

To:	All Community Arts Center Members
From:	Community Arts Center
Subject:	Summer Art Lecture Series
Date:	June 10
Attachment:	Summer_art_lecture_series

Dear Community Arts Center Members:

The Summer Art Lecture Series is nearly here! Please check out the attached schedule. All of our lecturers are new this year except for the one who gave a talk on the digital age of art, which we're bringing back due to high demand.

Order your tickets at www.commartscenter.org. Please note that we only accept group bookings (5 people or more) for events in our largest venues—the Rivas Room, with space for 150 people, and the Mercier Room, which accommodates 90 people.

Community Arts Center
Summer Art Lecture Series

Lecture Title	Lecturer	Date and Time	Location
Light and Watercolor	Annie Cho	June 29, 7-9 P.M.	Chester Room
Eco-Friendly Supplies	Samuel Delgado	July 2, 1-3 P.M.	Barron Room
The Digital Age of Art	Bianca Fallici	July 8, 3-5 P.M.	Rivas Room
Art in Architecture	Hugo Beckham	July 25, 3-4 P.M.	Chester Room
The Undiscovered History of Art	Hai Feng	July 31, 6-8 P.M.	Mercier Room
Mixed Media Creations	Yolanda Florez	August 4, 7-8 P.M.	Rivas Room

E-Mail

TO: Gerard McCray <gerardmccray@commartscenter.org>
FROM: Hai Feng <hfeng@hollowayinstitute.com>
DATE: August 5
SUBJECT: Thank you!

Dear Mr. McCray,

I wanted to thank you for inviting me to give a lecture for the Summer Art Lecture Series. I had a great experience, and I hope to participate again in the future. I was impressed with the venue for the event. Even though the room seemed rather empty, that was because it was such a large space. Actually, the number of attendees was much more than I expected, so I was very happy about that.

In addition, I was especially grateful to Tony Sheridan, who promptly responded to my request for technical assistance at the start of my talk and resolved the issue quickly. Fortunately, this meant that we only had to start 15 minutes late instead of having to cancel the talk.

Warmest regards,

Hai Feng

186. Which room can accommodate over 100 people?
    (A) The Barron Room
    (B) The Chester Room
    (C) The Mercier Room
    (D) The Rivas Room

187. Who has given a lecture at the event before?
    (A) Ms. Cho
    (B) Mr. Delgado
    (C) Ms. Fallici
    (D) Mr. Beckham

188. Who most likely is Mr. Sheridan?
    (A) A technician
    (B) An event planner
    (C) A researcher
    (D) A venue owner

189. Which lecture had a delayed start time?
    (A) Eco-Friendly Supplies
    (B) Art in Architecture
    (C) The Undiscovered History of Art
    (D) Mixed Media Creations

190. What is suggested about Mr. Feng?
    (A) He used to work with Mr. McCray.
    (B) He was pleased with the turnout.
    (C) He wished he had a larger room.
    (D) He traveled to attend the event.

Questions 191-195 refer to the following web page and e-mails.

http://www.treecarefoundation.org

The Tree Care Foundation (TCF) is dedicated to ensuring the health of trees in woodland areas. Our volunteers play an essential role in identifying tree diseases and pests and determining how and where they are expanding in the areas they affect. This helps us take measures to control outbreaks and reduce the loss of trees.

About Volunteering:
- Apply by completing an application form online and having brief phone interview
- Attend a training session to learn the skills you will need
- Commit to a minimum of 12 months of volunteer work at the TCF, conducting 2–3 survey sessions per month

---

TO:	Aida Ferreira, Kevin Murray, Sharad Dhibar, Ruth Bryson
FROM:	Ashley Jackson <jacksona@treecarefoundation.org>
DATE:	March 5
SUBJECT:	Training session

Dear Volunteers,

We're excited that you are joining our efforts at the Tree Care Foundation (TCF). Thanks to volunteers like you, we have been able to grow our charity considerably since Curtis Baxter founded it seven years ago.

The next step in the process is to complete an intensive training session. This is scheduled for Saturday, March 20, from 9 A.M. to 4 P.M. It will take place at the Aldredge Nature Center, and lunch will be provided. Mr. Baxter will be in charge of the session.

After the initial training, you will have one supervised survey session the following week with an experienced member, as below.

Name	Assigned Area
Aida Ferreira	Wesley Woodlands
Kevin Murray	Barnbrook Forest
Sharad Dhibar	Malham Forest
Ruth Bryson	Denton National Reserve

Please let me know if you have any questions,

Ashley Jackson

To:	Stanley Walton <s_walton@victoriamail.com>
From:	Ruth Bryson <ruth.bryson@gilbert-enterprises.com>
Date:	March 23
Subject:	Supervised survey

Dear Mr. Walton,

I'm looking forward to meeting you in person for my supervised survey session this Friday. I appreciate your adjusting your original start time to accommodate my work schedule. I plan to drive to the site, so I will meet you there at 2 P.M.

I will bring all of the gear that was distributed at the initial training session. However, I'm wondering if I have to wrap it up to protect it in some way. I'm just using a regular backpack, and I don't want to break any of the fragile components. Please let me know if there is anything special that I need to do.

Thank you,

Ruth Bryson

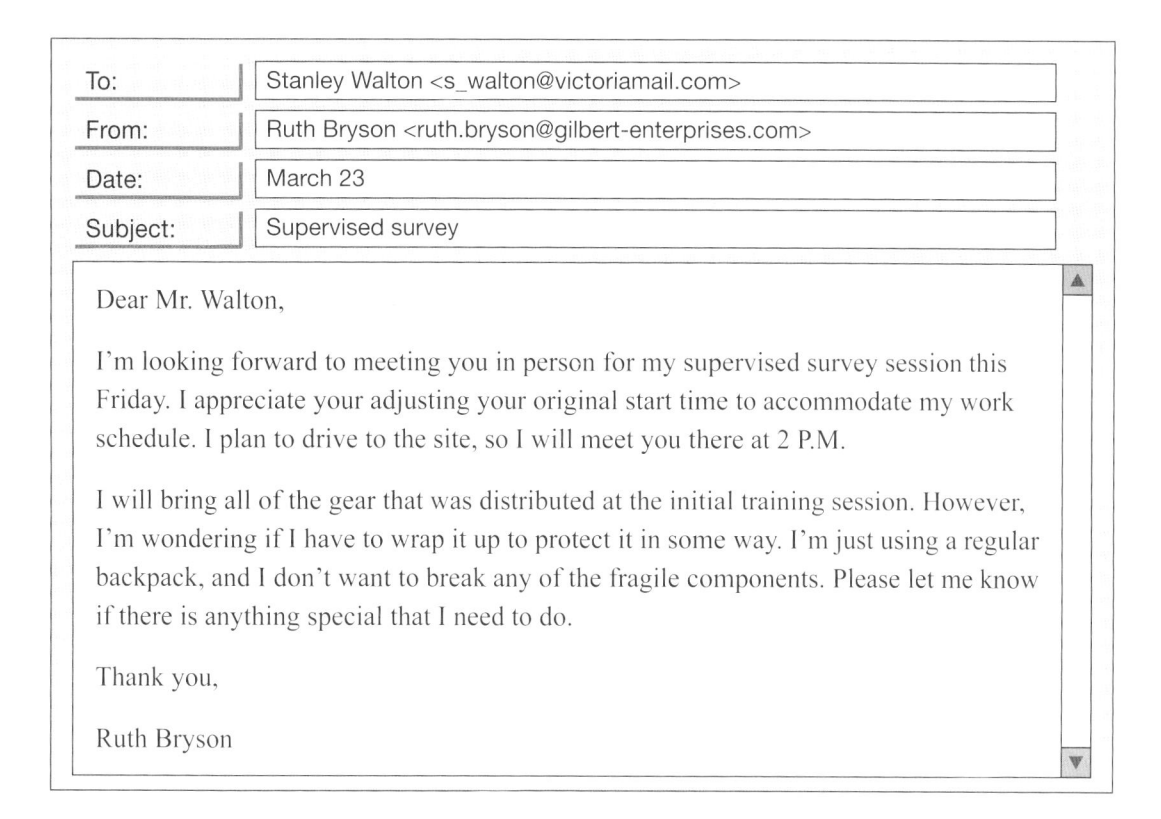

191. What is the main duty of TCF volunteers?

(A) Raising funds for tree projects
(B) Planting trees in woodland areas
(C) Tracking the spread of tree diseases
(D) Clearing away tree branches

192. What is suggested about the recipients of the first e-mail?

(A) They attended a group interview.
(B) They will work for TCF for at least one year.
(C) They will complete two to three surveys each week.
(D) They can choose the location where they work.

193. What is indicated about the training session on March 20?

(A) It was led by the charity's founder.
(B) It lasted for approximately three hours.
(C) It was conducted in several locations.
(D) It started in the afternoon.

194. Where will Mr. Walton most likely conduct a survey?

(A) At Wesley Woodlands
(B) At Barnbrook Forest
(C) At Malham Forest
(D) At Denton National Reserve

195. In the second e-mail, what does Ms. Bryson express concern about?

(A) Damaging some equipment
(B) Having parking difficulties
(C) Finding a remote location
(D) Purchasing the right gear

Questions 196-200 refer to the following e-mails and web page.

To:	Jeanette Patterson <jpatterson@charterhotel.com>
From:	Mason Emery <mason@emeryltd.com>
Date:	April 19
Subject:	Sprinkler system

Dear Ms. Patterson,

I'm more than happy to recommend a sprinkler system and installation company for your hotel. But to best meet your needs, I'll need you to answer the following questions:

1. *Will the system be for grass only or for flower beds as well?*

2. *Does the area get a lot of foot traffic?* Permanent sprinklers that don't pop up are less expensive, but they pose a trip hazard.

3. *Are there any building projects planned on your property in the next few years?*

4. *How soon do you need the system in place?* Summer is the busiest time of year as systems cannot be installed once the ground has frozen.

5. *Can the company work on a weekday while your business is open?* Some of the digging equipment can be disruptive. However, weekend work is in high demand.

Thank you in advance for providing this additional information.

Mason Emery

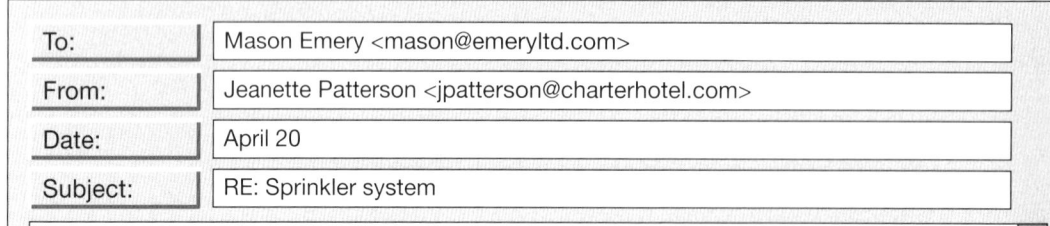

To:	Mason Emery <mason@emeryltd.com>
From:	Jeanette Patterson <jpatterson@charterhotel.com>
Date:	April 20
Subject:	RE: Sprinkler system

Dear Mr. Emery,

The grounds at the Bridgeview branch of Charter Hotel are completely fenced in. While we have a few raised flower beds, we want the system for our grassy area. We have a paved patio, so most guests spend their outdoor time there. Dogs often run around on the grass, but very few human guests utilize it.

The work crew can visit any day of the week, as we cannot shut down. Please note that we are willing to pay more for a high-quality system, and we want a company that has been in business for a long time.

Thank you for your assistance,

Jeanette Patterson

http://www.sprinklerexperts.com/bridgeview

Our website users have voted for the best installers of sprinkler systems in each region. You can find the results for Bridgeview below.

Company Name	Area of Specialization	Notes
Irrigation Solutions	Outdoor sprinklers	Newly opened; fast results
Lawn Doctors	Outdoor sprinklers	Opened last year; lowest prices
Tyler Landscaping	All categories	Operating locally for two decades
Waterworks Sprinklers	Indoor fire safety	Twenty-five years of experience; reasonably priced

196. Where does Mr. Emery most likely work?
    (A) At a manufacturing facility
    (B) At a consulting firm
    (C) At a property development company
    (D) At a marketing firm

197. What does Mr. Emery suggest about sprinkler systems?
    (A) They should be inspected by a professional regularly.
    (B) They must be installed when the ground is warm enough.
    (C) They can be hooked up to the city's water supply.
    (D) They will save the user money in the long run.

198. Which of Mr. Emery's questions is not addressed by Ms. Patterson?
    (A) Question 1
    (B) Question 2
    (C) Question 3
    (D) Question 5

199. According to the second e-mail, what is probably true about Charter Hotel?
    (A) It has recently opened a branch in Bridgeview.
    (B) It is closed for part of the year.
    (C) It allows pets on site.
    (D) It is located near a busy road.

200. Which company will Mr. Emery likely recommend?
    (A) Irrigation Solutions
    (B) Lawn Doctors
    (C) Tyler Landscaping
    (D) Waterworks Sprinklers

Stop! This is the end of the test. If you finish before time is called, you may go back to Parts 5, 6, and 7 and check your work.

ANSWER SHEET
ACTUAL TEST

ANSWER SHEET
ACTUAL TEST

ENERGY

生命的每個瞬間,
都該是美好的結束,
亦是嶄新的開始。

──法頂禪師

EZ TALK

New TOEIC 一本攻克新制多益聽力＋閱讀700+：
完全比照最新考題趨勢精準命題

作　　　者	：Eduwill語學研究所
譯　　　者	：關亭薇
主　　　編	：潘亭軒
責任編輯	：鄭雅方
封面設計	：兒日設計
內頁排版	：簡單瑛設
行銷企劃	：張爾芸

發　行　人	：洪祺祥
副總經理	：洪偉傑
副總編輯	：曹仲堯
法律顧問	：建大法律事務所
財務顧問	：高威會計師事務所

出　　　版	：日月文化出版股份有限公司
製　　　作	：EZ叢書館
地　　　址	：臺北市信義路三段151號8樓
電　　　話	：(02)2708-5509
傳　　　真	：(02)2708-6157
網　　　址	：www.heliopolis.com.tw
郵撥帳號	：19716071日月文化出版股份有限公司

總　經　銷	：聯合發行股份有限公司
電　　　話	：(02)2917-8022
傳　　　真	：(02)2915-7212
印　　　刷	：中原造像股份有限公司
初　　　版	：2024年11月
定　　　價	：520元
ＩＳＢＮ	：978-626-7516-46-1

New TOEIC 一本攻克新制多益聽力＋閱讀700+：完全比照最新考題趨勢精準命題／Eduwill語學研究所著；關亭薇譯. -- 初版. -- 臺北市：日月文化出版股份有限公司, 2024.11
360面；　19x25.7公分. -- (EZ talk)
ISBN 978-626-7516-46-1(平裝)
1.CST: 多益測驗

Copyright © 2023 by Eduwill Language Institute
All rights reserved.
Traditional Chinese Copyright © 2024 by HELIOPOLIS CULTURE GROUP
This Traditional Chinese edition was published by arrangement with Eduwill through Agency Liang

◎版權所有 翻印必究
◎本書如有缺頁、破損、裝訂錯誤，請寄回本公司更換

NEW TOEIC
一本攻克新制多益
聽力 + 閱讀
700+
解析本

**完全比照
最新考題趨勢精準命題**

不容錯過的多益應考攻略，透過短期密集訓練，培養高效解題思維，
一網打盡聽力閱讀 Part 1~Part 7 所有題型！

Eduwill語學研究所——著　關亭薇——譯

LC PART 1

UNIT 01　人物照片

PRACTICE
題本 p.25

1. (D)　**2.** (A)　**3.** (C)　**4.** (B)　**5.** (C)　**6.** (D)

1. 🎧 美國男子

(A) He's leaning against a fence.
(B) He's putting away a rake.
(C) He's picking some flowers.
(D) He's holding a gardening tool.

中譯
(A) 他正靠在圍欄上。
(B) 他正在收拾耙子。
(C) 他正在摘花。
(D) 他正拿著園藝工具。

單字　lean against 倚靠著⋯　put away 收拾
pick 摘（花、水果等）　gardening 園藝工具　tool 工具

2. 🎧 美國女子

(A) Products are displayed on shelves.
(B) A large basket is being used to carry goods.
(C) Customers are entering a shop.
(D) Display racks are being assembled.

中譯
(A) 商品陳列在貨架上。
(B) 大籃子被用來搬運商品。
(C) 客人正在進入商店。
(D) 展示架正在被組裝。

單字　display 陳列、展示　carry 搬運　enter 進入
rack 貨架、置物架　assemble 組裝

3. 🎧 美國男子

(A) They're pushing bicycles along a path.
(B) They're taking off their bicycle helmets.
(C) One of the people is riding a bicycle.
(D) One of the people is opening a bicycle lock.

中譯
(A) 他們沿著道路推著自行車。
(B) 他們正摘下自行車安全帽。
(C) 其中一人正在騎自行車。
(D) 其中一人正在打開自行車鎖。

單字　path 道路　take off 摘下、脫下　lock 鎖、鎖住

4. 🎧 美國女子

(A) The people are walking up some stairs.
(B) The people are leaving a building.
(C) The man is repairing a walkway.
(D) The woman is turning on a machine.

中譯
(A) 人們正在上樓梯。
(B) 人們正在走出大樓。
(C) 男子正在修理人行道。
(D) 女子正在啟動機器。

單字　leave 走出、離開　repair 修理　walkway 人行道、通道
turn on 打開（廣播、電視、電器等）

5. 🎧 澳洲男子

(A) He's driving a vehicle.
(B) He's closing a car door.
(C) He's examining a tire.
(D) He's looking for a parking spot.

中譯
(A) 他在開車。
(B) 他在關車門。
(C) 他在檢查輪胎。
(D) 他在找停車位。

單字 vehicle 車、車輛　examine 檢查　parking spot 停車位

6. 🎧 英國女子

(A) Some workers are carrying a ladder.
(B) Some workers are putting on hard hats.
(C) A wall is being painted.
(D) A roof is under construction.

中譯
(A) 一些工人正在拿著梯子。
(B) 一些工人正在戴上安全帽。
(C) 一面牆正在被粉刷。
(D) 屋頂正在施工中。

單字 ladder 梯子　put on 穿上、戴上　hard hat 安全帽　roof 屋頂　under construction 施工中

UNIT 02　事物照與風景照

PRACTICE
題本 p.27

1. (B)　2. (C)　3. (D)　4. (A)　5. (A)　6. (C)

1. 🎧 美國男子

(A) Several metal jugs are lying on their sides.
(B) Some containers have been placed on a platform.
(C) Lids have been fastened to some bottles.
(D) A wooden frame is covered in flowers.

中譯
(A) 幾個金屬罐側放著。
(B) 一些容器被放置在平台上。
(C) 一些瓶子被蓋上蓋子。
(D) 木製框架上覆蓋著花朵。

單字 metal 金屬　jug 瓶罐、壺　container 容器　be placed on 被放在…　platform 平台　lid 蓋子　fasten 固定、繫牢　wooden frame 木製框　be covered in 被覆蓋

2. 🎧 美國女子

(A) A fence is being repaired.
(B) Some umbrellas are shading a balcony.
(C) A picnic area has been set up outdoors.
(D) Diners are seated at some tables.

中譯
(A) 圍欄正在被修繕。
(B) 陽台上有幾把傘在遮陽。
(C) 戶外設有一個野餐區。
(D) 用餐者坐在幾張桌子旁。

單字 fence 圍欄　shade 遮蔽　set up 擺設、設置　diner 用餐的人

3. 🎧 美國男子

(A) Wooden furniture is being polished.
(B) A tool belt is hanging on a hook.
(C) Some hammers are scattered across a work area.
(D) Some tools have been left on a table.

中譯
(A) 木製家具正在被擦亮。
(B) 工具帶掛在掛鉤上。
(C) 幾把鐵鎚散落在工作區。
(D) 一些工具被放在桌上。

單字 polish 擦亮、拋光　hang 懸掛、吊　hammer 鐵鎚　be scattered 被散落

3

4. 🎧 美國女子

(A) **Merchandise is on display at an outdoor market.**
(B) A vendor is packing goods into shopping bags.
(C) Customers are waiting in a line.
(D) Some tents are being taken down.

中譯
(A) 商品陳列在露天市場上。
(B) 商人正在把商品裝進購物袋裡。
(C) 客人正在排隊等候。
(D) 一些帳篷正在被拆除。

單字 merchandise 商品　on display 陳列、展示　outdoor 戶外的　vendor 商人、賣家　pack 裝、包裝　wait in line 排隊　take down 拆除、拿下

5. 🎧 澳洲男子

(A) **There are some mountains in the distance.**
(B) People are relaxing under the trees.
(C) Some tree branches are being trimmed.
(D) A bench has been placed alongside a beach.

中譯
(A) 遠方有幾座山。
(B) 人們在樹下休息。
(C) 一些樹枝正在被修剪。
(D) 海灘旁放了一張長椅。

單字 in the distance 遠方　relax 放鬆　trim 修剪　alongside 旁邊、並肩

6. 🎧 英國女子

(A) A table has been set with dishes.
(B) Light fixtures are suspended above a fireplace.
(C) **A clock is mounted on a wall between some doors.**
(D) Chairs are stacked in a corner.

中譯
(A) 桌上擺放了盤子。
(B) 燈具懸掛在壁爐上方。
(C) 時鐘掛在門之間的牆壁上。
(D) 椅子堆放在角落。

單字 light fixture 燈具　suspend 懸掛、懸吊　be mounted on 安裝、固定　be stacked 被堆放　in a corner 在角落

PRACTICE
題本 p.29

1. (A)　**2.** (B)　**3.** (D)　**4.** (D)　**5.** (C)　**6.** (A)

1. 🎧 美國男子

(A) **Some people are wearing helmets.**
(B) Some people are getting into a vehicle.
(C) Some people are putting on safety vests.
(D) Some people are printing a document.

中譯
(A) 有些人戴著安全帽。
(B) 有些人正在上車。
(C) 有些人正在穿上安全背心。
(D) 有些人正在印文件。

單字 get into 上（車）　safety vest 安全背心　document 文件

2. 🎧 美國女子

(A) A lamp is being moved.
(B) **Artwork is hanging above a piece of furniture.**
(C) Some flowers have been planted in a garden.
(D) Some chairs are being occupied.

中譯

(A) 一盞燈正被移動。
(B) 藝術品掛在一件傢俱上方。
(C) 花園裡種了一些花。
(D) 一些椅子正被佔用。

單字 artwork 藝術品、插畫　plant 種植、植物
occupied 使用中的、佔據的

3. 🎧 美國男子

(A) A man is reaching into a toolbox.
(B) A man is pulling weeds from the ground.
(C) A paintbrush is propped against a building.
(D) A brick wall is being painted.

中譯

(A) 一名男子正把手伸進工具箱中。
(B) 一名男子正在拔地上的雜草。
(C) 油漆刷靠在建築物上。
(D) 一面磚牆正被粉刷。

單字 reach into 伸進　toolbox 工具箱　pull 拔、拉　weed 雜草　be propped against 靠著　brick wall 磚牆

4. 🎧 美國女子

(A) A tree is blocking a building.
(B) A car has stopped at a busy intersection.
(C) Items are being unloaded from a truck.
(D) Bicycles are parked under some tree branches.

中譯

(A) 一棵樹擋住了建築物。
(B) 一輛汽車停在繁忙的十字路口。
(C) 貨物正從卡車上被卸下來。
(D) 自行車停在一些樹枝下。

單字 block 擋住（道路、出口、視野等）
intersection 十字路口　unload 卸下　tree branch 樹枝

5. 🎧 澳洲男子

(A) The boat is passing under a bridge.
(B) Some people are tying a boat to a pier.
(C) Some people are taking a ride on a boat.
(D) The boat is being loaded with cargo.

中譯

(A) 船正從橋下駛過。
(B) 有些人正在把船拴在碼頭上。
(C) 有些人正在乘船。
(D) 船上裝載著貨物。

單字 tie 綁、拴　pier 碼頭　take a ride 乘坐　load 裝載
cargo 貨物

6. 🎧 英國女子

(A) A cushion is being arranged on a sofa.
(B) Some shelves are being stocked.
(C) Some potted plants are being watered.
(D) A window is being opened.

中譯

(A) 正在沙發上擺墊子。
(B) 正在一些貨架上進貨。
(C) 正在為一些盆栽植物澆水。
(D) 正在打開窗戶。

單字 stock 進貨、庫存　potted plant 盆栽　water 澆水

PART TEST　題本 p.30

1. (D)　2. (C)　3. (B)　4. (A)　5. (C)　6. (A)

1. 🎧 美國男子

(A) He's planting some flowers.
(B) He's putting on his gloves.
(C) He's pouring himself a drink.
(D) He's lifting a watering can.

中譯
(A) 他正在種一些花。
(B) 他正在戴手套。
(C) 他正在為自己倒飲料。
(D) 他正在舉起澆水壺。

單字 pour 倒、注入　lift 舉起、抬起　watering can 澆水壺

2. 🎧 美國女子

(A) She's pushing a shopping cart.
(B) She's waiting in a checkout line.
(C) She's holding a refrigerator door open.
(D) She's chopping some vegetables.

中譯
(A) 她正在推著購物車。
(B) 她正在排隊結帳。
(C) 她正在開著冰箱門。
(D) 她正在切一些蔬菜。

單字 checkout 收銀台　chop 切、剁碎

3. 🎧 英國女子

(A) Some of the men are shaking hands.
(B) Some of the men are wearing ties.
(C) The men are folding a document.
(D) The men are greeting one another.

中譯
(A) 有些男子正在握手。
(B) 有些男子繫著領帶。
(C) 男子們正在對折文件。
(D) 男子們正在互相打招呼。

單字 shake hands 握手　fold 折疊、對折
greet 打招呼、歡迎

4. 🎧 澳洲男子

(A) Some boats are docked in a row.
(B) A ship is passing under a bridge.
(C) Some boats are filled with passengers.
(D) Some people are diving off a pier.

中譯
(A) 有些船停泊成一列。
(B) 一艘船正從橋下駛過。
(C) 有些船載滿了乘客。
(D) 有些人正在碼頭跳水。

單字 dock 停泊　in a row 排成一列　be filled with 充滿
pier 碼頭

5. 🎧 美國男子

(A) They're cleaning off a countertop.
(B) They're fixing a coffee maker.
(C) One of the women is preparing a beverage.
(D) One of the women is arranging some baked goods.

中譯
(A) 他們正在清理檯面。
(B) 他們正在修理咖啡機。
(C) 其中一名女子正在準備飲料。
(D) 其中一名女子正在準備烘焙食品。

單字 countertop 檯面　beverage 飲料　baked goods 烘焙食品

6. 🎧 澳洲男子

(A) An outdoor area has been set up for dining.
(B) Some chairs have been arranged in a living room.
(C) A railing is being installed near some stairs.
(D) Some potted plants have been hung from a balcony.

中譯
(A) 已設置好戶外用餐區。
(B) 客廳裡擺放了一些椅子。
(C) 有些樓梯附近正在安裝欄杆。
(D) 陽台上掛著一些盆栽。

單字 set up 設置、設立　dining 用餐　railing 欄杆　install 安裝　hang 懸掛、吊著

LC PART 2

UNIT 03 Who, What, Which 問句

題本 p.38

1. (C)　**2.** (B)　**3.** (B)　**4.** (A)　**5.** (A)　**6.** (C)

1. 🎧 美國男子／美國女子

Who's creating the menu tomorrow?
(A) Twenty items for the event.
(B) Tomorrow at 3 o'clock.
(C) The new chef.

中譯
明天由誰來掌廚？
(A) 活動的二十個項目。
(B) 明天3點。
(C) 新廚師。

單字 create 製作、創作

2. 🎧 美國男子／美國女子

Who needs proof of my license renewal?
(A) No, I need to renew my membership.
(B) Angela does.
(C) You can park behind the building.

中譯
誰需要我的執照更新證明？
(A) 不,我需要更新我的會員資格。
(B) Angela需要。
(C) 你可以把車停在大樓後方。

單字 proof 證明　license 執照、許可　renewal 更新、更換

3. 🎧 美國男子／英國女子

Who's looking into the candidates' backgrounds?
(A) It's an impressive example.
(B) We don't know yet.
(C) In Conference Room 1.

中譯
誰在調查候選人的背景？
(A) 這是個令人印象深刻的例子。
(B) 我們還不清楚。
(C) 在第1會議室。

單字 look into 調查　candidate 候選人、申請人
background 背景　impressive 令人印象深刻的

4. 🎧 澳洲男子／美國女子

Who's going to inspect the apartment unit before move-in?
(A) The property manager.
(B) It's a popular residential building.
(C) Thanks, that would be great.

中譯
誰會在入住前檢查公寓？
(A) 物業經理
(B) 這是棟受歡迎的住宅大樓。
(C) 謝謝,那太好了。

單字 inspect 檢查、視察　property manager 物業經理
residential 住宅的

5. 🎧 澳洲男子／英國女子

Who transported the prototypes?
(A) A company in Seattle.
(B) You should finish this report.
(C) Yes, we built them in the lab.

中譯
誰運送了原型樣機？
(A) 西雅圖的一家公司。
(B) 你應該要完成這份報告。
(C) 是的,我們在實驗室裡製作的。

單字 transport 運送、輸送　lab(= laboratory) 實驗室

6. 🎧 澳洲男子／英國女子

Who's responsible for the budget report?
(A) They reported the news.
(B) Did you send a response?
(C) Andrew, I believe.

中譯
誰負責這份預算報告？
(A) 他們報導了這則新聞。
(B) 你回信了嗎？
(C) 據我所知是Andrew。

單字 be responsible for 對…負責　budget 預算
report 報告、報導　response 回信、答覆

② What, Which 問句

題本 p.39

1. (A)　**2.** (C)　**3.** (A)　**4.** (B)　**5.** (B)　**6.** (C)

8

1. 🎧 美國女子／美國男子

> Which post office is closest to your home?
> **(A) The one on Danvers Avenue.**
> (B) Yes, that's my neighborhood.
> (C) We don't open until ten.

哪間郵局離你家最近？
(A) Danvers大道的那間。
(B) 對，那是我的社區。
(C) 我們十點才開門。

單字 neighborhood 住宅區、街區、社區

2. 🎧 美國女子／美國男子

> What did Gregory say about the sales pitch?
> (A) A pitcher of water, please.
> (B) Right, I read something about it.
> **(C) He said he liked it a lot.**

Gregory對銷售演說有什麼看法？
(A) 請給我一壺水。
(B) 沒錯，我讀過一些相關內容。
(C) 他說他非常喜歡。

單字 sales pitch 說服他人購買的銷售演說　pitcher 壺、罐

3. 🎧 美國女子／澳洲男子

> What flight do you prefer for our upcoming trip?
> **(A) The later we depart, the better.**
> (B) I'm excited about meeting the clients.
> (C) No, it was less than one hundred dollars.

對於我們即將到來的旅程，你偏好哪個航班？
(A) 我們越晚出發越好。
(B) 我很高興能見到客戶。
(C) 不，不到一百美元。

單字 prefer 更喜歡、偏好　depart 出發
be excited about 對⋯感到興奮、高興　client 客戶
less than 少於⋯

4. 🎧 英國女子／美國男子

> What time does your train leave?
> (A) No additional stops.
> **(B) At one in the afternoon.**
> (C) That's a popular route.

你的火車幾點出發？
(A) 沒有額外的停靠站。
(B) 下午一點。
(C) 這是條受歡迎的路線。

單字 additional 額外的　stop 停靠站、車站
route 路線、路徑

5. 🎧 英國女子／澳洲男子

> What kind of cell phone package do you need?
> (A) That's too expensive.
> **(B) A standard plan.**
> (C) Here's my phone number.

你需要什麼樣的手機方案？
(A) 這太貴了。
(B) 標準方案
(C) 這是我的電話號碼。

單字 standard 標準的、一般的

6. 🎧 英國女子／澳洲男子

> Which car did Mr. Hobson drive to work?
> (A) An auto mechanic.
> (B) Turn off the engine, please.
> **(C) The black one in the first row.**

Hobson先生開了哪輛車去上班？
(A) 一位汽車維修技師。
(B) 請關掉引擎。
(C) 第一排黑色那輛。

單字 auto mechanic 汽車維修技師　row 排、列

UNIT 04　When, Where 問句

① When 問句

PRACTICE　題本 p.40

1. (B)　**2.** (C)　**3.** (A)　**4.** (C)　**5.** (A)　**6.** (B)

1. 🎧 美國男子／美國女子

> When do you move into your apartment downtown?
> (A) Yeah, occasionally.
> **(B) I found a better place.**
> (C) That's great.

中譯

你什麼時候搬進市中心的公寓？
(A) 是，偶爾會。
(B) 我找到一個更好的地方。
(C) 太好了。

單字 downtown 市中心　occasionally 偶爾

2. 🎧 美國男子／美國女子

> When will the board members meet?
> (A) The board decided to hire him.
> (B) Did you attend the track meet?
> **(C) It's scheduled for Thursday.**

中譯
董事會成員何時要開會？
(A) 董事會決定僱用他。
(B) 你參加田徑比賽了嗎？
(C) 預定於星期四。

單字 board member 董事會成員、高層
board 董事會、委員會　hire 僱用　attend 參加
track meet 田徑比賽

3. 🎧美國男子／英國女子

When did you visit the new office location?
(A) About two weeks ago.
(B) Yes, I've worked here a long time.
(C) They're transferring to the London branch.

中譯
你何時參觀了新辦公室地點？
(A) 大約兩週前
(B) 對，我在這裡工作了很長一段時間。
(C) 他們要調到倫敦分公司去。

單字 location 地點、地方　transfer 調職、調動
branch 分公司

4. 🎧澳洲男子／美國女子

When can you inform me about your days off?
(A) It was around 5:30.
(B) You should use black ink for the form.
(C) As soon as I check with my manager.

中譯
你何時能告訴我你的休假日期？
(A) 當時是五點半左右。
(B) 你應該用黑色墨水填寫表格。
(C) 待我跟經理確認完。

單字 inform 告知　form 表格、形式

5. 🎧澳洲男子／英國女子

When can we meet to discuss the proposed cover designs?
(A) I have a big deadline today.
(B) In the employee lounge.
(C) Fortunately, the company covers the cost.

中譯
我們何時能見面討論提議的封面設計？
(A) 我今天有個重要的截止日。
(B) 在員工休息室。
(C) 幸好公司承擔了費用。

單字 proposed 提議的　cover 封面、承擔
deadline 截止日

6. 🎧澳洲男子／英國女子

When will the hallway carpet be installed?
(A) It's very tall.
(B) Tomorrow afternoon.
(C) We're glad you're here.

中譯
何時要鋪設走廊地毯？
(A) 它非常高。
(B) 明天下午。
(C) 很高興你能來。

單字 hallway 走廊　install 安裝　tall 高、高大

② Where 問句

PRACTICE　題本 p.41

1. (A)　2. (B)　3. (C)　4. (B)　5. (C)　6. (A)

1. 🎧美國女子／美國男子

Where did he buy that leather jacket?
(A) At a shop in the Glendale Mall.
(B) They'll add a customized lining.
(C) A range of outerwear.

中譯
他在哪裡買到那件皮夾克？
(A) 在Glendale購物中心的一家商店。
(B) 他們會添加客製化的內襯。
(C) 一系列的外套。

單字 customized 客製化的　lining 內襯
a range of 多樣的　outerwear 外套、外衣

2. 🎧美國女子／美國男子

Where is the assistant editor's office?
(A) Yes, I have journalism experience.
(B) There's a floor plan right next to the elevators.
(C) The official release date.

中譯
助理編輯的辦公室在哪裡？
(A) 是的，我有新聞工作經驗。
(B) 電梯旁有樓層平面圖。
(C) 正式發行日。

單字 journalism 新聞工作、新聞業　floor plan 樓層平面圖
official 官方的、正式的　release 發行、公布

3. 🎧 美國女子／澳洲男子

> Where is Dr. Martinez?
> (A) Yes, that makes sense.
> (B) A new security badge.
> **(C) He should be in his office.**

中譯

Martinez醫生在哪裡？
(A) 是，這很有道理。
(B) 新的安全徽章。
(C) 他應該在他的辦公室。

單字 security 安全、保全

4. 🎧 英國女子／美國男子

> Where can I find the meeting agenda?
> (A) Several employees responded positively.
> **(B) Ms. McNeil still has to finalize it.**
> (C) Yes, that's what I heard.

中譯

哪裡可以找到會議議程？
(A) 多名員工積極回應。
(B) 仍需要McNeil女士做最終確認。
(C) 是的，那是我聽到的。

單字 agenda 議程　respond 回應　positively 積極地　finalize 最終確認

5. 🎧 英國女子／澳洲男子

> Where did these sofas come from?
> (A) The cushion colors can be changed.
> (B) Please take a seat.
> **(C) From a manufacturer in Germany.**

中譯

這些沙發是從哪裡來的？
(A) 靠墊顏色可以變更。
(B) 請坐。
(C) 來自德國的一家製造商。

單字 take a seat 坐下　manufacturer 製造商

6. 🎧 英國女子／澳洲男子

> Where should we leave our wet umbrellas?
> **(A) In the basket by the entrance.**
> (B) An easy-to-grip handle.
> (C) The weather forecast for today.

中譯

我們該把溼雨傘放在哪裡？
(A) 入口處的籃子裡。
(B) 手柄易於抓握。
(C) 今天的天氣預報。

單字 entrance 入口　easy-to-grip 易於抓握　weather forecast 天氣預報

UNIT 05　How, Why 問句

① How 問句

PRACTICE　　　　　　　　　題本 p.42

1. (C)　**2.** (A)　**3.** (B)　**4.** (C)　**5.** (A)　**6.** (B)

1. 🎧 美國男子／美國女子

> How much will it cost to get express delivery?
> (A) At a reliable courier.
> (B) No, they expressed interest.
> **(C) About twenty dollars.**

中譯

快遞寄送要多少錢？
(A) 透過可信賴的快遞公司。
(B) 不，他們表示有興趣。
(C) 約二十美元。

單字 express 快速的、表達、表現　reliable 可信賴的　courier 遞送員　interest 興趣

2. 🎧 美國男子／美國女子

> How many lunch boxes do we need for Saturday's hike?
> **(A) I'll bring my own food.**
> (B) The national park's open all summer.
> (C) Five and a half miles.

中譯

星期六的健行需要多少個午餐盒？
(A) 我會自備食物。
(B) 國家公園整個夏天都開放。
(C) 五英里半。

3. 🎧 美國男子／英國女子

> How did you like the dance festival?
> (A) There's a music stand.
> **(B) I'm going again tomorrow.**
> (C) That's what I did.

中譯

你覺得舞蹈節怎麼樣？
(A) 有個樂譜架。
(B) 明天我會再去。
(C) 我就是那麼做的。

單字 music stand 樂譜架

11

4. 🎧 澳洲男子／美國女子

> How long will your speech be?
> (A) A talk on economics.
> (B) In the conference center.
> **(C) About ninety minutes.**

中譯
你的演講時間多長？
(A) 經濟學講座。
(B) 在會議中心。
(C) 約九十分鐘。

單字 speech 演講　talk 講座、會談

5. 🎧 澳洲男子／英國女子

> How should we advertise our specialty cakes?
> **(A) By using social media sites.**
> (B) Sorry about the error.
> (C) Birthdays and anniversaries.

中譯
我們該如何宣傳我們的特色蛋糕？
(A) 透過社群媒體網站。
(B) 對於這個錯誤感到抱歉。
(C) 生日和週年紀念日。

單字 advertise 宣傳　specialty 特製品、名產
anniversary 週年紀念日

6. 🎧 澳洲男子／英國女子

> How often do you visit the headquarters?
> (A) Yes, I had a great time.
> **(B) About once a month.**
> (C) It has spacious offices.

中譯
你多久造訪一次總公司？
(A) 對，我玩得很開心。
(B) 約每個月一次。
(C) 擁有寬敞的辦公室。

單字 headquarters 總公司　spacious 寬敞的

② Why 問句

PRACTICE　題本 p.43

1. (A)　**2.** (C)　**3.** (C)　**4.** (B)　**5.** (A)　**6.** (B)

---

1. 🎧 美國女子／美國男子

> Why are you visiting the investors tomorrow?
> **(A) To demonstrate our new model.**
> (B) The Atlanta airport.
> (C) By 5 P.M.

中譯
明天你為什麼要拜訪投資者？
(A) 為了展示我們的新機型。
(B) 亞特蘭大機場。
(C) 下午五點前。

單字 investor 投資者　demonstrate 展示、示範

2. 🎧 美國女子／美國男子

> Why did the owner choose to hire a new cleaning company?
> (A) Mostly vacuuming and dusting.
> (B) Thanks, I worked really hard.
> **(C) Because we got a good rate.**

中譯
業主為何選擇僱用新的清潔公司？
(A) 主要是吸地和除塵。
(B) 謝謝，我真的很努力。
(C) 因為我們取得很好的價格。

單字 vacuuming 吸地　dusting 除塵　rate 費用、價格

3. 🎧 美國女子／澳洲男子

> Why is Mr. Bennett away from his desk?
> (A) No, on the second floor.
> (B) Yes, I'll give him the message.
> **(C) The IT team is away for training.**

中譯
Bennett先生為什麼不在他的辦公桌前？
(A) 不，在二樓。
(B) 對，我會轉達他。
(C) 資訊科技團隊外出接受訓練。

4. 🎧 英國女子／美國男子

> Why is there no furniture in this room?
> (A) No, it's a much bigger space.
> **(B) Because it's being replaced.**
> (C) An interior designer.

中譯
為什麼這間房間裡沒有傢俱？
(A) 不，這是一個更大的空間。
(B) 因為它正要被取代。
(C) 室內設計師。

單字 furniture 傢俱　space 空間　replace 替換、取代

5. 🎧 英國女子／澳洲男子

Why was the picnic canceled?
(A) Did you see the weather forecast?
(B) Please confirm your attendance.
(C) For a few days.

中譯
野餐為什麼被取消了？
(A) 你看到天氣預報了嗎？
(B) 請確認出席。
(C) 好幾天了。

單字 confirm 確認　attendance 出席

6. 🎧 英國女子／澳洲男子

Why have the commission payments not been made?
(A) Between ten and fifteen percent.
(B) Check with our manager.
(C) Yes, they accept credit cards.

中譯
為什麼還沒有支付佣金？
(A) 10%到15%之間。
(B) 請與我們的經理核對。
(C) 是的，他們接受信用卡。

單字 commission 佣金　payment 支付　accept 接受

UNIT 06 一般問句、表示建議或要求的問句

① 一般問句

PRACTICE　　　　　　　　　　　　題本 p.44

1. (B)　**2.** (A)　**3.** (B)　**4.** (C)　**5.** (C)　**6.** (A)

1. 🎧 美國男子／美國女子

Are you attending the awards ceremony?
(A) It departs at seven o'clock.
(B) No, I'll be on vacation that week.
(C) Thank you so much.

中譯
你會參加頒獎典禮嗎？
(A) 七點鐘出發。
(B) 不，那週我要去度假。
(C) 非常感謝。

單字 attend 參加　awards ceremony 頒獎典禮
depart 離開、出發　be on vacation 度假中

2. 🎧 美國男子／美國女子

Doesn't the pharmacy close at six on Saturdays?
(A) Yes, it does.
(B) Just basic medication.
(C) For this prescription, please.

中譯
星期六藥局不是六點關門嗎？
(A) 對，確實如此。
(B) 只是基本藥物。
(C) 請開給我這個處方箋。

單字 pharmacy 藥局　medication 藥物
prescription 處方箋

3. 🎧 美國男子／英國女子

Did you send out the party invitations?
(A) A larger venue.
(B) I'm waiting for the guest list.
(C) I thought it was.

中譯
你寄出派對邀請函了嗎？
(A) 更大的場地。
(B) 我正在等賓客名單。
(C) 我以為是那樣。

單字 invitation 邀請（函）　venue 場地

4. 🎧 澳洲男子／美國女子

Haven't you taken any language classes?
(A) Less than $100.
(B) Was your vacation overseas?
(C) I haven't had the chance.

中譯
你沒有上過任何語言課程嗎？
(A) 不到100美元。
(B) 你去國外度假了嗎？
(C) 我還沒有機會。

單字 overseas 在國外、海外

5. 🎧 澳洲男子／英國女子

Have the rugs in the lobby been cleaned?
(A) Next to the front office.
(B) Two leather couches.
(C) No, not yet.

中譯
大廳的地毯打掃乾淨了嗎？
(A) 在櫃檯旁邊。
(B) 兩張皮沙發。

13

(C) 不,還沒有。

單字 couch 沙發

6. 🎧 澳洲男子／英國女子

Will you join us for the team lunch?
(A) **Yes, I'd be glad to come along.**
(B) No, she's the newest staff member.
(C) The new Italian restaurant.

中譯
你願意和我們一起吃團隊午餐嗎?
(A) 好,我很樂意一起去。
(B) 不,她是最新進的員工。
(C) 新的義大利餐廳。

單字 come along 一起去、一起來

② 表達建議或要求的問句

PRACTICE 題本 p.45

1. (A)　2. (B)　3. (B)　4. (C)　5. (A)　6. (C)

1. 🎧 美國女子／美國男子

Could you please organize the supplies in the cabinet?
(A) **Sure, I have time now.**
(B) That surprised me, too.
(C) Our usual supplier, I think.

中譯
能麻煩你整理一下櫃子裡的用品嗎?
(A) 當然,我現在有空。
(B) 我也嚇了一跳。
(C) 我認為是我們平常往來的供應商。

單字 organize 整理　supplies 用品、供給　supplier 供應商

2. 🎧 美國女子／美國男子

Can you help me look over the candidates' résumés later today?
(A) The assistant manager position.
(B) **Sorry, I won't have time until tomorrow.**
(C) The salary is competitive.

中譯
今天稍晚你能幫我查看一下應徵者的履歷嗎?
(A) 副理的職位。
(B) 抱歉,我要到明天才有空。
(C) 薪資具有競爭力。

單字 look over 查看　candidate 應徵者　résumés 履歷
position 職位　salary 薪資　competitive 有競爭力的

3. 🎧 美國女子／澳洲男子

Why don't we go to the beach this weekend?
(A) Should we go home now or later?
(B) **I have some relatives visiting me.**
(C) Yes, the restaurant got great reviews.

中譯
我們這週末要不要來去海灘?
(A) 我們應該現在回家還是晚點?
(B) 有幾個親戚要來拜訪我。
(C) 是,餐廳獲得了好評。

單字 relative 親戚

4. 🎧 英國女子／美國男子

Would you mind turning up the heat?
(A) Benjamin turned down the offer.
(B) Yes, a coat and scarf.
(C) **Not at all.**

中譯
你介意把暖氣調強一點嗎?
(A) Benjamin拒絕了提議。
(B) 對,一件外套和圍巾。
(C) 一點也不(介意)。

單字 mind 介意、反對　turn up 調高(音量、溫度等)
heat 熱、溫度　turn down 拒絕　offer 提議

5. 🎧 英國女子／澳洲男子

Would you like to join me for a play on Friday?
(A) **Haven't you seen the work schedule?**
(B) That was an impressive performance.
(C) He plays basketball.

中譯
星期五要不要跟我一起去看話劇?
(A) 你沒看到工作時間表嗎?
(B) 這是場令人印象深刻的表演。
(C) 他在打籃球。

單字 impressive 令人印象深刻的　performance 表演

6. 🎧 英國女子／澳洲男子

Can I show you our dessert menu?
(A) Fifteen dollars each.
(B) I'll show you a picture.
(C) **We already ate too much.**

中譯
我可以給你看我們的甜點菜單嗎?
(A) 每人十五美元。
(B) 我給你看張照片。
(C) 我們已經吃太多了。

UNIT 07 附加問句、選擇疑問句

① 附加問句

PRACTICE　題本 p.46

1. (A)　**2.** (C)　**3.** (B)　**4.** (C)　**5.** (A)　**6.** (B)

1. 🎧 美國男子／美國女子

You have an extra phone charger, right?
(A) Of course, it's in the closet.
(B) No, I don't have enough experience.
(C) We're not in charge of recruiting.

中譯
你有多的手機充電器，對吧？
(A) 當然，它在衣櫥裡。
(B) 不，我沒有足夠的經驗。
(C) 我們不負責招募。

單字 extra 額外的、多出的　charger 充電器　in charge of 負責

2. 🎧 美國男子／美國女子

You used to live in a big city, didn't you?
(A) Let's use public transportation.
(B) Oh, I don't have any vacation time left.
(C) Yes, for most of my childhood.

中譯
你以前住在大城市，不是嗎？
(A) 我們搭乘大眾運輸工具吧。
(B) 哦，我已經沒有假了。
(C) 是的，在我童年大部分時間。

單字 public transportation 大眾運輸工具　childhood 童年

3. 🎧 美國男子／英國女子

This tablet will have a five-year warranty, won't it?
(A) Basic office software.
(B) Definitely.
(C) Major electronics stores.

中譯
這款平板電腦會有五年保固，不是嗎？
(A) 基本辦公軟體。
(B) 當然。
(C) 大型電子產品賣場。

單字 warranty 保固證明、保證書　electronics 電子產品

4. 🎧 澳洲男子／美國女子

The winner hasn't been announced, has it?
(A) Will the website be updated soon?
(B) Thanks, I'm honored.
(C) They're counting the votes now.

中譯
還沒有宣布當選者，是嗎？
(A) 網站很快就會更新嗎？
(B) 謝謝，我很榮幸。
(C) 他們現在正在計算選票。

單字 announce 宣布　honored 感到光榮的　count 計算　vote 選票

5. 🎧 澳洲男子／英國女子

The budget meeting is on the second floor, isn't it?
(A) Yes, it's in Room 205.
(B) No, I believe it starts at three.
(C) The prices have gone up.

中譯
預算會議在二樓舉行，不是嗎？
(A) 對，在 205 號會議室。
(B) 不，我想三點才會開始。
(C) 物價上漲了。

單字 budget 預算　price 價格、物價

6. 🎧 澳洲男子／英國女子

You're going to the clinic soon, aren't you?
(A) A routine checkup.
(B) My appointment was postponed.
(C) Sign the paperwork, please.

中譯
你很快就會去診所，不是嗎？
(A) 例行檢查。
(B) 我的看診時間被延後了。
(C) 請簽署文件。

單字 clinic 診所　routine 例行的、定期的　checkup （健康）檢查　appointment 預約　postpone 延後、推遲　paperwork 文件

② 選擇疑問句

PRACTICE
題本 p.47

1. (B) **2.** (B) **3.** (A) **4.** (A) **5.** (C) **6.** (B)

1. 🎧 美國女子／美國男子

> Do you want to walk to the theater or take a taxi?
> (A) A new musical performance.
> **(B) Well, it's only a block away.**
> (C) She recommended it.

中譯
你想走路還是搭計程車去電影院？
(A) 新的音樂表演。
(B) 嗯，電影院距離這裡只有一個街區。
(C) 她推薦的。

單字 recommend 推薦、建議

2. 🎧 美國女子／美國男子

> Would you rather discuss this over the phone or meet in person?
> (A) Any time before lunch, I think.
> **(B) Let's do a video conference.**
> (C) Here's a copy of the brochure.

中譯
你想在電話中討論這個問題，還是親自見面談？
(A) 我想午餐前的任何時間都可以。
(B) 我們開視訊會議吧。
(C) 這是小冊子的影本。

單字 discuss 討論 in person 親自
video conference 視訊會議 brochure 小冊子

3. 🎧 美國女子／澳洲男子

> Are you announcing your retirement before or after the meeting?
> **(A) Didn't you see my memo?**
> (B) I'll spend more time with my family.
> (C) Yes, that's my final day.

中譯
你要在會議前還是會議後宣布退休？
(A) 你沒看我的便條提醒嗎？
(B) 我會花更多時間陪伴我的家人。
(C) 是的，那是我的最後一天。

單字 retirement 退休 final 最後的

4. 🎧 英國女子／美國男子

> Would you prefer I print the manuals in color or black and white?
> **(A) In color is better.**
> (B) Only if you have to.
> (C) For the orientation session.

中譯
你希望我列印彩色還是黑白說明書？
(A) 彩色比較好。
(B) 僅在必要時才這樣做。
(C) 為了迎新會。

單字 manual 說明書 session 集會、期間

5. 🎧 英國女子／澳洲男子

> Do you store your towels in the bathroom or in another place?
> (A) Let's fold the laundry now.
> (B) The large one. Thanks.
> **(C) I put them in a closet.**

中譯
你把毛巾放在浴室還是其他地方？
(A) 現在來摺洗好的衣服吧。
(B) 大的，謝謝。
(C) 我把它們放在衣櫥裡。

單字 store 保管、收存 fold 摺疊、對折

6. 🎧 英國女子／澳洲男子

> Is the building inspection scheduled for this week or next week?
> (A) A city official.
> **(B) It's next Tuesday.**
> (C) The files are in order.

中譯
建築檢查安排在這週還是下週？
(A) 市政府公務員。
(B) 下週二。
(C) 檔案整理得井然有序。

單字 inspection 檢查 official 公務員 in order 按順序

UNIT 08 間接問句、直述句

① 間接問句

PRACTICE
題本 p.48

1. (C) **2.** (A) **3.** (A) **4.** (B) **5.** (B) **6.** (C)

16

1. 🎧 美國男子／美國女子

> Can you show me how to open a new account?
> (A) A well-respected local bank.
> (B) No, at least a few days.
> **(C) Let me send you the link.**

中譯
你能告訴我如何開立新帳戶嗎？
(A) 一家評價良好的當地銀行。
(B) 不，至少需要幾天。
(C) 我把連結傳給你。

單字 account 帳戶　well-respected 備受尊敬的、評價良好的　at least 至少

2. 🎧 美國男子／美國女子

> Can you tell me when the ferry departs?
> **(A) I can't connect to the Internet.**
> (B) I'll carry your suitcase.
> (C) The area's largest harbor.

中譯
你能告訴我渡輪何時出發嗎？
(A) 我連不上網路。
(B) 我幫你拿行李箱。
(C) 該地區最大的港口。

單字 harbor 港口

3. 🎧 美國男子／英國女子

> Do you know who's speaking at the banquet?
> **(A) Each of the department managers.**
> (B) The flowers in the front.
> (C) I can't remember how to register.

中譯
你知道誰要在宴會上致詞嗎？
(A) 各部門的經理。
(B) 前面的花。
(C) 我忘記要怎麼註冊。

單字 banquet 宴會、盛宴　register 註冊

4. 🎧 澳洲男子／美國女子

> Do you know where I can find the spices?
> (A) It's five ninety-nine in total.
> **(B) Over there, in aisle three.**
> (C) At noon on Wednesday.

中譯
你知道可以在哪裡找到香料嗎？
(A) 總共是五百九十九美元。
(B) 在那邊，三號走道。
(C) 星期三中午。

單字 spices 香料

5. 🎧 澳洲男子／英國女子

> Could you tell me where the dry cleaner is?
> (A) To bring in my suit.
> **(B) Actually, this neighborhood doesn't have one.**
> (C) The floor needs cleaning.

中譯
你能告訴我哪裡有乾洗店嗎？
(A) 把我的西裝拿進來。
(B) 其實這附近都沒有。
(C) 地板需要清潔。

單字 suit 西裝　neighborhood 鄰近地區

6. 🎧 澳洲男子／英國女子

> Can you show me how to reset my password?
> (A) A maintenance request.
> (B) Some security procedures.
> **(C) I'm about to leave for a training session.**

中譯
你能告訴我如何重設我的密碼嗎？
(A) 一個維修請求。
(B) 一些安全程序。
(C) 我正要去參加培訓課程。

單字 reset 重設　maintenance 維修、維護　procedure 程序　be about to 正要去做

② 直述句

PRACTICE　題本 p.49

1. (B)　**2.** (C)　**3.** (B)　**4.** (A)　**5.** (A)　**6.** (C)

1. 🎧 美國女子／美國男子

> Breakfast is served at 7 A.M.
> (A) Yes, dishes for vegetarians.
> **(B) Okay. We'll be there.**
> (C) The rooms are spacious.

中譯
早餐於上午7點供應。
(A) 是的，餐食適合素食者。
(B) 好，我們會去的。
(C) 房間很寬敞。

單字 serve 提供　vegetarian 素食者　spacious 寬敞的

17

2. 🎧 美國女子／美國男子

> The customer files were lost.
> (A) Yes, let's pile them here.
> (B) They work in customer service.
> **(C) Luckily, the system makes backups.**

中譯

客戶檔案遺失了。
(A) 是的，把它們堆放在這裡。
(B) 他們從事客戶服務工作。
(C) 幸運的是，系統有備份。

單字 lost 遺失　pile 堆積、堆放

3. 🎧 美國女子／澳洲男子

> This magazine cover looks perfect.
> (A) No, I have a subscription.
> **(B) I'm glad you like it.**
> (C) All the latest news stories.

中譯

這本雜誌封面看起來很完美。
(A) 不，我有訂閱。
(B) 我很高興你喜歡它。
(C) 全都是最新的新聞報導。

單字 subscription 訂閱　latest 最新的

4. 🎧 英國女子／美國男子

> I can set up the projector for you, if you'd like.
> **(A) Sure. That'll be helpful.**
> (B) It's an intense research project.
> (C) His suggestions were useful.

中譯

如果你想要的話，我可以幫你架設投影機。
(A) 當然，那會很有幫助的。
(B) 這是一個高強度的研究計畫。
(C) 他的建議很有用。

單字 set up 設定、準備好　intense 強烈的、極度的　suggestion 建議　useful 有用的

5. 🎧 英國女子／澳洲男子

> My security badge wouldn't work this morning.
> **(A) How did you access the building?**
> (B) Sometime after lunch.
> (C) Because of the high cost.

中譯

今天早上我的安全識別證無法使用。
(A) 那你是怎麼進入大樓的？
(B) 午餐後的某個時段。
(C) 因為高成本。

單字 access 進入

6. 🎧 英國女子／澳洲男子

> I'd like to change my mailing address.
> (A) I'd rather keep the schedule the same.
> (B) Thanks. It's my first home purchase.
> **(C) Let me transfer you to our account team.**

中譯

我想更改我的郵寄地址。
(A) 我想要維持同樣的行程安排。
(B) 謝謝，這是我第一次買房。
(C) 我把你轉交給我們的會計團隊。

單字 purchase 購買　transfer 轉移、移交

PRACTICE　　　　　　　　　　　題本 p.51

| **1.** (B) | **2.** (B) | **3.** (A) | **4.** (C) | **5.** (C) | **6.** (A) |
| **7.** (B) | **8.** (A) | **9.** (A) | **10.** (C) | **11.** (C) | **12.** (B) |

1. 🎧 美國男子／美國女子

> Who can help me renew my parking pass?
> (A) I'll take a bus. Thanks.
> **(B) It's undergoing maintenance right now.**
> (C) The storm will pass soon.

中譯

誰可以幫我更新停車證？
(A) 我要搭公車，謝謝。
(B) 停車場目前正在進行維護。
(C) 暴風雨很快就會過去。

單字 renew 更新　undergo 經歷　storm 暴風雨

2. 🎧 美國男子／美國女子

> Staff members who borrow equipment must complete this form.
> (A) A larger computer monitor.
> **(B) Okay, that won't take long.**
> (C) I'm sorry. The shipment is missing a box.

中譯

借用設備的工作人員必須完成填寫此表格。
(A) 更大的電腦螢幕。
(B) 好的，這不會花很多時間。
(C) 對不起，這批貨少一個箱子。

單字 borrow 借　complete a form 填寫表格　shipment 貨物、出貨、運送

3. 🎧 美國男子／英國女子

> Where should we stack the empty containers?
> **(A) We'll need to reorganize the warehouse.**
> (B) It doesn't weigh very much.
> (C) Early Thursday morning.

中譯
我們要把空的容器堆放在哪裡？
(A) 我們需要重新整理倉庫。
(B) 它並不是很重。
(C) 星期四清晨。

單字 stack 堆放　empty 空的　reorganize 重新整理、改造　weigh 秤…的重量

4. 🎧 澳洲男子／美國女子

> Why did we hire two part-time accountants recently?
> (A) A higher quality paper.
> (B) Because it wasn't on sale.
> **(C) We took on a major client.**

中譯
為什麼我們最近招募了兩名兼職會計師？
(A) 更高品質的紙張。
(B) 因為它沒有打折。
(C) 我們接了一個大客戶。

單字 part-time 兼職　accountant 會計師　quality 品質　on sale 打折、出售　take on 負責　major 重要的　client 客戶、委託人

5. 🎧 澳洲男子／英國女子

> Is the copy machine working?
> (A) I expect she can.
> (B) Yes, the coffee tastes delicious.
> **(C) Are you making handouts?**

中譯
影印機有正常運轉嗎？
(A) 我希望她可以。
(B) 是的，咖啡嚐起來很好。
(C) 你在製作講義嗎？

單字 taste 嚐起來、味道　handout 印刷品、講義

6. 🎧 澳洲男子／英國女子

> Where is the cafeteria?
> **(A) We only have a vending machine.**
> (B) Later this month, I think.
> (C) She usually arrives early.

中譯
自助餐廳在哪裡？
(A) 我們只有一台自動販賣機。
(B) 我想是這個月下旬。
(C) 她通常會提前抵達。

單字 vending machine 自動販賣機

7. 🎧 美國女子／美國男子

> How was the recent feedback from customers?
> (A) A colleague who recently left.
> **(B) We'll need further training support.**
> (C) In a few days.

中譯
客戶最近的反饋如何？
(A) 最近離職的一位同事。
(B) 我們需要進一步的訓練支援。
(C) 幾天後。

單字 recent 最近的、近期的　colleague 同事　further 進一步的　support 支援、支持

8. 🎧 美國女子／美國男子

> Who has a copy of the catalog?
> **(A) The products are listed online.**
> (B) There's plenty of space in this room.
> (C) Pamphlets and brochures.

中譯
誰有商品目錄的影本？
(A) 網站上有列出產品。
(B) 這個房間有足夠的空間。
(C) 手冊和小冊子。

單字 list 列表、清單　plenty of 大量的　brochure 小冊子

9. 🎧 美國女子／澳洲男子

> The print shop no longer offers overnight service.
> **(A) Do you know of another option?**
> (B) My office is on the fourth floor.
> (C) A long journey.

中譯
印刷廠不再提供通宵服務。
(A) 你知道哪裡還有提供相同的服務嗎？
(B) 我的辦公室在四樓。
(C) 長途旅行。

單字 offer 提供　overnight 隔夜、通宵　option 選項　journey 旅程

19

10. 🎧 英國女子／美國男子

> Who should I see about ordering a replacement part?
> (A) Yes, this is our newest branch.
> (B) A brand-new washing machine.
> **(C) I'd be happy to help you, ma'am.**

中譯
我應該聯絡誰才能訂購更換零件？
(A) 是的，這是我們最新的分公司。
(B) 一台全新的洗衣機。
(C) 我很樂意幫助您，女士。

單字 replacement 更換、替換　part 零件　newest 最新的
brand-new 新製的、全新的

11. 🎧 英國女子／澳洲男子

> There's a sale on used cars at Branson Autos.
> (A) The doors open automatically.
> (B) A standard loan agreement.
> **(C) I still don't have my license.**

中譯
Branson汽車公司有二手車促銷活動。
(A) 門會自動打開。
(B) 標準貸款協議。
(C) 我還沒有駕照。

單字 used 二手的　automatically 自動地　standard 標準的
loan 貸款　agreement 協議、合約　license 駕照、執照

12. 🎧 英國女子／澳洲男子

> The new office chairs are comfortable, aren't they?
> (A) Probably a few hundred dollars.
> **(B) My back feels better already.**
> (C) No, in three days.

中譯
新的辦公椅很舒適，不是嗎？
(A) 大概幾百美元。
(B) 我的背已經感覺好多了。
(C) 不，三天之後。

單字 comfortable 舒適的　back 背部

PART TEST
題本 p.52

7. (A)	8. (B)	9. (C)	10. (C)	11. (A)	12. (C)
13. (B)	14. (B)	15. (A)	16. (A)	17. (B)	18. (C)
19. (C)	20. (B)	21. (A)	22. (C)	23. (A)	24. (B)
25. (A)	26. (B)	27. (C)	28. (B)	29. (A)	30. (C)
31. (B)

7. 🎧 澳洲男子／美國女子

> When will the next bus depart?
> **(A) In about twenty minutes.**
> (B) A round-trip ticket.
> (C) The driver, I think.

中譯
下一班公車何時出發？
(A) 大約二十分鐘後。
(B) 來回票。
(C) 我認為是司機。

單字 depart 離開、出發　round-trip 來回旅程

8. 🎧 英國女子／澳洲男子

> Who is responsible for ordering company uniforms?
> (A) Professional clothing.
> **(B) Mr. Warren is.**
> (C) It's reasonable.

中譯
誰負責訂購公司制服？
(A) 專業服裝。
(B) Warren先生。
(C) 這是合理的。

單字 be responsible for 為…負責
professional 專業的、職業上的　reasonable 合理的、適當的

9. 🎧 美國女子／美國男子

> Where did you get that magazine?
> (A) Around the end of the month.
> (B) Yes, I always read it.
> **(C) The supermarket on the corner.**

中譯
你從哪裡拿到那本雜誌？
(A) 大約月底時。
(B) 是的，我總是會讀它。
(C) 街角的超市。

10. 🎧 澳洲男子／英國女子

> Why has this hallway been closed off?
> (A) We enjoyed the grand opening.
> (B) For three days.
> **(C) Because it's going to be painted.**

中譯
這條走廊為何被封閉？
(A) 我們很享受這場盛大的開幕式。
(B) 三天的時間。
(C) 因為要粉刷。

單字 hallway 走廊　grand opening 盛大的開幕、開業

11. 🎧 美國女子／美國男子

> How should we sort these résumés?
> **(A) By level of experience.**
> (B) An assistant manager.
> (C) Good luck with the interview.

中譯
我們該如何分類這些履歷呢？
(A) 依照經驗的程度。
(B) 副理。
(C) 祝面試順利。

單字 sort 分類　level 程度、水準

12. 🎧 美國男子／美國女子

> Should the train ticket be one-way or round-trip?
> (A) For Milton Station.
> (B) A trip to meet new clients.
> **(C) I just need a one-way ticket.**

中譯
火車票要單程票還是來回票？
(A) 前往Milton車站。
(B) 為了結識新客戶的旅程。
(C) 我只需要一張單程票。

單字 one-way 單程的　round-trip 來回的

13. 🎧 澳洲男子／英國女子

> Would you help to set up the projector?
> (A) An important sales presentation.
> **(B) Sure, I'm free now.**
> (C) The project was completed.

中譯
你能幫我安裝投影機嗎？
(A) 一場重要的銷售簡報。
(B) 當然，我現在有空。
(C) 專案已完成。

單字 presentation 簡報　complete 完成、結束

14. 🎧 美國女子／英國女子

> Who has the paper forms for ordering supplies?
> (A) I don't have enough space.
> **(B) We use an online system.**
> (C) Their prices are affordable.

中譯
誰有訂購用品的紙本表格？
(A) 我沒有足夠的空間。
(B) 我們使用線上系統。
(C) 他們的價格合理。

單字 paper form 紙本表格　supplies 用品　affordable 合理的、可負擔的（價格）

15. 🎧 美國男子／英國女子

> How was the workshop on designing brochures?
> **(A) I found it quite helpful.**
> (B) Yes, you should sign up.
> (C) She wants to be a fashion designer.

中譯
設計宣傳手冊的研討會如何？
(A) 我發現它很有幫助。
(B) 對，你應該報名。
(C) 她想成為一名時裝設計師。

單字 sign up 報名、註冊

16. 🎧 美國女子／澳洲男子

> Where can I find the fresh herbs?
> **(A) I can show you that section.**
> (B) That's a fresh approach.
> (C) Planting a variety of seeds.

中譯
我可以在哪裡找到新鮮的香草？
(A) 我可以帶你去那個區域。
(B) 那是一種新方法。
(C) 種下各式各樣的種子。

單字 approach 方法　a variety of 各式各樣的　seed 種子、籽

17. 🎧 英國女子／美國男子

> There are no empty seats on the main floor.
> (A) Yes, I'll fill them.
> **(B) The balcony is fine.**
> (C) I work on the third floor.

中譯
主樓層已經沒有空位。
(A) 是，我會填補它們。
(B) 陽臺也可以。
(C) 我在三樓工作。

單字 empty 空的　fill 填補

21

18. 🎧 英國女子／澳洲男子

Was Ms. Jackson pleased with the sales presentation?
(A) All right, I'll send her in.
(B) The head of the department.
(C) Everyone there loved it.

中譯
Jackson女士滿意這次的銷售簡報嗎？
(A) 好吧，我送她進去。
(B) 部門的負責人。
(C) 那裡所有人都喜歡。

單字 be pleased with 對…滿意、感到高興

19. 🎧 美國男子／美國女子

You're heading to the airport this afternoon, right?
(A) Sorry, your bag is too heavy.
(B) Five days in total.
(C) Yes, around three o'clock.

中譯
你今天下午要去機場，對吧？
(A) 抱歉，你的包包太重了。
(B) 總共五天。
(C) 是的，大約三點左右。

單字 be headed to 去、前往

20. 🎧 澳洲男子／美國女子

Haven't you received your security badge yet?
(A) The receipt for the meal.
(B) No, they're still processing it.
(C) I'll keep them confidential.

中譯
你還沒收到你的安全識別證嗎？
(A) 用餐收據。
(B) 沒有，他們仍在處理中。
(C) 我會保密。

單字 receive 收到　receipt 收據　process 處理
confidential 祕密的

21. 🎧 英國女子／美國男子

Do you want to set up the picnic in a sunny or shady spot?
(A) I love the sunshine.
(B) It is a beautiful park.
(C) Approximately twenty people.

中譯
你想在有陽光的地方野餐，還是在陰涼的地方？
(A) 我喜歡陽光。
(B) 這是個美麗的公園。
(C) 大約二十人。

單字 shady 陰涼的、成蔭的　spot 地方、地點
approximately 大約

22. 🎧 美國女子／美國男子

How much fabric should I order for the curtains?
(A) In alphabetical order.
(B) No later than 5 P.M., please.
(C) Well, we're covering ten windows.

中譯
我應該訂多少布料來做窗簾？
(A) 按字母順序排列。
(B) 請不要晚於下午5點。
(C) 我們要做十扇窗戶的窗簾。

單字 fabric 布料、織品　alphabetical order 字母順序
no later than 不晚於…

23. 🎧 澳洲男子／英國女子

Do we have a few staff members willing to work overtime?
(A) Yes, six people have already volunteered.
(B) The time on the clock was incorrect.
(C) I'm sorry you were overcharged.

中譯
我們有幾位員工願意加班嗎？
(A) 是，目前已有六人自願加班。
(B) 時鐘上顯示的時間是錯的。
(C) 很抱歉向你收取了過多費用。

單字 be willing to 願意…　work overtime 加班
volunteer 自願　incorrect 不正確的
overcharge 過度索價、被坑錢

24. 🎧 美國男子／美國女子

I need to change the address for my newspaper subscription.
(A) Maybe we should keep the same color.
(B) Please hold while I transfer your call.
(C) Thank you for the advice.

中譯
我需要更改訂閱報紙的地址。
(A) 也許我們應該維持同樣的顏色。
(B) 請稍等，我為您轉接電話。
(C) 謝謝您的建議。

單字 subscription 訂閱　hold （不掛斷電話）等候
transfer 轉換、調動

25. 🎧 英國女子／澳洲男子

> Doesn't Victor need to enroll in the Spanish class?
> **(A) He grew up in Spain.**
> (B) I applied for a leadership role.
> (C) A one-week vacation.

中譯
Victor不需要報名西班牙文課嗎？
(A) 他在西班牙長大。
(B) 我申請擔任領導者的職務。
(C) 一週的假期。

單字 enroll in 報名　apply for 申請　leadership 領導者　role 角色

26. 🎧 澳洲男子／美國女子

> How can I get a library card?
> (A) What kind of books do you like?
> **(B) You'll need proof of residency.**
> (C) Until the parking lot is full.

中譯
我要如何取得借閱證？
(A) 你喜歡什麼類型的書？
(B) 你需要居住證明。
(C) 直到停車場停滿為止。

單字 proof 證明（書）　residency 居住

27. 🎧 美國男子／英國女子

> This entrance is designated for deliveries only.
> (A) Because we eliminated shipping costs.
> (B) Sure, you can borrow my key.
> **(C) Oh, I have some packages.**

中譯
此入口僅供送貨使用。
(A) 因為我們省下了運送費用。
(B) 當然，你可以借用我的鑰匙。
(C) 哦，我有一些包裹。

單字 designate 指定　eliminate 消除　package 包裹

28. 🎧 英國女子／美國男子

> When are you free to mentor the interns?
> (A) To explain our company policies.
> **(B) I have several tight deadlines.**
> (C) They'll learn a lot about the industry.

中譯
你什麼時候有空指導實習生？
(A) 為了解釋我們公司的政策。
(B) 我有幾個緊迫的截止日。
(C) 他們會學到很多關於此行業的知識。

單字 mentor 指導　policy 政策　tight 緊迫的　industry 產業

29. 🎧 美國女子／澳洲男子

> Do you have experience with investments?
> **(A) Ranjit has a degree in finance.**
> (B) It's a good investment.
> (C) We need to weigh it first.

中譯
你有投資經驗嗎？
(A) Ranjit擁有金融學位。
(B) 這是一項很好的投資。
(C) 我們必須先秤重一下。

單字 investment 投資　degree 學位　finance 金融、財政　weigh 稱重

30. 🎧 美國男子／英國女子

> This is the address we should deliver the order to, isn't it?
> (A) The business is doing well.
> (B) An urgent staff meeting.
> **(C) Oh, that company moved recently.**

中譯
這是我們要送貨的地址，不是嗎？
(A) 事業做得很成功。
(B) 緊急員工會議。
(C) 哦，那家公司最近搬走了。

單字 urgent 緊急的

31. 🎧 澳洲男子／美國女子

> We should replace the carpet in the break room.
> (A) I think I've misplaced them.
> **(B) It still looks very new.**
> (C) The third door on the right.

中譯
我們應該要更換休息室的地毯。
(A) 我想我把它們放錯地方了。
(B) 它看起來仍然很新。
(C) 右側的第三扇門。

單字 replace 更換、替換　misplace 誤置、遺忘

LC PART 3

UNIT 09 詢問主旨或目的

PRACTICE 題本 p.59

1. (B)　2. (C)　3. (D)　4. (A)

1. 🎧 美國女子／美國男子
Question 1 refers to the following conversation.

> **W** Hi, Mr. Davis. This is Christina Whitley from the Westbury Small Business Association.
> **M** Oh, yes. Hello, Ms. Whitley.
> **W** I'm calling to let you know that the Digital Marketing Conference has been postponed until June 18.
> **M** I see. I can probably still attend it.
> **W** I hope so. I'll e-mail you an updated registration packet. Also, your travel and registration fees will be covered by us.
> **M** Thank you. I'll double-check whether or not I can participate in the event. If not, I will probably send my assistant manager in my place.

中譯
第 1 題，請參考下方對話。

女　嗨，Davis先生，我是Westbury中小企業協會的Christina Whitley。
男　哦，是，你好，Whitley女士。
女　**我打電話來通知您數位行銷會議已延期至6月18日。**
男　我明白了，但我應該還能參加。
女　但願如此。我會用電子郵件傳給您更新的報名資訊統整。另外，您的旅費和報名費將由我們負擔。
男　謝謝你。我會再確認一下能否參加該活動。如果不行，我可能會派我的副理代替參加。

單字 Small Business Association 中小企業協會
postpone 延期　attend 參加　registration 註冊
participate 參與　in one's place 代替某人

1. 女子為何打電話給男子？
(A) 要求支付帳單。
(B) 通知他行程的更動。
(C) 邀請他來演講。
(D) 分享一些管理策略。

單字 inform 通知　invite 邀請　strategy 策略

2. 🎧 英國女子／美國男子
Question 2 refers to the following conversation.

> **W** Have you heard about the negotiations with the Duluth Software representatives?
> **M** You mean the possible merger with that company? I think it'd give us a strong market position.
> **W** True, but I wonder what that means for our job security. I'm afraid they will downsize some departments.
> **M** Well, you can bring up that concern at the staff meeting on Friday. I know our executives are doing everything they can to protect our jobs. And there may be bonuses given to employees who stay with the company.
> **W** Well, I wonder how much they will be.
> **M** Hopefully enough to retain the best staff members.

中譯
第 2 題，請參考下方對話。

女　你是否聽說與Duluth軟體公司代表進行的談判？
男　**你是指可能和那家公司合併嗎？**我認為這會為我們帶來強大的市場定位。
女　沒錯，但我想知道這對於我們的就業保障意味著什麼。我擔心他們會縮減某些部門的規模。
男　嗯，你可以在週五的員工會議上提出這個問題。我知道我們的高階主管正在盡一切努力保護我們的工作。然後可能還會發放獎金給留在公司的員工。
女　嗯，我想知道獎金有多少。
男　希望是足以留住最優秀的員工的金額。

單字 negotiation 談判　representative 代表
merger 合併　market position 市場定位
job security 就業保障　downsize 縮減　bring up 提出
concern 擔心、擔憂　executive 高階主管、高層
retain 維持

2. 說話者主要在討論什麼？
(A) 總部搬遷
(B) 軟體升級
(C) 擬議合併
(D) 市場規定

單字 headquarters 總部　relocation 搬遷
proposed 提案的　regulation 規定

24

3. 🎧 澳洲男子／美國女子
Question 3 refers to the following conversation.

> M Thanks for calling the Burlington Parks and Recreation Department. What can I help you with?
>
> W Hi, my name is Rosa Garcia. I'd like to volunteer a few hours during the week, and I heard your department runs a volunteer program.
>
> M Yes, we do. We have several groups that assist with cleaning up our public parks. Unfortunately, though, you've just missed our recruitment event.
>
> W Oh, I was hoping to get to work quickly.
>
> M Well, I can take your contact information and let you know when we're recruiting new people. What's your number?

中譯
第 3 題，請參考下方對話。

男 感謝您致電Burlington公園和娛樂部門，有什麼需要幫忙的嗎？
女 嗨，我叫Rosa Garcia。**我想在平日做幾個小時的志工，聽說貴部門有一個志工計畫。**
男 是的，沒錯。我們有幾個小組協助清理我們的公共公園。但很遺憾的是，您剛好錯過了我們的招募活動。
女 哦，我本來希望能盡快開始工作的。
男 嗯，我可以記下您的聯絡方式，並於招募新人時通知您，您的號碼是？

單字 recreation 娛樂　assist with 協助
recruitment 招募、招收

3. 女人打電話的目的為何？
(A) 宣傳公園的活動
(B) 介紹清潔服務
(C) 安排參觀設施
(D) 詢問志工機會

單字 promote 宣傳　arrange 安排、計畫

4. 🎧 澳洲男子／英國女子
Question 4 refers to the following conversation.

> M So, we've been tasked with unpacking these boxes of sweaters that will go on sale tomorrow. We need to sort them by size and color.
>
> W That's a lot of boxes. Will it be just the two of us?
>
> M Unfortunately, yes. The rest of the staff members are working at the cash registers or assisting customers.
>
> W Well, we'll probably have to work all day on this.
>
> M I don't know. Let's get started and see how it goes. We can give Ms. Mallory an update closer to lunch.

中譯
第 4 題，請參考下方對話。

男 所以，我們的任務是拆箱這些將於明天上市的毛衣。我們要按照尺寸和顏色分類。
女 有很多盒啊，只有我們兩個做嗎？
男 很遺憾是這樣沒錯。其他員工正在收銀台工作或接待客人。
女 好吧，我們可能要工作一整天。
男 我不確定。先開始做，然後再看看進展如何。我們可以在接近午餐時，向Mallory女士報告最新進度。

單字 task 指派的工作、任務　unpack 打開（包裹）　sort 分類

4. 這段對話主要在談論什麼？
(A) 整理一些商品
(B) 培訓員工
(C) 更改櫥窗展示
(D) 為送貨箱貼上標籤

單字 merchandise 商品　display 陳列、展示

換句話說 unpacking these boxes of sweaters that will go on sale → Organizing some merchandise

UNIT 10 詢問說話者或地點

PRACTICE　題本 p.61

1. (A)　**2.** (D)　**3.** (C)　**4.** (B)

1. 🎧 美國女子／美國男子
Question 1 refers to the following conversation.

> W Welcome to the Camden Library. Are you a member here?
>
> M Actually, this is my first visit. I recently moved to the area.
>
> W Well, there is no charge to become a member. You just have to show proof of address, such as a utility bill or apartment lease.
>
> M Great. Do you offer any classes for the community?

25

W　Absolutely. We have a wide range of classes for adults. Here is the schedule for this month. But just so you know, we're closed next week because of the holiday.

M　Okay. Are there public computers as well?

W　Yes, just over there. You can use them anytime.

中譯

第 1 題，請參考下方對話。

女　**歡迎來到Camden圖書館**。你是這裡的會員嗎？

男　其實這是我第一次來訪。我最近剛搬到這個地區。

女　嗯，成為會員是免費的，你只需要出示地址證明，例如水電費帳單或公寓租約。

男　太好了。你們有為社區居民提供課程嗎？

女　當然有。我們為成人提供各類課程。這是本月的課程時間表。但提醒你一下，我們下週因為假期而閉館。

男　好的。這裡也有公用電腦嗎？

女　是的，就在那邊。你隨時都可以使用。

單字 charge 費用　proof 證明（書）　utility bill 水電費帳單　lease 租約

1. 對話最有可能發生在哪裡？
(A) 在圖書館
(B) 在房屋仲介機構
(C) 在電子產品商店
(D) 在健身中心

2. 🎧 英國女子／美國男子
Question 2 refers to the following conversation.

W　Good morning. What brings you into our leasing office today?

M　Hi. My name is Todd Morrison, and I'm in unit 310. My lease will expire in March, but I'm thinking about moving to a larger unit within the building.

W　Let me check what we have available. Hmm... it looks like apartment 501 will be available at that time. It's a three-bedroom unit for twelve hundred a month.

M　That sounds perfect. I don't mind spending more in order to have more space.

W　Great. I'll find out when you can have a look around the place.

中譯

第 2 題，請參考下方對話。

女　早安，今天怎麼會來我們的租賃辦公室？

男　嗨，我叫Todd Morrison，住在310號房。我的租約將於三月到期，但我正在考慮搬到大樓內更大的房間。

女　我確認一下我們有沒有空房。嗯… 看來到時候501號房應該會空出來。這間是三房的格局，每月租金1200美元。

男　聽起來很完美。我不介意多花點錢來獲得更多空間。

女　太好了。我確認一下什麼時候可以讓你參觀那裡。

單字 leasing office 租賃辦公室　expire 到期　available 空出的、可得到的

2. 女子最有可能是誰？
(A) 電工
(B) 清潔人員
(C) 室內裝潢師
(D) 物業經理

3. 🎧 美國女子／澳洲男子
Question 3 refers to the following conversation.

W　Hello, Mr. Elliot. You said you wanted to look into getting a loan for your business?

M　That's right. I own a company that sells medical supplies to hospitals and clinics.

W　Okay, I've looked over the paperwork regarding your business model. It seems you are doing well.

M　Yes, and we expect further growth. But we need to upgrade our website to help us attract more clients.

W　I understand. I can look over your financial records in more detail to find out how much funding would be available to you.

M　Thanks. I have all the documents right here.

中譯

第 3 題，請參考下方對話。

女　您好，Elliot先生，您說您想為您的企業貸款嗎？

男　沒錯，**我擁有一家向醫院和診所販售醫療用品的公司**。

女　好的，我查閱了關於您商業模式的文件，看起來您的生意做得很好。

男　是的，我們預期會有進一步的成長。而我們的網站需要升級，才能幫助我們吸引更多的客戶。

女　我明白了，我會詳細查閱您的財務紀錄，以了解您能獲得多少資金。

男　謝謝，所有的文件都在這裡。

單字 look into 調查　get a loan 貸款　medical supplies 醫療用品　paperwork 文件　growth 成長　attract 吸引　in more detail 更仔細地　funding 資金

3. 男子從事什麼行業？
(A) 出版業
(B) 餐飲服務
(C) 醫療保健
(D) 農業

4. 🎧 澳洲男子／英國女子

Question 4 refers to the following conversation.

> **M** I enjoyed your presentation on vegetarian cooking. I really learned a lot. I'm a producer at the Channel 5 TV Station.
>
> **W** Oh, really? I love your morning show.
>
> **M** Thanks! Actually, this kind of topic would be popular with our viewers. Would you be interested in being on the show?
>
> **W** Well, I've never done anything like that before, but it sounds like it would be interesting. Perhaps you could tell me more about it.
>
> **M** Of course. How can I reach you?

中譯
第4題，請參考下方對話。

男　我很喜歡你針對素食烹調的介紹。我真的學到了很多。**我是第五頻道電視台的製作人。**

女　噢，真的嗎？我很喜歡你的晨間節目。

男　謝謝！其實這類型的主題很受觀眾歡迎。你有興趣出演節目嗎？

女　嗯，我以前從未做過類似的事情，但聽起來很有意思。也許你可以告訴我更多相關內容。

男　當然，我要怎麼聯絡你呢？

單字　perhaps 也許、可能

4. 男子在哪裡工作？
(A) 在餐廳
(B) 在電視台
(C) 在商業機構
(D) 在電影院

UNIT 11　詢問相關細節

PRACTICE　題本 p.63

1. (B)　**2.** (A)　**3.** (C)　**4.** (D)

1. 🎧 美國男子／美國女子

Question 1 refers to the following conversation.

> **M** Hello, I'm supposed to meet Anthony Shaw here for an interview. I'm from the *Worthington Herald*.
>
> **W** Ah, yes. He's expecting you, so he'll be out in a moment. I know he's looking forward to telling your readers more about his coaching career.
>
> **M** Yes, he's been such a big part of the local basketball scene. A lot of people will miss him when he retires at the end of the season.
>
> **W** Right. He's very talented. Anyway, could I get you something to drink while you wait?
>
> **M** Thanks, but I'm fine.

中譯
第1題，請參考下方對話。

男　你好，我和Anthony Shaw約好見面進行採訪，我是Worthington Herald的員工。

女　啊，對。他在等你，馬上就會出來了。**我知道他期待向讀者介紹更多關於他教練生涯的故事。**

男　是，他是當地籃球界重要的一員。當他在賽季結束退役時，很多人都會想念他。

女　沒錯，他非常有才華。總之，在你等待期間，要喝些什麼嗎？

男　謝謝，不用沒關係。

單字　be supposed to 預定、應該要⋯
look forward to 期待　career 職涯　retire 退休
talented 有才華的

1. Anthony Shaw是誰？
(A) 一名維修工人
(B) 一名教練
(C) 一名接待人員
(D) 一名記者

2. 🎧 美國男子／英國女子

Question 2 refers to the following conversation.

> **M** Sumiyo, I didn't get a chance to talk to you after yesterday's meeting. What did you think of the result?
>
> **W** You mean about the proposal to acquire Anaheim Logistics? I was strongly in favor of it.
>
> **M** Yes, I thought it would be good for our company. I'm disappointed that the board didn't approve it.
>
> **W** Me, too. I feel like we missed an opportunity for future growth. I'm a bit worried we won't be able to keep up with our competition.
>
> **M** Hmm... I think there are other options that we can explore.

中譯
第2題，請參考下方對話。

男　Sumiyo，昨天會議結束後我沒機會找你談，你對結果有什麼看法？

女　你是指**收購Anaheim物流的提議**嗎？我強烈贊成。

男　是的，我認為這對我們公司有好處，**我很失望董事會沒有**

27

批准。

女　我也是，我覺得我們錯過了未來發展的機會。我有點擔心我們會跟不上競爭對手。

男　嗯……我想我們還可以探討其他選擇。

單字 acquire 取得　in favor of 贊成　approve 批准
keep up with 跟上…　competition 競爭對手
explore 探討、探索

2. 男子為什麼會失望？
(A) 一項提議遭否決。
(B) 一場會議被取消。
(C) 一名董事會成員離職。
(D) 一份簡報內含一些錯誤。

單字 reject 拒絕　resign 辭職

換句話說 didn't approve → was rejected

3. 🎧 澳洲男子／美國女子
Question 3 refers to the following conversation.

> M Excuse me, do you know why they're not boarding the bus to Cambridge? It's supposed to depart at 3 o'clock.
> W Yes, the Department of Transportation has closed several highways due to the severe storm.
> M I see. Are all bus trips canceled for today?
> W It's possible they can start clearing the roads soon, so another announcement will be made in about an hour.
> M Okay. I guess I'll get a coffee while I wait.
> W There's a nice café near the west entrance.

中譯
第 3 題，請參考下方對話。

男　不好意思，你知道他為什麼還不開放搭乘前往劍橋的公車嗎？原本預計3點要發車。
女　是的，由於嚴重的暴風雨，交通部關閉了多條高速公路。
男　我明白了。今天所有公車路線都會取消嗎？
女　他們可能很快就會開始清理道路，所以大約一個小時後會再通知。
男　好的，我想我會在等待期間喝杯咖啡。
女　西出口附近有家不錯的咖啡廳。

單字 board 搭乘　depart 出發　highway 高速公路
severe 嚴重的　storm 暴風雨

3. 女人提到什麼問題？
(A) 車票有印刷錯誤。
(B) 部分公車票價上漲。
(C) 天候不佳。
(D) 需要進行部分維修。

單字 misprint 印錯

4. 🎧 澳洲男子／英國女子
Question 4 refers to the following conversation.

> M Welcome to TC Hardware Store. How can I help you?
> W Hi, I'm doing some renovations in my bathroom. My coworker recommended your business for buying paint.
> M Oh, we always appreciate recommendations. Was there a particular brand that you had in mind?
> W Sweeny Interiors.
> M That's a good brand. Its paint is made from materials that last long and do not crack easily. Some other brands use cheaper materials, so the wall coverage isn't very good. Everything's in aisle 2.
> W Thank you.
> M And if you haven't signed up for our loyalty program yet, here's a brochure with all the details.

中譯
第 4 題，請參考下方對話。

男　歡迎來到TC五金行。有什麼需要幫忙的嗎？
女　嗨，我正在為我的浴室進行部分翻修，我同事推薦向貴店購買油漆。
男　啊，我們一直很感激大家的推薦。您心中是否有偏好的指定品牌？
女　Sweeny室內設計。
男　那是個好品牌。**他們家的油漆是由耐用且不易裂開的材料所製成**。其他幾個品牌使用較便宜的材料，因此牆面覆蓋率不是很好。它們家的所有產品都在2號走道。
女　謝謝您。
男　如果您尚未加入我們的會員回饋計畫，這裡有本包含所有詳細資訊的手冊。

單字 hardware store 五金行　renovation 修理、翻修
appreciate 感激　particular 特別的、特定的
have ~ in mind 想要、想到　material 原料、材料
last 持續　crack 裂開　aisle 走道　sign up 加入

4. 男子對該品牌有什麼看法？
(A) 它獲得許多正面評價。
(B) 它的價格實惠。
(C) 它目前缺貨。
(D) 它使用高品質的材料。

單字 positive 正面的　affordable (價格) 合理的
currently 現在　out of stock 缺貨中
high-quality 高品質的

換句話說 made from materials that last long and do not crack easily → uses high-quality materials

UNIT 12 詢問建議或要求

PRACTICE
題本 p.65

1. (D)　**2.** (C)　**3.** (A)　**4.** (A)

---

1. 🎧 美國男子／美國女子
Question 1 refers to the following conversation.

> **M** Mijin, I plan to apply for the assistant manager role, but I need a letter of evaluation for the application. Could you please write one?
>
> **W** I'd be happy to. You've been doing an excellent job on the sales team, and I'm really impressed with how hard you worked after being assigned to a new territory.
>
> **M** Thanks a lot. I'm actually quite proud of how I was able to exceed my sales targets by so much. It helped to boost my confidence.

中譯
第 1 題，請參考下方對話。

男　Mijin，我打算應徵副理一職，但**申請會需要需要評鑑表，能麻煩你寫一份嗎？**

女　我很樂意。你在銷售部門的工作表現非常好，而且在被分配到新地區後，你在工作上的努力讓我留下深刻的印象。

男　非常感謝。其實我對自己能遠遠超過銷售目標感到自豪，這有助於增強我的自信心。

單字 apply for 應徵　evaluation 評價、評鑑　assign 指派
territory 地區、領土　exceed 超過　target 目標
boost 提升、增強　confidence 自信、信心

1. 男子要求女子做什麼？
(A) 校對銷售目錄
(B) 拜訪客戶
(C) 發表簡報
(D) 撰寫評價

單字 proofread 校對

---

2. 🎧 英國女子／美國男子
Question 2 refers to the following conversation.

> **W** I just got a phone call from the building owner. She'd like us to add a flower bed to the shared outdoor area, by the fence on the east side. She thinks it will create a more relaxing atmosphere for tenants.
>
> **M** Okay. Let's go take some measurements now. Also, I think we have some gardening materials left over from our last project.
>
> **W** That's right. There is some potting soil and a few tools. I'll check what's there after we figure out the size of the flower bed we need.

中譯
第 2 題，請參考下方對話。

女　我剛接到大樓業主的電話。她希望我們在東側柵欄旁的公共戶外空間增加一個花圃，她認為這能為住戶創造更輕鬆的氛圍。

男　好的，我們現在就去測量尺寸。另外，我們上個專案應該還有**留下一些園藝材料**。

女　沒錯，有一些盆栽土壤和工具。待我們弄清楚花圃大小後，**我再確認看看有些什麼。**

單字 flower bed 花圃　relaxing 使人放鬆的
atmosphere 氛圍　tenant 住戶
take measurements 測量尺寸　gardening 園藝
left over 剩下的　figure out 弄清楚

2. 女子願意做什麼事？
(A) 在週末工作
(B) 訂購一些花
(C) 尋找一些材料
(D) 召開住戶會議

換句話說 check → look for

---

3. 🎧 澳洲男子／美國女子
Question 3 refers to the following conversation.

> **M** Have you seen the sales figures for the latest quarter? Online sales of our home furnishings have now surpassed in-person sales at the store.
>
> **W** Yes, I noticed that trend, and it's probably going to continue. We need to find a way to help online customers find new products naturally, like they would if they were browsing the shelves in the store.
>
> **M** Why don't we create some videos to showcase our best home accessories?
>
> **W** I like that idea. Actually, I have a friend who's an interior designer. She could collaborate with us to give decorating tips using our products. I'll give her a call this afternoon.

中譯
第 3 題，請參考下方對話。

男　你看過最近一季的銷售數據了嗎？我們家居用品的線上銷售額已經超過實體店面的銷售額。

女　是的，我有注意到這個趨勢，而且很有可能持續下去。我們要想辦法幫助線上顧客自然地找到新產品，就像他們逛實體商店內貨架上的商品一樣。

男　**我們何不製作一些影片，來展示我們最好的家居用品呢？**

女　我喜歡這個主意。其實，我有個朋友是室內設計師。她可以與我們合作，使用我們的產品並提供裝飾技巧。今天下午我會打電話給她。

單字 sales figures 銷售額　quarter 季度　surpass 超過
browse 瀏覽　showcase 展示、介紹　collaborate 合作
decorating 裝飾的

3. 男子建議做什麼事？
(A) 製作宣傳影片
(B) 邀請名人到店裡
(C) 發放優惠券
(D) 舉辦裝飾比賽

單字 promotional 宣傳的　celebrity 名人

4. 🎧 澳洲男子／英國女子
Question 4 refers to the following conversation.

> M Thanks again for all of your planning for the company picnic, Wendy. I've heard a lot of positive comments about it.
> W Oh, I'm glad that people had a good time.
> M Yeah, everyone loved the activities and the food. Speaking of food, the cherry pie that you made was amazing. Would you mind sharing its recipe?
> W It's not my own, just one I found on a website. I can e-mail you the link. It was pretty easy to make, so you should definitely give it a try.
> M Thanks, I will.

中譯
第 4 題，請參考下方對話。
男 再次感謝你為公司野餐活動做的所有計畫，Wendy。我聽到很多此事的正面評價。
女 哦，我很高興大家度過了美好的時光。
男 是的，每個人都喜歡野餐的活動和食物。說到食物，你做的櫻桃派真是太讓人驚艷了。**你願意分享它的食譜嗎？**
女 這不是我自己的食譜，是我在網路上找到的。我可以把連結用電子郵件傳給你。它非常容易製作，所以你一定要試試看。
男 謝謝，我會的。

單字 speaking of 說到⋯　give it a try 嘗試看看

4. 男子要求什麼？
(A) 甜點食譜
(B) 宣傳手冊
(C) 邀請函影本
(D) 聯絡人名單

UNIT 13　詢問下一步的行動

PRACTICE　　　　　　　題本 p.67

1. (D)　**2.** (B)　**3.** (B)　**4.** (A)

30

1. 🎧 美國女子／美國男子
Question 1 refers to the following conversation.

> W Hi, I tried to use the library's self-checkout machine, but there was a message saying that I owe a fine. Here is my card.
> M Let me see... Yes, it looks like one of your books was returned late. You'll have to pay a fine of $1.25 before checking out anything new.
> W Oh, that's no problem. I can pay it now. Sorry about that.
> M It happens. And just a reminder that we'll be holding a fundraiser next Saturday. We're selling used books to purchase new computers for the library.

中譯
第 1 題，請參考下方對話。
女 嗨，我本來想使用圖書館的自動借還機，但它顯示我要繳交罰款的訊息。這是我的借閱證。
男 我來看一下⋯⋯是的，你有一本書逾期歸還了。在借新書之前，你必須繳交 1.25 美元的罰款。
女 哦，沒有問題。我現在可以付款。對此我很抱歉。
男 這是常有的事。**還有通知你一聲，我們下週六將舉辦募款活動。**我們將出售一些舊書，為圖書館購置新電腦。

單字 owe 欠錢　fine 罰款

1. 下週六將會發生什麼事？
(A) 寫作研討會
(B) 詩歌朗誦
(C) 電腦課程
(D) 募款活動

2. 🎧 美國男子／英國女子
Question 2 refers to the following conversation.

> M Thanks for meeting, Ms. Jackson. As I said on the phone, I'm relocating my jewelry shop to a building on Donovan Street. Because so much of our stock is delicate, the moving company needs to handle everything carefully.
> W I understand. I can assure you that our crew members take great care when it comes to fragile items. So, why did you decide to relocate?
> M Well, we've been growing rapidly, so we need a bigger space.
> W That's great. And what's your target move day?
> M July 12. Can you help on that day?
> W Let me open the calendar app on my phone.

中譯

第 2 題，請參考下方對話。

男　謝謝你來見我，Jackson 女士。正如我在電話中所提到，我的珠寶店要搬到位在 Donovan 街的大樓裡。由於庫存中很大一部分商品都是易碎的，搬家公司要小心處理一切。

女　我明白了，我可以向你保證，我們的工作人員在處理易碎物品時會非常小心。那麼，你為什麼決定搬遷呢？

男　嗯，我們一直在快速成長，所以需要更大的空間。

女　那太好了。你想要搬家的日期是哪一天？

男　7 月 12 日，那天你能幫忙嗎？

女　我開一下手機的行事曆應用程式。

單字　relocate 搬遷　stock 庫存　delicate 脆弱的、易碎的　assure 保證、擔保　fragile 易碎的　target 目標

2. 女子接下來最有可能做什麼事？
(A) 寫下地址
(B) 確認時間表
(C) 介紹一名工作人員
(D) 提供成本估算表

單字　confirm 確認　cost estimate 成本估算表

3. 🎧 澳洲男子／美國女子
Question 3 refers to the following conversation.

M　Rhonda, I'm glad I caught you after today's rehearsal. I wanted to talk to you about an issue that some of the actors mentioned, about the curtains being opened and closed between acts.

W　What seems to be the problem?

M　They're moving smoothly enough, but they're really squeaky. I think even audience members sitting far from the stage could be distracted by that noise. Do you know what might be causing it?

W　It's probably easy to fix. I'll try to oil the curtain track to see if that helps.

M　Thank you. Since opening night is next week, we need to make sure everything is perfect. I think this will be our best show yet.

中譯

第 3 題，請參考下方對話。

男　Rhonda，我很高興今天彩排後能見到你。我想和你談談有些演員提到的問題，是有關在表演之間布幕的開關。

女　問題出在哪裡呢？

男　它們移動得夠順暢，但會發出吱吱聲。我想即使是坐在離舞台很遠的觀眾，也會因為噪音而分心。你知道是什麼原因造成的嗎？

女　這應該很容易修好。我會試著在布幕軌道上塗油，看看是否有幫助。

男　謝謝。**因為下週是開幕之夜，**所以我們要確保一切都很完美。我認為這將是我們迄今為止最好的演出。

單字　smoothly 順暢地、平滑地　squeaky 吱吱作響的　distracted 注意力分散的　oil 上油

3. 下週將會發生什麼事？
(A) 劇院將被翻新。
(B) 一齣舞台劇即將開演。
(C) 將會印製海報。
(D) 將頒發表演獎項。

單字　renovate 翻修　present 給、頒發

4. 🎧 澳洲男子／英國女子／美國男子
Question 4 refers to the following conversation with three speakers.

M1　Thanks for stopping by in person to talk about the designs for our new dental clinic. Our grand opening will be September 3.

W　My pleasure. I can see that this space has a lot of natural light. That's great. The waiting area is small, though.

M2　Yes, but we hope you can find a way to make the best use of the space.

M1　That's right. And we'd like to make sure the area has a calming atmosphere.

W　I have a few ideas to make that happen. I'll start out by measuring each room so I know what I have to work with.

中譯

第 4 題，請參考下方三人對話。

男1　感謝妳親自前來討論我們新開牙醫診所的設計。我們將於 9 月 3 日盛大開幕。

女　不客氣。我注意到這個空間有很多自然光，太好了。不過等候區域很小。

男2　是的，但是我們希望你能找到充分利用空間的方法。

男1　沒錯，而且我們希望該區域能有平靜的氛圍。

女　我有些想法能實現這點。**我先來測量每個診間的大小，才能知道接下來該怎麼做。**

單字　make the best use of 充分利用　calming 平靜的　atmosphere 氛圍　measure 測量

4. 女子說她會做什麼事？
(A) 進行一些測量
(B) 粉刷房間
(C) 簽訂合約
(D) 安裝一些燈具

單字　install 安裝

換句話說　measuring each room → take some measurements

UNIT 14 詢問說話者的意圖

PRACTICE
題本 p.69

1. (C)　**2.** (A)　**3.** (D)　**4.** (B)

1. 🎧 美國女子／美國男子
Question 1 refers to the following conversation.

> **W** Hi, Mr. Fox. Our team of consultants has gone over your business model, and we've come up with some ideas to expand your footwear brand.
> **M** That's great. We've been struggling to make a name for ourselves in the market, so your insights will be helpful.
> **W** All right. So, what do you think about displaying your footwear in hardware stores?
> **M** They usually market to an older clientele.
> **W** Hmm... Let me see what you think of some of our other ideas.

中譯
第 1 題，請參考下方對話。

女　嗨，Fox先生。我們的顧問團隊已經研究過貴公司的商業模式，並提出了一些拓展您鞋子品牌的點子。
男　太好了。我們一直努力想在市場上出名，因此你的見解會有所幫助。
女　好的。那麼，對於在五金行陳列貴公司的鞋子，您有什麼看法？
男　它們通常會販售給較年長的顧客。
女　嗯…我來看一下您對我們其他點子有什麼看法。

單字　consultant 諮詢、顧問　expand 擴張　footwear 鞋子　struggle 努力、奮鬥　insight 洞察力　hardware store 五金行　market 交易；市場　clientele 顧客

1. 男子為何會說：「它們通常會販售給較年長的顧客。」？
(A) 表達失望
(B) 同意計畫
(C) 否決建議
(D) 提供協助

2. 🎧 美國男子／英國女子
Question 2 refers to the following conversation.

> **M** Hello. I have a reservation for six people at 12:30. My name is Lawrence Scott.
> **W** Oh, yes. We have your reservation right here, Mr. Scott.
> **M** When I called a few days ago, I had asked to sit at a table on the rooftop. However, it's very cold today.
> **W** Hmm... I can move your group to table 8 in the indoor dining area.
> **M** Thank you. Also, I took public transportation here, but some of the others in our group are driving. There didn't seem to be much room in the parking lot.
> **W** We have more spots behind the building, and customers can park there for free.
> **M** Oh, thanks. I'll let them know.

中譯
第 2 題，請參考下方對話。

男　你好，我預訂了12點半六個人。我叫Lawrence Scott。
女　啊，好的。我們這裡有您的訂位記錄，Scott先生。
男　前幾天我打電話來時，有要求要坐在頂樓的位置。但是今天天氣很冷。
女　嗯……我可以把你們改安排至室內用餐區的8號桌。
男　謝謝你。另外，我是搭大眾運輸工具來的，但我們這群人當中有些人會開車過來。停車場好像沒有太多單位。
女　我們大樓後方有更多停車位，顧客可以免費停在那裡。
男　哦，謝謝。我會告訴他們。

單字　rooftop 頂樓　take public transportation 搭乘大眾運輸工具　spot 位置、地點

2. 男子說：「今天天氣很冷」是什麼意思？
(A) 他提出想要換座位的要求。
(B) 搭乘大眾運輸工具很不舒服。
(C) 應該調高暖氣溫度。
(D) 他可能要延後會議。

單字　uncomfortable 不舒適的

3. 🎧 美國女子／澳洲男子
Question 3 refers to the following conversation.

> **W** Hi, Rahul. Are you busy? I've created a one-year lease agreement that I'd like you to check. I want to make sure I didn't miss anything.
> **M** Okay. I need to show an apartment in the Clifton Building to prospective tenants at eleven, but I've got some time right now. Which property is the lease for?
> **W** The three-bedroom unit in the Meadowview neighborhood. I showed it to a couple this morning, and they loved it.
> **M** That property was just posted a few days ago.
> **W** I guess Meadowview neighborhood is becoming more popular.

中譯
第 3 題，請參考下方對話。

女　嗨，Rahul，你在忙嗎？我做了一份為期一年的租約，希望你能檢查一下。我想確保我沒有漏掉任何東西。

男　好的，我11點要帶潛在租客參觀Clifton大廈的公寓，但我現在有些時間。出租的是哪一間公寓？

女　Meadowview社區內一間三房的公寓。**今天早上我帶了一對夫妻參觀，他們很喜歡那裡。**

男　那間公寓才剛發布沒幾天。

女　我覺得Meadowview社區好像變得越來越受歡迎了。

單字　lease agreement 租約　　prospective 潛在的、將來的　　tenant 租客　　property 房產、建築物

3. 男子為何會說：「那間公寓才剛發布沒幾天」？
(A) 提出提案
(B) 提供藉口
(C) 解釋錯誤
(D) 表示驚訝

單字　excuse 藉口、理由

4. 🎧 英國女子／澳洲男子
Question 4 refers to the following conversation.

> W　Hi, Ron. I just spoke to Ms. Murphy, and she said that your crew didn't finish the landscaping work at her property today. What's going on?
>
> M　The wood chipping machine stopped working. I thought it was checked for maintenance issues a few weeks ago.
>
> W　Well, that equipment gets used a lot.
>
> M　You're right. I'm planning to borrow one from the other crew and go back tomorrow. That way, we won't have to wait for any repairs.

中譯

第4題，請參考下方對話。

女　嗨，Ron。我剛才和Murphy女士通過電話，她說你的工程團隊今天沒有完成她家的景觀美化工程。這是怎麼回事？

男　**劈柴機停止運轉，我以為幾週前已經定期維護檢查過了。**

女　嗯，但經常會用到那項設備。

男　你說得對。我打算向其他工程組借一台，明天再回去做工程。如此一來，我們就不必等到維修完成。

單字　landscaping 景觀美化　　chip 削、切

4. 女子說：「但經常會用到那項設備」，意味著什麼？
(A) 買了高品質的產品。
(B) 出問題並不意外。
(C) 不需要培訓課程。
(D) 費用合理。

單字　purchase 購買　　expense 費用　　reasonable 合理的

UNIT 15 圖表整合題

PRACTICE　　　　　　　　　　　　題本 p.71

1. (A)　　**2.** (B)　　**3.** (D)

1. 🎧 美國女子／美國男子
Question 1 refers to the following conversation and list.

> W　I missed the staff meeting yesterday. Is there anything I need to know about?
>
> M　Well, the planning for the city's Environmental Awareness Day is going well. There's going to be a cleanup project at Hartford Park in the morning. We'll also be collecting recyclable items at city hall.
>
> W　Great. Did we find any sponsors for the event?
>
> M　Yes. Finch Landscaping is donating three hundred saplings that people can plant at home. We've chosen the tallest of these four varieties because it's the easiest to take care of.

中譯

第1題，請參考下方對話和表格。

女　我錯過了昨天的員工會議。有什麼我需要知道的嗎？

男　嗯，城市環境意識日的規劃進展得很順利。明天早上將會在Hartford公園進行清掃工作。我們還會在市政府收集可回收物品。

女　太棒了。我們找到這次活動的贊助商了嗎？

男　是的，Finch景觀公司捐贈了三百棵樹苗，供人們在家中種植。**我們在四個品種中選了高度最高的品種，因為它最容易照顧。**

單字　recyclable 可回收再利用的　　sponsor 贊助商　　sapling 樹苗　　variety 品種、種類

樹木	高度
橙木	15公尺
霍桑	10公尺
灰柳	8公尺
冬青	6公尺

1. 請查看圖表。哪一種樹苗會被捐贈？
(A) 橙木
(B) 霍桑
(C) 灰柳
(D) 冬青

33

2. 🎧 美國男子／英國女子

Question 2 refers to the following conversation and map.

- **M** Have you seen the map for shooting next week's commercial?
- **W** I'll check it now. Let's see. In the scene, the driver will be heading north on 11th Street. Hmm...
- **M** Is something wrong?
- **W** I think we'll have to adjust our original plan to make the filming easier.
- **M** What did you have in mind?
- **W** Originally, the driver was supposed to turn left on Hines Avenue. Instead, we should have her turn right and then stop in front of the flower shop.
- **M** Okay. We can get that road closed temporarily on the filming day. I'll make the necessary arrangements.

中譯

第 2 題，請參考下方對話和地圖。

男 你看過下週廣告拍攝的地圖了嗎？

女 我現在確認。我來看看，在場景中，駕駛人將會沿著11街向北行駛。嗯……

男 有什麼問題嗎？

女 我認為我們必須調整一下原計畫，才能更容易拍攝。

男 你有什麼想法？

女 **駕駛人原本應在Hines大道左轉。但我們應該讓她右轉，然後停在花店前面。**

男 好的，**我們可以在拍攝當天暫時封閉那條路。**我會做好必要的準備。

單字 shoot 拍攝　commercial 廣告　scene 場景
adjust 調整　temporarily 暫時
make arrangements 做準備、安排

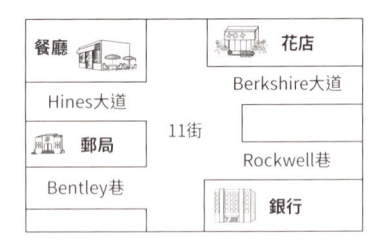

```
┌─────────────────────────────────┐
│ 餐廳              花店           │
│                  Berkshire大道   │
│ Hines大道                        │
│         11街                     │
│ 郵局              Rockwell巷     │
│ Bentley巷         銀行           │
└─────────────────────────────────┘
```

2. 請查看圖表。哪條道路會被封閉？

(A) Hines大道

(B) Berkshire大道

(C) Bentley巷

(D) Rockwell巷

3. 🎧 澳洲男子／英國女子

Question 3 refers to the following conversation and flight schedule.

- **M** Hi, Bethany. I thought I might run into you here. You're headed to Berlin for the manufacturing trade fair, right?
- **W** That's right. Custer Manufacturing isn't hosting a booth this year, so I'm just going as an attendee. Are you still working at Goodwin Production?
- **M** Yes, I am. I've recently been promoted to team leader, so I've been pretty busy.
- **W** Congratulations! I'm sure you'll do a great job in that role.
- **M** Thanks! Say, it looks like my flight is boarding soon. Are you also taking the Powell Airlines flight?
- **W** No, I'm flying with GT Airways. Have a good trip. I'll see you tomorrow at the event.

中譯

第 3 題，請參考下方對話和航班時刻表。

男 嗨，Bethany。我想說可能會在這裡碰到妳。妳要去柏林參加製造業貿易博覽會對吧？

女 沒錯，Custer製造公司今年沒有參展，所以我單純作為與會者參加。你還在Goodwin生產公司工作嗎？

男 是的。最近升遷為組長，所以很忙。

女 恭喜你！我相信你會在這個職位上表現得很出色。

男 謝謝！我的航班好像快登機了。你也是搭乘Powell航空的班機嗎？

女 不，**我搭的是GT航空的班機**。祝你旅途愉快。明天活動上見。

單字 run into 偶然碰到　trade fair 貿易博覽會
attendee 出席者　promote 升遷

```
┌─────────────────────────────────┐
│        飛往柏林的航班            │
│  起飛時間         航空公司       │
│  下午 1 點 35 分   Kershaw廉航   │
│  下午 3 點 58 分   Rosco天合聯盟 │
│  下午 7 點 31 分   Powell航空    │
│  下午 8 點 02 分   GT航空        │
└─────────────────────────────────┘
```

3. 請查看圖表。女子的航班何時起飛？

(A) 於下午1點35分

(B) 於下午3點58分

(C) 於下午7點31分

(D) 於下午8點02分

32. (D)	33. (C)	34. (B)	35. (B)	36. (D)
37. (A)	38. (B)	39. (C)	40. (A)	41. (A)
42. (C)	43. (B)	44. (C)	45. (D)	46. (A)
47. (D)	48. (C)	49. (B)	50. (A)	51. (D)
52. (A)	53. (B)	54. (D)	55. (C)	56. (A)
57. (B)	58. (C)	59. (C)	60. (A)	61. (B)
62. (C)	63. (D)	64. (A)	65. (C)	66. (B)
67. (B)	68. (A)	69. (A)	70. (C)	

32-34. 🎧 澳洲男子／美國女子
Questions 32-34 refer to the following conversation.

> M Victoria, sales of ³²our athletic shoes have declined. ³³How about we hold a 3-on-3 basketball tournament to bring more attention to our store?
> W Good idea! We could fence off an area of the parking lot and hold it there.
> M Yes, and spectators would come, too, so we could get a pretty big crowd.
> W We've never done anything like it. It'll take a lot of planning.
> M That's true. ³⁴I'll e-mail the staff now to see who's interested in helping.

第 32-34 題，請參考下方對話。

男　Victoria，**我們的運動鞋**銷量下降了。**我們要不要舉辦一場3對3的籃球比賽，讓更多人關注我們的商店？**
女　好主意！我們可以用柵欄圍住停車場的一個區域，在那裡舉行比賽。
男　沒錯，而且觀眾也會來，所以可能會有眾多人潮。
女　我們從來沒有做過這樣的事，這需要詳細計畫。
男　你說得對。**我現在就發電子郵件給員工，看看是否有人願意提供協助。**

單字 athletic shoes 運動鞋　decline 下降
bring attention to 帶來關注　fence off 用柵欄隔開
spectator 觀眾　crowd 人潮、人群

32. 對話最有可能發生在哪裡？
(A) 在五金行
(B) 在社區中心
(C) 在汽車經銷商
(D) 在鞋店

33. 男子建議做什麼？
(A) 僱用兼職人員
(B) 重新整理商品排列
(C) 舉辦運動比賽
(D) 聯絡供應商

單字 rearrange 重新排列、改變　competition 比賽
換句話說 3-on-3 basketball tournament → sports competition

34. 男子接下來會做什麼？
(A) 與主管交談
(B) 發送訊息
(C) 更新網站
(D) 查看一些數據

單字 supervisor 主管　review 查看　figures 數據
換句話說 e-mail the staff → send a message

35-37. 🎧 美國男子／美國女子／英國女子
Questions 35-37 refer to the following conversation with three speakers.

> M Hi, I'm Ronald. ³⁵The landlord called me this morning and said you were having some issues with your ceiling.
> W1 Yes, the problem is over here in my coworker's office. Hey, Carol. ³⁵The facility manager's here.
> W2 Oh, thanks for coming. During last week's heavy rain, ³⁶I noticed water running down the wall. Look, you can see the damp patch there.
> M Hmm... We often have these problems after a major storm. In this case, the floor above needs to be examined first. Anyway, ³⁷it will take some time to figure out the exact cause and get it repaired. Is that all right?

第 35-37 題，請參考下方三人的對話。

男　嗨，我是Ronald。**今天早上房東打電話給我，說你們的天花板有點問題。**
女1 是的，問題出在我同事的辦公室裡。嘿，Carol，**設施經理來了。**
女2 哦，謝謝你過來。上週下大雨時，**我注意到水沿著牆流下來。**你看，那裡可以看到潮溼的小區塊。
男　嗯⋯⋯我們經常在暴風雨過後遇到這樣的問題。在這種情況下，需先檢查上方樓層。總之，**需要一些時間弄清楚確切原因，並修好它。**這樣可以嗎？

單字 landlord 房東、地主　ceiling 天花板
facility 設施　damp 潮濕的　patch 小區塊
major 重大的、主要的　examine 檢查

35. 男子最有可能是誰？
(A) 房東
(B) 設施經理
(C) 水管工人
(D) 電工

36. 根據Carol的說法，問題出在哪裡？
(A) 某些指示並不正確。
(B) 有名同事缺勤。
(C) 她缺少一些零件。
(D) 她注意到漏水。

單字 instruction 說明　component 零件　leak 漏水處

37. 男子針對維修提到什麼？
(A) 無法立即完成。
(B) 可能需要特殊零件。
(C) 目前沒有必要。
(D) 最近收費有漲價。

單字 complete 完成　charge 收費

換句話說 it will take some time → it cannot be completed right away

38-40. 🎧 英國女子／美國男子
Questions 38-40 refer to the following conversation.

> W　Good morning. I saw your advertisement about open positions at your company.
> M　Yes, ³⁸we're taking on more and more building projects, so we need more people to assist with that.
> W　Is there any previous experience required?
> M　No, but ³⁹you must have completed an occupational safety certification course for the general industry. If you don't have a certificate, it's easy to obtain one.
> W　Can I get information about where I can take those courses?
> M　Actually, ⁴⁰we're going to hold an online information session this Friday, where all your questions can be answered. Would you like me to sign you up for that?

第 38-40 題，請參考下方對話。

女　早安，我有看到貴公司的徵人廣告。
男　是的，**我們承接越來越多的建築專案，所以需要更多人的協助。**
女　有需要任何過往相關經驗嗎？
男　不用，但**您必須完成一般行業的職業安全認證課程。如果您目前沒有認證，也能輕鬆取得。**
女　我能在哪裡取得參加該課程的資訊呢？
男　其實**我們將於本週五舉行線上資訊說明會，**您所有的問題都能得到解答。要我幫您報名參加嗎？

單字 open position 職缺　assist with 協助…
previous 先前的　occupational 職業的
certification 證照、認證　certificate 證書　obtain 獲得

38. 男子最有可能在哪裡工作？
(A) 在政府機關
(B) 在建設公司
(C) 在診所
(D) 在職業介紹所

39. 根據男子所述，應徵者需要提供什麼？
(A) 推薦信
(B) 郵件地址
(C) 認證證書
(D) 附照片的身分證影本

40. 星期五有什麼安排？
(A) 資訊說明會
(B) 訪談
(C) 員工晚餐
(D) 董事會會議

41-43. 🎧 美國女子／澳洲男子
Questions 41-43 refer to the following conversation.

> W　Hi, I'm interested in buying ⁴¹the Damaro digital camera, but I'm having trouble finding it. I'm wondering if your store has any in stock.
> M　It's a really popular item, so, unfortunately, we've just sold the last one.
> W　That's too bad. ⁴²I'm taking pictures at an outdoor concert this weekend, and I wanted to use a new camera for that event. ⁴³Do you know how I can get one?
> M　Hmm... our system is showing that there's one left in stock at our Springdale branch. I can call them and ask them to hold it for you, if you can pick it up today.

第 41-43 題，請參考下方對話。

女　嗨，我想要買**Damaro數位相機**，但我找不太到。我想知道貴商店是否還有庫存。
男　這是一款非常受歡迎的商品，可惜我們剛剛賣出了最後一台。
女　太可惜了。**這個週末我要在戶外音樂會上拍照**，我想在那場活動中使用新相機。**你知道怎樣才能買到嗎？**
男　嗯… 我們的系統顯示Springdale分店還有一台庫存。如果您今天能取貨的話，我可以打電話給他們，請他們幫您保留。

單字 have trouble -ing 做…有困難　have in stock 有庫存

41. 說話者正在討論什麼樣的產品？
(A) 數位相機
(B) 電玩遊戲系統
(C) 印表機
(D) 智慧型手機

42. 這個週末將舉行什麼活動？
(A) 電影放映
(B) 一年一度的遊行
(C) 音樂表演
(D) 商務會議

換句話說 concert → musical performance

43. 女子針對什麼提問？
(A) 保固期有多長
(B) 如何取得物品
(C) 運費多少
(D) 如何退貨

單字 warranty 保固　return 返還

44-46. 🎧 美國男子／美國女子
Questions 44-46 refer to the following conversation.

> M　Good afternoon, Ms. Cooper. ⁴⁴ I'm here to plant the flowers and bushes that you ordered for your front garden.
>
> W　⁴⁵ Thanks for coming so quickly. I want to get this project started as soon as possible. I plan to put my house on the market, and I want it to look its best.
>
> M　I understand. We'll make sure that it makes a good first impression. Now, is it all right if I leave my truck parked on the street?
>
> W　Actually, street parking is only for residents. But ⁴⁶ I'll pull my car into the garage so you can use the driveway.
>
> M　That's perfect. Thank you.

第 44-46 題，請參考下方對話。

男　午安，Cooper女士。**我來這裡種植您為前方庭院訂購的花卉和灌木。**
女　**謝謝你這麼快過來。**我想盡快開始這項工作，我打算把我的房子放到市場上出售，因此希望它看起來是最佳狀態。
男　我明白了。我們會確保它給人留下良好的第一印象。請問我現在可以把卡車停在街上嗎？
女　事實上，只有住戶才能在路邊停車。但**我會把我的車開進車庫裡**，這樣你就可以使用車道了。
男　那太好了，謝謝您。

單字 bush 灌木　first impression 第一印象　resident 居民　garage 車庫　driveway 車道

44. 女子需要什麼幫忙？
(A) 安裝窗戶
(B) 建造車庫
(C) 在庭院種植
(D) 移除樹木

45. 女子為何要感謝男子？
(A) 他提供了折扣。
(B) 他提出了建議。
(C) 他解釋了流程。
(D) 他很快就抵達。

單字 procedure 流程

46. 女子接下來最有可能做什麼？
(A) 移動她的車
(B) 取得電源線
(C) 付款
(D) 選擇顏色

換句話說 pull my car into the garage → move her vehicle

47-49. 🎧 澳洲男子／英國女子
Questions 47-49 refer to the following conversation.

> M　Thanks for calling Augusta's. How may I help you?
>
> W　Hi. This is Lauren Rodriguez. ⁴⁷ You're making dinner for our office on Friday.
>
> M　Oh, yes. Holt Insurance Services, right?
>
> W　Yes, that's right. ⁴⁸ I'm arranging an anniversary party to commemorate twenty-five years in business.
>
> M　That's wonderful. ⁴⁷ You're booked in for a delivery at 6:30 P.M. Do you need any changes?
>
> W　Actually, I just found out that three of our employees are vegetarians. ⁴⁹ Would it be possible to change three of the entrees to meat-free dishes?
>
> M　I was going to order everything today, so you're in luck.

第 47-49 題，請參考下方對話。

男　感謝您致電Augusta's。請問有什麼需要幫忙的嗎？
女　你好，我是Lauren Rodriguez。**星期五貴店要為我們公司準備晚餐。**
男　啊，是的。您是Holt保險公司對吧？
女　對，沒錯。**我正在準備一個週年紀念派對，以慶祝開業25週年。**
男　太棒了。**您預約晚上6點30分送達。**有任何需要更改的部分嗎？
女　事實上，我剛才發現我們有三名員工是素食主義者。能否將其中三道主菜改成不含肉的餐點？
男　我本來預計今天要訂購所有食材，您運氣真好。

單字 insurance 保險（業）　commemorate 紀念、慶祝　book in 預約

37

47. 女子打電話給什麼樣的公司？
(A) 飯店
(B) 保險公司
(C) 電影院
(D) 餐飲公司

48. 為何女子要策劃一場活動？
(A) 宣傳盛大開幕
(B) 頒發一些獎項
(C) 慶祝公司週年
(D) 為專案籌措資金

單字 promote 宣傳　present 頒發　raise funds 籌措資金

換句話說 commemorate twenty-five years in business → celebrate a company anniversary

49. 為何男子會說：「我本來預計今天要訂購所有食材」？
(A) 感謝女子的提醒
(B) 確認能夠實現要求
(C) 接受更改截止日期
(D) 要求付款

單字 reminder 提醒　fulfill 滿足、實現

50-52. 🎧 美國男子／英國女子／美國女子
Questions 50-52 refer to the following conversation with three speakers.

> **M** Joanne and Stacey, we're continually trying to make improvements to the working conditions ⁵⁰here at our law firm. I'd like your help, since you're part of the IT team.
> **W1** Is there anything specific you have in mind?
> **M** Well, ⁵¹a lot of people have been complaining about the sign-in system for logging their working hours. It takes a long time to load each page. Employees say that it's frustrating.
> **W2** I've noticed that, too. If there's room in the budget, ⁵²the company should upgrade the existing software program. That would help a lot.
> **M** Thanks, Stacey. I'll see what I can do.

第 50-52 題，請參考下方三人對話。
男　Joanne和Stacey，我們一直在努力**改善律師事務所**的工作條件。你們是資訊科技團隊的一員，我需要你們的幫助。
女1　你有什麼具體的想法嗎？
男　嗯，很多人一直在抱怨記錄工作時間的登入系統。載入每個頁面都需要很長的時間，員工們表示這令人沮喪。
女2　我也有注意到這件事。如果預算允許，**公司應該升級現有軟體程式**。這會有很大的幫助。
男　謝謝，Stacey。我看看我能做什麼。

單字 continually 不斷地　make improvements 改善

working condition 工作條件　log 記錄
frustrating 令人沮喪的　existing 原有的

50. 說話者在哪裡工作？
(A) 在律師事務所
(B) 在職業介紹所
(C) 在報紙出版社
(D) 在攝影工作室

51. 男子提到什麼問題？
(A) 某些設備遺失。
(B) 分享了一些機密資訊。
(C) 員工的工作量過多。
(D) 系統運作緩慢。

單字 confidential 機密的

換句話說 It takes a long time to load each page. → A system is running slowly.

52. Stacey認為公司應該做什麼？
(A) 升級部分軟體
(B) 收集員工的意見回饋
(C) 更改營業時間
(D) 提供年度獎金

單字 the hours of operation 營業時間

53-55. 🎧 澳洲男子／英國女子
Questions 53-55 refer to the following conversation.

> **M** Hi, Kimberly. ⁵³Thank you for your interest in working here at Lafayette. According to your résumé, you have a lot of experience cleaning guest rooms.
> **W** That's right. I'm currently on the housekeeping staff at the Maloy Inn. ⁵⁴I'm hoping to buy a house later this year, so I'm taking on a second job so I can save up.
> **M** Well, ⁵⁵the shift for this job is 7 A.M. to noon on weekdays. Can you work then? I hope it doesn't conflict with your current work schedule.
> **W** Not at all. I only work afternoons at the Maloy Inn.
> **M** That's perfect.

第 53-55 題，請參考下方對話。
男　你好，Kimberly。**感謝你有興趣在Lafayette工作**。根據你的履歷，你有很多清掃客房的經驗。
女　沒錯。我目前在Maloy Inn.當房務清潔人員。**我想在今年年底買房子**，所以才想做第二份工作，以便存錢。
男　嗯，**這個工作的輪班時間是平日上午7點到中午。這段時間你能工作嗎**？希望不會與你目前的工作班表衝突。

女　完全不會。我在 Maloy Inn.只有下午會工作。
男　那太好了。

單字　housekeeping 房務管理、家務　save up 存（錢）
shift 輪班工作時間　conflict 衝突

53. 男子最有可能是誰？
(A) 高級會計師
(B) 飯店經理
(C) 大樓清潔工
(D) 服飾店老闆

54. 女子想要在今年年底做什麼？
(A) 搬到新城市
(B) 出國旅遊
(C) 自行創業
(D) 買房子

換句話說　buy → purchase

55. 男子詢問女子什麼事？
(A) 她的職業目標
(B) 她可以開始工作的日期
(C) 她的工作時間安排
(D) 她的期望薪資

56-58. 🎧 美國女子／澳洲男子
Questions 56-58 refer to the following conversation.

> W　⁵⁶Have we finished all of the testing for the project along the Aimes River? I need to send the completed report by May 7.
> M　⁵⁶Yes, we've checked the environmental impact, and it seems that there will be very little disruption to wildlife in the area.
> W　That's great. Unless something unexpected happens, ⁵⁷the city will approve this project by next month. Residents will be happy to finally get a walking and jogging trail.
> M　I'm excited about it. ⁵⁸It'll be good for encouraging people to work out and take better care of their health.

第 56-58 題，請參考下方對話。
女　我們已經完成 Aimes 河沿岸項目的所有測試了嗎？我必須在 5月7日前發送完成的報告。
男　是的，我們已經檢查過對環境的影響，幾乎不會干擾該地區的野生動物。
女　太好了。除非有預期之外的事發生，**市政府將於下個月前批准該項目**。居民會很高興終於有一條可以散步和慢跑的步道。
男　我對此感到很興奮。這將有助於鼓勵人們運動，並更好地照顧自身健康。

單字　completed 完成的

environmental impact 環境影響
disruption 干擾、環境破壞　wildlife 野生動物
unexpected 意外的　approve 批准　work out 健身、運動

56. 說話者最有可能是誰？
(A) 環境科學家
(B) 公司投資者
(C) 市議員
(D) 建築工人

57. 市府預計會批准什麼？
(A) 舉辦節慶活動
(B) 修建人行道
(C) 擴建停車場
(D) 翻修體育場

單字　pedestrian 步行的、人行的　path 道路

換句話說　get a walking and jogging trail → building a pedestrian path

58. 對話中提到專案的優點為何？
(A) 能夠省錢。
(B) 創造就業機會。
(C) 促進健康。
(D) 吸引遊客。

單字　promote 促進、宣傳

59-61. 🎧 美國男子／英國女子
Questions 59-61 refer to the following conversation.

> M　⁵⁹Sandra, our application to be one of the presenters at the Home Appliance Trade Show has been approved!
> W　That's great news!
> M　It really is. We were among only eight companies selected. For the event, we need to choose a recipe to demonstrate our blender.
> W　⁶⁰We could make a fresh fruit smoothie.
> M　Well, everyone is familiar with that.
> W　⁶⁰Hmm... you're right. We should think of something new and exciting.
> M　⁶¹How about we go to the grocery store? Seeing the options for ingredients might inspire us.
> W　⁶¹Good idea. I have time to do that with you today after work.

第 59-61 題，請參考下方對話。
男　Sandra，**我們申請成為家電貿易展的發表者之一，已經獲得批准了！**
女　真是個好消息！
男　確實如此。我們是獲選的八家企業之一。在這次活動中，我們需要選擇一個食譜來展示我們的攪拌機。

39

女　我們可以製作新鮮的水果冰沙。
男　嗯，那是每個人都很熟悉的甜點。
女　嗯… 你說得對。我們應該想一些新穎和令人興奮的料理。
男　我們要不要去超市看看？看到可以選擇的材料可能會為我們帶來靈感。
女　好主意。我今天下班後有空跟你一起去。

單字　application 申請　demonstrate 展示　ingredient 材料、成分　inspire 帶來靈感、啟發

59. 對話的主要內容為何？
(A) 出版一本食譜
(B) 開始做網路廣播
(C) 在貿易展覽會上發表
(D) 推出家用電器

單字　launch 推出　household appliance 家用電器

60. 為何男人會說：「那是每個人都很熟悉的甜點」？
(A) 拒絕建議
(B) 確認調查結果
(C) 稱讚戰略
(D) 認可成果

單字　praise 稱讚　acknowledge 認可
accomplishment 成果、業績

61. 說話者同意做什麼事？
(A) 聯絡一些供應商
(B) 一起逛商店
(C) 錄製演示
(D) 瀏覽網站

單字　browse 瀏覽

換句話說　go to the grocery store → visit a shop

62-64. 🎧 澳洲男子／英國女子
Questions 62-64 refer to the following conversation and list.

> M　Hello. ⁶²I'm wondering if the community center offers ballet classes. My daughter is interested in joining one.
> W　Yes, we do. You can take a look at this list of classes to see the fees.
> M　All right. What day is the class?
> W　That depends. ⁶³Is your daughter at the beginner, intermediate, or advanced level?
> M　She's never done dancing before.
> W　Okay. Then I'd recommend the Saturday morning class. This is the registration form. ⁶⁴And, if you'd like to see some footage of past shows, there's a brief video on our website.
> M　I'll check that out.

第 62-64 題，請參考下方對話和名單。

男　你好。**我想知道社區中心是否有提供芭蕾舞課程**，我女兒有興趣加入。
女　是的，我們有。您可以查看此課程表以了解費用。
男　好的。星期幾上課？
女　視情況而定。**您女兒的程度是初級、中級還是高級？**
男　她從來沒有跳過舞。
女　好的，那我推薦星期六早上的課程。這是報名表。另外，**如果您想看過去演出的一些片段，我們網站上有簡短的影片。**
男　我會去查看的。

單字　fee 費用、學費　beginner 初學者、初級的
intermediate 中級的　advanced 高級的
footage 影片、片段

詩歌	10美元
水彩畫	18美元
⁶²芭蕾舞	14美元
縫紉	22美元

62. 請查看圖表。男子最有可能付多少錢？
(A) 10美元
(B) 18美元
(C) 14美元
(D) 22美元

63. 女子詢問什麼資訊？
(A) 信用卡號碼
(B) 電子郵件地址
(C) 開始日期
(D) 難度分級

64. 女子建議做什麼事？
(A) 觀看影片
(B) 租用一些裝備
(C) 穿著特殊服裝
(D) 列印手冊

65-67. 🎧 美國女子／澳洲男子
Questions 65-67 refer to the following conversation and map.

> W　Hello, ⁶⁵I'm here for the lecture on economics.
> M　That's in the main auditorium, just to your right. The auditorium is nearly full, so I'd recommend heading straight in.
> W　⁶⁶Oh, I didn't realize that so many people would be here. Could I ask you one more question?
> M　Of course.

40

W I took a taxi here, but can I get a public bus back to the Ramsey Hotel?

M Let's see...according to the map, you can take bus 47. ⁶⁷The nearest stop to your hotel is TG Pharmacy.

第65-67題，請參考下方對話和地圖。

女 你好，**我是來聽經濟學講座的。**

男 那個講座在主禮堂，就在你的右手邊。禮堂幾乎坐滿了，我建議你直接進去。

女 啊，**沒想到會有這麼多人來。**我可以再問你一個問題嗎？

男 當然可以

女 我是搭計程車來的，我能改搭公車回Ramsey飯店嗎？

男 我看一下…… 根據地圖，你可以搭47號公車。**離你飯店最近的公車站是TG藥局。**

單字 auditorium 禮堂

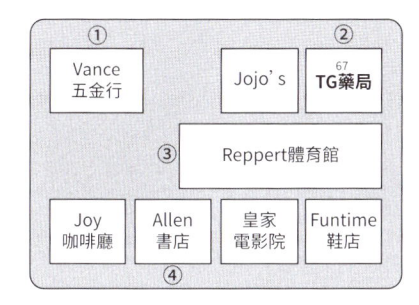

```
①
┌─────────┐ ┌─────────┐ ┌─────────┐
│ Vance   │ │ Jojo's  │ │⁶⁷TG藥局 │
│ 五金行  │ │         │ │         │
└─────────┘ └─────────┘ └─────────┘
      ③  ┌──────────────┐
         │ Reppert體育館│
         └──────────────┘
┌──────┐┌──────┐┌──────┐┌──────┐
│ Joy  ││Allen ││皇家  ││Funtime│
│咖啡廳││書店  ││電影院││鞋店  │
└──────┘└──────┘└──────┘└──────┘
      ④
```

65. 女子為何造訪該地點？
(A) 與投資者見面
(B) 進行檢查
(C) 聽講座
(D) 參加工作面試

單字 site 地點　inspection 檢查、檢驗

66. 女子對什麼感到驚訝？
(A) 交通費
(B) 參加人數
(C) 交通時間
(D) 場地大小

單字 transportation 交通運輸　attendee 參與者

67. 請查看圖表。女子最有可能在哪裡下車？
(A) 第1站
(B) 第2站
(C) 第3站
(D) 第4站

68-70. 🎧 美國男子／英國女子
Questions 68-70 refer to the following conversation and weather forecast.

M Hi, Ms. Chilton. ⁶⁸I'm sorry to have to bother you today. My colleague measured the property lines for your fence inaccurately, so it has to be done again.

W No problem.

M Thanks for understanding. ⁶⁹And it's great that you've decided to have metal instead of wood.

W Yes, I think it will last longer in any kind of weather.

M Speaking of the weather, my team needs a dry day to do the fence installation. ⁷⁰It's rainy now, but we'll return on the first sunny day this week.

第68-70題，請參考下方對話和天氣預報。

男 您好，Chilton女士。**很抱歉在今天打擾您。我的同事量錯了您房地產的柵欄邊界，所以需要重新測量。**

女 沒問題。

男 感謝您的諒解。**另外，很高興您決定使用金屬而不是木頭。**

女 是的，我認為金屬在任何天氣下，都更為耐用。

男 說到天氣，我的團隊需要一個乾燥的日子來安裝柵欄。**現在正在下雨，但我們會在本週的第一個晴天過來。**

單字 bother 打擾　measure 測量
property line 房地產邊界　inaccurately 不準確地、不精準地
last 持久、持續　installation 安裝

	費城 一週天氣預報			
星期一	星期二	⁷⁰**星期三**	星期四	星期五
雨天	雨天	晴天	陰天	晴天

68. 男子為何要道歉？
(A) 必須重新進行一些測量。
(B) 一個工作估價單不準確。
(C) 有些用品尚未送達。
(D) 一位員工沒有提供請款單。

單字 measurement 測量　estimate 估價　bill 請款單、帳單

69. 男子認為什麼是個好主意？
(A) 使用不同的材料
(B) 換成其他公司
(C) 評估房地產的價值
(D) 要求趕工

單字 assess 評估　value 價值

70. 請查看圖表。男子的團隊最有可能什麼時候回來？
(A) 星期一
(B) 星期二
(C) 星期三
(D) 星期四

LC PART 4

UNIT 16 通話訊息

PRACTICE 題本 p.81

1. (A) 2. (D) 3. (C) 4. (C) 5. (B) 6. (D)
7. (C) 8. (A) 9. (D)

1-3. 🎧 美國男子
Questions 1-3 refer to the following telephone message.

> M Hi, Sandra. I'm sorry I didn't call you back sooner. I was in Boston last week attending a medical association convention. Regarding your interview, everyone on our hiring panel was very impressed with your career history. [1,2]I would like to offer the position of healthcare assistant at our practice. Now, I realize that our job posting said the start date would be August 25. [3]However, Amar, our training coordinator, will be out of town at that time. So, that's been moved to September 1.

第 1-3 題,請參考下方電話留言。

男 你好,Sandra。我很抱歉沒有早點回電給你。上週我在波士頓參加醫學協會會議。關於你的面試,我們招募小組的每個人都對你的工作經歷印象深刻。**我想提供我們診所的醫療助理一職**。但我現在發現我們的徵人啟事上寫到職日為 8 月 25 日。**但是我們的培訓協調員Amar那段時間要出差。所以到職日會改到 9 月 1 日**。

單字 panel 專門小組　practice (醫療) 工作場所
coordinator 協調員

1. 說話者最有可能在哪裡工作?
(A) 在醫療診所
(B) 在律師事務所
(C) 在職業介紹所
(D) 在軟體公司

2. 說話者為何打電話來?
(A) 要求聽者提供推薦函
(B) 邀請聽者演講
(C) 更改面試地點
(D) 提供工作機會

單字 reference 推薦函、推薦人

換句話說 offer the position of healthcare assistant → make a job offer

3. 延後的原因為何?
(A) 委員會必須召開會議。
(B) 場地預訂已滿。
(C) 員工無法到場。
(D) 部分用品尚未送達。

單字 venue 場地

換句話說 out of town → unavailable

4-6. 🎧 美國女子
Questions 4-6 refer to the following telephone message.

> W Hi, Vijay. I have some exciting news. [4]Country Living magazine would like to feature our bakery in the July issue. A reporter will be visiting us on Friday to interview our staff and learn more about our unique baked goods. Since you're the executive pastry chef, [5]I'll need you to stay late on Thursday to make sure everything is well organized so we can make a good impression. Unfortunately, I'm too busy to help much, as [6]I'm still planning to attend the Rockford Career Fair this weekend. Thanks.

第 4-6 題,請參考下方電話留言。

女 嗨,Vijay。我有個令人振奮的消息。《鄉村生活》雜誌打算在七月號上刊登我們麵包店的特別報導。有位記者將於週五來拜訪,採訪我們的員工,並進一步了解我們獨特的烘焙食品。因為你是糕點行政主廚,所以**我需要你在週四晚上待晚一點**,確保一切都能順利進行,並給人留下好印象。可惜的是,我太忙了,沒辦法幫上忙,因為**我仍打算參加這個週末的Rockford職業博覽會**。謝謝。

單字 feature (在報章雜誌上) 專題報導、特輯
issue (刊物的) 版、期號　executive 行政上的、經營管理的
pastry chef 糕點師傅　organized 有規劃的
make a good impression 留下好印象

4. 留言的主要內容為何?
(A) 海外出差
(B) 新產品上市
(C) 雜誌採訪
(D) 企業搬遷

單字 launch 上市　relocation 搬遷

5. 說話者要求聽者星期四做什麼事?
(A) 簽訂合約
(B) 比平常工作到更晚
(C) 烘烤額外品項
(D) 預訂晚餐

換句話說 stay late → work later than usual

42

6. 這個週末說話者要去哪裡？
(A) 參加培訓研討會
(B) 參加董事會會議
(C) 參加音樂節
(D) 參加職業博覽會

換句話說 career fair → job fair

7-9. 🎧 澳洲男子
Questions 7-9 refer to the following recorded message.

> M ⁷Thank you for calling Westlake Bus Services. Due to the severe storm in the area, several of our journeys have been delayed. We are very sorry for any inconvenience this may cause. ⁸We will confirm the new schedule for the departure times as soon as we can. However, at this time, we are monitoring the situation. ⁹For the most updated details about our services, we ask that you visit our website.

第 7-9 題，請參考下方語音留言。

男 感謝您撥打西湖客運服務電話。由於該地區的嚴重風暴，造成我們部分班次延誤。對此造成您的不便，我們深表歉意。**我們將盡快確認新的發車時間。但就目前來看，我們仍在監測狀況。**關於我們的服務，欲知更多最新消息，請至我們的網站查詢。

單字 severe 嚴重的　journey 行程、路程
inconvenience 不便　monitor 監測

7. 聽者撥打至什麼類型的公司？
(A) 汽車維修廠
(B) 公用事業供應商
(C) 運輸公司
(D) 電器行

換句話說 bus services → a transportation company

8. 說話者提到：「我們正在監測狀況」，意味著什麼？
(A) 無法確定出發時間。
(B) 將會提出申訴。
(C) 將評估客戶回饋。
(D) 採納新的政策。

單字 uncertain 不確定的　file 提出
assess 評估、評價　adopt 採納

9. 聽者如何獲取最新消息？
(A) 與司機交談
(B) 訂閱電子報
(C) 發送電子郵件
(D) 查詢線上資訊

UNIT 17 公告與導引

PRACTICE 題本 p.83

1. (A)　**2.** (A)　**3.** (B)　**4.** (D)　**5.** (B)　**6.** (C)
7. (D)　**8.** (B)　**9.** (A)

1-3. 🎧 美國女子
Questions 1-3 refer to the following announcement.

> W Attention, customers. ¹Thank you for shopping at Highland Apparel. Today's special is 20% off all leather jackets. And don't forget to register for our new loyalty rewards program. ²Each month, we offer one accessory at no charge to members of the program. So, don't miss out. Also, ³please be aware that we're going to carry out some building work at the rear of the store to expand our display space. We'll be starting that project next Monday.

第 1-3 題，請參考下方公告。

女 各位顧客請注意，**感謝您在Highland服裝購物**。今日的特價活動為所有皮革夾克享八折優惠。也別忘了註冊我們新的顧客回饋計劃。**每個月我們都會免費提供一件飾品給該計劃的會員**，千萬不要錯過。另外，**為了擴大陳列空間，我們將於賣場後方進行部分建築工程，敬請注意。**我們預計於下週一開始施工。

單字 at no charge 免費提供　carry out 進行、執行
rear 後方的

1. 聽者最有可能在哪裡？
(A) 在服飾店
(B) 在五金行
(C) 在電子產品商店
(D) 在書店

2. 說話者表示會提供什麼加入給顧客回饋計劃的會員？
(A) 免費物品
(B) 優惠券
(C) 快遞服務
(D) 預售通知

單字 advance 預先的

換句話說 one accessory at no charge → a free item

3. 什麼活動將於下週一開始？
(A) 延長營業時間
(B) 一些工程
(C) 週年慶活動
(D) 清倉拍賣

單字 extended 延長的

43

4-6. 🎧 美國男子

Questions 4-6 refer to the following excerpt from a meeting.

> M ⁴Next Friday, Dixon Furniture will deliver three leather sofas that we will place in our employee lounge. ⁵Research has shown that taking breaks regularly can improve productivity significantly. So, we are doing our best to provide a relaxing space for our staff. We'll also be replacing everyone's office chair. If you'd like to see the options that are available, ⁶please take a look at the product catalog at the reception desk. The ones that are within our budget will be marked with a star.

第 4-6 題，請參考下方會議摘錄。

男　下週五Dixon傢俱將送來三張皮製沙發，我們會將這些沙發擺放在員工休息室中。研究結果顯示，定期休息可以顯著提高工作生產力。因此，我們竭盡全力為我們的員工提供一個可以放鬆的空間。我們也將替換每個人的辦公椅。如果你想查看可供選擇的品項，**請至接待櫃檯查看產品目錄**。在我們預算之內的項目會標記星號。

單字 place 放置、擺設　productivity 工作效率
significantly 顯著地　take a look at 查看…
mark 標記

4. 下週五會有什麼東西送來？
(A) 名片
(B) 盆栽
(C) 輕食茶點
(D) 皮製沙發

5. 關於工作生產力，提到了什麼？
(A) 最近辦公室的生產力有提高。
(B) 可透過定期休息來增加。
(C) 直接帶來更高的利潤。
(D) 新管理團隊的關注點。

單字 result in 導致　profits 利潤、獲利

6. 根據說話者所述，接待櫃檯有什麼東西？
(A) 合約
(B) 調查表
(C) 目錄
(D) 更新的時間表

7-9. 🎧 英國女子

Questions 7-9 refer to the following excerpt from a meeting and pie chart.

> W Good afternoon, everyone. ⁷Welcome to our monthly gardening club meeting. Last time, I gave you a list of topics related to gardening and asked you to select which ones you would like to learn more about. You can see the results here. I'm still working on finding a speaker for a workshop on the most requested topic, Seasonal Planning. ⁸So, in the meantime, we'll hold a workshop on the second most requested topic. That'll take place on August 10. I'll send some information about that later this week, so ⁹please be sure to update the e-mail address and phone number we have for you.

第 7-9 題，請參考下方會議摘錄和圓餅圖。

女　大家午安。**歡迎參加我們每月一次的園藝社團會議**。上次我提供了園藝相關的主題清單，並要求大家選出想深入了解的主題。你可以在此處看到結果。我仍在努力尋找研討會的講者，來探討最受歡迎的主題「季節性規劃」。**所以在此期間，我們將先以第二受歡迎的主題舉辦研討會**。活動將於8月10日舉行。我會在本週稍晚發送相關資訊，所以**請務必更新提供給我們的電子郵件地址和電話號碼**。

單字 requested 要求的

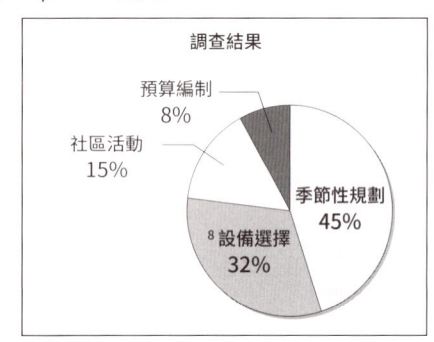

調查結果
預算編制 8%
社區活動 15%
季節性規劃 45%
⁸設備選擇 32%

7. 聽者是哪一類型社團的成員？
(A) 繪畫
(B) 縫紉
(C) 自行車
(D) 園藝

8. 請查看圖表。根據說話者所述，可能會先舉行哪個研討會？
(A) 季節性規劃
(B) 設備選擇
(C) 社區活動
(D) 預算編制

9. 說話者要求聽者做什麼？
(A) 更新聯絡資訊
(B) 推薦研討會的地點
(C) 解釋調查的答覆
(D) 招募新團隊成員

單字 recruit 招募

換句話說 the e-mail address and phone number → some contact information

UNIT 18 演說與講座

PRACTICE 題本 p.85

1. (B) **2.** (A) **3.** (B) **4.** (A) **5.** (C) **6.** (B)
7. (C) **8.** (D) **9.** (A)

1-3. 🎧 美國男子
Questions 1-3 refer to the following speech.

> M ¹Before the benefit concert begins, I want to thank everyone for the support you have given to the Stonebrooke Community Center. ²I'm sure you're all aware that our building has been in need of a new roof for a long time. We've raised about half the money we need for the replacement, but there's still more to be done. After the show, ³I want to encourage you to purchase our community center T-shirts and sweatshirts. Profits from those sales will go toward the project. Thank you!

第 1-3 題，請參考下方演講。

男 在慈善音樂會開始之前，我想感謝大家對Stonebrooke社區中心的支持。我相信大家都知道，**我們大樓長期以來一直需要一個新屋頂**。我們已經籌措到更換屋頂所需資金的一半左右，但仍需要更多。演出結束後，**我鼓勵大家購買我們社區中心的T恤和運動衫**。銷售的收入將用於該工程。謝謝你們！

單字 benefit 慈善活動、義演　support 支持、資助
aware 知道的、察覺的　in need of 需要⋯
replacement 更換　go toward 助於促成某件事

1. 將會舉行什麼活動？
(A) 藝術節
(B) 募款活動
(C) 音樂課
(D) 烘焙比賽

換句話說 the benefit concert → A fundraising event

2. 該組織計畫做什麼事？
(A) 更換屋頂
(B) 培訓志工
(C) 更改開放時間
(D) 提供線上服務

3. 說話者鼓勵聽者做什麼事？
(A) 觀看演出
(B) 購買服飾
(C) 享用茶點
(D) 盡快再訪

換句話說 T-shirts and sweatshirts → clothing

4-6. 🎧 美國女子
Questions 4-6 refer to the following talk.

> W Hello, and welcome to today's panel discussion. My name is Esther Yang, and ⁴I'm a senior associate here at the Ministry of Education. I'm delighted to be moderating this debate on the use of technology to track performance. ⁵We're excited about hearing from our four debate participants. We chose them because they are well known as specialists in their field. I'm sure you'll find their insights to be fascinating. Now, before we begin, ⁶I see that some of you have pens and paper out. Just so you know, this session will be recorded.

第 4-6 題，請參考下方談話。

女 大家好，歡迎來到今天的小組討論會。我叫Esther Yang，**是教育部的資深專員**。我很高興主持這場關於使用科技追蹤績效的辯論會。**我們很期待聽到四位辯論參與者的意見。我們之所以選擇他們，是因為他們是各自所屬領域的知名專家**。相信大家會發現他們的見解非常有意思。現在，在我們開始之前，**我看到你們有些人已經拿出筆和紙**。讓各位知道一下，本次討論會將全程錄音。

單字 panel discussion 小組討論會　moderate 節制、主持
track 追蹤　insight 見解　fascinating 吸引人的、有意思的

4. 說話者是誰？
(A) 公務人員
(B) 大學教授
(C) 教科書編輯
(D) 軟體專家

換句話說 a senior associate here at the Ministry of Education → a government employee

45

5. 根據說話者所述，為何選擇特定的辯論參與者？
(A) 他們最近出版了書籍。
(B) 他們來自不同的國家。
(C) 他們被視為專家。
(D) 他們已經開創自己的事業。

換句話說 they are well known as specialists in their field → They are considered to be experts

6. 說話者提到：「本次討論會將全程錄音」，意味著什麼？
(A) 問題會在最後得到回答。
(B) 不需要做筆記。
(C) 應該收起手機。
(D) 觀眾應留在座位上。

7-9. 🎧 英國女子
Questions 7-9 refer to the following speech.

> W Good morning. I'm your instructor, Abigail Lambert, and I've been a financial planner for the past fifteen years. ⁷Today, I'll share my tips and tricks to help you prepare for your retirement and ensure that you are financially secure. ⁸I'd like to thank those participants who wrote down their questions and submitted them to me before the workshop. I'll address as many of them as possible. Now, before we get started, ⁹I want to make sure that all of you have the seminar handouts. If you haven't picked them up yet, they're on the table near the side entrance.

第 7-9 題，請參考下方演講。

女　早安，我是您們的講師Abigail Lambert，過去十五年間，我一直擔任理財規劃顧問。**今天我將分享我的技巧和竅門，幫助各位為退休做好準備，並確保您的財政狀態穩定。我想感謝在研討會前寫下問題並交給我的參加者**。我會盡可能回答這些問題。現在，在我們開始之前，**我想確認大家是否都有拿到研討會的講義。如果您還沒有拿到，它們就放在側門的桌子上。**

單字 financial planner 理財規劃顧問　trick 竅門
ensure 確保　secure 安心無慮的、安全的
address 解決、處理

7. 研討會的主題為何？
(A) 節省時間的方法
(B) 溝通技巧
(C) 退休規劃
(D) 求職

8. 說話者為何要感謝某些聽者？
(A) 他們提早報名。
(B) 他們換了座位。
(C) 他們準備好會議室。
(D) 他們提出問題。

單字 register 報名

9. 說話者為何會提到側門？
(A) 可以在那裡找到活動資料。
(B) 在整個研討會期間會被鎖住。
(C) 那裡有提供參加者飲料。
(D) 可於緊急情況下使用。

單字 in case of emergency 在緊急情況下

UNIT 19　廣告與廣播

PRACTICE　題本 p.87

1. (B)　**2.** (A)　**3.** (D)　**4.** (D)　**5.** (A)　**6.** (C)
7. (C)　**8.** (A)　**9.** (B)

1-3. 🎧 美國男子
Questions 1-3 refer to the following advertisement.

> M At Sure-Tech Assistants, we're proud to serve the Omaha community. ¹We offer fast and affordable computer upgrades and repairs. Our technicians have a lot of experience, and they carefully listen to customers to fully understand their needs. ²For the third consecutive year, the Omaha Business Bureau has nominated us for the Best Customer Service Award. And to celebrate, we're offering 15% off all automated data backup packages, our newest service. ³To get this deal, you must schedule an appointment either by phone or online. Call us today at 555-2899 for more information.

第 1-3 題，請參考下方廣告。

男　Sure-Tech Assistants很榮幸能為Omaha社區服務。**我們提供快速且經濟實惠的電腦升級和維修**。我們的技術人員擁有豐富的經驗，且會仔細傾聽客戶的意見，充分了解他們的需求。**Omaha商業促進局連續三年提名我們為最佳客戶服務獎**。為了慶祝，推出我們最新的服務，提供所有資料自動備份套組八五折優惠。**欲獲得此優惠，您必須透過電話或線上預約**。請立即致電555-2899了解更多資訊。

單字 serve 提供（服務）　affordable 負擔得起的、價格合理的
consecutive 連續的　nominate 提名　automated 自動化的、自動的

46

1. 正在廣告的是什麼類型的業務？
(A) 職業介紹所
(B) 電腦維修商店
(C) 醫療保健診所
(D) 汽車租賃服務

2. 企業為何要慶祝？
(A) 獲得獎項提名。
(B) 將開設新分店。
(C) 已經經營了二十年。
(D) 收購了競爭對手。

單字 acquire 取得、收購

3. 聽者需要做什麼才能獲得優惠？
(A) 參加現場活動
(B) 訂閱電子報
(C) 完成問卷調查
(D) 安排預約

4-6. 🎧 美國女子
Questions 4-6 refer to the following podcast.

> W Welcome to this week's episode of my podcast, *Taking Control*, ⁴where you'll get your weekly inspiration on preparing the right food for your nutritional needs. Today, I'll interview Maya Dalavi. ⁵Ms. Dalavi is a registered nurse who has just launched her own website with special meal plans to help individuals reach certain goals. We'll discuss her methods and the research behind them. Also, ⁶if you haven't signed up as a member of my podcast yet, please consider doing so. You'll receive exclusive content every week.

第 4-6 題，請參考下方網路廣播。

女 歡迎收聽本週這一集的網路廣播《取得控制》，每週都會從本節目獲得靈感，了解如何準備符合您營養需求的食物。今天我要採訪Maya Dalavi。Dalavi女士是名註冊護士，她剛剛開設自己的網站，提供特殊的飲食計畫，幫助個人實現特定目標。我們將探討其背後的方法及研究。另外，如果您尚未註冊成為我的網路廣播會員，請考慮加入。每週您將會收到獨家內容。

單字 inspiration 靈感　nutritional 營養上的
need 需求、要求　registered 註冊的
individual 個人　exclusive 獨家的

4. 網路廣播的主要內容為何？
(A) 職業轉換
(B) 寫作技巧
(C) 醫學突破
(D) 營養建議

單字 breakthrough 突破、進展　nutrition 營養

5. Maya Dalavi最近做了什麼事？
(A) 她開設網站。
(B) 她教授課程。
(C) 她贏得比賽。
(D) 她發表雜誌文章。

換句話說 launched → started

6. 講者提到網路廣播會員資格的什麼？
(A) 隨時都可以取消。
(B) 按月收取費用。
(C) 提供額外的好處。
(D) 有助於僱用新員工。

7-9. 🎧 澳洲男子
Questions 7-9 refer to the following broadcast and map.

> M ⁷In local news, the city broke ground on the new Kembery Sports Arena yesterday. The designs show that the structure will have space for two cafés, a souvenir shop, and administrative offices. There will also be a seating capacity of eight thousand spectators, more than the original plan of six thousand. ⁸This is thanks to a generous donation of two thousand padded seats from Braun Manufacturing. Although on-site parking will be available at the arena, a new bus stop will be added to encourage the use of public transportation. ⁹It will be at the intersection of Rose Avenue and Huntz Street. A map of the area can be found online.

第 7-9 題，請參考下方廣播和地圖。

男 當地新聞報導，該城市新的Kembery體育競技場於昨天開始動工。從設計上來看，該建築會包含兩間咖啡館、一間紀念品店和行政辦公室。例外，總座位數還能容納八千名觀眾，多於原定計畫的六千名。這要歸功於Braun製造商慷慨捐贈的兩千張軟墊座椅。儘管場館中設有停車場，但為鼓勵使用大眾運輸工具，仍會增設新的公車站。它將位在玫瑰大道和Huntz街的交叉口。網站上可找到該地區的地圖。

單字 break ground 開始動工　structure 結構
seating capacity 座位數量　generous 慷慨的、大方的
on-site 現場的　intersection 十字路口

```
              Berry巷  →
           ┌──1──┐
              玫瑰大道⁹
       ┌─2─┐        ┌─4─┐
  Huntz街⁹→      Blair街
                        ┌─┐
                        │ │Fox河
                   3
```

7. 廣播的主要內容為何？
(A) 道路修繕
(B) 百貨公司開幕
(C) 體育設施的建設
(D) 即將到來的遊行路線

單字 route 路線、路程

8. 公司捐贈了什麼東西？
(A) 畫作
(B) 座位
(C) 木材
(D) 機械

9. 請查看圖表。公車站位在哪裡？
(A) 地點 1
(B) 地點 2
(C) 地點 3
(D) 地點 4

UNIT 20 觀光與參訪

PRACTICE
題本 p.89

1. (A)　**2.** (D)　**3.** (B)　**4.** (D)　**5.** (A)　**6.** (C)
7. (B)　**8.** (D)　**9.** (C)

1-3. 🎧 美國女子
Questions 1-3 refer to the following talk.

> W ¹Thanks again for joining me on today's tour of the Darcy Ceramics Studio. I hope you enjoyed learning more about the process of making ceramics by hand. This concludes the main part of the tour, but you are welcome to explore the site on your own, especially our gift shop. ²And don't forget that we will be screening a short documentary about ancient pottery at three o'clock in our lecture hall. It is free to attend. One of our employees, Ashley Mendoza, will answer questions afterward. She is very knowledgeable, as ³she just published her second book about the topic, entitled *The First Step*.

第 1-3 題，請參考下方談話。

女　再次感謝大家今天來參觀Darcy陶瓷工作室。希望大家能學習到更多手工製陶的過程。行程的主要部分到此結束，但歡迎各位自行探索此處，尤其是我們的禮品店。**還有別忘了三點我們將在演講廳放映有關古代陶器的紀錄短片**，可以免費觀賞。隨後我們其中一名員工Ashley Mendoza 將會回答各位的問題。她的知識淵博，且**剛出版了第二本關於該主題的書籍，書名為《第一步》**。

單字 ceramics 陶瓷　conclude 結束　explore 探索
screen 放映　pottery 陶器　knowledgeable 博學多聞的
entitled 標題為⋯

1. 說話者最有可能是誰？
(A) 導遊
(B) 電影導演
(C) 店經理
(D) 藝術評論家

2. 三點將會發生什麼事？
(A) 將會有歌手表演。
(B) 將會提供一些食物。
(C) 將會停止營業。
(D) 將會播放一段影片。

換句話說 we will be screening a short documentary → a video will be shown

3. 《第一步》是什麼？
(A) 社團
(B) 書籍
(C) 廣播節目
(D) 舞台劇

4-6. 🎧 美國男子
Questions 4-6 refer to the following tour information.

> M Welcome to Hamilton Manor. This is one of the most popular tourist attractions in the area. ⁴Hamilton Manor is best known for having the country's largest private collection of watercolor paintings, most of which you can see on display today. ⁵Like many visitors before you, I'm sure you'll want to make a wish at the stone fountain by tossing in a coin. You can find the fountain in the East Garden. ⁶We'll stop here for about an hour, after which time you should return to the bus. That way, we can leave on time for our next stop.

第 4-6 題，請參考下方旅遊資訊。

男　歡迎來到Hamilton莊園。這裡是該地區最受歡迎的旅遊景點之一。**Hamilton莊園以擁有全國最多的私人水彩畫收藏而聞名**，今天你可以看到其中大部分的作品展出。如同許多先前來訪的遊客，相信你也會想在石頭噴水池中投擲一枚硬幣來許願。你可以在東側花園找到噴水池。**我們預計在此停留一個小時左右，之後大家要回到巴士上**，這樣我們才能準時出發前往下一站。

單字 attraction 觀光景點　watercolor painting 水彩畫
on display 展出　make a wish 許願　fountain 噴水池
toss 投擲

4. Hamilton莊園為何出名？
(A) 曾是電影拍攝地點。
(B) 由知名建築師設計。
(C) 是舉辦受歡迎節慶的場地。
(D) 擁有大量的藝術收藏品。

單字 filming location 電影拍攝地點　prominent 知名的
extensive 廣泛的、大量的

換句話說 the country's largest private collection of watercolor paintings → an extensive art collection

5. 根據說話者所述，遊客喜歡在Hamilton莊園做什麼？
(A) 許願
(B) 試吃食物
(C) 游泳
(D) 收集花朵

6. 聽者被要求在一小時後做什麼？
(A) 拍攝團體照
(B) 觀看演出
(C) 返回巴士上
(D) 在咖啡廳碰面

換句話說 return to the bus → get back on the bus

7-9. 🎧 英國女子
Questions 7-9 refer to the following tour information.

> W ⁷Welcome to Vista Nature Park. It's my pleasure to lead you through the region's most diverse collection of plants and wildlife. We've made significant improvements to the hiking trails in the park, ⁸a project that was funded by local business owner Annette Harvey. She loves being in nature and wanted to make sure everyone could enjoy this beautiful site for many years to come. ⁹I know that some of you were worried about the recent mudslides due to the heavy rains. It's true that these can pose a risk, but that area is closed to visitors. If everyone's ready, let's get started.

第 7-9 題，請參考下方旅遊資訊。

女　歡迎來到Vista自然公園。我很高興帶領你們參觀該地區最多樣化的植物和野生動物群。我們對公園的登山步道進行了重大的改善，該計畫由當地企業家Annette Harvey資助。她喜歡親近大自然，並希望在未來的幾年，確保每個人都可以享受這個美麗的地方。我知道你們當中有些人擔心近期因暴雨引發的土石流。這確實可能帶來風險，但該區域已停止對遊客開放。如果大家都準備好了，我們就開始吧。

單字 diverse 多種的、多樣的　wildlife 野生動物
hiking trail 登山步道　fund 提供資金　mudslide 土石流
pose 造成、引起　risk 風險

7. 導覽地點在哪裡？
(A) 在製造工廠
(B) 在自然公園
(C) 在音樂廳
(D) 在購物中心

8. Annette Harvey做了什麼事？
(A) 她建造了一座橋。
(B) 她拍攝了一個廣告。
(C) 她設計一棟建築。
(D) 她捐了一些錢。

單字 commercial 廣告

9. 說話者說：「該區域已停止對遊客開放」，是什麼意思？
(A) 行程會比平常短。
(B) 會有部分退款。
(C) 聽者不用擔心。
(D) 應遵循指示標誌。

單字 partial 部分的　issue 核發、發放

PART TEST
題本 p.90

71. (C)	72. (B)	73. (A)	74. (A)	75. (C)
76. (D)	77. (A)	78. (B)	79. (C)	80. (D)
81. (B)	82. (C)	83. (C)	84. (B)	85. (A)
86. (B)	87. (A)	88. (A)	89. (D)	90. (A)
91. (C)	92. (C)	93. (D)	94. (D)	95. (C)
96. (D)	97. (B)	98. (A)	99. (C)	100. (D)

71-73. 🎧 英國女子
Questions 71-73 refer to the following advertisement.

> W Do you love playing sports and keeping active? ⁷¹Parker Sporting Goods has a great selection of equipment for athletes. We're conveniently located in the Finwood Mall, with an outdoor entrance on Snyder Street. Our prices can't be beat, and ⁷²we even offer a ten percent discount to anyone with a Parker Gold Card, as we appreciate their continued patronage. Our staff is highly knowledgeable. That's why ⁷³we're famous for offering useful guidance about the right equipment to buy. Stop by today. We're open daily from 9 A.M. to 9 P.M.

第 71-73 題，請參考下方廣告。

女　你喜歡運動並保持活力嗎？Parker運動用品店為運動員提供各式各樣的裝備。我們位於Finwood購物中心，於Snyder街設有戶外入口。我們的價格無人能敵，且為感謝持續光顧的顧客，我們甚至會提供Parker金卡持有者九折的優惠。我們的員工擁有豐富的知識。因此，我們以提供實用建議，

49

讓顧客可以買到合適的裝備而聞名。今天就過來逛逛吧。

我們的營業時間為每天上午9點至晚上9點。

單字 athlete 運動員　appreciate 感謝
continued 持續不斷的　patronage 光顧、資助
guidance 引導、指引

71. 正在廣告的是什麼類型的公司？
(A) 汽車租賃公司
(B) 舞蹈工作室
(C) 運動用品店
(D) 園藝用品店

72. 根據廣告內容，誰可以獲取優惠？
(A) 企業所有人
(B) 卡片持有者
(C) 慈善工作者
(D) 大學生

73. 該間公司以什麼聞名？
(A) 實用的建議
(B) 大型設施
(C) 眾多分店
(D) 現代化的網站

單字 numerous 眾多的

換句話說 useful guidance → helpful advice

74-76. 🎧 美國男子
Questions 74-76 refer to the following telephone message.

> M　Hi, Ms. Evans. ⁷⁴This is Leon from the Melville Tower property management office. As you requested, I've arranged for a crew to replace the carpet in your bedroom. ⁷⁵The thing is, you'll have to remove everything from the room before their visit. I'm sure it's full of furniture, so I hope you understand. The crew may be able to assist with large items. ⁷⁶Please call me back at 555-4982 to let me know which day this week would work best for you. Thanks.

第74-76題，請參考下方電話留言。

男　嗨，Evans女士。我是Melville大廈物業管理辦公室的Leon。按照您的要求，我已經安排工作人員來更換您臥室的地毯。但有個問題是在他們來訪之前，您得把房間裡的東西通通搬走。我想裡面應該擺滿了傢俱，還希望您能諒解。工作人員也許能協助搬運大型物件。請撥打電話555-4982給我，讓我知道這週您哪一天時間最為方便，謝謝。

單字 management office 管理辦公室　assist with 協助…

74. 說話者是誰？
(A) 物業經理
(B) 房屋仲介
(C) 安全檢查員
(D) 建築工人

75. 說話者說：「我想裡面應該擺滿了傢俱」，意味著什麼？
(A) 入口可能被堵住。
(B) 倉儲空間可能正在使用中。
(C) 完成任務可能會有難度。
(D) 選出一種風格需要時間。

單字 block 堵住　storage 保管、儲存

76. 為何聽者要回電給說話者？
(A) 繳交押金
(B) 確認顏色
(C) 提供證明
(D) 選擇方便的日子

單字 deposit 押金　reference 證明、參考資料
convenient 方便的

77-79. 🎧 澳洲男子
Questions 77-79 refer to the following talk.

> M　Good morning, and welcome to Hana Beverages. ⁷⁷We've asked you here today to try our new line of herbal teas. There are some feedback forms that you can use to review our products, and we ask that you be as detailed as possible in your comments. Of course, we're excited about the delicious taste of our tea. ⁷⁸We're also proud of how we use significantly less packaging than other brands, hardly any at all. We'll begin in just a few minutes. ⁷⁹And when the session is over, don't forget to pick up your coupon for sixty percent off your next purchase of our products.

第77-79題，請參考下方談話。

男　早安，歡迎來到Hana飲品店。今天我們邀請大家來此試飲我們新推出的花草茶系列。你可以填寫回饋表來評論我們的產品，請盡可能詳細填寫你的意見。我們當然對於花草茶的美味寄予厚望。同時讓我們也感到自豪的是，相較於他牌，我們使用極少的包裝材料，幾乎沒有包裝。我們將於幾分鐘後開始。待活動結束後，別忘了領取優惠券，下次購買我們的產品時，可享有四折優惠。

單字 detailed 詳盡的　comment 意見
hardly any 幾乎沒有　at all 完全、根本

77. 聽者最有可能是誰？
(A) 產品審查員
(B) 銷售代理商
(C) 求職者
(D) 新聞記者

78. 說話者對於產品的哪一方面感到自豪？
(A) 在國內生產。
(B) 使用極少包裝材料。
(C) 許多國家皆有販售。
(D) 由科學家開發的。

單字 domestically 在國內

79. 說話者於活動結束後會提供聽者什麼？
(A) 一盒樣品
(B) 免費餐食
(C) 折價券
(D) 結業證書

單字 complimentary 贈送的、免費的　certificate 證書　completion 結業、結束

80-82. 🎧美國男子
Questions 80-82 refer to the following broadcast.

> M　You're listening to *City Seekers*, the radio show that explores all of the exciting things going on in our city. My guest today is ⁸⁰Valentino Arruda, who works at Olivia Bistro. He's been creating delicious dishes there for the past decade. Mr. Arruda loves to try new and exotic flavors, and ⁸¹he gets his inspiration from the many trips overseas that he takes throughout the year. ⁸²Our team has been chasing him for an interview for months, as he has a very busy schedule. ⁸²You're in for a treat. We hope you all enjoy hearing more about Mr. Arruda's fascinating career history and working process. Stay tuned.

第 80-82 題，請參考下方廣播節目。

男　你現在正在收聽的是《城市探索者》，本節目探討所有發生在我們城市中令人興奮的事情。今天的來賓是在Olivia餐酒館工作的Valentino Arruda。過去十年以來，他一直在製作美味佳餚。Arruda先生喜愛嘗試全新的異國風味，他的靈感源自於他全年多次的海外旅行。由於他的行程非常繁忙，我們團隊這幾個月一直追著他接受採訪。想必各位一定會滿意。希望大家會喜歡聽到更多關於Arruda先生精彩的職業生涯史和工作歷程。敬請繼續收聽節目。

單字 decade 十年　exotic 異國風味的　flavor 味道、風味　inspiration 靈感

80. Valentino Arruda是誰？
(A) 科學家
(B) 畫家
(C) 作家
(D) 廚師

81. 根據說話者所述，是什麼給予Arruda先生靈感？
(A) 聽音樂
(B) 海外旅遊
(C) 與專家合作
(D) 花時間接觸大自然

82. 說話者提到：「他的行程非常繁忙」，意味著什麼？
(A) 無可避免取消。
(B) 與嘉賓談話的時間很短暫。
(C) 本次採訪是個難得的機會。
(D) Arruda先生已經開創了新事業。

單字 cancellation 取消

83-85. 🎧美國女子
Questions 83-85 refer to the following talk.

> W　Thank you all for being here for this planning meeting. ⁸³As the structural engineer for the Webster Stadium project, I've been asked to review a proposed change. ⁸⁴In the original plan, the roof only partially covered the field and seating areas. Some people on this committee want a full roof for the structure. I've assessed the plans, and I can confirm that making this change is still possible at this point. Additional support beams will need to be added. ⁸⁵I've prepared a new schedule to account for the added work. Please take a look now so we can have a discussion about it.

第 83-85 題，請參考下方談話。

女　感謝大家來此參加本次的策劃會議。作為Webster體育場專案的結構工程師，我被要求審查一項變更提議。在原本的計畫中，屋頂僅覆蓋部分的場館和座位區。委員會當中一些人希望有個完整覆蓋體育場的屋頂。我已經評估過計畫，並確認目前仍能能進行此項更動，還需要增加額外的支撐樑柱。我已準備好一個新的行程表，來說明增加的工作。請各位現在看一下，以便我們進行討論。

單字 structural engineer 結構工程師　proposed 提議的　partially 部分的　field 運動場　assess 評估　account for 說明

83. 誰在主講？
(A) 職業運動員
(B) 財務顧問
(C) 結構工程師
(D) 市長

51

84. 根據說話者所述，有些人提出了什麼建議？
(A) 使用回收材料
(B) 改變屋頂設計
(C) 增加入場費
(D) 擴建停車設施

單字 recycled 回收的　admission fee 入場費

85. 聽者接下來最有可能做什麼事？
(A) 查看行程表
(B) 觀看現場示範
(C) 分享他們的問題
(D) 結識新同事

86-88. 🎧英國女子
Questions 86-88 refer to the following broadcast.

> W　Are you looking for a way to take your writing to the next level? Our guest today can help you! [86]Brittany Morrison will be sharing her top tips for thinking more creatively in your writing projects. This is perfect for poets, screenwriters, or anyone writing for fun. Ms. Morrison teaches classes at the McKinney Institute. [87]They're so popular that they're fully booked for the next three terms. We'll talk to Ms. Morrison in a moment. [88]And be sure to tune in to our next show, as I'll be revealing the winner of our annual contest.

第 86-88 題，請參考下方廣播節目。

女　你是否正在尋找能讓寫作能力更上一層樓的方法？今天的來賓能夠幫助你！Brittany Morrison將會分享她的重要技巧，讓大家在寫作項目中能夠更有創意地思考。這非常適合詩人、編劇，或任何為了樂趣而寫作的人。Morrison女士任教於McKinney學院。她的課非常受歡迎，接下來的三個學期都已滿堂。稍後我們會與Morrison女士談話。還請務必收聽下一期的廣播，我將會揭曉年度比賽的獲勝者。

單字 screenwriter 編劇　term 學期　reveal 揭曉

86. 廣播的主要內容為何？
(A) 設計網站
(B) 增強創造力
(C) 提升溝通技巧
(D) 培養健康習慣

單字 enhance 提升、增強

87. 說話者對於Morrison女士的課程提到了什麼？
(A) 已經額滿。
(B) 針對初學者。
(C) 可線上觀看。
(D) 免費提供。

單字 be at full capacity 滿載、額滿
aimed at 目標針對、瞄準…

換句話說 fully booked → at full capacity

88. 說話者說下次節目中會發生什麼事？
(A) 宣布比賽獲勝者。
(B) 介紹新的主持人。
(C) 會回答一些聽眾的問題。
(D) 販售活動門票。

換句話說 I'll be revealing the winner of our annual contest → A contest winner will be announced

89-91. 🎧美國女子
Questions 89-91 refer to the following telephone message.

> W　Hi, Gary. [89]I wanted to update you on the wooden chairs we're making for Stewart Insurance. The designs have been finalized, and we need to have them shipped by February 6. [90]You said that you were concerned that I had accepted such a small order for customized goods. Well, I know that we don't usually do this, but we've had a lot of cancellations. In fact, [91]I'm going to let some employees go home early today and tomorrow because we don't have enough work for them to do. Fortunately, our busy season will be starting soon, so I'm not too worried.

第 89-91 題，請參考下方電話留言。

女　嗨，Gary。我想向你更新我們為Stewart保險公司製作木椅的進度。設計已經定案了，且我們需要在2月6日以前出貨。你說你擔心我接下這麼小規模的客製化訂單。嗯，我知道我們通常不會做這種事，但是我們有很多筆取消的訂單。其實，因為今天和明天都沒有足夠的工作要做，所以我會讓幾名員工提早回家。幸運的是，我們的旺季馬上就要開始了，所以我不太擔心。

單字 finalize 最終確認　customized 客製化的

89. 說話者最有可能在哪裡工作？
(A) 在攝影工作室
(B) 在汽車維修廠
(C) 在文具店
(D) 在傢俱工廠

90. 為何說話者會說：「我們有很多筆取消的訂單」？
(A) 對於決定作出解釋
(B) 確認自己有空
(C) 提出申訴
(D) 建議需要更多廣告

91. 說話者提出要為員工做什麼事？
(A) 訂購餐食
(B) 提供休假
(C) 讓一些人提前離開
(D) 舉辦培訓活動

92-94. 🎧 澳洲男子
Questions 92-94 refer to the following speech.

> M Welcome, everyone. I'd like to thank the event planners for inviting me to give a talk ⁹²**here at the Melbourne Health Fair**. Today I'm going to tell you more about the new blood pressure tracker from Dominick Enterprises. This compact device records information throughout the day. In addition, ⁹³**if your blood pressure gets out of the desired range, it sends a message to your phone to alert you to the issue.** ⁹⁴**A recent survey of our customers showed that the instructions for our previous model were hard to understand.** So, we've made changes to address this issue.

第 92-94 題，請參考下方演講。

男 歡迎大家。感謝活動策劃者邀請**我在墨爾本健康博覽會上發表演說**。今天我將向各位詳細介紹Dominick企業新推出的血壓追蹤器。這個小型設備能夠全天記錄資訊。另外，**如果你的血壓超出適當範圍，它會向你的手機發送訊息，提醒你注意**。最近我們對客戶進行的調查結果顯示，我們**先前機型的說明指示很難理解**。因此，我們已做出一些改變，來解決這個問題。

單字 desired 要求的、希望的   range 範圍   alert 通知
instructions 說明、指示   address 處理、解決

92. 聽者在哪裡？
(A) 在員工入職訓練活動
(B) 在盛大的開幕式
(C) 在健康博覽會
(D) 在慈善募款晚宴

93. 根據說話者所述，該產品如何幫助使用者？
(A) 藉由追蹤出貨
(B) 藉由減少開銷
(C) 藉由快速充電
(D) 藉由發送通知

94. 說話者從調查中了解到什麼事？
(A) 需要現代化的設計
(B) 價格過高
(C) 使用者有安全上的疑慮
(D) 部分說明令人困惑

換句話說 hard to understand → confusing

95-97. 🎧 美國女子
Questions 95-97 refer to the following tour information and map.

> W I'd like to let you know about a change to our itinerary. Unfortunately, the grand opening event at the Clifton Concert Hall has been postponed. ⁹⁵**Construction was supposed to be completed by now, but it is a few days behind schedule.** Therefore, you'll have some free time between 1 and 3 P.M. this afternoon. ⁹⁶**I suggest browsing Henderson's Antique Shop.** We'll have an additional activity during tomorrow's scheduled free time to make up for this change. So, ⁹⁷**at dinner tonight, I'll give you a list of options, and you can tell me which you prefer.** We'll do the most popular one.

第 95-97 題，請參考下方旅遊資訊和地圖。

女 我想通知各位我們的行程有所更動。很遺憾的是，Clifton音樂廳的開幕活動延期了。**原本應於現在完工，但比預定時間晚了幾天**。因此，今天下午1點到3點之間，大家會有一些自由活動時間。**我推薦各位可以逛逛Henderson古董店**。我們將在明天的自由活動時間進行額外活動，以補償這項變動。所以**今晚的晚餐時間，我會給各位一份選擇清單，各位可以告訴我你偏好哪個項目**。我們會採用最受歡迎的項目。

單字 itinerary 旅遊行程表
behind schedule 比預定時間晚、延期   browse 瀏覽、逛
make up for 補償

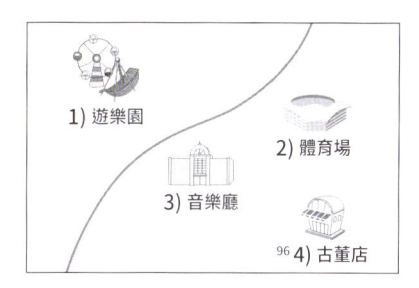

1) 遊樂園
2) 體育場
3) 音樂廳
⁹⁶ 4) 古董店

95. 根據說話者所述，是什麼導致問題發生？
(A) 交通繁忙
(B) 惡劣天氣
(C) 施工延誤
(D) 電腦錯誤

96. 請查看圖表。說話者推薦今天下午去哪裡？
(A) 地點 1
(B) 地點 2
(C) 地點 3
(D) 地點 4

97. 聽者在晚餐時間可以做什麼？
(A) 要求部分退款
(B) 表達活動偏好
(C) 參加額外行程
(D) 選擇隔天餐食

單字 preference 偏好、喜好

98-100. 🎧 美國男子
Questions 98-100 refer to the following excerpt from a meeting and fact sheet.

> M　Next, I'd like to discuss the building expansion project. [98]The new wing will allow us to host larger exhibitions or have separate spaces for two different artists. [99]Now, we've hired a new marketing manager to help with promoting these larger-scale events. She'll be at next week's meeting, so you'll have the chance to find out more about her then. About the project itself, [100]the original plan included twelve hundred square meters of new space. However, because we decided to remove two trees from the property, [100]it'll be fifteen hundred instead. So, I've changed that on the fact sheets I gave you.

第 98-100 題，請參考下方會議摘錄和概要說明書。

男　接下來，我想討論一下建築擴建專案。新的建築將允許我們舉辦更大規模的展覽，或為兩位不同的藝術家提供單獨空間。我們現在聘請到了一位新的行銷經理，來協助推廣這些大型活動。她將參加下週的會議，所以屆時大家會有機會認識她。就專案本身而言，最初的計畫包括1200平方公尺的新空間。然而，我們決定從該地區中移除兩棵樹，所以會變成1500平方公尺。因此，在我給你的概要說明書中，已經修改了這一項。

單字 expansion 擴建　separate 分開的
larger-scale 大規模的

產品概要說明書		
第1欄	費用	800,000 美金
第2欄	建築師	Steven Gray
第3欄	完工日期	9月1日
[100]第4欄	面積	1,200 平方公尺

98. 最有可能擴建哪一種建築？
(A) 藝術畫廊
(B) 學校
(C) 健身場所
(D) 郵局

99. 聽者會在下次會議上做什麼事？
(A) 自願參加活動
(B) 查看設計藍圖
(C) 認識新員工
(D) 提供預算報告書

單字 blueprints 設計圖、藍圖

100. 請查看圖表。哪一欄有被更動？
(A) 第1欄
(B) 第2欄
(C) 第3欄
(D) 第4欄

54

RC PART 5

UNIT 01 名詞

CHECK-UP
題本 p.100

1. supply
2. appointments
3. surprise
4. Deliveries
5. director
6. commitment
7. creation
8. sales

1.
解說 畫底線處前方為不定冠詞，後方要連接單數名詞，因此答案為 supply。

中譯 Kenway建設公司已開始保留更多材料的庫存在手邊，以防於額外接到的專案中會用到。

單字 on hand 手邊、在手上　in case 以防萬一　available 可用的、有空的

2.
解說 appointment 當可數名詞使用時，意思為「約定、預約」。若使用單數形態，需搭配不定冠詞一起使用。該句話的底線前方沒有不定冠詞，因此答案為複數名詞 appointments。

中譯 由於未預期的設備問題，Retha牙醫直到下週才會開始安排預約。

單字 unexpected 未預期的、意外的

3.
解說 畫底線處置於動詞 have expressed 後方的受詞位置，因此答案為名詞 surprise。

中譯 許多活動策劃者對Villa大廳的租金表示驚訝。

單字 express 表現　rental fee 租金、租借費用

4.
解說 畫底線處後方連接介系詞片語，接著又連接動詞 arrive，表示畫底線處的單字應使用名詞，扮演主詞的角色，因此答案為 Deliveries。

中譯 Del運輸公司的貨物有時會提前兩到三天抵達。

單字 occasionally 有時候　ahead of schedule 比預期提前

5.
解說 根據文意，反對削減預算者應為人物，因此答案要選 director，意思為「經理、高層主管」。

中譯 總經理強烈反對公司提出的削減預算方案。

單字 strongly 強烈地、激烈地　oppose 反對　propose 提出、提議

6.
解說 根據前後文，表達「由於對品質的堅持，獲得顧客的青睞」語意最為通順，因此答案要選 commitment，意思為「堅持、保證、承諾」。

中譯 幾十年來Mantique傢俱因其對品質的堅持而受到顧客的青睞。

7.
解說 畫底線處與前方單字 job 搭配，表示「創造就業機會」最符合文意，因此答案為 creation。

中譯 稅額扣抵將為小型企業創造大量的就業機會。

單字 result in 導致…　substantial 大量的

8.
解說 畫底線處與後方單字 figures 搭配，表示「銷售數據」最符合文意，因此答案為 sales。

中譯 根據Jerome's科技公司發布的銷售數據顯示，公司於上一季度的獲利成長了3%。

單字 release 公開、發布、上市　profit 獲利、收益

UNIT 02 代名詞與限定詞

CHECK-UP
題本 p.102

1. she
2. itself
3. those
4. any
5. every
6. any
7. All
8. each

1.
解說 畫底線處前方為連接詞，後方連接動詞，表示畫底線處扮演主詞的角色，因此答案為人稱代名詞主格 she。

中譯 因為塞車，Cailot女士上班遲到了五分鐘。

單字 stuck 被堵住、無法移動

2.
解說 畫底線處置於動詞 prides 後方的受詞位置，而根據文意，畫底線處指的是前方出現的 The grocery store，因此答案為反身代名詞 itself。

中譯 這家超市以只使用當地供應商生產的農產品而自豪。

單字 produce 農產品、生產

3.

解說 畫底線處為介系詞 including 的受詞，受到過去分詞片語 issued online 的修飾，且用來代替前方出現過的複數名詞 coupons，因此答案為複數形態 those。

中譯 Zack's 餐館所有的優惠券，包含線上發行的優惠券，將於 12月31日到期。

單字 including 包含…　issue 發行、核發　expire 到期

4.

解說 根據前後文，表達「可以參加任何活動」的語意最為通順，因此答案為 any，用於肯定句中的意思為「任何」。

中譯 會議與會者可以參加任何他們感興趣的活動。

單字 interest 感興趣

5.

解說 畫底線處前方出現主詞和動詞，表示其連接的是結構完整的子句。而畫底線處後方連接名詞，表示畫底線處應填入適合修飾名詞的字詞，因此答案為限定詞 every。

中譯 祕書每週四都會訂購辦公用品，所以若有任何要求，請在那之前發送電子郵件給他。

單字 secretary 祕書　office supplies 辦公用品

6.

解說 畫底線處後方連接不可數名詞，因此答案為 any。a few 用來修飾複數名詞，因此並非答案。

中譯 JC's 露營用品店對 Flash Sailing Co. 製造的所有商品提供折扣。

單字 merchandise 商品、物品　manufacture 製造

7.

解說 畫底線處後方連接名詞 staff，而後方使用的是複數動詞 are，因此答案為 All。staff 可以當成單數或複數名詞使用，因此作答該類題型時，一定要確認後方連接的是單數還是複數動詞。

中譯 目前出差的所有員工，均可免除參加義務月會。

單字 business trip 出差　be exempt from 免除…　mandatory 義務的、強制的

8.

解說 畫底線處後方連接［of＋複數名詞］，而後方連接單數動詞 was，因此答案為 each。

中譯 委員會將標誌設計大賽的候選人從358名縮減至5名，並聯絡每位候選人會面。

單字 narrow down（選擇範圍）縮小、減少　candidate 候選人、應徵者　contact 聯絡、接觸

PRACTICE UNIT 01~02　題本 p.104

1. (D)　**2.** (B)　**3.** (B)　**4.** (C)　**5.** (B)　**6.** (A)
7. (A)　**8.** (A)　**9.** (C)　**10.** (C)　**11.** (C)　**12.** (D)
13. (B)　**14.** (D)　**15.** (B)　**16.** (B)

1. 填入名詞［冠詞後方］

解說 空格前方有定冠詞，且後方連接介系詞片語，表示空格應填入名詞，因此答案為 (D) renovation。

中譯 Henson 公寓的業主批准了翻修主大廳的資金。

單字 approve 批准、認可　renovation 翻修、改造

2. 人稱代名詞［受格］

解說 空格置於不定詞 to compare 後方的受詞位置上，選項中僅有 (A) themselves 和 (B) them 可以當作受詞使用。根據文意，空格所指的是 unlimited paint samples，因此答案為 (B)。

中譯 Ian 油漆店允許顧客把不限數量的油漆樣品帶回家，讓他們可以與現在的裝潢進行比較。

單字 unlimited 無限制的、無限量的　compare 比較

3. 限定詞 every

解說 空格後方連接單數名詞，表示空格應填入適當的字詞，修飾後方的單數名詞，因此答案為 (B) every。(A) few 用來修飾複數名詞；(C) other 用來修飾複數名詞或不可數名詞，兩者並非答案。

中譯 櫃檯人員的職責之一是接聽每一通來電。

單字 receptionist 櫃檯接待人員

4. 人物名詞 vs 事物／抽象名詞

解說 空格後方連接動詞 will have，表示空格為主詞，應填入名詞。(A) Subscriptions 和 (C) Subscribers 皆為名詞，根據文意，應為人物，因此答案要選 (C)，意思為「訂閱者」。

中譯 訂閱者在首次付款後，即可點閱所有 Greenwich 新聞的高級內容。

單字 have access to 可獲得、進入…

5. 填入限定詞

解說 空格前方為動詞，後方連接名詞當作受詞，表示空格應填入適當字詞，修飾後方名詞，因此答案為限定詞 (B) which。

中譯 人力資源部門尚未決定該職位要僱用哪位應徵者。

6. 可數名詞 單數形態 vs 複數形態

解說 空格應填入適當的字詞，與 sign language 組合後，當作動詞 have employed 的受詞。選項中僅有 (A) interpreters 和 (B) interpreter 為名詞，而空格前方有限定詞 several，因此答案為複數可數名詞 (A)。

中譯 主辦單位為國際會議聘請多位手語翻譯員。

單字　sign language 手語

56

7. 指示代名詞those
解說 空格受到形容詞子句（主格）who wish to park in this lot 的修飾。選項中，僅有 (A) those 可以受到形容詞子句的修飾，故為正解。
中譯 想在此停車場停車的人，需持有停車許可證。
單字 permit 許可（證）

8. 填入名詞［形容詞後方］
解說 空格前方為形容詞，後方連接介系詞片語，表示空格應填入名詞，因此答案為 (A) distinction。
中譯 這兩種洗衣機機型的關鍵差別在於其中一種有節能設定。
單字 crucial 關鍵的、重要的

9. 不定代名詞others
解說 空格前方為連接詞，後方連接動詞，表示空格要填入適當的主詞。選項中 (C) others 和 (D) anyone 皆可當作主詞使用，根據文意，表示「其中一名住戶不在意噪音，但其他人在意」較為通順，因此答案為 (C)，意思為「其他的人」。(B) whoever 當作複合關係代名詞使用時，可以當作主詞，但若置於連接詞後方，whoever 引導的子句無法單獨使用，因此並非答案。
中譯 其中一名住戶Victor Guerrero表示，施工噪音並不構成干擾，但其他人則表示對此感到困擾。
單字 occupant 住戶、使用者　nuisance 干擾、討厭的人或事　report 報告、描述　bother 打擾、感到困擾

10. 人物名詞vs事物／抽象名詞
解說 空格前方為形容詞，後方連接介系詞片語，表示空格應填入名詞。選項中僅有 (A) instructors 和 (C) instructions 為名詞，根據文意，表示「使用手冊中的說明混亂，獲得較低的客戶服務評分」較為通順，因此答案為 (C)，意思為「說明、指示」。
中譯 由於使用手冊中的說明混亂，Reway製造公司獲得較低的客戶服務評分。

11. 填入所有格形容詞
解說 空格前方有動詞，後方連接名詞片語，表示空格要填入適當的字詞，修飾後方的名詞片語，因此答案為所有格形容詞 (C) her。
中譯 McGuire女士讓她的團隊成員在輪班期間定期排休。
單字 break 休假、休息　shift 輪班

12. 名詞的功能［主詞］
解說 空格前方為連接詞，後方連接動詞，表示空格要填入名詞，當作主詞，因此答案為 (D) profits。
中譯 如果利潤繼續保持在高點，董事會將考慮把業務擴展到其他企業。
單字 board of trustees 董事會　consider 考慮、視為　venture （伴隨風險的）事業　profit 利潤　remain 保持、剩下

13. 人物名詞vs事物／抽象名詞
解說 空格前方為定冠詞，後方連接動詞 must make sure，表示空格應填入名詞，受到現在分詞片語 working on the audit 的修飾。選項中僅有 (B) accountants 和 (C) accounts 為名詞，根據文意，從事稽核工作的主體為人，因此答案為 (B)，意思為「會計師」。
中譯 從事稽核工作的會計師，必須盡可能確保數字準確。
單字 audit 會計稽核　make sure (that) 確保…

14. 人稱代名詞［主格］
解說 空格前方為連接詞，後方連接動詞，表示空格要填入適當的主詞，因此答案為 (D) he。
中譯 Brightwood自來水公司退還 80 美元給Gilmore先生，因為他被多收了錢。
單字 overcharge 多收錢

15. 複合名詞
解說 空格應與前方的tourist組合，根據文意，表示「旅遊景點、觀光地點」最為適當，因此答案為 (B) attractions。
中譯 這間公寓可以步行到達許多旅遊景點，使其成為頂級住宅。
單字 within walking distance 在步行距離內　prime 頂級的、一流的　real estate 房地產

16. 限定詞all
解說 空格應填入適當的字詞，修飾後方的複數名詞，因此答案為 (B) All。其他選項皆用來修飾單數名詞，因此並非答案。
中譯 所有文件都要經過符合資料保護法的批准程序。
單字 document 文件　approval 批准　undergo 經歷（變化、壞事等）　process 過程、程序

UNIT 03　形容詞與副詞

CHECK UP　　　　　　　　　　　題本 p.106

1. initial　　　　　　2. mandatory
3. actively　　　　　4. efficiently
5. still　　　　　　　6. therefore
7. more evenly　　　8. most important

1.
解說 畫底線處前方有定冠詞，後方連接名詞片語，表示畫底線處要填入適當的字詞，修飾後方的名詞片語，因此答案為形容詞 initial。
中譯 就Ortiz女士擁有碩士學位和五年的工作經驗而論，最初的薪資待遇相當低。
單字 considering (that) 考慮到、就…而論　fairly 相當地、公正地

57

2.

解說 畫底線處置於 be 動詞 is 後方的主詞補語位置上，表示畫底線處用來具體說明主詞 Following safety regulations，因此答案為形容詞 mandatory。

中譯 所有訪客都必須遵守施工現場的安全規定。

單字 follow 跟隨、遵守　safety 安全　regulation 規定
construction 建設、施工　site 現場、場所
mandate 命令、指令、授權

3.

解說 畫底線處置於助動詞 has 和過去分詞 pursued 之間，應填入副詞，因此答案為 actively。

中譯 大學畢業後，Shaw先生積極從事電影事業。

單字 pursue 從事、追求

4.

解說 畫底線處用來修飾動詞 is working，因此答案為副詞 efficiently。

中譯 空氣清淨機上的濾網應定期更換，以確保其能有效運轉。

單字 air purifier 空氣清淨機　replace 替換、更換
at regular intervals 定期地、每隔一段時間
ensure 確保、保障

5.

解說 畫底線處置於 be 動詞 were 和現在分詞 trying 之間，應填入副詞，因此答案為 still。

中譯 當執行長在活動中發表開幕致詞時，有些觀眾仍在尋找座位。

單字 opening remarks 開幕致詞

6.

解說 畫底線處置於助動詞 must 和動詞 be 之間，應填入副詞，因此答案為 therefore。

中譯 我們近期大部分的行銷策略都沒有成功，因此需要重新評估和調整。

單字 strategy 策略、計畫　largely 大部分、主要地
re-evaluate 重新評估　revise 調整、修改

7.

解說 畫底線處前方有副詞 much，用來強調比較級，且後方用介系詞 than 連接比較對象，表示畫底線處應填入比較級，因此答案為 more evenly。

中譯 相較於舊冷氣，新冷氣的冷空氣循環更為均勻。

單字 circulate 循環

8.

解說 根據文意，表示「最重要的資格條件」最為通順。畫底線處前方有定冠詞 the，因此答案為 most important，組合成形容詞最高級用法。

中譯 強大的人際溝通能力是應徵該職位最重要的資格條件。

單字 interpersonal skills 人際溝通能力
qualification 資格條件

UNIT 04 介系詞與連接詞

CHECK-UP　題本 p.108

1. in　　　　2. until
3. Prior to　　4. along with
5. both　　　6. When
7. Because　　8. despite

1.

解說 畫底線處後方連接一段較長的時間 the third quarter，因此答案為 in。on 用於連接明確的時間，和比 in 短的時間範圍。on 後方可連接日期、星期幾、特定日子。

中譯 我們在第三季度獲得成功歸功於積極的行銷活動。

單字 quarter 季度、四分之一　result 結果、導致
aggressive 積極進取的

2.

解說 根據文意，表示「持續至特定時間點」較為適當，因此答案為 until，意思為「直到…為止」。介系詞 by 表示在特定時間之前，完成某個行為或動作，強調「完成」的概念，因此不適合填入底線處。

中譯 從星期一起，新自助餐廳每天早上8點開放至晚上8點。

單字 daily 每日、每日的

3.

解說 畫底線處後方連接動名詞片語，表示畫底線處應填入介系詞。選項中 In front of 和 Prior to 為介系詞。根據文意，表示「Jane Hamilton 在 Hosto 公司工作之前，曾受僱於 Popka 公司」較為通順，因此答案為 Prior to，意思為「（時間上）在…之前」。

中譯 在Hosto公司工作之前，Jane Hamilton曾受僱於Popka公司。

單字 employ 僱用

4.

解說 畫底線處後方連接名詞片語，表示畫底線處應填入介系詞。選項中 on account of 和 along with 為介系詞。根據文意，表示「可在網站上找到更多資訊以及公園的最新照片」較為通順，因此答案為 along with，意思為「與…一起」。In short 為連接副詞，意思為「總而言之、簡而言之」，不適合作為答案。

中譯 有關該項目的更多資訊，以及公園的最新照片，均可在我們的網站上找到。

5.

解說 畫底線處後方使用 and 連接 current (employees) 和 former employees，表示畫底線處可填入適當的字詞，與 and 組合成相關連接詞，因此答案為 both。

中譯 人力資源部門保有現任員工和前任員工的相關資訊。

單字 current 現在的、當前的　former 從前的、前者的

6.

解說 畫底線處後方連接一個結構完整的子句（主詞＋動詞），而逗點後方又連接一個新的子句，表示畫底線處應填入連接詞，因此答案為 When。Above 可以當作形容詞、副詞或介系詞使用。當形容詞使用時，意思為「上文的、前述的」；當副詞使用時，意思為「在上面、（特定數字或標準）更高、更多」；當介系詞使用時，意思為「在…之上、超過」。

中譯 當你的電腦遇到問題時，請撥打分機56與金先生聯絡。

單字 encounter 遇到、遭遇　contact 聯絡、接觸　extension 分機號碼

7.

解說 畫底線處後方連接一個結構完整的子句（主詞＋動詞），而逗點後方又連接一個新的子句，表示畫底線處應填入連接詞，因此答案為 Because。

中譯 由於設計與網站上的不一樣，客戶提出抱怨。

8.

解說 畫底線處後方連接名詞片語，表示畫底線處應填入介系詞，因此答案為 despite。

中譯 儘管首間分店的成功率很低，Beanie咖啡店仍在巴黎開設了另一家分店。

單字 branch 分店、分公司　success 成功、成果

UNIT 03~04　　題本 p.110

1. (D)	2. (A)	3. (B)	4. (C)	5. (B)	6. (A)
7. (A)	8. (C)	9. (D)	10. (B)	11. (B)	12. (B)
13. (D)	14. (C)	15. (D)	16. (A)		

---

1. 填入副詞［及物動詞前方］

解說 空格用來修飾動詞 believe，應填入副詞，因此答案為 (D) firmly。

中譯 大多數選民堅信城市的主要道路需要更好地去維護。

單字 firmly 堅定地、穩固地　maintain 維持（關係、狀態、標準等）

2. 表示地點的介系詞［on vs. in］

解說 on 可表示在東西的表面上方，因此答案為 (A)。

中譯 牆上有幾個活動標誌，應於本月之內拆除。

單字 take down 拆除、取下　as 以…的身分

3. 填入形容詞［名詞前方］

解說 空格前方有不定冠詞，後方連接名詞，表示空格要填入適當的字詞，修飾後方的名詞，因此答案為形容詞 (B) secure。

中譯 Hensley女士建立了一個安全資料庫，可以儲存來自Globe汽車公司客戶的評論。

單字 secure 安全的、安心的　store 儲存、保管

4. 對等連接詞 as well as

解說 空格前後連接同樣詞性的名詞片語 hands-on workshops 和 short lectures，因此答案為對等連接詞 as well as。(A) for instance 為連接副詞，意思為「舉例來說」，不適合作為答案。

中譯 Parmona博物館提供實作工作坊以及簡短講座。

單字 hands-on 實作的

5. 表示一段時間的介系詞 throughout

解說 根據文意，表示「整個七月份持續舉辦夏季促銷活動」較為適當，因此答案為 (B) throughout。(C) even so 為連接副詞，意思為「儘管如此」，不適合作為答案。

中譯 將會在整個七月份持續舉辦夏季促銷活動。

單字 last 持續、繼續　inside 在…內部

6. 介系詞 vs. 從屬連接詞

解說 空格後方連接一個結構完整的子句（主詞＋動詞），而逗點後方又連接一個新的子句，表示空格應填入連接詞，因此答案為 (A) After。(D) Especially 為副詞，意思為「尤其」。

中譯 Caruso女士重新佈置等候區的傢俱後，空間顯得寬敞許多。

單字 rearrange 重新佈置　waiting area 等候區

7. 填入副詞［助動詞和動詞之間］

解說 空格置於助動詞 will 和動詞 release 之間，應填入副詞，因此答案為 (A) soon。(D) timely 為形容詞，意思為「及時的、適時的」，並非答案。

中譯 Bea's美容用品公司很快就會在網站上推出新的泡沫洗面乳。

8. 形容詞的功能［補語］

解說 空格置於 be 動詞 is 後方的位置上，應填入主詞補語，用來補充說明主詞 it。選項中只有 (C) suitable 為形容詞，故為正解。

中譯 該建築物需進行大規模翻修，才適合當作辦公室使用。

單字 property 建築物、房地產、財產、所有物
extensive 大規模的、範圍廣的　renovation 翻修、改裝

9. 填入形容詞［名詞前方］

解說 空格前方為動詞，後方連接名詞，表示空格應填入適當的字詞，修飾後方的名詞，因此答案為形容詞 (D) helpful。

中譯 本簡報包含執行防範詐騙技術的有用提示。

單字 implement 實施、執行　anti-fraud 防範詐騙

10. 從屬連接詞 so that

解說 空格前後各連接一個結構完整的子句，表示空格應填入連接詞。(A) given that 和 (B) so that 皆為連接詞，而根據文意，表示「應在會議前閱讀提案，以便充分了解情況」較為適當，因此答案為 (B)，意思為「以便…」。

中譯 董事會成員應在會議前閱讀提案，以便在討論細節時，能夠充分了解情況。

單字 well-informed 充分了解的　detail 細節

11. 填入副詞＋比較級用法

解說 空格修飾動詞 looks，應填入副詞。且空格後方出現介系詞 than，連接比較的對象，表示空格要填入副詞的比較級，因此答案為 (B) more closely。

中譯 這位導演的新紀錄片比第一部更深入探討石油產業。

單字 look at 研究、探討

12. 形容詞的功能［補語］

解說 空格置於不及物動詞 remains 的後方，應填入主詞補語，補充說明主詞 Martin Textiles，因此答案為形容詞 (B) dependent。

中譯 Martin 紡織公司仍然仰賴棉纖維的銷售來獲取利潤。

單字 remain 維持、剩下　dependent 仰賴、依賴
cotton fibers 棉纖維　profit 收益、利潤

13. 介系詞 vs. 從屬連接詞

解說 空格前後各連接一個結構完整的子句，表示空格應填入連接詞，因此答案為 (D) unless。

中譯 所有機密文件都必須存放在上鎖的櫃子裡，除非有人需要使用。

單字 confidential 機密的

14. 填入副詞［不及物動詞後方］

解說 空格用來修飾動詞 has increased，應填入副詞，因此答案為 (C) significantly。

中譯 自去年以來，企業參與數量大幅增加。

單字 participating 參與的　significantly 大幅地、顯著地、重要地

15. 從屬連接詞 before

解說 空格前後各連接一個結構完整的子句，表示空格應填入連接詞。選項中 (B) although 和 (D) before 皆為連接詞，而根據文意，表示「在規劃之前，需要先取得市議會的同意」較為適當，因此答案為 (D)，意思為「在…之前」。(A) rather（寧願、倒不如）(C) also（並且）皆為副詞，不適合作為答案。

中譯 我們需要得到市議會的同意，才能著手規劃把這塊住宅區改造成商業區。

單字 get consent 取得同意　residential 住宅的
commercial 商業的

16. 介系詞片語 according to

解說 根據文意，表示「根據僱傭合約，有權成立工會」較為適當，因此答案為 (A) According to，意思為「根據」。

中譯 根據僱傭合約，勞動者有權成立工會。

單字 employment contract 僱傭合約　retain 保有
form 成立、組織　labor union 工會

UNIT 05　動詞

CHECK-UP　　　　　　　　　　　　　題本 p.112

1. expect
2. supplies
3. be informed
4. are required
5. will open
6. has improved
7. are issued
8. are monitoring

1.

解說 主詞 Executives 為複數名詞，動詞也要使用複數形態，才符合主動詞的單複數一致性，因此答案為 expect。

中譯 Murphy 汽車公司的經營管理高層預計下個月至少會銷售 100 輛二手車。

單字 at least 至少

2.

解說 主詞 Thornton Textiles 為單數名詞，動詞也要使用單數形態，才符合主動詞的單複數一致性，因此答案為 supplies。請特別留意，公司名稱最後加上 s，同樣視為單數形。

中譯 棉織物製造商 Thornton 紡織廠，為全國 50 多家服裝廠供貨。

單字 producer 製造商、生產者　supply 供貨

3.

解說 畫底線處後方並未連接受詞，先行詞 Audience members 為行為接受者，表示畫底線處使用被動語態「be ＋過去分詞」較為適當，因此答案為 be informed。

中譯 希望得知即將到來演出資訊的觀眾，應填寫一份包含聯絡資料的表格。

單字 inform 告知、通知　upcoming 即將到來的、即將來臨的　complete 完整填寫（表格等）、完成、結束

4.

解說 畫底線處後方連接不定詞 to V，表示畫底線處適合填入 require 的被動語態「be ＋過去分詞」的形態，因此答案為 are required。

中譯 所有用戶在使用我們的雲端軟體之前，都必須驗證他們的帳戶。

單字 authenticate 驗證　account 帳戶、帳號

5.

解說 畫底線處後方出現 next month，適合搭配未來式使用，因此答案為 will open。

中譯 Newbury國家公園將於下個月開放給登山客和露營者。

6.

解說 畫底線處後方出現 since July，適合搭配現在完成式使用，因此答案為 has improved。

中譯 自七月以來，Bailey運動服飾公司新的服裝系列有顯著的改善。

單字 significantly 顯著地、相當地、重要地

7.

解說 主詞 the permits 為複數名詞，為符合主動詞單複數的一致性，動詞也要使用複數形態。are issued 和 were issuing 皆為複數形態，而畫底線處後方並未連接受詞，且主詞 the permits 為行為接受者，表示畫底線處適合使用「be ＋過去分詞」的形態，因此答案為 are issued。

中譯 一旦核發許可證，將會在Vivitech總部展開下一階段的建設。

單字 permit 許可證　issue 核發、發行

8.

解說 畫底線處後方連接受詞 their spending，且主詞 department heads 為行為者，表示畫底線處應使用主動語態。had monitored 和 are monitoring 皆為主動語態，而根據文意，表示「更謹慎地監控」較為適當，因此答案為現在進行式 are monitoring。過去完成式用於表示較過去某個特定時間點更早發生的事情，因此該句子並不適用。

中譯 在公司新業主的體制下，部門負責人比以前更謹慎地控管支出。

單字 ownership 業主、所有權者　monitor （定期）監控、監看

UNIT 06 動狀詞

CHECK-UP　　　　　　　　　題本 p.114

1. to arrange　　2. to perform
3. locking　　　4. substituting
5. to increase　6. continuing
7. rising　　　　8. qualified

1.

解說 畫底線處前方為 would like，後方連接名詞片語 a group interview，表示畫底線處應填入適當的字詞，既能當作 would like 的受詞，又能連接後方名詞片語，當作受詞，因此答案為不定詞 to arrange。

中譯 Waite女士想在下週五安排一場團體面試。

單字 arrange 安排、準備

2.

解說 畫底線處前方連接一個結構完整的子句，表示畫底線處至句末需扮演副詞的角色，因此答案為不定詞 to perform。

中譯 大樓內所有電梯將從上午十點起停用一小時，以進行必要的維護。

單字 out of service 停用　required 必要的、被要求的　maintenance （建築、機器等）維護

3.

解說 畫底線處前方為介系詞片語，後方連接名詞，表示畫底線處應填入適當的字詞，既能當作介系詞片語的受詞，又能連接後方名詞當作受詞，因此答案為動名詞 locking。

中譯 最後一個離開辦公室的人，必須確保在鎖門前設定好安全警報裝置。

單字 security alarm 安全警報裝置

4.

解說 畫底線處置於動詞 suggest 的受詞位置上，suggest 可連接動名詞當作受詞，因此答案為 substituting。

中譯 我們建議在你最喜歡的食譜中，用天然甜味劑代替人工甜味劑。

單字 substitute A for B 用 A 代替 B　natural 天然的、自然的　sweetener 甜味劑　artificial 人工的

5.

解說 be able 後方要連接不定詞，因此答案為 to increase。

中譯 在更多投資者的支持下，公司得以增加產量。

單字 with the backing of 在…的支持、支援下　production 產量

6.

解說 look forward to 後方要連接動名詞，因此答案為 continuing。

中譯 我們感謝您的支持，並期待繼續為您服務。

單字 appreciate 感謝、賞識、欣賞

7.

解說 畫底線處前方有定冠詞，後方連接名詞，表示畫底線處要填入適當的字詞，修飾後方的名詞，因此答案為現在分詞 rising。

中譯 居民主要最擔心的是公共服務費用上漲。

單字 be concerned about 擔心⋯

8.

解說 根據文意，表示「吸引符合資格的求職者」最為適當，因此答案為 qualified，意思「有資格的、勝任的」。

中譯 Corbett女士主張增加公司福利，可吸引適任的員工。

單字 argue 主張、議論　benefit 福利
attract 吸引、引誘

UNIT 07 關係代名詞

CHECK-UP 題本 p.116

1. who 2. which
3. contained 4. he
5. where 6. that
7. Whoever 8. wherever

1.

解說 畫底線處前方為人物名詞，因此答案為 who。

中譯 所有完成問卷調查的顧客，皆可獲得折價券。

單字 complete 完整填寫（表格等）、完成、結束　voucher 禮券、優惠券

2.

解說 畫底線處前方為介系詞 after，表示畫底線處應填入適當的字詞，當作介系詞的受詞，因此答案為關係代名詞（受格）which。原本的句子應為「which the account is suspended after」，但在關係子句句末的介系詞，可移至關係代名詞前方。

中譯 影音串流中心公司在向客戶發出關於逾期付款的三次警告後，帳戶將會被停用。

單字 warning 警告　account 帳戶、帳號
suspend 停用、中止

3.

解說 修飾對象 Some information 與畫底線處為被動關係，因此答案為過去分詞 contained。另外，該句話中 contained in the documents 修飾前方的 Some information，因此省略 contained 前方的「關係代名詞（主格）＋ be 動詞」，即為 which is。

中譯 文件中包含的某些資訊已經過時。

單字 outdated 過時的、陳舊的

4.

解說 畫底線處前方為一個結構完整的子句，'------ can' 為形容詞子句，用來修飾 everything，表示畫底線處要填入適當的字詞，當作動詞 can (do) 的主詞，因此答案為人稱代名詞主格 he。另外，該句話省略了 everything 和 he 之間的關係代名詞（受格）。

中譯 執行長竭盡全力支持他的員工。

5.

解說 畫底線處前後方各連接一個結構完整的子句，表示畫底線處要填入兼具副詞和連接詞功能的關係副詞，因此答案為 where。what 包含先行詞和關係代名詞，因此 what 前方不能出現先行詞。其用法為「what ＋不完整的子句」置於主詞、補語或受詞的位置上，扮演名詞的角色。

中譯 該品牌的忠實粉絲，在發售限量版運動鞋的商店前方排起了隊伍。

單字 dedicated 忠實的、盡心的　be lined up 排隊
release 發售、公開、上市

6.

解說 畫底線處後方連接一個缺少主詞的子句，表示畫底線處要填入關係代名詞主格，因此答案為 that。

中譯 該款手機的製作材料可承受五公尺以下因摔落而導致的損傷。

單字 be comprised of 由⋯製成　resist 承受（損傷）、抵抗

7.

解說 「------ leaves the office last」扮演主詞的角色，表示畫底線處應填入適當的字詞，引導名詞子句，因此答案為複合關係代名詞 Whoever，用來引導缺少主詞的不完整子句。

中譯 最後離開辦公室的人應該要關燈。

單字 be expected to do 應該要⋯、被期望做⋯、預計要⋯

8.

解說 畫底線處前後各連接一個結構完整的子句，表示畫底線處要填入適合連接子句的字詞，因此答案為複合關係副詞 wherever。

中譯 Pawan科技公司開發了一個手機應用程式，無論用戶去哪裡，都能為他們提供最新的交通狀況。

單字 develop 開發

PRACTICE UNIT05~07　　題本 p.118

1. (B)　2. (B)　3. (D)　4. (C)　5. (D)　6. (D)
7. (A)　8. (C)　9. (C)　10. (C)　11. (D)　12. (B)
13. (D)　14. (A)　15. (B)　16. (A)

1. 填入分詞［名詞前方］
解說　空格前方有定冠詞，後方連接名詞，表示空格應填入能修飾名詞的字詞。選項中僅有過去分詞能修飾名詞，因此答案為 (B) preferred。
中譯　Zeller女士邀請了幾位求職者參加面試，儘管他們並不具備初級研究員職位的優先條件資格。
單字　preferred 優先的　qualification 資格

2. 填入關係代名詞主格
解說　空格前方為一個結構完整的子句「主詞（A retirement party）＋動詞（will be held）＋副詞片語（next week）＋介系詞片語（for Mr. Schmidt）」；空格後方連接一個缺少主詞的不完整子句，表示空格應填入兼具連接詞和主詞功能的字詞，連接前後兩個子句，同時當作不完整子句的主詞，因此答案為關係代名詞主格 (B) who。
中譯　下週將為Schmidt先生舉辦退休派對，他已經在Melon科技公司工作超過30年。

3. 主動詞單複數的一致性
解說　主詞 Mr. Farrow 為單數名詞，表示動詞也要使用單數形態，才符合主動詞單複數的一致性。選項中，(A) are inspecting 和 (C) inspect 為複數動詞，不適合作為答案；(B) having inspected 不適合置於動詞位置上，並非答案。刪去其餘三個選項後，可選出答案為 (D) will inspect。
中譯　Farrow先生將檢查車輛的引擎，並報告有無任何問題。
單字　inspect 檢查、檢驗　report 報告　issue 問題、議題、主題、爭議

4. 介系詞＋關係代名詞
解說　空格前後各連接一個結構完整的子句，表示答案可能是 (A) when 或 (C) for which（介系詞＋關係代名詞）。空格前方沒有表示特定時間的先行詞，且空格後方有形容詞 grateful，適合搭配介系詞 for 使用，因此答案為 (C)。
中譯　我們的資金來自基金會和讀者的支持，我們對此表示感謝。
單字　foundation 基金會　B as well as A 不僅A還有B　grateful 感謝的

5. 不定詞 to V
解說　空格前方為一個結構完整的子句，表示空格至句末要扮演副詞的角色。選項中僅有不定詞 (D) to understand 能扮演副詞的角色。
中譯　所有員工都必須參加下週的研討會，以了解如何操作新型機器。
單字　machinery 機器

6. 主動詞單複數的一致性與語態
解說　主詞 renovations 為複數名詞，表示動詞也要使用複數形態，才符合主動詞單複數的一致性，因此答案可能是 (A) will be completing 或 (D) are being completed。而空格後方並未連接受詞，表示空格要填入被動語態「be＋過去分詞」，因此答案為 (D)。
中譯　Carsen健身房將於翻修期間關閉約兩個月。
單字　be shut down 關閉、停業

7. 現在分詞 vs. 過去分詞
解說　空格前方為動詞，後方連接名詞，表示空格應填入能修飾名詞的字詞。選項中，過去分詞 (A) used 和現在分詞 (D) using 皆可修飾名詞，而句中的 computers 與空格間屬於被動關係，為「被使用」的東西，因此答案為 (A)。
中譯　客戶服務部門會購買二手電腦是因為他們的預算很少。
單字　budget 預算

8. 未來進行式
解說　空格前方出現 Later this afternoon，適合搭配使用的時態為未來式，因此答案為 (C) will be renegotiating。
中譯　今天下午稍晚的時候，Bullock女士將與一間建築材料公司重新協商合約條款。
單字　renegotiate 重新協商　terms 條款

9. 現在分詞 vs. 過去分詞
解說　空格前方為定冠詞，後方連接名詞，表示空格應填入能修飾名詞的字詞。選項中，過去分詞 (C) returned 和現在分詞 (D) returning 皆可修飾名詞。而句中的 product 與空格間屬於被動關係，為「被退還」的東西，因此答案為 (C)。
中譯　我們收到郵寄的退貨商品後，將為您退款。

10. 語態與時態
解說　空格後方出現 last Friday，適合搭配使用的時態為過去式，表示空格應填入動詞過去式，答案可能是 (C) gave 或 (D) was given。而空格後方連接受詞，表示主詞 Mr. Grimes 為行為者，因此空格應使用主動語態，答案為 (C)。
中譯　Grimes先生上週五在資訊科技和安全會議上發表了主題演講。
單字　address 演講、地址

11. 填入動名詞［介系詞後方］
解說　空格前方為介系詞 of，後方連接名詞片語 its business，表示空格應填入適當的字詞，既能當作介系詞的受詞，又能連接名詞片語當作受詞。因此答案要選動名詞 (D) extending。
中譯　Cannon公司正在探索將其業務擴展到亞洲的可能性。
單字　explore 探索、探究　possibility 可能性　extend 擴展（事業、勢力等）、延長

12. 被動語態vs.主動語態

解說 空格後方並未連接受詞，且主詞 Mosquito pesticide spraying operations 為行為接受者，表示空格適合填入被動語態「be ＋過去分詞」，因此答案為 (B) are scheduled。

中譯 噴灑滅蚊殺蟲劑的行動，預計在遊客來度假前開始。

單字 pesticide 殺蟲劑　spray 噴灑　on vacation 度假中

13. 填入複合關係代名詞

解說 「------ they prefer」用來修飾前方的子句，扮演副詞的角色，因此空格應填入適當的字詞，引導副詞子句。選項中僅有複合關係代名詞可以引導副詞子句，因此答案為 (D) whichever。

中譯 為了慶祝Chonie沙龍成立10週年，顧客可以依據自己的喜好，免費獲得所有護髮產品的樣品。

單字 in celebration of 慶祝…、迎接…

14. 不定詞的語態

解說 空格前方為動詞 plans，表示空格要填入適當的字詞，當作動詞的受詞。選項中的不定詞 (A) to turn 和 (B) to be turned 皆有可能為答案，而空格後方連接受詞 an abandoned building，表示空格適合填入主動語態，因此答案為 (A)。

中譯 Smallville的市長計畫將一棟廢棄建築物改造成圖書館。

單字 abandoned 廢棄的、被遺棄的

15. 現在分詞vs.過去分詞

解說 空格前方為定冠詞，後方連接名詞片語，表示空格應填入能修飾名詞片語的字詞。選項中，過去分詞 (B) accomplished 和現在分詞 (C) accomplishing 皆可修飾名詞。根據文意，表示「優秀的產品設計師獲獎」最為適當，因此答案為 (B)，意思為「優秀的、傑出的」。

中譯 這位優秀的產品設計師榮獲業界的最高榮譽。

單字 be awarded with 獲頒…　top honors 最高榮譽

16. 填入關係代名詞主格

解說 空格前方為一個結構完整的子句「主詞（Mr. Barbour）＋動詞（showed）＋間接受詞（the electrician）＋直接受詞（the light fixture）」；空格後方連接一個缺少主詞的不完整子句，表示空格應填入兼具連接詞和主詞功能的字詞，連接前後兩個子句，同時當作不完整子句的主詞，因此答案為關係代名詞主格 (B) that。

中譯 Barbour先生給水電工看了故障的燈具。

單字 light fixture （固定在天花板或牆上的）燈具
malfunction 故障

UNIT 08 詞彙

CHECK-UP　名詞　題本 p.121

| 1. (B) | 2. (C) | 3. (A) | 4. (D) | 5. (A) |
| 6. (B) | 7. (A) | 8. (B) | 9. (A) | 10. (A) |

1.

中譯 在修復好結構上的缺陷之前，博物館無法對外開放。

單字 public 大眾、大眾的、公共的　structural 結構的
defect 缺陷　definition 定義、意義　communication 溝通
uncertainty 不確定性

2.

中譯 若在費城市區範圍內送貨，乾洗公司不收取額外費用。

單字 make a delivery 送貨　charge 費用、責任
pressure 壓力、壓迫　provider 提供者、供應者
area 地區、區域

3.

中譯 儘管雪量比預測來得少，但仍在整個尖峰時段造成了交通堵塞。

單字 predict 預測、預報　delay 延遲、耽擱
refund 退款　route 道路、路線　suggestion 提案、提議

4.

中譯 如果您申請汽車保險理賠，我們將於三個工作日內審查該請求。

單字 file a claim 申請索賠（補償金等）、求償
examine 調查、檢視　request 要求、請求（書）
expertise 專業知識、專業性　account 帳戶、帳號
registration 報名

5.

中譯 除了擁有知名大學學位外，Harris女士還有多張證書。

單字 in addition to 除了…之外
prestigious 有聲望的、名聲好的　certification 證書
assignment 課題、任務　estimate 報價（單）、估計（值）
recipient 收件者、接受者

6.

中譯 一筆小額的企業貸款，幫Joslin先生克服了阻擋他生意的障礙。

單字 overcome 克服、戰勝　obstacle 障礙（物）
hold back 抑制、控制　attempt 嘗試　reaction 反應
opposite 反對

7.

中譯 圖書館讀者完成了問卷調查，分享值得購買的書籍建議。

單字 share 分享　recommendation 推薦（信）、建議
reimbursement 償還、退款、賠償　retrieval 回收
resolution 決議案、解決

8.

中譯 Tingley旅行社為學生推出暑期歐洲短程旅行。

單字 excursion （短程）旅行　settlement 協議、解決、結帳
institution 機構　accomplishment 成就、成果

9.

中譯 儘管該店家的網站上已明確說明退款政策，但有些消費者仍對此感到困惑。

單字 policy 政策、方針　clearly 明確地、確實地　state 說明
shelter 居住地、避難所　preference 偏好、偏愛的事物
appointment 約定、預約

10.

中譯 Verity餐廳的私人宴會廳提供任何特殊活動的預約，最多可容納三十人。

單字 private 私人的、專用的　reserve 預約、單獨安排（座位等）
occasion 活動、時候、情況　turnover 離職率、營業額
competence 能力　intention 意圖

CHECK UP　形容詞　題本 p.123

| 1. (C) | 2. (B) | 3. (B) | 4. (B) | 5. (C) |
| 6. (D) | 7. (A) | 8. (D) | 9. (C) | 10. (A) |

1.

中譯 在安裝新軟體前，員工花費大量時間更新客戶的帳戶。

單字 install 安裝　substantial 相當的、多的
consecutive 連續不斷的　direct 直接的、直達的
visible 顯而易見的

2.

中譯 Henley學院的公開演講課適合企業團體和學生個人。

單字 public speaking 公開演講　be suitable for 適合…
corporate 企業的　individual 單獨的、個別的
beneficial 有益的　deliberate 故意的、蓄意的
distant （距離）遠的

3.

中譯 具有豐富管理經驗的求職者，有很大的機會被錄用。

單字 applicant 求職者　extensive 廣泛的、大規模的
management 經營、營運、管理　straight 筆直的、端正的
compact 小型的、簡潔的　attentive 留意的、體貼的、專心的

4.

中譯 專家擔心氣候變遷可能對全球經濟帶來巨大的影響。

單字 massive 大規模的、非常多 [大、巨大] 的

5.

中譯 影音串流服務在過去一個季度中，增加了大量的新用戶。

單字 sizeable 相當大的　current 現在的、近期的
defective 有缺陷的　preserved 保存的

6.

中譯 如果Kellogg先生的國家認可證書有效，他將獲得高級會計的職位。

單字 turn out 結果是…、　valid 有效的
successive 連續的、依次的　familiar 熟悉的、常見的
informal 非正式的、不拘禮節的

7.

中譯 在首次行程很快就售罄後，投資者對於郵輪公司的潛力抱持樂觀的態度。

單字 optimistic 樂觀的、樂天的　potential 潛力、可能性
sell out 售罄　superior 優秀的、優越的
rare 罕見的、稀有的　unique 獨特的、唯一的

8.

中譯 在Rosewood飯店，客人的舒適度至關重要。

單字 comfort 舒適、安逸、安慰　utmost 極度的
constant 接連不斷的、持續的　diminished 變少的、減輕的
joint 共同的、聯合的

9.

中譯 新的稅收減免措施，使鎮上新成立的小企業數量產生重大的變化。

單字 incentive 獎勵的、鼓勵的
significant 相當的、有意義的、重要的
difficult 困難的　prepared 準備好的　capable 有能力的

10.

中譯 發電廠升級後，該市的電力供應將會更加穩定。

單字 following 在…以後、隨著
power plant 發電廠　dependable 可靠的
supply 供應　patient 有耐心的
enthusiastic 熱情的、熱烈的　grateful 感謝的

CHECK UP　副詞　題本 p.125

| 1. (A) | 2. (D) | 3. (C) | 4. (A) | 5. (C) |
| 6. (B) | 7. (C) | 8. (A) | 9. (B) | 10. (D) |

1.
中譯 Riddell農牧場直接供應牛奶給當地餐廳，以保持較低的成本。
單字 supply 供應　directly 直接、正好地　neatly 整潔地
hardly 幾乎不　unusually 不尋常地、非常

2.
中譯 我們的技術專家正在努力恢復辦公室的網路服務。
單字 diligently 勤奮地、努力地　restore 恢復、復原
financially 財政上、金融上　seemingly 表面上、似乎是
particularly 尤其

3.
中譯 辦公室經理Charles Yarger出人意料地要求與Arlow女士會面，因此她不得不調整自己的行程安排。
單字 unexpectedly 出乎意料地、意外地
request 要求、請求　adjust 調整
commonly 通常地、一般地　indefinitely 無限期地
nearly 幾乎

4.
中譯 這家廚具公司於比利時成立，總部設在比利時，目前正在興建新工廠。
單字 found 成立　headquartered 以…為總部所在地的
currently 現在、目前　extremely 極度地、非常
solidly 堅固地、牢靠地　immediately 立刻、馬上

5.
中譯 天空宴會廳最多可容納50位客人，而微風宴會廳可輕鬆容納80至100人。
單字 accommodate 容納　seat （特定數量的）座位
comfortably 輕鬆地、無負擔地；舒適地、便利地
consequently 結果、因此　widely 廣泛地
exceedingly 極度地、非常地

6.
中譯 Lamora水果園最近證實將在下一個季度進行所有權變更。
單字 recently 最近　ownership 所有權
approximately 大概、大約　heavily 沈重地
randomly 隨意地

7.
中譯 與競爭對手相比，Clotherly生產的棉質T恤明顯比較柔軟。
單字 noticeably 明顯地　competitor 競爭對手
hurriedly 匆忙地　respectively 分別地、各自地
closely 接近地、密切地

8.
中譯 Waldeck新推出的平板電腦配有高解析度螢幕。
單字 newly 最近　feature 以…為特色、特徵
high-resolution 高解析度　absolutely 絕對地
naturally 當然、自然地　considerably 相當地

9.
中譯 在四樓裝修期間，銷售部門將暫時搬遷至五樓。
單字 temporarily 暫時地、臨時地　renovate 裝修、改造
faintly 微弱地　sincerely 真誠地
competitively 競爭地、有競爭力地

10.
中譯 其中一名學員因為不熟悉該軟體，不小心為Traylyn公司多印了十條橫幅。
單字 unfamiliar 不熟悉的
accidentally 不小心地、偶然地、意外地
extra 額外的、外加的　mainly 主要地、大部分地
vigorously 活潑地、強而有力地　necessarily 必定、必然地

CHECK-UP　動詞　題本 p.127

1. (A)　**2.** (B)　**3.** (C)　**4.** (C)　**5.** (B)
6. (A)　**7.** (B)　**8.** (D)　**9.** (B)　**10.** (B)

1.
中譯 Midco通訊公司和Trant公司宣布了一項聯合慈善活動，將為低收入戶家庭提供網路服務。
單字 announce 宣布、通知　joint 聯合的、共同的
charity 慈善（團體）　endeavor 努力、嘗試
household 戶、家庭　install 安裝
treat （用特定的態度）對待、看待　calibrate 使標準化、校準

2.
中譯 請注意，請假必須提前一週獲得主管批准。
單字 note 注意、提到　request 要求、請求
time off 請假、休假　approve 批准、認可、讚許 (~ of)
assess 評估　secure 取得、獲得
reschedule 重新安排時間、改期

3.

中譯 利潤減少促使Liang工業公司增加其行銷預算。

單字 prompt 促使　license 准許
restock 重新進貨、補貨、裝滿　outline 略述、概述

4.

中譯 Kirtfield銷售公司的首席會計師審查了公司的財務狀況，確定該公司無法負擔翻修大樓的費用。

單字 determine 決定、確定、（以具體證據）判斷、查明
afford （金錢和時間上）可負擔、買得起
admit 承認、允許進入
maintain 維持（關係、狀態、標準等）　remember 記得

5.

中譯 一年一度的遊戲大會聚集了來自全國各地的電玩開發商。

單字 bring together （人們）齊聚一堂
carry out 執行、實行　use up 耗盡…
take down 取下、記下

6.

中譯 名列年度最暢銷的懸疑小說是《The Door to Sandra's》。

單字 top 獲得第一名；超過（數量、記錄等）；蓋上
impress 留下印象、使銘記　generate 產生
seek 尋找、探索

7.

中譯 商品通常來自兩個或多個倉庫，因此您的訂單可能會被分裝成不同的包裹。

單字 separate 分開、分成　mandate （官方上）命令、授權
prioritize 按優先順序處理　demolish 拆除（建築物）

8.

中譯 根據預購的數量，該公司預期新款遊戲機的推出將取得巨大的成功。

單字 unit 單位、單元　anticipate 預想、期待、預期
compile 編輯、匯編　condense 縮減（文章等）、濃縮
delegate 委託（工作、任務等）、委任、代表

9.

中譯 Vance銀行提醒旅客，由於貨幣市場的波動，銀行無法保證有相同的匯率。

單字 remind 提醒　guarantee 保障、保證
exchange rate 匯率　fluctuation 波動、變動、變化
currency market 貨幣市場
convey 傳達（想法、感受等）、運送　undergo 經歷、體驗
obscure 模糊的、含糊不清

10.

中譯 記者詢問了股價與經營管理團隊變動之間的關係。

單字 inquire 詢問　executive 經營管理的、行政的
formulate 規劃、制訂　persuade 說服
occupy 佔領、佔據

PART TEST

題本 p.128

101. (B)	102. (B)	103. (C)	104. (D)	105. (B)
106. (A)	107. (D)	108. (B)	109. (B)	110. (C)
111. (C)	112. (C)	113. (C)	114. (D)	115. (A)
116. (C)	117. (C)	118. (B)	119. (B)	120. (D)
121. (D)	122. (D)	123. (A)	124. (D)	125. (C)
126. (C)	127. (B)	128. (A)	129. (B)	130. (D)

101. 填入動詞

解說 空格前方為主詞 Many tutors，後方連接受詞 their services，表示空格應填入動詞，因此答案為 (B) advertise。

中譯 許多家教在社區論壇上宣傳他們的服務，因為它具有成本效益。

單字 tutor 導師、家教　advertise 宣傳、廣告
cost-effective 有成本效益的

102. 填入所有格形容詞

解說 空格前方為連接詞，後方連接名詞，表示空格要填入能修飾名詞的字詞，因此答案為所有格形容詞 (B) their。

中譯 除非公開內容物，否則郵局不接受國際包裹。

單字 unless 除非　disclose 公開、透露

103. 副詞詞彙題 quickly

中譯 工廠管理者對Benson製造公司工作人員迅速修復損壞機器的表現感到滿意。

單字 supervisor 管理者、監督人
be pleased with 對…感到滿意、高興　quickly 迅速地
machinery 機器　electronically 電子化地
increasingly 逐漸地、越來越多地　highly 非常、很

104. 名詞的功能［受詞］

解說 空格置於不定詞 to exceed 後方的受詞位置上，選項中只有名詞能當作受詞使用，因此答案為 (D) expectations。

中譯 Poole女士和Johnson先生在他們管理職位上的表現持續超出預期。

單字 exceed 超越　managerial 經營的、管理的
expectation 預期、期待　expectant 期待著的

67

105. 介系詞詞彙題 by
中譯 兩房公寓的租約必須在10月6日之前續約。
單字 lease 租賃　renew 更新、延長　by 在…之前
with 一起、帶著…　in 在…裡面　of …的

106. 動詞詞彙題 clean
中譯 會議室通常會在平日晚上8點鐘左右關閉，以進行清潔工作。
單字 clean 清潔、打掃　approximately 大概、約莫
dispose 處置、處理　speak 說話　paint 油漆

107. 現在式
解說 主要子句為現在式，而該句話中描述「填寫報關單時」屬於一般事實，空格適合填入現在式，因此答案為 (D) complete。
中譯 當你填寫政府提供的海關申報表時，請全部使用大寫字母填寫。
單字 capital letter 大寫字母
customs declaration form 海關申報表

108. 形容詞詞彙題 current
中譯 Delgado女士解釋道，她目前與設計公司的合約僅為短期合約。
單字 current 現在的、目前的　steep 陡峭的
natural 天然的、自然的　occasional 偶爾的

109. 介系詞詞彙題 up to
解說 空格前方有主詞和動詞，為一個結構完整的子句，且空格後方連接名詞，表示空格應填入介系詞。(D) in case 為從屬連接詞，因此並非答案。
中譯 乘客最遲可在航班起飛前24小時，免費更改座位預訂。
單字 up to 直到…　charge 費用、責任、掌管
since 自從　as for 說到…　in case 以防萬一

110. 副詞詞彙題 temporarily
中譯 Greenwich五金行停車場的部分區域，因樹木倒塌而暫時關閉。
單字 be shut down 遭關閉、封鎖
temporarily 暫時地、臨時地　potentially 潛在地
significantly 相當地、重要地　annually 每年一次

111. 填入關係代名詞主格
解說 空格前方為一個結構完整的子句「主詞（Vensa Airways）＋動詞（provided）＋受詞（travel vouchers）＋介系詞片語（to everyone）」；空格後方連接一個缺少主詞的不完整子句，表示空格應填入兼具連接詞和主詞功能的字詞，連接前後兩個子句，同時當作不完整子句的主詞，因此答案為關係代名詞主格 (C) who。
中譯 Vensa航空公司有為所有因航班取消而導致行程延誤的人，提供旅遊優惠券。
單字 voucher 禮券、優惠券　cancellation 取消

112. 被動語態 vs. 主動語態
解說 主詞 Spectators 為動詞 ask 的行為接受者，表示空格應使用被動語態「be ＋過去分詞」較為適當，因此答案為 (C) are asked。
中譯 觀眾被要求避免攜帶不必要的個人物品進入體育場。
單字 spectator 觀眾　be asked to do 被要求…
refrain from 避免…　unnecessary 不必要的

113. 填入形容詞
解說 空格前方為冠詞，後方連接名詞，表示空格應填入修飾後方名詞的字詞，因此答案為形容詞 (C) acceptable。
中譯 Sunderland保險公司的政策有包括將撥打緊急電話納入工作中允許使用個人電話的範疇。
單字 emergency 緊急、突發狀況

114. 填入從屬連接詞＋詞彙題
解說 空格前後各連接一個結構完整的子句，表示空格要填入連接詞。(C) except 和 (D) before 皆為連接詞，而根據文意，表示「送到賣場之前，都會經過嚴格檢查」較為適當，因此答案為 (D)，意思為「在…之前」。
中譯 我們所有服裝在送到AJ時裝店之前，都會經過嚴格審查。
單字 garment 服裝、衣服　closely 緊密地、嚴密地
inspect 檢查、審查　except 除…之外

115. 填入副詞
解說 空格位在 be 動詞 was 和過去分詞 confirmed 之間，應填入副詞，因此答案為 (A) reliably。
中譯 合併消息由其中一個組織證實消息來源可靠。
單字 merger 合併　reliably 可靠地、確實地
confirm 證實、確定　source 消息來源、提供消息者、出處
organization 機構、組織、團體　reliable 可信賴的、可靠的
reliability 信賴度、可信度

116. 填入介系詞＋詞彙題
解說 空格後方連接動名詞片語，表示空格應填入適當的字詞，連接動名詞片語當作受詞。選項中 (B) According to 和 (C) Prior to 為介系詞，皆有可能是答案。而根據文意，表示「完成碩士學位之前，花了兩年的時間」較為適當，因此答案為 (C)，意思為「在…之前」。
中譯 在完成碩士學位之前，Lewis女士花了兩年時間嘗試推出自己的餐飲事業。
單字 launch 推出、上市　catering 餐飲服務
according to 根據…

117. 動詞詞彙題 depart

中譯 前往電影院的巴士將從藥局正門出發，終點站為 Yorkshire 街。

單字 depart 出發　conduct 執行、指揮（特定活動）
extend 延長、擴大（事業、勢力等）
withdraw 提取（錢）、收回、撤退

118. 填入分詞

解說 空格前方為動名詞，後方連接名詞片語，表示空格要填入修飾名詞片語的字詞，選項中只有過去分詞能修飾名詞，因此答案為 (B)。

中譯 為了降低創業成本，可以購買二手辦公設備。

單字 start-up costs 創業成本

119. 名詞詞彙題 site

中譯 Brow 用品公司計畫開發新的安全帽，以改善工作現場的安全性。

單字 hard hat 安全帽　site 現場、場所　notice 公告、通知
goal 目標、目的　calendar 日曆、行事曆

120. 動詞詞彙題 contact

中譯 如欲詢問更換老舊設備的問題，請連落資訊科技部門的 Arrieta 先生。

單字 inquiry 詢問、諮詢　replace 替換
outdated 老舊的、過時的　contact 聯絡、接觸
determine 決定、確定　apply 申請、應徵、適用
hire 僱用、任用

121. 填入介系詞＋詞彙題

解說 空格前方的句子有主詞和動詞，為一個結構完整的子句，且空格後方連接名詞片語，表示空格要填入適當的字詞，連接名詞片語當作受詞。選項中適合填入的詞性為介系詞 (A) onto 或 (D) until，而根據文意，表示「直到八月底為止都會提供免費導覽活動」較為適當，因此答案為 (D)，意思為「直到⋯」。

中譯 博物館將在週六上午提供免費的幕後導覽活動，直至八月底。

單字 behind-the-scenes 幕後、未公開地
onto 到⋯之上、在⋯之上

122. 介系詞詞彙題 between

中譯 前往 Clerrick 國家公園的遊客，應向位於咖啡廳和兒童遊樂場之間的國家公園管理站報告過夜的露營計畫。

單字 report 報告、告知　overnight 整夜的　ranger station（森林的）國家公園管理站　locate 位在、座落於（特定位置）
between A and B 在 A 和 B 之間　including 包含⋯
into 到⋯裡面　throughout 遍及、貫穿

123. 副詞詞彙題 soon

中譯 Arden 製鞋公司宣布很快就會擴大其登山靴系列。

單字 soon 很快地、不久、即將　expand 擴大、擴充
wherever 無論在哪裡、無論什麼情況下
most 最、非常、很　so 非常、如此、多麼

124. 名詞詞彙題 combination

中譯 室內設計師在客戶選擇淺灰色和黃色作為廚房用色之前，提出了幾種組合。

單字 present 提出、展示　combination 組合、團體
region 地區　impression 印象、感想　function 功能

125. 填入形容詞

解說 空格置於 be 動詞 are 後方，適合填入主詞補語，補充說明主詞 salary increases。因此答案要選形容詞 (C) negotiable。

中譯 根據 Redding 科技公司的新政策，將不再進行加薪協商，因此員工薪資取決於年資等級。

單字 under one's policy 根據⋯的政策
no longer 不再　compensate 補償

126. 填入副詞

解說 空格位在助動詞 have 和過去分詞 publicized 之間，應填入副詞，因此答案為 (C) widely。

中譯 由於其對一些行業所造成影響，媒體廣泛宣傳了貿易協議的細節。

單字 media outlet 新聞媒體管道、媒體　publicize 宣傳

127. 從屬連接詞＋詞彙題

解說 空格後方句中有主詞和動詞，表示為一個結構完整的子句，因此空格要填入從屬連接詞，才能連接逗點後方的子句。(A) While 和 (B) If 皆為從屬連接詞，而根據文意，表示「如果物品有所損壞，可免費換貨」較為適當，因此答案為 (B)，意思為「如果⋯」。

中譯 在 Strike 運動品店網站上購買的物品，若到貨時有損壞，可以免費換貨。

單字 at no cost 免費　while 當⋯的時候、在⋯期間

128. 填入名詞

解說 空格前方為形容詞，表示空格應填入名詞，因此答案為 (A) applause。

中譯 RadioWave 家電行的新產品示範操作贏得了熱烈的掌聲。

單字 demonstration 實地示範、示範操作、說明

129. 形容詞詞彙題extensive

中譯 由於Max Punja在藥物研究領域擁有豐富的知識，將由他來擔任高級顧問。

單字 owing to 由於⋯　extensive 廣泛的、大規模的
knowledge 知識、理解　pharmaceutical 藥物的、製藥的
consultant 顧問、諮詢者　amicable 友善的、溫和的
charitable 慈善的、慈悲為懷的
gratifying 令人心滿意足的、令人高興的

130. 填入介系詞＋詞彙題

解說 空格前方句中有主詞和動詞，表示為一個結構完整的子句。且空格後方連接名詞片語，表示空格要填入適當的字詞，連接名詞片語當作受詞。選項中 (C) rather than 和 (D) as a result of 為介系詞，後方適合連接名詞片語，但根據文意，表示「由於天氣狀況惡劣，因此高速公路禁止非緊急車輛通行」較為適當，因此答案為 (D)，意思為「結果、因此」。

中譯 由於天氣狀況惡劣，從即日起19號高速公路的所有車道將禁止非緊急車輛通行。

單字 immediately 即刻、立即　non-emergency 非緊急的
severe weather condition 惡劣的天氣狀況
so that 以便　as though 彷彿
rather than 而不是⋯

RC　PART 6

段落填空
題本 p.134

131. (D)　**132.** (B)　**133.** (C)　**134.** (A)

131-134. 說明指示

Baldrick飾品店　透過Baldrick飾品店的網站可輕鬆製作帶有你的名字或其他文字的獨特飾品！只要選擇你想要的產品，並輸入文字，然後選擇字體、大小和顏色即可。在下訂單之前，請務必仔細檢查樣品圖片。**此外**，如果有任何需要修改的地方，你可以使用「返回」鍵。**請注意商品售出後不提供退換貨服務。**由於我們的產品屬於客製化商品，所以無法重複利用。訂購完成後，你將於幾分鐘內**收到**包含收據的**電子郵件**。當你的產品**準備就緒**時，還會發送另一封電子郵件。根據我們訂單數量的多寡，最多可能需要五天的時間。

單字 unique 獨特的、唯一的　simply 僅僅、簡單地
input 輸入　examine 調查、檢查　place an order 下單
make a change 變更、修改　necessary 必要的、需要的
custom 客製化的　up to 直至⋯　depend on 取決、視⋯而定
volume 容量、音量

131. 連接副詞詞彙題additionally
(A) Consequently 結果、因此
(B) For example 舉例來說
(C) Conversely 相反地
(D) Additionally 此外、附加地

132. 句子插入題
(A) 訂閱我們的電子報可享有折扣。
(B) 請注意商品售出後不提供退換貨服務。
(C) 不要忘記定時回來查看是否有新商品。
(D) 將會顯示配送選項。

單字 subscriber 訂閱者　receive a discount 獲得折扣
be aware that 察覺、意識到⋯　merchandise 產品、物品
all sales are final 商品售出後不可退換貨
present 展示、提出、呈現、交出

133. 未來式
解說 空格後方連接的句子為「當你的產品準備就緒時，還會發送另一封電子郵件。」，表示空格前方會說明下單後將會發生的事情，因此答案為未來式 (C) will be e-mailed。

134. 形容詞詞彙題ready
(A) ready 準備就緒的
(B) brief 簡單的、簡短的
(C) similar 相似的
(D) exempt 被免除的、被豁免的

UNIT 09　時態
題本 p.136

1. (B)　**2.** (A)　**3.** (D)　**4.** (A)　**5.** (A)　**6.** (D)
7. (B)　**8.** (C)

1-2. 網頁

春季插花課程一現已開放報名
Tidwell社區大學**將**於今年春季學期為當地社區**開設**一門新課程。履獲殊榮的花藝師Jennifer Goldsmith將向學生展示如何為特殊場合打造完美的花藝作品，並教授學生如何延長插花作品壽命的技巧。課程**安排於**每週二和週五晚上7點至10點。

最後將會於6月2日展出學生的學期作品。購票詳情請至社區大學網站www.tidwellcc.com。

單字 flower arrangement 插花、花藝
occasion 時候、情況、場合
B as well as A 不僅有A 也有B
creation 創作（作品）　last 持續、繼續　piece 一件（作品）

1. 未來式
解說 根據文章，今年春季學期將會開設新課程，並由花藝師Jennifer Goldsmith授課，因此答案要選未來式 (B) will be opening。

2. 現在式
解說 前一句話具體說明授課內容，後方應告知何時上課較為適當，因此答案為現在式 (A) are held。未來即將發生的事，若為已確定的事實，可使用現在式代替未來式。

3-4. 公告

經典汽車廠團隊的重大消息！
我們要恭喜Nathaniel Foreman晉升為團隊經理，自8月16日起生效。Foreman先生透過我們與Russel學院合作的實習計畫，成為實習生**加入**經典汽車廠。在過去的15年間，他超越員工的期望並為公司做出重大貢獻，不斷地為我們的金融團隊尋找新穎又創新的解決方案。我們相信Foreman先生將在他的新職位上**表現出眾**。下次見到他時，請向他致以熱烈的祝賀。

單字 congratulate A on B 針對B 事恭喜A
effective 起到作用的、有效的
go above and beyond 表現超乎預期
make a contribution 貢獻　look for 尋找⋯
innovative 創新的、革新的　certain 確信的、有把握的

71

3. 過去式

解說　空格後方提到過去 15 年的工作狀況，前方說明當年以實習生身分加入公司較為適當，因此答案為過去式 (D) entered。

4. 未來式

解說　前方提到過去 15 年間對公司的貢獻，空格所在的句子表示 Foreman 先生將會在新的職位上大放異彩較為適當，因此答案為未來式 (A) will shine。

單字　shine 發光、顯露

5-6. 廣告

> Emerald 製鞋公司成立 25 週年了！
>
> 25 年前，Emerald 製鞋公司在 Plainsman 賣場以一個小攤位的形式開業。如今我們擁有兩層樓的獨棟建築，還有寬敞的展示區。我們高品質的產品和知識淵博的員工，**幫助**我們成為一家值得信賴的鞋子零售商。為了感謝顧客多年來對我們的支持，我們將於 9 月 8 日推出特別優惠活動。
>
> 購買一雙鞋後，第二雙可享四折優惠。此優惠**適用**於任何品牌，價格較低的那雙可獲得優惠。請注意，此優惠不可與其他額外的優惠券合併使用。

單字　kiosk （通常販售報紙或飲料的）小型攤位
story （建築物的）樓層　spacious 寬敞的、廣闊的
knowledgeable 知識淵博的　trusted 值得信賴的
patronage 光顧　offer 優惠、提供　note 注意、提到
additional 額外的

5. 語態和時態複合題

解說　主詞 high-quality products and knowledgeable staff 為行為者，表示空格應填入主動語態。選項中的主動語態有 (A) have helped 和 (D) were helping，而根據文意，從以前至今多虧有高品質的產品和知識淵博的員工幫助，Emerald 製鞋公司現在才能擁有一棟兩層樓的獨棟建築，因此答案為現在完成式 (A)。

6. 現在式

解說　空格前方說明優惠活動為何，而空格所在的句子提及什麼樣的產品適用優惠較為適當，因此答案為現在式 (D) applies。

7-8. 顧客評論

> 我剛剛收到在居家必備品店訂購的 100 張餐巾紙，它們讓我留下了深刻的印象！我從事餐飲業，經常需要訂購餐桌佈置用品。但因為我常訂購的公司缺貨，所以我決定給居家必備品店一個機會。這些用品製作得更為精美，而且公司**提供**更多種顏色和設計的選擇。從現在開始，我只會在居家必備品店**訂購**產品。
>
> — Martin Quinn

單字　order 訂購、下單　thoroughly 完全地、徹底地

impress 給…深刻的印象、使感動　supplies 用品
out of stock 缺貨　give…a chance 給予…一個機會
construct 製造、構成　a wide range of 各式各樣的
exclusively 專門地、獨家地　from now on 從現在起

7. 現在式

解說　逗點前方提到產品製作的更為精美，空格後方連接的子句補充說明更多優點較為適當，因此答案為現在式 (B) offers。

8. 未來式

解說　空格前一句話提到用品製作更為精美，公司還提供更多種顏色和設計的選擇，後方表示往後只會在居家必備品店訂購產品較為適當。另外，空格後方出現 from now on，通常會搭配未來式一起使用，因此答案為未來式 (C) will be ordering。

UNIT 10　詞彙

題本 p.138

1. (B)　**2.** (D)　**3.** (B)　**4.** (B)　**5.** (C)　**6.** (D)
7. (B)

1. 電子郵件

> 我們來信通知您，Graystone Printer X302 已經停產，您的訂單已自動取消。然而，最近有許多客戶都喜歡上**類似的**機型 X430。請致電 555-2098 與我們聯絡，以便訂購新產品或討論退款選項。
>
> Alex's 辦公用品店

單字　inform 告知、通知　discontinue 停產
automatically 自動地　place an order 訂購　refund 退款

(A) accountable 有解釋義務的、有責任的
(B) comparable 比得上的、可比較的
(C) amicable 友善的、溫和的
(D) applicable 適用的、可應用的

2. 廣告

> 快來 Auto Masters，我們將在短短兩個小時內為您整輛車提供完整的服務。包括更換機油、**重新補充**擋風玻璃清洗液、進行輪胎旋轉等等。我們位於 Fairhills 購物中心旁邊，當您在與家人共度時光時，我們可以同時整頓您的車輛。請致電 555-2840 預約此服務或其他各種服務。

單字　service 維修保養車輛、服務、檢修　washer fluid 清洗液
rotate 轉動、更換（車輛前後輪胎）
locate 位於、設置於（特定地點）　book 預約

(A) remarking 說出（事實、意見等）

(B) rounding 使變圓、環繞
(C) reloading 重新裝載
(D) refilling 重新裝滿

3. 公告

> 九月標誌著多倫多歌劇院新歌劇季的開始。開幕之夜為9月12日，一直持續到12月31日。今年歡迎大眾參加每週二下午2點到下午4點的**公開**彩排。如要預訂彩排門票，請至網站www.torontooc.org。

單字 **mark** 表示…的特徵、標誌
run （舞台劇、電影）上映、開演　　**sit in** 旁聽、參加
reserve 預約、預訂

(A) seasonal 季節的、季節性的
(B) public 公開的、公眾的、公共的
(C) domestic 國內的、家庭的
(D) challenging 有挑戰性的、考驗能力的

4. 招聘公告

> Rainbow玩具公司正在尋找一名新的社群行銷經理。應徵者將致力於讓我們的社群媒體平台更容易使用，並為我們的客戶創造更**有吸引力的**內容。因此，應徵者應具備影片創作、社群媒體平台管理或文案撰寫方面的經驗。

單字 **look for** 尋找　　**applicant** 應徵者
work on 致力於、努力做…
accessible 容易使用的、易進入的

(A) lengthy 冗長的、無聊的
(B) engaging 吸引人的、有魅力的
(C) impersonal 客觀的、沒有人情味的
(D) accelerated 加速的

5. 廣告

> Booker為我們最受歡迎的閱讀計畫提供特別的新年優惠！註冊豪華閱讀計畫，即可**存取**超過50萬本書，並享有本月最新出版書籍的七折優惠。只有Booker有提供無限量的圖書租借服務。今天就上www.booker.com/newyear享有此優惠。

單字 **sign up** 報名、註冊　　**release** 出版、公開、推出
unlimited 無限制的、無數的　　**take advantage of** 利用

(A) claim 主張、聲稱、請求（賠償金等）
(B) control 控制、支配
(C) access 存取、使用權利
(D) entry 進入、入場、參加

6-7. 顧客評論

> 多年來我一直使用Manaray的傢俱，並且始終對我購買的產品感到滿意。然而，在參觀Logan傢俱的展示廳後，我覺得幸好我有這樣做。他們傢俱的品質完成是在另一個等級！
>
> 他們的皮沙發採用高檔柔軟的皮革製成。所有沙發的設計都可以客製化，來包含活動躺椅。我們還找到了一款完美的桃花心木餐桌椅。桌子和椅子感覺很**堅固**，肯定能用一輩子。
>
> 請注意，大多數產品均未**組裝**，可額外支付一小筆費用進行專業組裝。但由於所有產品都附有易於遵循的說明書，因此可能不一定需要。

單字 **purchase** 購買、購入、所購之物　　**customize** 客製化
as well 同樣地　　**be sure to** 肯定會…　　**last** 持續、繼續
be aware that 察覺、發現到…　　**assemble** 組裝
available 可利用的、有空的　　**additional** 額外的
necessary 必需的、必要的　　**instructions** 說明書、指示

6.
(A) separate 分開的、個別的
(B) stiff 僵硬的
(C) simple 簡單的
(D) sturdy 堅固的、耐用的

7.
(A) fixed 固定的
(B) assembled 組裝的
(C) crumbled 粉碎的、弄碎的
(D) pieced （一塊塊）拼湊而成的

UNIT 11 連接副詞

題本 p.140

1. (B)　　**2.** (C)　　**3.** (B)　　**4.** (D)

1. 信件

> 敬啟者，
>
> 我們誠摯邀請您成為Forever健身房會員。我們在占地40英畝最先進的場所中，擁有該地區最齊全的頂級設備。我們專門為那些經常使用社群媒體的人提供一項獨特的功能——拍照區。**否則**，在事先未經同意的情況下，一律不允許在我們的普通健身房樓層拍攝照片。我們健身房提供超過40種最多樣化的健身項目。所有指導者和教練都擁有多項國家資格證照，為您提供最佳體驗。
>
> 請致電555-2109進行免費諮詢，並獲得1日免費通行證。我們相信您會再次光臨。

祝好，

店主Kelly Vasquez

單字 an array of 多數的　top-of-the-line 最高級的
state-of-the-art 最新的　feature 功能、特色
maintain 維持（關係、狀態、標準等）　presence 存在
consent 同意　a wide range of 多樣的
national certification 國家資格證照　consultation 諮詢

(A) Besides 此外
(B) Otherwise 否則
(C) If not 不然
(D) Regardless 無論如何

2. 廣告

讓你的事業受到關注！

你是否擁有一家出色的企業，但似乎沒有人知道呢？我們可以解決這個問題！Frankfurt媒體公司擁有一支專家團隊，隨時準備為你的事業制訂正確的廣告策略。我們將製作完美的電視或廣播廣告，並將其傳達給你的目標受眾。**與此同時**，你將會有更多時間專注在你的事業上。

立即上www.frankfurtmedia.com，一週內便會準備好你的廣告！

單字 notice 關注、注意到、通知　strategy 策略、計畫
craft （熟練地）製作、手藝　commercial 廣告的、商業的
intended 預期的、故意的

(A) Nevertheless 然而
(B) Even so 儘管如此
(C) Meanwhile 與此同時
(D) Recently 最近

3. 電子郵件

收件者：Mark Klein <kleinm@solarnet.com>
寄件者：Jane Lorowitz <jlorowitz@greatconstructs.com>
日期：4月20日
主旨：行程變動

親愛的Klein先生，

特此通知您施工進度有所變動。目前的行程已經排定至6月12日。然而，由於這幾天暴雨頻繁，我們不得不在這段時間停止施工。**因此**，我們無法完成築牆工程。新的預估完工日期為6月20日。

如果您希望進一步討論行程安排，我很樂意與您談談。

祝安好，

Jane Lorowitz

單字 construction 建設、施工　be unable to do 無法做…

put up 建造、築牆　estimated 預估的　end date 完工日

(A) Nonetheless 然而、但是
(B) Consequently 因此、結果
(C) Finally 終於、最後
(D) Lastly 最後、最終地

4. 資訊

經過六個月的整修後，Craftsbury圖書館很高興能宣布重新開放。新的特色包括一個配備坡道的輪椅無障礙入口，以及五個新教室，可舉辦更多受歡迎的課後活動。**此外**，我們還建立了一個職業準備中心，幫助Craftsbury居民尋找並獲取就業機會。欲了解圖書館的所有新特色，請至我們的網站www.craftsburylibrary.gov。

單字 renovation 整修、重新裝修　feature 特色、功能
accessible 可使用的、可進入的　ramp 坡道
establish 建立、設立、創辦　occupation 職業
preparation 準備、預備　look for 尋找…
secure 獲得、確保、保證　head to 前往

(A) Hence 因此
(B) Accordingly 因此
(C) Therefore 因此
(D) Additionally 此外

UNIT 12 句子插入題

題本 p.142

1. (D)　**2.** (A)　**3.** (D)　**4.** (B)

1. 電子郵件

收件者：所有顧客
寄件者：Keritz音響公司客戶服務團隊
日期：12月2日
主旨：年底閉店休息

Keritz音響公司將於12月23日開始進入年底假期，**您在年底之前可以訂購的最後日期為12月22日**。此日期之後的所有訂單都將於新的一年出貨。另外，請記得交貨日期將根據您確切的交貨地點有所不同。要查看您所在地區的預估交貨時間表，請至我們網站的送貨部分。

感謝您一如既往的支持，期待向您展示我們為新的一年準備的新產品。

Keritz音響公司團隊敬上

單字 closure 關閉　effective 實行的、生效的、起作用的
place an order 訂購　ship 出貨　vary 變化、使多樣化

depend on 取決於…、依靠、信賴　estimated 預估的
look forward to 期待…　line up 準備、整隊

(A) 請聯絡快遞公司並提供您的訂單確認號碼。
(B) 快遞服務額外收費5.99美元。
(C) 營業時間為上午9點至下午5點。
(D) 您在年底之前可以訂購的最後日期為12月22日。

單字　courier 快遞公司　confirmation number 確認號碼
express delivery 快遞服務　available 可利用的、有空的

2. 公告

來造訪美麗的Catskills水上樂園，全家大小度過歡樂刺激的一天。我們不僅是該地區最大的水上樂園，也是最環保的樂園。我們是全國唯一擁有完全環用水系統的水上樂園。**所有的水都是從自然來源收集而來，如雨水和天然水庫。**這有助於減少對當地供水的影響。該樂園甚至使用水力發電為所有遊樂設施和潮汐池供電。我們希望家庭世世代代都能享受Catskills水上樂園。若想知道門票和資訊，請上我們的網站 www.catskillswaterpark.com。

單字　not only A (but) also B 不僅A還有B
feature 以…為特色、以…為主打　completely 完全地、徹底地
environmentally friendly 環保的
be used to do 用於…（比較：be used to (doing) something 習慣於…）
hydroelectricity 水力發電　power 供電
for generations 歷經世世代代

(A) 所有的水都是從自然來源收集而來，如雨水和天然水庫。
(B) 在樂園中時，我們要求所有遊客撿起自己的垃圾。
(C) 造訪期間請勿使用過多的水。
(D) 所有紙製品均由再生紙製成。

單字　collect 收集、聚集　source 源頭、根源、來源
reservoir 水庫、貯水池　pick up 撿拾…
refrain from 避免…、抑制…　recycled paper 再生紙

3. 公告

最近我們得知目前的供應商全球生產製造公司已決定縮減其供應鏈。這意味著我們將無法把柑橘類水果出口到北歐。**該地區是我們今年擴張計畫的重點部分。**因此，我們需要努力尋找新的經銷商。

我們引以為傲的一點為擁有豐富的異國水果種類。看看能否找到需要補充該地區柑橘類水果的公司。如果你有找到任何公司，請讓我知道。

我希望在週五下午之前拿到一份潛在業者名單，並在每週的經理會議上提出。

單字　vendor 供應商　downsize 縮減、縮小
supply chain 供應鏈　be unable to do 無法…
export 出口　put effort into 付出努力在…

distributor 經銷商　an array of 大量的
exotic 異國的、外來的　supplement 補充、增補
a list of leads 潛在顧客名單
present 提出、繳交、現在的、參加的

(A) 我們團隊中的人員都從未去過北歐。
(B) 請給我們一份詳細的柑橘類水果清單。
(C) 我們必須努力增加我們的供應量。
(D) 該地區是我們今年擴張計畫的重點部分。

單字　work on 從事…、努力…　expansion 擴張

4. 資訊

Hartman景觀公司的老闆Charles Hartman，20多年來一直致力於美化該地區。他的團隊專門從事商業和公共領域房產的景觀工程。

他們以建造該地區最受歡迎的休閒公園和空間而聞名。**他們負責設計了獲獎的Campbell公園**，這片佔地100英畝的區域是每年舉辦George街頭音樂節的場地。

如欲將您的房產變成一件藝術品，請今日立即聯絡Hartman景觀公司。他們將根據您的預算和要求，建造完美的草坪。

單字　beautify 美化　specialize in 專門從事…
commercial 商業的、廣告
public 大眾的、公共的、公開的
property 房地產、建築物、財產、所有物
construction 建築、工程

(A) 他們的辦公室位在當地郵局旁邊。
(B) 他們負責設計了獲獎的Campbell公園。
(C) 因此，他們偏好使用所有本土的花卉和灌木。
(D) 他們是年度活動最大的贊助商。

單字　be responsible for 負責…　native 本土的　shrub 灌木

PART TEST　題本 p.144

131. (C)　**132.** (B)　**133.** (B)　**134.** (B)　**135.** (C)
136. (D)　**137.** (B)　**138.** (B)　**139.** (C)　**140.** (D)
141. (C)　**142.** (D)　**143.** (A)　**144.** (D)　**145.** (D)
146. (A)

131-134. 電子郵件

收件者：Edward Sandoval <sandovaledward@warrenmail.com>
寄件者：Brunswick Studios <accounts@brunswickstudios.com>
日期：2月22日
主旨：會員資格

親愛的Sandoval先生，

感謝您註冊成為Brunswick錄音室一年期的會員。我們的網站致力於幫助您吸引新粉絲、創作有意義的歌曲，並提升您的表演水準。我們網站上的內容為由像您一樣的音樂家**撰寫而成**。您將收到一封電子郵件，提供您所需產品的特別優惠，例如**針對**需要編輯之專案的軟體程式。如要**自訂**發送到收件匣的內容，請登入您的帳戶並選擇想了解的選項。每月只需額外支付5.99美元，就能升級為金卡會員，並享有更多內容。**您可以隨時取消，不會收取任何罰款。**既然零風險何不試試看呢？

致上最溫暖的問候，
Tara Nelson
Brunswick錄音室

單字 sign up 報名、註冊　be devoted to 致力於…
require 需要、要求　desired 想要的、希望的
give it a try 嘗試看看

131. 語態和時態複合題

解說 空格後方連接 by musicians 為「by＋行為者」，表示空格要填入被動語態「be＋過去分詞」，(C) is written 和 (D) had been written 皆為被動語態，空格前方介紹 Brunswick 錄音室的網站，後方接著提及目前網站上的內容，應使用現在式，因此答案為 (C)。

132. 介系詞詞彙題for
(A) into 在…裡面
(B) for 為…
(C) our 我們的
(D) at 在…

解說 空格後方連接名詞，表示空格要填入介系詞，因此答案為 (B) for。

133. 動詞詞彙題personalize
(A) deliver 運送
(B) personalize 個人化、自訂
(C) calculate 計算
(D) dispute 爭論

134. 句子插入題
(A) 我們很高興獲得提名。
(B) 您可以隨時取消，不會收取任何罰款。
(C) 您的回饋有助於我們改善服務。
(D) 速度取決於您的網路服務。

單字 nominate 提名…　depend on 取決…、視…而定

135-138. 電子郵件

收件者：Redhawk大樓所有住戶
寄件者：Jennifer Milligan
日期：2月20日
主旨：停電通知

親愛的Redhawk大樓住戶，

第12大道和第14大道之間的Jennings街和Pine街上的所有建築物**預定**停止供電。為執行必要的維護工作，將中斷電力供應。工程將於2月25日和26日上午9點進行，直至中午。

為應對**每一天**的停電，請提前制定計劃。電腦應在停電前關機。**電源保持開啟狀態，可能會因突然關機而受到損壞。**如果冰箱和冷凍庫的門保持關閉，存放其中的食物就不會受到影響。感謝您的**合作**與耐心。

Jennifer Milligan
Redhawk大樓物業經理

單字 tenant 住戶　power outage 停電　interruption 中斷
shut off 關閉（電源等）　essential 必要的
maintenance 維護（建築、機器等）　take place 發生、舉行
prior to 在…之前

135. 被動語態vs.主動語態

解說 空格後方並未連接受詞，且主詞 An interruption 為行為接受者，表示空格應填入被動語態「be＋過去分詞」較為適當，因此答案為 (C) is scheduled。

136. 限定詞each

解說 空格後方為單數名詞 day，表示空格要填入適合修飾單數名詞的字詞，因此答案為 (D) each。(B) most 和 (C) all 用來修飾複數名詞或不可數名詞，因此並非答案。

137. 句子插入題
(A) 現在有幾間公寓可供使用。
(B) 電源保持開啟狀態，可能會因突然關機而受到損壞。
(C) 我們可以確認有認真對待安全問題。
(D) 噪音將不再對大家造成干擾。

單字 unit （公寓的）單位、空間、一個　available 可供使用的、有空的　unexpected 預料之外的、突發的
shutdown 中斷（營運、運轉等）、關閉
confirm 確定、確認　take~seriously …受到認真看待
no longer 不再…　disturbance 干擾、擾亂

138. 名詞詞彙題cooperation
(A) donation 捐贈
(B) cooperation 合作
(C) destination 目的地
(D) confirmation 確認

139-142. 部落格摘錄

> 水管工車輛
> 如果你是一名獨立作業的水管工人，擁有一輛車是至關重要的事。起初，你可能認為尋找**最便宜的**選項是個不錯的主意。然而，最好從一開始就投資一台可靠的車輛。**你應該花點時間考慮你需要的車輛大小**。例如，你是否必須停在狹窄的車位，或在車內放置大型**工具**，像是電鋸呢？務必閱讀你正在考慮車輛型號的評論。**最終**，你購買的車輛將在工作旅程中支持著你甚至可能激勵你。

單字　plumber 水管工人　independent 獨立自主的
essential 不可或缺的　look for 尋找…
reliable 可靠的、值得信賴的　power saw 電鋸
motivate 激勵

139. 最高級用法
解說　空格前方為定冠詞，後方連接名詞 option，表示空格應填入形容詞，修飾後方的名詞。根據文意，表示「最便宜的選項」最為適當，且最高級用法會搭配定冠詞 the 一起使用，因此答案為 (C) cheapest。

140. 句子插入題
(A) 車輛的燃油效率非常重要。
(B) 建立客戶群可能需要幾個月的時間。
(C) 管道工作全年的需求穩定。
(D) 你應該花點時間考慮你需要的車輛大小。

單字　efficiency 效率　steadily 穩定地、平穩地
in demand 有需求的

141. 名詞詞彙題 tool
(A) electricians 水電工
(B) uniforms 制服
(C) tools 工具
(D) pipes 管道

142. 連接副詞詞彙題 ultimately
(A) Lately 最近
(B) On the other hand 另一方面
(C) Otherwise 除此之外、否則
(D) Ultimately 最終

143-146. 信件

> 3月3日
>
> 親愛的西北公用事業顧客，
>
> 對於最近一期**能源**帳單造成的混亂，我們深感抱歉。我們的帳務部門遇到了軟體故障，因此導致二月份**發送**的帳單含有錯誤的資訊。**儘管**我們努力準確反映顧客的使用情況，但有時仍難以避免這種錯誤。
>
> **請忽略這份帳單，並等待新的帳單核發**。您預計會在接下來的五個工作天內收到它。由於本次的錯誤，我們將繳費截止期限延長兩週。感謝您在此過程中的耐心和理解。
>
> 西北公用事業
> 4190 Woodland Terrace
> 塔科馬華盛頓州 98412

單字　confusion 混亂、混淆　malfunction 發生故障、功能失常
strive to do 努力…　usage 使用量
extend 延長、擴展（事業、勢力等）、擴大

143. 填入名詞
解說　空格前方為所有格代名詞 your，表示空格要填入名詞，因此答案為 (A) energy。

144. 片語動詞 send out
(A) given away 洩漏（秘密）、贈送
(B) cashed in 兌現
(C) brought down 降低（程度、數量）
(D) sent out 發出、寄出

145. 從屬連接詞詞彙題 although
(A) Despite 儘管
(B) Except 除…之外
(C) Once 一旦、一經…就
(D) Although 儘管

解說　空格後方連接一個結構完整的子句（主詞＋動詞），而逗點後方又連接一個新的子句，表示空格要填入從屬連接詞。
(A) Despite 為介系詞，因此不能作為答案。

146. 句子插入題
(A) 請忽略這份帳單，並等待新的帳單核發。
(B) 部分電力來自再生能源。
(C) 我們的網站上已清楚概述了該政策。
(D) 感謝您迅速支付服務費用。

單字　ignore 忽略　issue 發行、發布
electricity 電力　renewable 可再生的
outline （簡略）說明　prompt 迅速的

RC PART 7

UNIT 13 電子郵件與信件
題本 p.152

文章結構與脈絡

1. (D)　**2.** (B)　**3.** (B)

收件者：Bonnie Rosario <b.rosario@glendalehotel.com>
寄件者：Philip Hawley <philip@charackconstruction.com>
日期：4月24日
主旨：游泳池施工

親愛的Rosario女士，

Charack建設公司已收到貴飯店興建室外游泳池的保證金。這類規格的項目一般需要6-8週左右的時間。但是按照您的要求，我們能在3週內完成這項工程。我們深知在夏季旺季開始前，開放該設施的重要性。我方團隊將於4月28日開始施工，初步包含清理和前期準備工作。

該項目的細節大部分已經敲定，但仍需要您挑選磁磚圖案。今日稍晚我方一名員工將送上一箱樣品，請瀏覽一下樣品，並於4月30日的會議上告訴我您偏好哪一款。我方僅提供尚有庫存的磁磚，因此不會出現供應鏈延遲的問題。

祝好，
Philip Hawley
Charack建設公司經理

單字 deposit 保證金、押金　approximately 大約、約莫　request 要求、請求、需求　initially 起初　finalize 完成　drop off 放下　look over 查看　supply chain 供應鏈

1. 該封電子郵件的目的為何？
(A) 建議變更工作計畫
(B) 申請保證金資金
(C) 介紹工程業務
(D) 提供工程項目的最新進展

2. 第二段第3行中的「drop off」一詞意思最接近何者？
(A) 收集
(B) 遞送
(C) 減少
(D) 打瞌睡

3. 根據電子郵件的內容，在4月30日的會議之前Rosario女士該做什麼事？
(A) 確認尺寸
(B) 選擇一些素材
(C) 簽訂合約
(D) 瀏覽一些草圖

PRACTICE
題本 p.154

1. (B)　**2.** (D)　**3.** (D)　**4.** (D)　**5.** (B)　**6.** (A)

1-2. 電子郵件

收件者：Ravi Singh<singhr@nayarsecurities.com>
寄件者：Emerald Gardening Supplies<orders@emerald-garden.com>
日期：5月2日
主旨：訂購編號#03795
附件：RG7_使用手冊

親愛的Singh先生，

感謝您最近在Emerald園藝用品店購物！在過去的10年裡，我們一直為客戶提供設備和裝飾品，讓他們的花園看起來更漂亮。我們希望您會喜歡您所訂購的**RG7太陽能燈籠**。請參考附件的使用手冊，**其中提供放置燈籠的建議，讓燈籠在白天接受最大程度的陽光照射。**

如果您有拍攝在花園裡燈籠的照片，請在我們的社群媒體網站上分享。您將能參加抽獎，並有機會贏得100美元的禮券。

致上最溫暖的問候
Emerald園藝用品店

單字 provide A with B A 向 A 提供 B
solar-powered 太陽能的　maximize 增加至最大限度
exposure 曝曬　drawing 抽籤　voucher 禮券、折價券

1. 關於燈籠，文中指出什麼？
(A) 不應暴露在潮濕的環境中。
(B) 可以透過陽光充電。
(C) 有多種尺寸可供選擇。
(D) 提供十年的保固。

解說 事實與否
Singh先生訂購了太陽能燈籠，使用說明中提到白天曝曬在陽光下的建議，表示燈籠可以靠太陽光充電，因此答案為(B)。

單字 be exposed to 暴露於…　charge 充電、收取（費用等）
a variety of 各式各樣的　warranty 保固（書）

2. Singh先生被要求做什麼事？
(A) 撰寫產品評論
(B) 提供發送禮券的地址
(C) 向公司出示購買證明
(D) 在社群媒體上發布照片

解說 相關細節
文中提到若有在花園裡拍攝燈籠的照片，請分享至社群媒體網站上，因此答案為(D)。

單字 proof of purchase 購買證明（書）　post 發布

3-6. 信件

2月19日

Melissa Hammond
Eastbourne 太陽能公司人力資源總監
Malvern大廈203號
Eastbourne, BN20 7AF

親愛的Hammond女士，

很高興能在貴公司面試時見到您，我很榮幸您邀請我加入Eastbourne太陽能公司的團隊並擔任資深銷售人員。**很遺憾的是，我無法接受這個職位，因為我決定接受另一間公司的工作，該職位不需要出差。**我對貴公司充滿敬意，**我相信貴公司將會繼續增加市佔率並擴增員工數。**

正如我所承諾的，**隨信附上我在面試中提到的網路電子簽名工具清單。**雖然我與這些公司並無關聯，但我相信這些資訊對您會有用處。我計畫**參加**今年年末的年度太陽能貿易展覽，希望有機會在那裡見到您，並進一步討論業界情況。

致上最溫暖的問候，
Spencer Ingram
附件

單字 unfortunately 遺憾的是、不幸地
be unable to do 無法做… require 要求、需要
a great deal of 大量 expand 擴大、擴張
be affiliated with 與…有來往

3. Ingram先生這封信的目的為何？
(A) 詢問工作職責
(B) 介紹他的公司
(C) 安排面試
(D) 拒絕工作機會

解說 主旨或目的
文中提到他決定去別間不需出差的公司，所以無法接受該工作機會，因此答案為(D)。

單字 inquire 詢問 schedule 安排

4. Ingram先生對Eastbourne太陽能公司有何看法？
(A) 它專注於團隊合作。
(B) 它應該行銷方面加強投資在。
(C) 它提供很好的薪資待遇。
(D) 它未來將會成長。

解說 事實與否
文中提到Eastbourne太陽能公司往後將會擴大市場佔有率並增加員工數，因此答案為(D)。

換句話說 It will continue to gain market share and expand its staff → It will grow in the future.

單字 compensation package 薪資待遇

5. Ingram先生寄了什麼東西給Hammond女士？
(A) 已簽名的合約
(B) 線上工具清單
(C) 提議的面試時間表
(D) 網站調查表

解說 相關細節
文中提到隨信附上網路電子簽名工具的清單，因此答案要選(B)。

6. 第二段第3行中的「attend」一詞意思最接近何者？
(A) 前往
(B) 相符、同時發生
(C) 巧遇
(D) 照顧

解說 找出同義詞
attend 所在的句子為「I plan to attend the Annual Solar Trade Exhibition」，意思為「我計畫參加年度太陽能貿易展覽」，表示 attend 指的是「參加」之意，因此答案要選 (A)。

UNIT 14 文字簡訊與線上聊天　題本 p.156

1. (C)　**2.** (D)

Gina Quan［上午8點25分］嗨，Bruno，我在前往Barraza會議中心的路上碰到了一些麻煩。我需要改搭計程車，但希望費用能由公司支付。

Bruno Mota［上午8點28分］**沒問題，但請務必保留你的收據。**Shelby飯店不再提供接駁車服務了嗎？

Gina Quan［上午8點29分］有，但需要事先預約。我猜他們更改了政策，因為上次我沒有預約就搭到了接駁車。

Bruno Mota［上午8點31分］需要我幫你查找計程車服務嗎？

Gina Quan［上午8點32分］謝謝，但我已有電話號碼可以聯繫。

單字 cover 負擔費用、包含　run 營運
in advance 事先、提前

1. 上午8點28分，Mota先生寫道「沒問題」最有可能是什麼意思？
(A) 他將代替Quan女士前往會議中心。
(B) 他可以在其他地方和Quan女士見面。
(C) 他同意簽核交通費。
(D) 他找到了預約收據。

單字 in one's place 代替某人　authorize 授權

2. 關於Quan女士文中提到什麼？
(A) 她是Mota先生的主管。
(B) 她需要協助尋找聯絡電話。
(C) 她弄丟了飯店預訂號碼。
(D) 她以前住過Shelby飯店。

PRACTICE　題本 p.158

1. (A)　2. (C)　3. (D)　4. (B)　5. (C)　6. (C)

1-2. 文字簡訊

> Betsy Braun（下午1點46分）
> 嗨，Matthew，**你或你的團隊成員是否有一直在監控Haven街的入口？**
>
> Matthew Alvarado（下午1點48分）
> 除了影像監控之外，我們大約在20分鐘前進行了每小時例行的人工檢查，為什麼要這樣問？
>
> Betsy Braun（下午1點49分）
> **我注意到門沒有鎖**。我以為門應該要一直鎖著。
>
> Matthew Alvarado（下午1點51分）
> 確實如此，除非是在收貨的時候。Anchorage用品公司剛才完成卸下所有貨物。**我已經通知Eric。**
>
> Betsy Braun（下午1點53分）
> 好，我知道了。我很高興有人已經著手處理了。

單字　monitor （定期地）確認、監控
in addition to 除了⋯之外　　usual 平常的、慣常的
in person 親自　　notice 注意到、通知、察覺
unlock 打開（上鎖的門）　　be supposed to do 應該要⋯
at all times 隨時　　except 除了
unload 從（卡車、船上等）卸下貨物　　notify 告知、通知
take care of 留意、處理、照顧⋯

1. Alvarado先生最有可能是誰？
(A) 警衛
(B) 駕駛教練
(C) 影片剪輯者
(D) 接待人員

解說　**推論或暗示**
Braun女士於下午1點46分詢問對方是否一直在監控Haven街的入口，而後Alvarado先生回答除了影像監控之外，還有親自進行檢查，由此段工作內容可推論出Alvarado先生為警衛，因此答案為(A)。

2. 在下午1點51分時，Alvarado先生寫道：「我已經通知Eric。」是什麼意思？
(A) Eric會提早來上班。
(B) Eric將從卡車上卸下貨物。
(C) Eric會把門上鎖。
(D) Eric將與Braun女士見面。

解說　**掌握意圖**
Braun女士於下午1點49分指出門似乎沒有上鎖，而後Alvarado先生表示只有在收貨時才會打開，貨物卸下後會通知Eric，指的是會請Eric上鎖，因此答案為(C)。

3-6. 線上聊天

> Kathleen Arcand［上午10點03分］ 我今天在為我們下週**與Bancroft簽署合約**的會議訂火車票。
>
> Gordon Walters［上午10點04分］ 我們是星期二出發，對吧？
>
> Kathleen Arcand［上午10點07分］ **事實上，因為會議要到星期三下午才開始**，我想我們可以當天早上去，然後在星期四早上回來。
>
> Gordon Walters［上午10點08分］ 好，我們要攜帶宣傳手冊嗎？
>
> Kathleen Arcand［上午10點10分］ 有需要帶嗎？他們已經看過**我們的心臟監測設備**了。
>
> Gordon Walters［上午10點11分］ 我們可以介紹一些其他產品，供他們日後考量。
>
> Kathleen Arcand［上午10點13分］ 好，我會記得帶一些過去。他們還會帶我們去吃晚餐和看表演。**Bancroft的Macy Oliver想知道我們想看什麼樣的表演，我必須回覆她這件事。**
>
> Peter Zhang［上午10點16分］ 聽起來很有意思。
>
> Kathleen Arcand［上午10點17分］ 我不確認現在有什麼表演。**Peter，你能查一下嗎？**
>
> Peter Zhang［上午10點19分］ **我會研究一下當地劇院有哪些表演。**
>
> Kathleen Arcand［上午10點20分］ 太好了，但盡量越快越好。
>
> Peter Zhang［上午10點22分］ 沒問題，我會在一小時內發訊息給你。

單字　book 預約　　necessary 必要的、必需的
be sure to do 肯定要⋯　　pack 收好、打包
wonder 想知道　　would like to do 想要做⋯
have got to do 必需做⋯　　get back to 之後再聯絡⋯
look into 調查、研究

3. 訊息撰寫者最有可能從事哪個行業？
(A) 娛樂業
(B) 教育
(C) 出版業
(D) 醫療保健

解說　推論或暗示
Arcand 女士於上午 10 點 10 分提到「我們的心臟監測設備」，表示撰文者從事與醫療設備有關的行業，因此答案為 (D)。

4. 大概會在什麼時候簽訂合約？
(A) 星期二
(B) 星期三
(C) 星期四
(D) 星期五

解說　推論或暗示
Arcand 女士於上午 10 點 03 分提到為了要與 Bancroft 簽署合約，正在預訂火車票。之後於 10 點 07 分提到會議時間在星期三下午，因此答案為 (B)。

5. Oliver女士想了解什麼資訊？
(A) 用餐的飲食限制
(B) 開會客人的抵達時間
(C) 對於表演的偏好
(D) 交通費

解說　相關細節
Arcand 女士於上午 10 點 13 分提到 Macy Oliver，並表示對方想知道他們想看什麼樣的表演，因此答案為 (C)。

單字　dietary 飲食的　restriction 限制、約束
preference 喜好、偏好的事物

6. 早上 10 點 20 分，Arcand女士寫道：「盡量越快越好」是什麼意思？
(A) 她擔心錯過截止日。
(B) 她認為有些火車票會賣光。
(C) 她想盡快給予回覆。
(D) 她很快就要去開會了。

解說　掌握意圖
Arcand 女士於上午 10 點 17 分請 Peter 查一下有哪些表演，而後 Peter 回應會研究一下當地劇院的表演。接著 Arcand 女士回應「盡量越快越好」，表示她想盡快回覆 Oliver 女士，因此答案為 (C)。

單字　sell out 售完　shortly 立刻、不久

UNIT 15　報導、公告、廣告　題本 p.160

1. (B)　**2.** (A)　**3.** (C)

Beaverton圖書館重新開放

（7月29日）Beaverton圖書館將於9月25日重新開放。一[1]一。居民期待能夠再次使用圖書館。該圖書館原定於18個月前重新開放。

為加速專案的進展，Cowan建設公司和Brock建設公司均被選中。一[2]一。然而，此決定終究是一個錯誤，**因為雙方往往在互相不知情的情況下，完成同樣的工作，因此浪費了大量的時間。**

此外，由於該專案開局不利，所以受到公眾的監督和壓力越來越大。一[3]一。該專案的預估完成時間並不合理，尤其是與類似的工程相比。

該專案原本還包括一間小型館內咖啡廳。一[4]一。在未來的提案中，可能會重新審視咖啡廳這個選項。

單字　take place 舉行、發生　turn out 結果是
get off to a bad start 開局不順利　scrutiny 監督
pressure 壓力、壓迫　estimated 預估的、估價的
complete 完成、結束　reasonable 合理的、妥當的
be supposed to do 應該要做　be likely to do 可能會做
revisit 重新討論、再訪

1. 關於Brock建設公司文中暗示了什麼？
(A) 這是該公司第一個建設專案。
(B) 員工與Cowan建設公司溝通不良。
(C) 很快就會停業。
(D) 計劃與Cowan建設公司合併。

單字　go out of business 停業　merge 合併

2. 針對圖書館用地，本篇文章指出了什麼？
(A) 規劃者不得不縮小專案的原始範圍。
(B) 第二階段的建設排定於明年。
(C) 由咖啡廳收入提供部分資助。
(D) 這是Beaverton的第二間圖書館分館。

單字　partially 部分地　fund 提供資金　proceeds 收益

3. 文章的[1]、[2]、[3]、和[4]當中，何處最適合填入下方句子？
"This ultimately resulted in the creation of an impossible work schedule."
這最終造就了一個無法完成的工作行程。

單字　ultimately 最終地　result in 結果⋯
creation 創造、創作

題本 p.162

1. (D)　**2.** (C)　**3.** (B)　**4.** (D)　**5.** (B)　**6.** (B)
7. (C)　**8.** (A)　**9.** (C)　**10.** (B)　**11.** (A)　**12.** (B)

81

1-2. 招募公告

> **企業招募服務**
>
> **誠徵倉儲工人**
>
> Laird傢俱店目前正在為位於Wilmar的工廠尋找倉儲工人。我們會提供一些在職培訓，但以具備在倉庫環境工作過的相關經驗為優先考量。職責包括根據送貨路線分類包裹、裝卸貨品到車輛上，以及維持儲藏區域的整潔。應徵者必需有可靠的交通方式自行前往倉庫，因為附近沒有公車站或火車站。
>
> 請點擊此處應徵。

單字 seek 尋找、探索
on-the-job training 在職培訓、在職訓練
previous experience 過往經驗　　sort 分類
according to 根據⋯　applicant 應徵者
dependable 可靠的　　on one's own 自行
apply 應徵、申請、適用

1. 招募公告中包含哪些資訊？
(A) 預期時薪
(B) 工作時間
(C) 培訓時間安排
(D) 該工作的職責

解說 相關細節
文中提到應徵者的職責涵蓋包裹分類、裝卸貨品到車輛上與整理好儲藏區域，因此答案為 (D)。

單字 hourly wage 時薪　　duties 業務

2. 該職位有什麼資格要求？
(A) 安全證照
(B) 優秀的電腦技能
(C) 可前往倉庫的可靠交通方式
(D) 該領域的相關經驗

解說 相關細節
文中提到附近沒有公車站或火車站，所以要有方法自行前往倉庫，因此答案為 (C)。有在倉庫工作過的經驗僅為優先考量（preferred），並非必要條件，因此 (D) 不是答案。另外，在多益測驗中，招募的相關文章中會出現 requirements（應徵資格）、required（必需具備的）和 preferred（優先的），答題時請留意這三者的差異。

單字 certificate 證照、資格證　　reliable 可靠的、值得信賴的

3-5. 公告

> 分享吸引人的創意，獲得Spring Sensations禮券！
>
> 在Spring Sensations，我們很自豪能夠提供受顧客喜愛的獨特產品。在您的幫助下，我們可以讓產品線變得更好！**我們正在尋找開發新香氣的創意點子，以用於廣受歡迎的身體乳和護手霜**。如果您提供的香氣為被選中的三者之一，您將收到價值500美元的Spring Sensations禮券，而這些禮券永遠不會過期！
>
> 欲參加比賽，請至Spring Sensations社群媒體頁面，在評論中留下您的創意點子。新香氣可以包含多達三種主要香氣的組合，並請您為其取一個獨特的名稱。請務必上www.springsensations.com確認我們現有的產品線，以確保您不會推薦我們目前現有的產品！
>
> 比賽將於3月5日至4月20日舉行，預計於4月25日在我們的網站和社群媒體上公布得獎者。禮券將於5月1日透過電子郵件發送。

單字 winning 獲勝的、吸引人的、有魅力的　　look for 尋找
expire 到期　　contain 包含、容納　　up to 多達
dominant 佔首位的、支配的　　come up with 想出
as well 同樣地　　check out 查看　　existing 現存的
run 持續（特定期間）

3. Spring Sensations最有可能是什麼？
(A) 行銷公司
(B) 保養品製造商
(C) 年度慶典活動
(D) 服飾零售店

解說 推論或暗示
文中提到公司正在尋找新香氣的創意點子，用於廣受歡迎的身體乳和護手霜。表示該公司是與保養品有關的產業，因此答案為 (B)。

單字 retail 零售的

4. 何者並非繳交作品必備的要求？
(A) 使用不同氣味的數量限制
(B) 包括創作作品的名稱
(C) 確認香氣組合尚未被使用
(D) 提供包裝上的建議

解說 事實與否
文中並未要求提供包裝上的建議，因此答案為(D)。

換句話說 (B) should come up with a unique name for it
→ Including a name for the creation

單字 submission 繳交、呈遞

5. 繳交參賽作品的最後期限是什麼時候？
(A) 3月5日
(B) 4月20日
(C) 4月25日
(D) 5月1日

解說 相關細節

文中提到比賽時間為 3 月 5 日至 4 月 20 日，表示最後繳交期限為 4 月 20 日，因此答案為 (B)。

單字 entry 參賽作品、進入、加入、參加

6-8. 廣告

Maurita檢測分析公司一開放職缺

Maurita檢測分析公司（MAI）自從在Plainview開設第一家分公司，並迅速擴展到Lubbock以來，**一直是農業用地和建築項目上，土壤測試領域值得信賴的品牌。**我們為員工提供良好的工作環境、組織內職涯發展的機會、以及**有競爭力的薪資和有薪假。**

現場團隊負責人
監督現場 4-5 名土壤技術員的團隊。準備土壤採集地點的地圖，並分配任務給團隊成員。主要在Lubbock工作，**但可能需要在該地區以外的地方工作。**

土壤技術員
參訪Lubbock及其周邊地區，採集和標記土壤樣本。由於採集過程的步驟繁複，必須注重細節。技術員採分組工作，並提供培訓。

高級實驗室技術員
帶領由八名技術人員組成的團隊，在Hereford的實驗室進行精確的土壤測試。需具備環境科學或相關專業的學士學位。**偶爾需要出差。**

單字 open position 開放職缺　trusted 值得信賴的
agricultural 農業的　expand 擴展、擴大
provide A with B 向 A 提供 B
supportive 支援的、給予幫助的　competitive 競爭的
oversee 監督　assign 指派、分配
based in 在（某地點）打下根基　label 貼標籤
attention to detail 注重細節、細心　conduct 實施、執行
occasional 偶爾的

6. 關於Maurita檢測分析公司，文中指出什麼？
(A) 該地區唯一提供測試服務的公司。
(B) 擁有良好的聲譽。
(C) 仍由原來的創始人經營。
(D) 已停止農業服務。

解說 事實與否

文中提到該公司一直是農業用地和建築項目上，土壤測試領域值得信賴的品牌，因此答案為(B)。

換句話說 has been a trusted name → has a good reputation

單字 have a good reputation 擁有良好聲譽
operate 經營　founder 創始人、創立者
discontinue 中斷、停止

7. 第一段第4行中的「competitive」一詞意思最接近何者？
(A) 矛盾的、衝突的
(B) 侵略的、好鬥的
(C) 適當的、合理的、價錢公道的
(D) 有野心的、野心勃勃的

解說 找出同義詞

competitive 所在的句子指的是 competitive wages，意思為「有競爭力的薪資」，表示當中的 competitive 意思為「有競爭力的」。換句話說，薪資與其他公司相比，算是「不差的、過得去的」，所以可以把 competitive 替換成 reasonable，因此答案為 (C)。

8. 所有職缺的共同點為何？
(A) 需要出差。
(B) 僅開放大學畢業生。
(C) 每年支付獎金。
(D) 包含管理其他人。

解說 相關細節

現場團隊負責人需要在 Lubbock 以外的地方工作、土壤技術員需要參訪 Lubbock 及其周邊地區、高級實驗室技術員偶爾需要出差，因此答案為 (A)。

9-12. 報導

藝術角落

Lance Colbert撰寫

當商業和藝術的世界交融時，有時很難找到平衡點。但當地企業家Elizabeth Sanders和Timothy Marlowe正在尋找一種讓兩者融合的方法。**他們的新公司Art Phase為商業場所提供出租原創畫作的服務。這對希望擁有精緻裝飾，卻無法大量投資在藝術品上的Asheville地區企業來說非常合適。**

Sanders女士和Marlowe先生是在共同經營會計師事務所時，萌生了這個想法。Sanders女士表示：「我們想裝飾我們的辦公室，以給客戶留下良好的第一印象。**然而，我們才剛起步，所以還有很多其他物品需要購買。**我們也對於在藝術品上進行前期投資感到有些緊張。這是因為流行趨勢經常變動，所以畫作過一段時間後可能會顯得過時。」

Marlowe先生是一位業餘藝術家，活躍於當地藝術界。他和Sanders女士創立了Art Phase作為副業，並預期它會受到歡迎。Art Phase提供多種畫作出租，其中大部分由當地藝術家所創作。有興趣租賃藝術品的人，可以請Art Phase的顧問造訪他們的地方，並根據房間的顏色和個人風格進行推薦。一旦選定，畫作就會運送到現場，並在租賃期結束後幫客戶免費回收。客戶可以每季度更換藝術品，甚至可以收到有關作品靈感的藝術家註記。

Asheville藝術家協會會長Neil Patterson解釋道：「Art Phase對於那些尚未成名的藝術家來說是個絕佳的機會。他們可以讓他們的藝術作品被更多人看到，同時還能賺取一定比例的租金。對於那些無法負擔在陽光街市集租攤位或沒有畫廊空間的人來說，這是一個具有吸引力的選擇。」

單字 entrepreneur 企業家、創業者
commercial 商業的、廣告　premises 房屋建築、場地
sophisticated 精緻的、精密的
afford to do 負擔得起、買得起⋯　heavily 非常地、厲害地
operate 運作　first impression 第一印象
outdated 老舊的、過時的
after a while 一段時間後、過了一會　found 創立
a wide range of 各式各樣的　recommendation 推薦、建議
inspiration 靈感　established 受認可的、有地位的

9. 報導的目的為何？
(A) 引進投資機會
(B) 突顯當地藝術家的畫作
(C) 說明新提供的服務
(D) 鼓勵參加藝術課程

解說　主旨或目的
本文主要在介紹 Sanders 女士和 Marlowe 先生創立的新公司 Art Phase，因此答案為 (C)。文中並未介紹當地藝術家的畫作，因此 (B) 並非答案。

單字 highlight 強調　newly 最近　available 可使用的、有空的
encourage 建議、鼓勵　participation 參加

10. 根據文章，Art Phase 不提供什麼服務？
(A) 取貨和送貨
(B) 免費試用期
(C) 親自諮詢
(D) 藝術家的評論

解說　事實與否
文中並未提到有免費試用期，因此答案為 (B)。

單字 trial 試用、試驗　in-person 親自

11. Patterson 先生暗示了陽光街市集的什麼特質？
(A) 收費高。
(B) 裝飾得很有吸引力。
(C) 靠近一個藝廊。
(D) 設有不同大小的展位。

解說　推論或暗示
他提到對於那些無法負擔在陽光街市集租攤位的人來說，這是一個具有吸引力的選擇。表示對於金錢上沒有餘裕的藝術家來說，可能無法負擔陽光街市集的攤位租金，因此答案為 (A)。

12. [1]、[2]、[3]、[4] 當中，何處最適合填入下方句子？
「我們也對於在藝術品上進行前期投資感到有些緊張。」
(A) [1]
(B) [2]
(C) [3]
(D) [4]

解說　句子插入題
題目提供的句子中出現「also（也）」，表示前後句脈絡需一致。題目句寫道：「我們也對於在藝術品上進行前期投資感到有些緊張。」，而 [2] 前方 Sanders 女士提到：「我們才剛起步，

所以還有很多其他物品需要購買。」，與題目句同為困難之處，因此句子置於其後方的 [2] 最為適當，答案要選 (B)。

單字 upfront 預付的、坦白的

UNIT 16　雙篇與多篇文章　題本 p.166

1. (D)　**2.** (C)

感謝您在 Holly 居家用品店的訂購！
訂單編號：068379
出貨方式：1-3 個工作天內出貨
運送至：685 Aspen Lane, Irvine, CA 92614

產品	描述	樣式	價格
H190	10.5 英吋盤子，6 入一組	森林樹葉	35.99 美元
B836	6 英吋碗，6 入一組	森林樹葉	25.99 美元
M331	咖啡杯，6 入一組	藍色波紋	32.99 美元
W275	茶壺，2 入一組	森林樹葉	49.99 美元
		小計	144.96 美元
* 首次購買的顧客 使用代碼 WELCOME 可享消費總額九折優惠		代碼*：WELCOME	-14.49 美元
		運費	5.99 美元
		合計	136.46 美元

Holly 居家用品店：申請退貨
客戶：Howard Erickson
訂單編號：068379
退貨商品：M331
申請退貨理由：
[ ] 物品損壞　　　　　[✓] 其他（請說明）：
[ ] 寄錯商品　　　　　顏色與預期不符

單字 damage 損壞

1. 關於 Holly 居家用品店文中提到了什麼？
(A) 致力於環境責任。
(B) 允許顧客訂購客製化樣式。
(C) 擁有各種材料製成的產品。
(D) 為新顧客提供折扣。

單字 be dedicated to 致力於、專注於⋯　custom 客製的

2. Erickson 先生退回什麼樣的產品？
(A) 盤子
(B) 碗
(C) 杯子
(D) 茶壺

84

1. (A)	2. (A)	3. (D)	4. (B)	5. (D)	6. (D)
7. (D)	8. (B)	9. (C)	10. (D)	11. (A)	12. (D)
13. (D)	14. (B)	15. (B)	16. (B)	17. (B)	18. (C)
19. (A)	20. (D)				

1-5. 報導與線上評論

CALGARY（7月13日）— Rocky服飾店是一家提供男女款夾克、滑雪褲、打底衣物等一系列滑雪服裝的公司。五年前，**合夥人Noella Purcell和Travis Byler**在Clagary開了一家小型零售店，從此以後，生意開始**蓬勃發展**。在Edmonton開設了第二家分店，消費者對Rocky服飾店商品的需求也有大幅增長。**由於公司嚴格測試其服裝，以確保能夠抵禦極端溫度和被粗魯對待**，因此建立了一批忠實的顧客群。衣服成品也十分色彩繽紛又兼具時尚感。

Rocky服飾店先前僅在其零售店販售商品，但上個月推出了線上商店，使其能接觸到世界各地的顧客。**現在Purcell女士和Byler先生計劃於11月在Lake Louise開設第三家零售店**。選擇該地點是因為儘管Lake Louise是一個小村莊，但它位於熱門滑雪區的中心，周圍有許多度假村。該商店僅在十一月下旬至四月底的滑雪旺季期間開放。合夥人還在考慮與滑雪教練建立合作關係，以提供滑雪課程的折扣。

單字 base layer 基礎層、為保暖而穿在裡面的衣服
merchandise 物品、商品
significantly 相當地、有意義地、重要地
loyal customer 忠實顧客　rigorously 嚴格地
make sure (that) 確實做到⋯　withstand 抵擋
extreme 極端的　rough 粗暴的　treatment 對待、治療、處置
reach 到達、抵達　area 地區　surround 圍繞
run（在特定期間）持續　look into 調查、研究

發文時間：11月30日	發文者：Daniel Blair

今天我參觀了Rocky服飾店最新的零售分店，其商品種類讓我留下深刻的印象。我遇到了其中一位合夥人Noella Purcell，她對滑雪非常了解，因為她曾經是一名專業滑雪員。聽她講述如何與她的合作夥伴創立這間公司很有意思。**她的合作夥伴負責公司的會計工作**，她則專注於時尚和顧客。店內的氣氛充滿活力，整個商店的螢幕上不斷播放著滑雪員的有趣片段。我找到了一些我喜愛的品項。我可能會在冬季經常光顧這家店，**因為我就住在附近，可以步行抵達！**如果你喜歡滑雪，Rocky服飾店絕對值得光顧。

單字 selection 選擇、精選品　knowledgeable 博學的
used to do 過去常常做⋯　found 設立　handle 處理、處置
footage 片段、畫面　within walking distance 走路就能到的距離　definitely 肯定、確實地　worth 有⋯的價值
check out 確認、查看

1. 文章中關於Rocky服飾店提到了什麼？
(A) 對其產品進行重要測試。
(B) 在世界各地開設零售分店。
(C) 被提名時尚獎項。
(D) 自行生產布料。

解說 事實與否
文章提到公司對其產品進行嚴格的測試，確保服裝能夠抵禦極端溫度和被粗魯對待，因此答案為 (A)。

單字 conduct 進行、執行　nominate 提名
manufacture 製造

2. 關於Byler先生，文中指出什麼？
(A) 他負責公司的記帳工作。
(B) 他在訪談期間遇到Blair先生。
(C) 他曾經是一名職業滑雪員。
(D) 他自行設計了一些衣服。

解說 雙篇文章整合題—事實與否
第一篇文章提到合夥人為 Noella Purcell 和 Travis Byler。而後第二篇文章中提到 Blair 先生遇到 Purcell 女士，聽她講述如何與她的合作夥伴創立這間公司很有意思，以及她的合作夥伴 Byler 先生負責公司的會計工作，因此答案為 (A)。

換句話說 handles the accounting side of the business
→ is in charge of the business's bookkeeping

單字 be in charge of 負責⋯　bookkeeping 記帳、會計工作

3. 文章第一段第7行中「taken off」一詞的意思最接近何者？
(A) 消失
(B) 出發
(C) 去除
(D) 成功

解說 找出同義詞
taken off 所在句為「the business has taken off」，指「生意開始蓬勃發展」。當中的 taken off 表示「快速成長」之義，因此答案為 (D)。

4. 關於Blair先生，文中提到什麼？
(A) 他是位經驗豐富的滑雪員。
(B) 他住在Lake Louise。
(C) 他應徵了Rocky服飾店的工作。
(D) 他與Purcell女士一起工作。

解說 雙篇文章整合題—推論或暗示
第二篇文章為 Blair 先生於 11 月 30 日撰寫的評論，當中提到他參觀了新開的 Rocky 服飾店零售分店，並表示他住在走路可以到達的地方。回到第一篇文章，當中提到 Purcell 女士和 Byler 先生計劃於 11 月在 Lake Louise 開設第三家零售店。由此可知 Blair 先生造訪的是位在 Lake Louise 的分店，可推論他住在該地區，因此答案為 (B)。

單字 experienced 有經驗的、老練的　apply for 應徵⋯

5. 關於Rocky服飾店的最新商店，文中指出什麼？
(A) 其規模與第二家分店一樣。
(B) 顧客可以在那裡預約滑雪課程。
(C) 全年無休。
(D) 有為顧客播放影片。

解說 事實與否
第二篇文章中提到整個商店的螢幕上不斷播放著滑雪員的有趣片段，因此答案為 (D)。

換句話說 they were showing interesting footage of skiers on the screens → It has videos playing for customers.

單字 book 預約

6-10. 報導

> 仍會持續建設新體育場
> Courtney Wallace撰寫
>
> Davenport（1月2日）— 一位於Davenport西北部的新體育場館Apex體育場的建設仍按計畫進行，即將展開內部工程。這座體育場由Sigley集團所擁有，該集團旗下有許多棟建築物，其中大部分是表演場地，**這是他們首次涉足體育場館**。
>
> 該項目的**目標**之一為透過大型體育賽事，吸引更多遊客來Davenport。**最初的設計是8000個座位，但如果可以修改成容納至少10,000個座位，其規模就符合主辦區域半職業錦標賽的資格。**
>
> 該體育場的首場比賽定於5月2日舉行，由Davenport老虎隊對上Waterloo獵鷹隊。

單字 venue 場地　be on track 如期進行中、按計劃進行　venture into 涉足⋯　alter 改變、修改　accommodate 容納　be eligible to do 具備⋯的資格　host 主辦

> 棒球迷對新球場感到興奮
> Jerry Lambert撰寫
>
> Davenport（5月3日）— 昨晚Apex體育場舉行了Davenport老虎隊和Waterloo獵鷹隊之間的比賽。**儘管有很多前來支持Waterloo獵鷹隊的球迷**，主場隊仍以3比1獲勝。Davenport老虎隊的總教練Stephen Wilson對球隊的表現感到驕傲。「Waterloo隊是一支很難擊敗的球隊，但是**多虧了Rob Sanchez和他隊友們的努力，我們才能獲勝。**」Wilson先生說。
>
> 許多觀看比賽的觀眾對於這座由建築師Howard Torres設計的新建築印象深刻。**該體育場將成為今年末區域半職業錦標賽的主辦地點**。欲查看所有即將舉行的活動，請至www.apexstadium.com/events。

單字 matchup 比賽　thanks to 多虧⋯　pull off 成功完成（困難的事）　attendee 在場者　upcoming 即將到來的、來臨的

6. 關於Sigley集團，文中指出什麼？
(A) 它收購了一家建築公司。
(B) 它已搬遷至Davenport。
(C) 它處於新的管理體系之下。
(D) 它只經營一座體育場。

解說 事實與否
第一篇文章中提到這是他們首次涉足體育場館，表示Sigley集團旗下只有一座體育場，因此答案為(D)。

單字 relocate 搬遷　management 經營、管理、營運　operate 經營

7. 第一篇文章中第二段第1行「points」一詞的意思最接近何者？
(A) 意義
(B) 特色
(C) 地點
(D) 目標

解說 找出同義詞
points 所在的句子為「One of the points of the project is to bring more tourists to Davenport」，意思是「該項目的目標之一為透過大型體育賽事，吸引更多遊客來到 Davenport」。當中的 points 等同於「重點目標」之意，因此答案為 (D)。

8. 關於Apex體育場，文中提到什麼？
(A) 其建設由市政府資助。
(B) 擴增了原定的座位數量。
(C) 開幕時間晚於預期。
(D) 每年都會舉辦一場區域錦標賽。

解說 雙篇文章整合題—推論或暗示
第一篇文章中提到 Apex 體育場最初的設計是 8000 個座位，但如果可以修改成容納至少 10,000 個座位，其規模足以符合主辦區域半職業錦標賽的資格。第二篇文章中則提到 Apex 體育場今年末將主辦區域半職業錦標賽。綜合上述，Apex 體育場的座位數量至少擴增為 1 萬個，因此答案為 (B)。

單字 fund 資助　expand 擴增、擴大　capacity 容量、容納數量、能力

9. 關於Waterloo獵鷹隊，文中指出什麼？
(A) 本賽季贏球次數不多。
(B) 其體育場規模小於Apex體育場。
(C) 它的許多球迷專程前去觀看比賽。
(D) 為粉絲們保留了特殊座位。

解說 事實與否
第二篇文章中提到有許多球迷前來支持 Waterloo 獵鷹隊，因此答案為 (C)。

換句話說 the Waterloo Falcons had a great showing of fans → Many of its fans traveled to attend a game.

單字 reserve 保留（座位）、預約

10. Rob Sanchez是誰？
(A) 體育記者
(B) 建築師
(C) 教練
(D) 運動員

解說 相關細節
第二篇文章中提到 Davenport 老虎隊的總教練在採訪中表示多虧 Rob Sanchez 和隊友們的努力，才能獲勝，由此可知 Rob Sanchez 是位運動員，因此答案為 (D)。

11-15. 時間表、時事文章與表格

Megalith健身房加盟店業主年度會議 10月21日星期六時間表			
上午7點15分	茶飲、咖啡和甜甜圈		麻雀會議室
上午8點	歡迎致辭 執行長Pranav Chetti		老鷹會議室
上午8點30分	從全國至個別的 推廣行銷 行銷總監 Sanhana Adwani		老鷹會議室
上午10點30分	了解您的客戶 資深研究員 Priya Vadekar		金翅雀會議室
下午12點30分	報名時包含的自助式 午餐		麻雀會議室
下午1點30分	加盟業主演講： 應對競爭 團體課程管理		孔雀會議室 金翅雀會議室
下午3點	新設備展示 採購總監 Ganesh Munshif		孔雀會議室

單字 promotion 宣傳、促銷、升遷、晉升
deal with 處理、處置　demonstration 示範演練、說明

對加盟店業主的支持

William Lowery撰寫

上個週末，經營Megalith健身房加盟店的小型企業業主參加了該公司在Dallas舉行的年度會議。來自美國各地超過三百多人參加了為期兩天的活動。**行銷總監Sanhana Adwani概述了母公司正在推廣連鎖品牌的健身中心，以及如何在有限的預算下推廣各別分公司。會議上選了幾位加盟店業主進行演說。與會者還搶先看到電動跑步機Marietta和直立式划船機Netzer。**這兩種器材即將在今年年底送至各健身房。

單字 operate 運作　outline 簡略說明
parent company 母公司　individually 單獨地、個別地
get a sneak peek 搶先看（尚未正式公開）
motorized 電動的、裝上發動機的　upright 直立的、筆直的

Megalith健身房加盟店業主年度會議回饋表	
感謝您花時間與我們分享您的意見。請根據您參加的講座，給予1（差）至5（優秀）的評分。

演講	評分
了解您的客戶	5
應對競爭	不適用
團體課程管理	5
保持顧客的積極性	5
成功的關鍵步驟	不適用
Megalith任務	5

意見：我選擇在活動會場預訂一晚的住宿，所以我沒有遇到任何問題，但與我交談過的一些人說，他們遲到是因為不熟悉這座城市，而且要在交通堵塞的情況下前往現場。**我覺得各場次間的時間過於倉促，建議每場活動提前一點結束。**

姓名：Peggy Kearns

單字 overnight 整夜的　accommodation 住處、住宿
rushed 匆忙的

11. 與會者可以在哪裡聽到開幕致辭？
(A) 在老鷹會議室
(B) 在金翅雀會議室
(C) 在孔雀會議室
(D) 在麻雀會議室

解說 相關細節
第一篇文章中寫歡迎致辭地點在老鷹會議室，因此答案為 (A)。

12. 文章的其中一個目的為何？
(A) 說明Adwani女士的新角色
(B) 提供即將開設課程的詳情
(C) 鼓勵人們參與加盟
(D) 強調公司會議上的活動

解說 主旨或目的
文章針對在 Dallas 舉行的年度會議進行說明，因此答案為 (D)。

單字 upcoming 即將來臨的、即將到來的
encourage 鼓勵、建議　highlight 強調

13. 與會者最有可能在何時看到Marietta和Netzer？
(A) 上午8點
(B) 上午10點30分
(C) 下午1點30分
(D) 下午3點00分

解說 雙篇文章整合題—推論或暗示
Marietta 和 Netzer 出現在第二篇文章中，分別是電動跑步機和直立式划船機的名稱，文中提到與會者將搶先在年度會議上看到這些器材。回到第一篇文章的時間表，與機器有關的講座為「新設備展示」，對應的時間為下午 3 點，因此答案為 (D)。

87

14. 關於Kearns女士，哪一項敘述是正確的？
(A) 她去年參加過活動。
(B) 她下午參加了一場講座。
(C) 她參加活動遲到。
(D) 她住在會議舉辦的城市。

解說 雙篇文章整合題—事實與否
Kearns 女士為第三篇文章回饋表的撰寫者，文中她給「團隊課程管理」5 分，表示她有參加該場講座。回到第一篇文章，「團隊課程管理」的時間為下午 1 點 30 分，因此答案為 (B)。

15. Kearns女士不太滿意這次會議的哪一方面？
(A) 場地缺乏重要的設施。
(B) 場次之間沒有足夠的緩衝時間。
(C) 很難聽到講者的聲音。
(D) 部分會議同時舉行。

解說 相關細節
第三篇文章 Kearns 所撰寫的意見中提到各場次間的時間過於倉促，建議每場活動提前一點結束，因此答案為 (B)。

單字 lack 不足、缺乏的 amenities （便利）設施

16-20. 邀請函、宣傳手冊與電子郵件

> 化學工程大會
> www.chemicalengineeringconf.com
>
> 在 4 月 9 日開始的第五屆年度化學工程大會上，度過一個充實的週末，聆聽資訊豐富的講座，並與專業人士建立人脈。我們的目標是向在該領域工作的人介紹最新趨勢、安全措施和新興技術。本次大會將首次在 Parkview Hall 舉行，我們很高興邀請到 Dalton化學公司的執行長 **Wyatt Faber擔任我們的主講者。**
>
> 有關詳細的贊助資訊，請參閱附件的宣傳手冊。

單字 informative 有幫助的（資訊） networking 人脈
emerging 新興的、浮現的 attach 附加、貼上

> 化學工程大會
> 贊助方案
>
> 企業贊助對我們大會的成功有重要的作用，因為它使我們能夠維持價格合理的註冊費。**透過成為贊助商，您可以向數百名該領域的專業人士介紹您的公司，使他們對您的品牌更加熟悉。**
>
> 經濟型—500 美元
> • 在我們印刷的大會企劃中展示貴公司的標誌
> • 享註冊九折優惠，最多可適用於 10 名員工
>
> 基本型—1,500 美元
> • 在我們印刷的大會企劃和報到區橫幅上展示貴公司的標誌
> • 享註冊九折優惠，最多可適用於 15 名員工

> 高級型—2,500 美元
> • 在所有區域展示貴公司的標誌，包含舞台上
> • 貴公司所有員工皆享註冊九折優惠
>
> 菁英型—4,500 美元
> • 在所有區域展示貴公司的標誌，包含舞台上
> • **貴公司所有員工皆享註冊八五折優惠**
> • **貴公司員工可使用我們的貴賓休息室**，當中設有印表機和影印設備、免費茶點、手機充電站等。

單字 tier （組織、系統等）層級 corporate 企業的
play an important role 發揮重要作用
affordable 價格合理的 feature 以…為特色
complimentary 免費的 refreshments 茶點

> 收件者：Holbrook公司 全體員工 <stafflist@holbrookinc.com>
> 寄件者：Nancy Turner <n.turner@holbrookinc.com>
> 日期：3月28日
> 主旨：化學工程大會
>
> 親愛的員工，
>
> 化學工程大會即將到來。**我需要填寫註冊表單，所以我想知道誰想參加該活動。我們是今年的活動贊助商，因此所有想參加的員工都具備註冊費優惠的資格。**此外，在參加活動的同時，你還可以使用貴賓休息室。許多人應該會認出今年的主講者，去年他曾來訪我們公司舉辦一場研討會，介紹了最先進的化學工具。
>
> Nancy Turner
> Holbrook公司行政總監

單字 wonder 想知道 be eligible for 有…的資格
state-of-the-art 最先進的

16. 關於大會，邀請函中指出什麼？
(A) 每年都在Parkview Hall舉行。
(B) 為期兩天。
(C) 可免費參加。
(D) 首次舉行。

解說 事實與否
邀請函中寫道：「在 4 月 9 日開始的第五屆年度化學工程大會上，度過一個充實的週末」，表示大會舉行時間為週末兩天，因此答案為 (B)。

單字 take place 舉行、發生 last 持續

17. 宣傳手冊中提到贊助的好處為何？
(A) 贊助商可以在會議上設置攤位。
(B) 贊助商可以提高品牌知名度。
(C) 贊助商可以獲得標誌設計的協助。
(D) 贊助商可以線上推廣他們的業務。

解說 事實與否
宣傳手冊中提到成為贊助商可以向數百名專業人士介紹公司，讓他們更熟悉公司的品牌，因此答案為 (B)。

單字 operate 營業　recognition 知名度、認可
assistance 協助、支援　promote 推廣、升遷

18. 電子郵件的主旨為何？
(A) 解釋作出決定的理由
(B) 招募志工進行演講
(C) 找出誰有興趣參加活動
(D) 安排前往會議的交通

解說 主旨或目的
電子郵件的撰寫者表示：「我需要填寫註冊表格，所以我想知道誰想參加該活動」，因此答案為 (C)。

單字 recruit 招募　arrange transportation 安排交通工具

19. 何者為關於Faber先生的描述？
(A) 他在Holbrook公司舉辦了培訓活動。
(B) 他因贊助事宜聯絡了Turner女士。
(C) 他將成為Holbrook公司的員工。
(D) 他開發了新技術。

解說 雙篇文章整合題—事實與否
Faber 先生的名字最先出現在第一篇邀請函裡，提到他將擔任大會的主講者。而在第三篇文章中，再度提及他是今年的主講者，以及去年他曾在 Holbrook 公司舉辦研討會，介紹了最先進的化學工具，因此答案為 (A)。

話句話說 teach a workshop → led a training event

20. Holbrook公司是屬於哪種方案的贊助商？
(A) 經濟型
(B) 基本型
(C) 高級型
(D) 菁英型

解說 雙篇文章整合題—相關細節
第三篇文章中提到Holbrook公司為今年的活動贊助商，因此有資格按照想參加的員工數量享有註冊優惠，還有使用貴賓休息室的權利。而在第二篇文章中，菁英型方案享有的福利為：「所有員工皆享註冊八五折優惠」以及「可以使用貴賓休息室」，因此答案為(D)。

題本 p.176

147. (D)	148. (A)	149. (D)	150. (D)	151. (B)
152. (B)	153. (B)	154. (B)	155. (C)	156. (C)
157. (B)	158. (A)	159. (A)	160. (D)	161. (A)
162. (B)	163. (D)	164. (B)	165. (C)	166. (B)
167. (B)	168. (D)			

147-148. 說明書

> 如何設定新的Lanette可視門鈴
>
> 安裝後，請保存本手冊。
>
> 1. 從www.lanettetech.com下載Lanette智慧型手機應用程式，並建立一個新帳戶。
> 2. 在應用程式中，點選「裝置設定」，並選擇「門鈴」。
> 3. 掃描裝置背面的條碼。完成此操作後，會向您發送一封包含產品編號的核准電子郵件。請在此寫下電子郵件中的產品編號：730950R。
> 4. 輸入您的地址以指定您的所在位置。請注意，可選擇是否執行此步驟，但如果您跳過此步驟，將無法使用門鈴的某些功能。
> 5. 在應用程式中，點選「確認」。裝置將自動連接到您的Wi-Fi，但您需要輸入Wi-Fi密碼。
> 6. 按住前方的紅色按鈕三秒鐘來測試裝置。一旦綠燈開始閃爍，您的設備即可使用。請在此處填寫測試日期：_____。
>
> 如果您有任何問題或疑慮，請撥打1-800-555-4950聯絡我們的客服團隊。

單字 set up 設定　installation 安裝　account 帳戶、帳號
approval 批准、認可、同意　input 輸入
specify 具體指定、詳細說明　optional 可選擇的
feature 功能、特色　function 作用　flash 閃爍、閃光

147. 用戶為何要提供位置？
(A) 確定由哪個辦公室處理詢問事宜
(B) 提供運費估算
(C) 收取替換零件
(D) 確保所有功能正常運作

解說 相關細節
文中提到需要輸入地址以指定確切的所在位置，若跳過此步驟，將無法使用門鈴的某些功能，因此答案為 (D)。

單字 determine 決定、確定　handle 處理、處置
inquiry 詢問、諮詢　estimate 估價、估算
replacement 替換（品）　ensure 確保、保障

148. 文中提到使用說明書用戶的什麼？
(A) 用戶掃描了代碼。
(B) 用戶發送了一封確認電子郵件。
(C) 用戶沒有收到產品編號。
(D) 用戶進行了測試。

解說 推論或暗示
文中用戶在產品編號欄寫下了編號，表示用戶已經掃描過裝置背面的條碼，並收到包含產品編號的核准電子郵件，因此答案為 (A)。測試日期欄位為空白，表示用戶尚未進行測試，因此 (D) 並非答案。

89

149-151. 邀請函

平面設計藝術慶典
Findlay宴會廳
Ardmore路827號

7月1日 星期五
下午7點至9點30分

Findlay平面設計協會（FSGD）將舉辦年度宴會！我們邀請您參加這個令人振奮的活動，屆時將播放有關我們今年活動的影片、介紹即將來臨的計劃，以及一場如何在自由業界工作的主題演講。**我們還將頒發幾個獎項，以表彰那些今年不辭辛勞地工作，使我們社團變得更棒的人。**這是一個可享用美味的四道佳餚，同時**與其他FSGD參與者進行社交活動的機會**。在用餐期間，將由Rio弦樂四重奏提供現場音樂演奏。參加此活動無需任何費用，因為這是由我們的會費所支付。

如果您計劃參加此活動，請在6月16日之前發信至pslater@fsgd.org聯絡Patrick Slater。**聯絡時，請務必註明您的同行者有多少人。**

我們希望能在活動現場見到您！

單字 celebration 慶祝活動　feature 以…為特色、特別展示
keynote speech 主題演講　navigate 導航、引導
socialize 與人交流、參與社交　fellow 會員、同事
dues 會費　no later than 不晚於…　indicate 指出、明示
party （同行的）團體

149. 邀請函最有可能是給誰的？
(A) 私人捐款者
(B) 民選官員
(C) 電腦程式設計師
(D) 社團成員

解說 推論或暗示
文中提到將會頒發獎項給FSGD社團成員，還能與其他FSGD參與者進行社交活動，表示該邀請函是提供給社團成員，因此答案為(D)。

150. 第一段第4行中「recognize」一詞的意思最接近何者？
(A) 回想
(B) 領悟
(C) 確認、識別
(D) 承認、（正式）表達感謝之意

解說 找出同義詞
recognize 所在的句子為「We'll also be presenting several awards to recognize the people who have worked so hard」，意思為「頒發幾個獎項以表彰那些今年不辭辛勞工作的人」。當中的recognize 表示「認可、表彰」之意，因此答案為(D)。

151. 關於本次活動，文中提到什麼？
(A) 應在6月16日之前繳交入場費。
(B) 受邀者可攜伴參加。
(C) 場地很快就會敲定。
(D) 活動將被拍攝下來。

解說 暗示或推論
邀請函最後寫道：「聯絡時，請務必註明您的同行者有多少人。」，表示受邀的人可以攜伴參加，因此答案為(B)。

單字 admission fee 入場費　recipient 收件者
finalize 最終確定、完成

152-154. 報導

Valley公園的升級項目獲得批准

（2月13日）— 市長Christopher Wilcher已證實聯合市將會推進Valley公園的升級項目。這項工程的**部分資金來自聯合市的年度公園和娛樂預算**。該市還收到了**當地企業家Gary Austin的慷慨捐贈**。此外，**當地社區團體還舉行了募款活動，為該項目作出貢獻**。例如：UC朋友社團舉辦了一場二手書義賣活動。

預計將會填平公園西北部棒球場上的坑洞，並在需要的地方種植新的草坪。將會拆除停車場附近的花圃，**以便騰出空間給能容納10張桌子的頂棚野餐區**。儘管有人提議建造第二個停車場，但規劃者決定擴建現有的停車場。

大多數人都期待能夠使用這些公園的改良設施。儘管如此，有些人認為當地官員應該專注於其他領域。居民Elizabeth Arnold說道：「在我看來，我們有更迫切的問題需處理，比如道路的狀況不佳。」

單字 approve 批准、贊成（~ of）　confirm 證實、確認
partially 部分地　fund 出資　generous 慷慨的、大方的
entrepreneur 企業家　fundraiser 募款活動
contribute to 對…有貢獻　flower bed 花圃
propose 提案、提議　expand 擴大、擴展
look forward to 期待　take advantage of 利用…
improvement 改良、改善、進步　pressing 急迫的

152. 文中並未提到何者為升級的資金來源？
(A) 居民捐款
(B) 書店
(C) 年度預算
(D) 社區組織

解說 事實與否
文中並未提到有書店提供資金，因此答案為(B)。

153. Valley公園的新特色為何？
(A) 運動場
(B) 野餐區
(C) 花圃
(D) 第二個停車場

解說 相關細節
文中提到會拆除停車場附近的花圃，騰出空間建設頂棚野餐區，因此答案為(B)。

154. [1]、[2]、[3]、[4]當中，何處最適合填入下方句子？
「儘管如此，有些人認為當地官員應該專注於其他領域。」
(A) [1]
(B) [2]
(C) [3]
(D) [4]

解說 句子插入題
題目提供的句子出現「Nonetheless（儘管、雖然如此）」，表示前後句為相互對照的內容。題目句寫道：「儘管如此，有些人認為當地官員應該專注於其他領域。」，而 [4] 前方提到大多數人都期待能夠使用這些公園的改良設施，題目句適合置於該句話後方。而 [4] 後方則列出居民提出的意見，詳述應該專注於什麼領域，因此答案為 (D)。

單字 focus on 專注於…

155-158. 線上聊天

Naomi Rutledge［上午10點03分］早安，各位成員。我想和大家討論一下Concord公寓大樓的事。

Jared Padilla［上午10點04分］《西北生活》雜誌的一名記者同意撰寫一篇關於即將舉行之竣工儀式的文章。她想要附加一些照片。我需要聯絡攝影師Jonathan Webb，安排拍攝更多照片嗎？

Naomi Rutledge［上午10點05分］我們已經有夠多照片了。我會轉發照片集的連結給你，方便你選擇適當的照片。

Rupert Burke［上午10點06分］我很高興我們能獲得額外的宣傳。我們的預售目標是達到八成，但我們現在連七成都還沒達到。

Naomi Rutledge［上午10點07分］雜誌文章會有所幫助，我會繼續尋找其他方案。

Rupert Burke［上午10點09分］我們以前從未經手過如此大型的建物，所以這次做好很重要。

Naomi Rutledge［上午10點10分］我同意。但要記得Katie Sullivan離開團隊後，中間損失了一些時間。

Varuni Goyal［上午10點11分］確實如此。在Naomi接手後，她需讓自己熟悉這項工作。

Naomi Rutledge［上午10點12分］我感覺現在已經有跟上進度了，所以我們可以加快執行速度。

單字 check in with （主要是為了獲得新資訊而）檢查
accompany 陪同、附加　arrange 籌備、安排
forward 轉發　appropriate 適當的　publicity 宣傳
reserve 預約、特別安排（座位等）　pursue 追求、繼續進行
get... right 把…做好　step in 投入（困難的情況）
up to speed 跟上進度、了解最新狀況

155. Rutledge女士最有可能是誰？
(A) 室內設計師
(B) 建築承包商
(C) 物業經理
(D) 雜誌記者

解說 推論或暗示
聊天的內容主要針對出售 Concord 公寓大樓一事，討論宣傳相關事實，並提到首次經手這種大型建物，由此可以推測 Rutledge 女士為管理房地產租賃的人，因此答案為 (C)。

156. 上午10點05分，Rutledge女士寫道：「我們已經有夠多照片了」，是什麼意思？
(A) 她有信心有時間完成工作。
(B) 她正在考慮增加儲藏空間。
(C) 她不需要更多Webb先生的作品。
(D) 她認為他們能夠負擔Webb先生的服務。

解說 掌握意圖
Jared Padilla 於上午 10 點 04 分詢問是否需要聯絡攝影師 Jonathan Webb，安排拍攝更多照片。而後 Rutledge 女士回應照片已經夠多了，會轉發照片集的連結對方選擇適合的照片。表示不需要要求 Webb 先生拍攝，因此答案為 (C)。

單字 confident 有信心的、肯定的　afford 負擔得起、買得起

157. 聊天中提到了什麼問題？
(A) 帳單尚未付清。
(B) 未達成團隊目標。
(C) 建築未通過檢核。
(D) 預算低於預期。

解說 事實與否
Rupert Burke 於上午 10 點 06 分提到預售目標是達到八成的數量，但現在還沒達到七成，表示尚未達成目標，因此答案為 (B)。

158. 關於Rutledge女士，文中提到什麼？
(A) 她並非從一開始就參與這項專案。
(B) 她計劃聘請Sullivan女士提供額外的協助。
(C) 她想儘快造訪現場。
(D) 她擔心團隊成員經驗不足。

解說 推論或暗示
Rutledge 女士於上午 10 點 10 分提到 Katie Sullivan 離開團隊一事，而後 Varuni Goyal 回應 Rutledge 女士接手後，需讓自己熟悉這項工作。由此可知 Rutledge 女士並非一開始就參與這項專案，因此答案為 (A)。

單字 work on 著手、努力…
be concerned about 對…感到擔憂

PART 7

91

159-163. 線上文章與讀者評論

> 《橡樹論壇》8月15日,「神祕列車」
>
> 火車啟程,沿著軌道發出喀噠喀噠的聲響。乘客們坐在座位上,享用著茶點。突然間,有演員走進車廂,一場充滿戲劇性的神祕事件隨之展開。觀眾必須找出線索解開謎團。根據時代搭配的服裝、引人入勝的角色,以及**每個月都不同的情節**,神祕列車在一個獨特的「舞臺」——一輛老式蒸汽火車上呈現令人興奮的現場表演!
>
> 神祕列車已經運行了十年,當地的劇團一直在尋找籌措資金的方法。**Adrian Urbano在當前的演出中擔任主角**,他也從一開始就在大部分神祕列車的表演中演出。Urbano先生說道:「我喜歡看觀眾投入於我們的表演中,在破案之際,看到他們的喜悅之情非常有趣。」
>
> 神祕列車的演出時間為每週四、週五、週六和週日晚上,以及週六和週日下午。**演出時間長達兩個半小時,唯獨週日下午的演出時長為90分鐘**,成為家庭的熱門選擇。門票可在 www.mysterytrainboxoffice.com購買。

單字 clickety-clack 喀噠喀噠(聲響) refreshments 茶點
unfold 展開、呈現 pick up on 注意到⋯
intriguing 引人入勝的 plot 情節、策劃
old-fashioned 舊式的、老派的
in operation 運行中、運作中 look for 尋找⋯
raise money 募資、籌款 run (舞臺劇、電影)上演、表演
feature 以⋯為特色、特別展示 case 案件
with the exception of 除⋯之外

> 我最近剛剛看完神祕列車的演出,實在是太棒了!**我很喜歡看主角表演**。不僅是因為他才華洋溢,而且我個人和他也有關係,我們是從同一所高中畢業的。我記得他當時就很喜歡上戲劇課。**因神祕列車演出的許多劇本都由橡樹寫作協會(OWS)的成員所創作,所以我希望在下一期有機會看到關於這些人的專題報導**。我訂閱貴公司的刊物多年,所以我知道你們經常做這類的報導。
>
> Gloria Ramirez

單字 not only A but also B 不僅A而且B
personal 個人的、私人的 connection 關聯、連結、接觸
at that time 當時、那個時候 edition 刊號、版
frequently 頻繁地 subscribe 訂閱
publication 刊物、出版物

159. 關於神祕列車的演出,文中提到什麼?
(A) 定期更動故事情節。
(B) 觀眾會四處走動。
(C) 有知名演員演出。
(D) 每週舉行四次。

解說 推論或暗示
第一篇文章中提到每個月都有不同的情節,由此可推論故事情節會定期更動,因此答案為 (A)。演出時間為週四至週日,每周四天。若計算次數的話為週四、週五、週六和週日晚上,以及週六和週日下午,加起來共六次,因此 (D) 並非答案。

換句話說 a different plot to enjoy every month → Their storylines change regularly.

單字 storyline 故事情節 take place 發生、舉行

160. 關於週日下午的演出,何者敘述正確?
(A) 專門提供給家庭。
(B) 價格最便宜的演出。
(C) 最受歡迎的表演。
(D) 較其他演出的時間短。

解說 事實與否
第一篇文章中提到演出時間長達兩個半小時,唯獨週日下午的演出時長為 90 分鐘,因此答案為 (D)。

單字 exclusively 專門地、僅僅

161. 關於Urbano先生,文中提到什麼?
(A) 他曾和Ramirez女士上同個學校。
(B) 他計劃開設表演課程。
(C) 他為演出設計正宗的服裝。
(D) 他是劇團的創始人。

解說 雙篇文章整合題—推論或暗示
第一篇文章中提到 Adrian Urbano 在近期的演出中擔任主角。第二篇文章為 Ramirez 女士撰寫的讀者評論,當中提到她很喜歡看主角表演,並表示他們是同一所高中畢業的,因此答案為 (A)。

單字 authentic 真實的、正宗的 founder 創始人、創辦人

162. Ramirez女士有興趣做什麼事?
(A) 向報社投稿她的作品
(B) 閱讀關於OWS編劇的文章
(C) 提前審閱劇本
(D) 加入當地的寫作團體

解說 相關細節
第二篇文章中提到她希望往後有機會看到關於 OWS 成員的專題報導,因此答案為 (B)。

單字 in advance 提前、事先

163. 關於Ramirez女士,讀者評論中提到什麼?
(A) 她經常參加當地的活動。
(B) 她童年大部分時間都在橡樹鎮度過。
(C) 她多次觀看神祕列車的演出。
(D) 她長期以來都是《橡樹論壇》的訂閱者。

解說 推論或暗示
在第二篇文章中,Ramirez 女士提到她訂閱《橡樹論壇》的刊物多年,因此答案為 (D)。

單字 participate in 參加⋯ subscriber 訂閱者

164-168. 線上留言板、電子郵件與網頁

Aldridge社區論壇

類別：教育

問題：Rowley學院的課程值得上嗎？

提問者：Evan McLean，3月9日

> 去年我在Rowley學院上了法語加強課程。講師Paulette Rancourt是一位法語母語人士，她真的非常有活力。雖然課業量龐大，但我學到很多。**學院還在它的網站上提供許多可下載的補充資料。**
>
> 整體而言，儘管學費偏高，我還是推薦這間學院。事實上，我省下了一筆錢，**因為學院的副經理與她旅行社的朋友合作，給所有學生一張可用在法國旅遊的優惠券。**
>
> ─ Sophie Faulkner，3月10日

單字 intensive 加強的、密集的
make arrangements with 與…商定

收件者：全體員工<staff@rowleyinstitute.co.uk>

寄件者：Lara Hurst <l.hurst@rowleyinstitute.co.uk>

日期：5月30日

主旨：Manchester

親愛的各位，

今天是**我在Rowley學院的最後一天**。為了能和家人住得更近，我將要搬到Manchester，**但我真的會很想念大家**。作為副經理，我有機會在個人與專業層面上了解你們所有人。我對各位致力於學生成功的精神印象深刻。我要特別感謝**Dominic Archer聘請我**，給予我提升管理技能的機會。

我很高興能在這裡工作，希望我們繼續保持聯絡。

祝一切順利，

Lara Hurst

單字 close 靠近的 personal 個人的、私人的
commitment 致力、獻身、承諾 particularly 特別是

Aldridge地方企業獎

類別：支持地方教育

金獎：Jack Talbot，Aldridge社區中心

銀獎：Dominic Archer，Rowley學院

銅獎：Holly Khan，Rowley學院

榮譽獎：Ava Conway，Crafton職業學校

這些得獎者由Aldridge居民提名，並由市府官員和小型企業主組成的評審團所選出。得獎者將接受《Community Cares》雜誌記者的採訪，他們的貢獻將在Aldridge政府網站上簡要介紹。明年的提名將於7月10日後受理。

單字 trade school 職業學校 nominate 提名
panel 評審團、專門小組 contribution 貢獻
outline 簡略說明

---

164. 關於Rowley學院，Faulkner女士提到了什麼？
(A) 作業量合理。
(B) 網路上有提供額外資料。
(C) 所有講師均為母語人士。
(D) 有遠距課程的選項。

解說 事實與否
Faulkner女士為在線上留言板（第一篇文章）上回答的人，她在文中提到學院在網站上提供許多可下載的補充資料，因此答案為(B)。Faulkner女士有提到她的講師Paulette Rancourt是一位法語母語人士，但無法從文中確認所有講師皆為母語人士，因此(C)並非答案。

換句話說 offers a lot of extra downloadable materials on its website → It provides additional materials online.

單字 reasonable 合理的、妥當的 additional 額外的
option 選項 remote 遠端的、遙遠的

---

165. 關於Faulkner女士，文中提到什麼？
(A) 她的導師是有出過書的作家。
(B) 她的學費由她公司支付。
(C) 她收到Hurst女士給的優惠券。
(D) 她打算搬到法國。

解說 雙篇文章整合題─推論或暗示
第一篇文章中Faulkner女士提到學院的副經理與她旅行社的朋友合作，給所有學生一張可用在法國旅遊的優惠券。而第二篇文章（電子郵件）的撰寫者為Lara Hurst，並在郵件中提到自己是Rowley學院的副經理。綜合兩篇文章的內容，可推論出給Faulkner女士優惠券的人便是Hurst女士，因此答案為(C)。

---

166. 電子郵件的主旨為何？
(A) 恭喜員工的成就
(B) 向同事道別
(C) 尋求Manchester的相關推薦
(D) 指名員工作為接任人選

解說 主旨或目的
該郵件發送給全體員工，並於開頭處寫道：「我在Rowley學院的最後一天」，以及「我真的會很想念大家」，表示向大家道別，因此答案為(B)。

單字 congratulate A on B 針對B事情恭喜A
say farewell 告別、道別 recommendation 推薦、建議
replacement 接任者、替換（品）

---

167. 僱用Hurst女士的人獲頒什麼獎項？
(A) 金獎
(B) 銀獎
(C) 銅獎
(D) 榮譽獎

解說 雙篇文章整合題─相關細節
第二篇文章中Hurst女士提到Dominic Archer聘請她。檢視第三篇文章的獲獎名單，可以得知Dominic Archer獲頒銀獎，因此答案為(B)。

168. 網頁上提到什麼？
(A) 得獎者可以在《Community Cares》雜誌上免費刊登廣告。
(B) Talbot先生之前曾得過商業獎。
(C) 預計於 7 月 10 日頒發獎項。
(D) Archer先生和Khan女士為同位僱主工作。

解說 **推論或暗示**
得獎者的名字旁邊有列出所屬公司，Archer 先生任職於 Rowley 學院；Khan 女士同樣任職於 Rowley 學院，由此可推論兩人在相同的地方工作，因此答案為 (D)。

單字 **advertise** 刊登廣告　**previously** 先前、之前
distribute 分發、分配、（產品）流通

LISTENING TEST

1. (D)	2. (B)	3. (A)	4. (D)	5. (C)
6. (B)	7. (A)	8. (B)	9. (C)	10. (B)
11. (A)	12. (C)	13. (B)	14. (A)	15. (B)
16. (C)	17. (A)	18. (B)	19. (C)	20. (A)
21. (B)	22. (A)	23. (C)	24. (B)	25. (C)
26. (A)	27. (B)	28. (C)	29. (A)	30. (B)
31. (A)	32. (D)	33. (D)	34. (C)	35. (A)
36. (D)	37. (B)	38. (B)	39. (A)	40. (C)
41. (B)	42. (D)	43. (C)	44. (C)	45. (A)
46. (D)	47. (B)	48. (A)	49. (C)	50. (D)
51. (D)	52. (C)	53. (C)	54. (A)	55. (B)
56. (D)	57. (A)	58. (B)	59. (C)	60. (B)
61. (A)	62. (D)	63. (C)	64. (B)	65. (D)
66. (A)	67. (B)	68. (B)	69. (D)	70. (B)
71. (C)	72. (C)	73. (A)	74. (D)	75. (C)
76. (B)	77. (D)	78. (A)	79. (A)	80. (C)
81. (D)	82. (A)	83. (D)	84. (C)	85. (C)
86. (D)	87. (B)	88. (A)	89. (B)	90. (D)
91. (A)	92. (B)	93. (C)	94. (D)	95. (A)
96. (D)	97. (B)	98. (A)	99. (D)	100. (B)

READING TEST

101. (A)	102. (A)	103. (C)	104. (D)	105. (A)
106. (A)	107. (D)	108. (D)	109. (A)	110. (D)
111. (C)	112. (B)	113. (B)	114. (A)	115. (C)
116. (A)	117. (B)	118. (A)	119. (A)	120. (B)
121. (D)	122. (C)	123. (B)	124. (A)	125. (A)
126. (A)	127. (C)	128. (D)	129. (B)	130. (B)
131. (D)	132. (B)	133. (B)	134. (C)	135. (B)
136. (B)	137. (A)	138. (D)	139. (C)	140. (D)
141. (A)	142. (B)	143. (B)	144. (C)	145. (C)
146. (A)	147. (C)	148. (C)	149. (B)	150. (C)
151. (A)	152. (B)	153. (B)	154. (A)	155. (D)
156. (D)	157. (B)	158. (B)	159. (C)	160. (B)
161. (B)	162. (C)	163. (B)	164. (C)	165. (B)
166. (C)	167. (A)	168. (A)	169. (A)	170. (B)
171. (D)	172. (D)	173. (A)	174. (A)	175. (C)
176. (A)	177. (C)	178. (B)	179. (A)	180. (D)
181. (C)	182. (D)	183. (B)	184. (D)	185. (A)
186. (D)	187. (C)	188. (A)	189. (C)	190. (B)
191. (C)	192. (B)	193. (A)	194. (D)	195. (A)
196. (B)	197. (B)	198. (C)	199. (C)	200. (C)

---

1. 澳洲男子

(A) A bucket is being filled with soil.
(B) A pole is being positioned in a hole.
(C) A person is putting away some tools.
(D) A person is working in a field.

中譯

(A) 水桶裡裝滿泥土。
(B) 杆子被放在孔洞裡。
(C) 有人在收拾一些工具。
(D) 有人在田裡工作。

單字 bucket 水桶　be filled with 裝滿　pole 杆子
hole 孔洞　position 放置、決定位置　field 田地、原野

2. 英國女子

(A) They're walking through a construction site.
(B) They're resting against a railing.
(C) They're inspecting some safety helmets.
(D) They're painting items on a balcony.

中譯

(A) 他們正穿越建築工地。
(B) 他們倚靠在欄杆上。
(C) 他們正在檢查一些安全帽。
(D) 他們在陽台上粉刷物品。

單字 construction site 建築工地　rest against 倚靠
railing 欄杆　inspect 檢查　safety helmet 安全帽

3. 美國女子

(A) The man is holding a tray.
(B) The man is moving a table.
(C) The man is standing near an entrance.
(D) The man is paying for some food.

中譯

(A) 男子拿著一個托盤。
(B) 男子正在搬一張桌子。
(C) 男子站在入口附近。
(D) 男子正在付錢買一些食物。

單字 tray 托盤　entrance 入口

4. 美國男子

(A) Some cups are being stored in a cupboard.
(B) Water is flowing from a faucet.
(C) Some wall tiles are lined up for sale.
(D) Eating utensils have been placed in a rack.

中譯

(A) 有些杯子被放在櫥櫃裡。
(B) 水正從水龍頭流出來。

95

(C) 有些牆磚排成一列販售。
(D) 餐具被放置在架子上。

單字 store 存放、保管　cupboard 櫥櫃　flow 流動
faucet 水龍頭　line up 排成一列
eating utensil 餐具　rack 架子、層架

5. 🎧美國女子

(A) He's reaching for a pair of gloves.
(B) He's jogging along a walkway.
(C) Leaves are scattered on the ground.
(D) A broom is leaning against a tree.

中譯
(A) 他伸手去拿一副手套。
(B) 他沿著人行道慢跑。
(C) 樹葉散落在地上。
(D) 一把掃帚靠在樹上。

單字 reach for 伸手去抓　walkway 步道、人行道
scatter 散落　broom 掃帚　lean against 靠在…

6. 🎧美國男子

(A) Some cushions are being stacked near a container.
(B) Some sofas have been arranged in a display area.
(C) Some furniture is piled onto a truck.
(D) Some light fixtures are hanging above a dining room.

中譯
(A) 有些靠墊堆放在容器附近。
(B) 展示區擺放著一些沙發。
(C) 有些傢俱堆放在卡車上。
(D) 餐廳上方懸掛著一些燈具。

單字 stack 堆放　furniture 傢俱　pile 堆積
dining room 餐廳

7. 🎧澳洲男子／英國女子

Where is the nearest dry cleaner?
(A) On Cardinal Avenue.
(B) I'm nearly finished.
(C) It's for all clothing.

中譯
最近的乾洗店在哪裡？
(A) 在Cardinal大道。
(B) 我快完成了。
(C) 適合所有服裝。

單字 nearest 最近的　nearly 幾乎

8. 🎧美國女子／澳洲男子

Should we send the package today or tomorrow?
(A) Five pounds.
(B) Today is better.
(C) An international address.

中譯
我們應該今天還是明天寄包裹？
(A) 五磅。
(B) 今天比較好。
(C) 國際地址。

單字 international 國際的

9. 🎧澳洲男子／英國女子

Does the printer need a new ink cartridge?
(A) A double set of prints, please.
(B) Jamie has the posters.
(C) No, I just replaced it.

中譯
印表機需要新的墨水匣嗎？
(A) 請列印兩份。
(B) Jamie有海報。
(C) 不用，我剛換過了。

單字 replace 替換、替代

10. 🎧美國男子／美國女子

Who set up this display?
(A) The new winter boots.
(B) Jessica did.
(C) Mostly on the weekend.

中譯
誰佈置了這個展示區？
(A) 冬季新款靴子。
(B) Jessica做的。
(C) 主要是在週末。

單字 display 擺設、陳列品

11. 🎧英國女子／美國男子

The company retreat is in the summer, right?
(A) Right. It's scheduled for July.
(B) She's a repeat customer.
(C) The venue is modern.

中譯
公司的度假會議是在夏天對吧？
(A) 沒錯，預定在七月。
(B) 她是常客。
(C) 場地很現代化。

單字 retreat 度假會議　repeat customer 常客
venue 場地　modern 現代化的

12. 🎧美國女持／美國男子

> Can I try on these dresses?
> (A) I can take your shift.
> (B) Our dress code has changed.
> **(C) The shop is closing soon.**

中譯

我可以試穿這些衣服嗎？
(A) 我可以替你值班。
(B) 我們的服裝規定已更改。
(C) 商店很快就要關門了。

單字 try on 試穿　take a shift 代班　dress code 服裝規定

13. 🎧澳洲男子／英國女子

> Is there a secure place to leave my luggage?
> (A) A new credit card.
> **(B) Sure, behind the front desk.**
> (C) At the maximum weight.

中譯

有安全的地方可以寄放我的行李嗎？
(A) 新的信用卡。
(B) 當然，在櫃檯後方。
(C) 最大重量。

單字 secure 安全的、有把握的　luggage 行李
maximum 最大限度的　weight 重量

14. 🎧美國女子／澳洲男子

> Are you attending the trade fair on Friday or on Saturday?
> **(A) My ticket is for Saturday.**
> (B) The Valentine Hotel.
> (C) Yes, I was impressed.

中譯

你參加的是星期五還是星期六的貿易展覽會？
(A) 我的票是星期六的。
(B) Valentine飯店。
(C) 是的，令我印象深刻。

單字 attend 參加　trade fair 貿易展覽會
impressed 令人印象深刻的

15. 🎧美國男子／美國女子

> Why don't you reserve your table through the app?
> (A) Once a month.
> **(B) Can you show me how?**
> (C) She went out for lunch.

中譯

你為何不透過應用程式預訂座位呢？
(A) 每月一次。
(B) 你能演示給我看嗎？
(C) 她出去吃午餐了。

單字 reserve 預約

16. 🎧英國女子／澳洲男子

> When do I need to make a payment?
> (A) More than five hundred dollars.
> (B) For a magazine subscription.
> **(C) By the end of the week.**

中譯

我何時需要付款呢？
(A) 超過五百美元。
(B) 為了雜誌訂閱。
(C) 本週之前。

單字 make a payment 付款、支付

17. 🎧英國女子／美國男子

> Which taxi service do you usually use?
> **(A) I prefer to take the bus.**
> (B) No, these are brand-new.
> (C) It takes about twenty minutes.

中譯

你通常會用哪家計程車服務？
(A) 我比較喜歡搭公車。
(B) 沒有，這些是全新的。
(C) 大約需要二十分鐘。

18. 🎧美國女子／澳洲男子

> Could you work on preparing the orientation?
> (A) Five new employees.
> **(B) Certainly, I'd be happy to.**
> (C) I sat near the front.

中譯

你能準備一下迎新活動嗎？
(A) 五名新進員工。
(B) 當然，我很樂意。
(C) 我坐在靠前面。

19. 🎧美國女子／美國男子

> I ordered the banners two days ago.
> (A) The shop's grand opening.
> (B) Yes, she's a graphic designer.
> **(C) Custom orders take a week.**

中譯
我兩天前訂購了橫幅。
(A) 商店的盛大開幕。
(B) 是的,她是位平面設計師。
(C) 客製訂單需要一週的作業時間。

單字 grand opening 盛大開幕　custom 客製的

20. 🎧美國男子／英國女子

Where are the watermelons in your store?
(A) Those are only seasonal.
(B) I'll stop by the store.
(C) Forty-five cents per pound.

中譯
你們店裡的西瓜在哪裡?
(A) 只有當季才有。
(B) 我去店裡看看。
(C) 每磅45美分。

單字 seasonal 季節性的、當季的　stop by 順路造訪

21. 🎧澳洲男子／美國女子

Is this a good price for a tennis racket?
(A) The court in the corner.
(B) Not really. I've seen lower prices.
(C) Here is the lesson schedule.

中譯
這個網球拍的價格合理嗎?
(A) 在角落的球場。
(B) 並非如此。我看過更低的價格。
(C) 這是課程時間表。

單字 court 球場、場地

22. 🎧英國女子／澳洲男子

How was the conference call this morning?
(A) The committee had to reschedule.
(B) The main conference room.
(C) I'll check our inventory.

中譯
今天早上的電話會議怎麼樣?
(A) 委員會必須重新安排時間。
(B) 主會議室。
(C) 我會檢查我們的庫存。

單字 committee 委員會　reschedule 重新安排、改期
inventory 商品庫存

23. 🎧澳洲男子／美國女子

Doesn't the ferry leave at 2?
(A) I prefer to stand.
(B) That's too heavy.
(C) I believe so.

中譯
渡輪不是2點出發嗎?
(A) 我比較喜歡站著。
(B) 那太重了。
(C) 我想是的。

單字 stand 站立

24. 🎧英國女子／美國男子

We're replacing this machine, aren't we?
(A) Yes, he changed menu options.
(B) The budget isn't large enough.
(C) Around fifteen minutes.

中譯
我們要更換這台機器,不是嗎?
(A) 是,他更改了主選單的選項。
(B) 預算不夠多。
(C) 大約十五分鐘。

25. 🎧澳洲男子／英國女子

Do you think you can organize a party for Sumin's last day?
(A) Who gave them a gift?
(B) The updated organization chart.
(C) Of course, I'm confident I can.

中譯
你覺得你能為Sumin的最後一天籌備一場派對嗎?
(A) 誰送了他們禮物?
(B) 更新後的組織架構圖。
(C) 當然,我有信心可以做到。

單字 organize 籌備　organization 組織、結構
confident 有信心的、確信的

26. 🎧美國男子／美國女子

Why isn't the keypad at the laboratory entrance working?
(A) The manager sent an e-mail this afternoon.
(B) Down the hall on the right.
(C) No, after 7:00 P.M.

中譯
為何實驗室入口處的鍵盤無法使用?
(A) 今天下午經理發了一封電子郵件。
(B) 在走廊盡頭的右側。

(C) 不是,晚上7點以後。

單字 laboratory 實驗室　hall 走廊

27. 🎧 美國女子／美國男子

> We have just launched a new loyalty program.
> (A) I'm busy at lunchtime.
> **(B) Great, I'll check it out.**
> (C) She studied computer programming.

中譯

我們剛推出新的客戶回饋計劃。
(A) 午餐時間我很忙。
(B) 太好了,我會去查看。
(C) 她主修電腦程式設計。

單字 launch 推出、開始

28. 🎧 美國男子／英國女子

> Would you rather go to a concert or watch a movie?
> (A) Oh, is that your new watch?
> (B) Probably sometime this weekend.
> **(C) I love live performances.**

中譯

你比較想去看演唱會還是看電影?
(A) 啊,那是你的新手錶嗎?
(B) 可能在這週末的某個時段。
(C) 我喜歡現場表演。

29. 🎧 英國女子／美國男子

> Is the company's Internet service working?
> **(A) I couldn't get connected.**
> (B) No, we store them upstairs.
> (C) My username and password.

中譯

公司的網路運作是否正常?
(A) 我沒辦法連上。
(B) 不,我們把它們存放在樓上。
(C) 我的用戶名稱和密碼。

單字 username 用戶名稱

30. 🎧 澳洲男子／美國女子

> Who should we choose to take over as assistant manager?
> (A) Some clear production goals.
> **(B) The current one may not retire yet.**
> (C) Thank you for your assistance.

中譯

我們該選誰來接任副理呢?
(A) 一些明確的生產目標。
(B) 現任者可能還沒要退休。
(C) 謝謝你的協助。

單字 take over 接任　production 生產(量)
current 現在的　retire 退休　assistance 協助、支援

31. 🎧 美國女子／澳洲男子

> When can I expect my laptop to be repaired?
> **(A) We're waiting for some new components.**
> (B) At least two hundred dollars.
> (C) They're usually sold as a pair.

中譯

我的筆記型電腦預計何時可以修好?
(A) 我們正在等一些新零件。
(B) 至少兩百美元。
(C) 它們通常成對出售。

單字 component 零件、要素　pair 一雙、一對

32-34. 🎧 英國女子／美國男子

Questions 32-34 refer to the following conversation.

> W　Hi, this is Samantha from Daisy Flower Shop. ³²You left a message about the retirement party you're having on June 8.
>
> M　Yes, I wanted to confirm the delivery time. The event is scheduled to start at 7 P.M. So, could you deliver the flowers at 5:30?
>
> W　All right. ³³It's hard to estimate how long the driving time will be at that time of day. If our driver arrives early, will there be someone there to accept the delivery?
>
> M　Yes, I'll be there from four o'clock.
>
> W　Okay, ³⁴I'll send you the invoice for the flowers later today.

中譯

第 32-34 題,請參考下方對話。

女　嗨,我是Daisy花店的Samantha。**您留下一則有關6月8日舉行退休派對的訊息。**

男　是的,我想確認配送時間。活動預計晚上7點開始。請問花能在5點半送達嗎?

女　我知道了。**但難以預測當天那個時段需要多長的運送時間。** 如果我們的司機提前抵達,會有人來收貨嗎?

男　有的,我四點開始就會在那裡。

女　好,今天稍晚**我會把花朵訂單的發票寄給你。**

單字 estimate 預測　invoice 發票、請款單

99

32. 男子正在策劃什麼活動？
(A) 週年慶祝會
(B) 開幕活動
(C) 慈善募款活動
(D) 退休派對

33. 女子說什麼難以預測？
(A) 運費
(B) 可用的顏色
(C) 勞力成本
(D) 運送時間

換句話說 the driving time → the travel time

34. 女子會寄給男子什麼？
(A) 部分樣品
(B) 一些照片
(C) 發票
(D) 手冊

35-37. 🎧 澳洲男子／美國女子
Questions 35-37 refer to the following conversation.

> M ³⁵ The turnout for the open house at the Emerson Street property was so low. Only two potential buyers stopped by.
>
> W I know. ³⁶ Unfortunately, the wrong address was printed in our ad for the event. This made it difficult for people to find the site.
>
> M Well, the owner wants to sell this property as quickly as possible. ³⁷ We'd better hold another open house this weekend. I know that none of us were planning to work this weekend, but we need to make up for our mistake.

中譯
第 35-37 題，請參考下方對話。

男 Emerson街開放看屋日的到場人數非常少。只有兩名潛在買家停留參觀。
女 我知道。**不幸的是，活動廣告上的地址印錯了，導致人們很難找到正確地點。**
男 嗯，屋主希望盡快賣掉這間房屋。**我們最好於本週末再次開放看屋。**我知道我們本來都沒有計劃在這週末工作，但我們必須彌補錯失。

單字 turnout 到場人數　potential 潛在的
make up for 彌補

35. 說話者最有可能從事哪一種行業？
(A) 房地產
(B) 教育
(C) 製造業
(D) 醫療保健

36. 根據女子所述，是什麼導致問題發生？
(A) 惡劣的天氣狀況
(B) 錯過最後期限
(C) 部分設備損壞
(D) 廣告中的錯誤

37. 男子建議做什麼？
(A) 增加預算
(B) 舉辦另一場活動
(C) 雇用更多工人
(D) 閱讀一些評論

換句話說 open house → event

38-40. 🎧 澳洲男子／英國女子
Questions 38-40 refer to the following conversation.

> M Hi, Allison. It's Jake. ³⁸ I wanted to talk to you about the tour of the Harrisburg historical district that you're leading tomorrow.
>
> W I've just been reviewing my notes. It departs from the Waldeck Building at 9 A.M., right?
>
> M Yes, that's right. ³⁹ But I wanted to remind you about the new policy. You have to be at the departure point forty-five minutes before the scheduled start time, not twenty minutes.
>
> W I'll be sure to do that. Do you know if it's a large group?
>
> M ⁴⁰ I can see how many people have signed up. Just a moment, please.

中譯
第 38-40 題，請參考下方對話。

男 嗨，Allison，我是Jake。**我想談談明天你負責帶領的Harrisburg歷史街區之旅。**
女 我剛剛複習了我的筆記。上午9點從Waldeck大樓出發，對嗎？
男 是，沒錯。**但我想提醒你一項新政策。**你必須在預定開始時間前45分鐘就抵達出發地點，而不是20分鐘。
女 我一定會那樣做。你知道這是否為大團嗎？
男 **我可以看到有多少人報名，請稍等一下。**

單字 historical district 歷史街區　lead 帶領　departure point 出發地點　scheduled 預定的　sign up 報名

38. 女子最有可能從事什麼工作？
(A) 雜誌記者
(B) 導遊
(C) 博物館館長
(D) 公車司機

39. 男子為何打電話來？
(A) 提供提醒
(B) 提議升遷
(C) 取消活動
(D) 安排面試

單字 promotion 升遷

40. 男子接下來會做什麼事？
(A) 更新網站
(B) 發送時間表
(C) 確認參加者名單
(D) 解釋政策

單字 timetable 時間表、日程表　participant 參加者

41-43. 🎧 美國女子／美國男子
Questions 41-43 refer to the following conversation.

> W　Marco, ⁴¹I've found a new supplier for the wallpaper and floor coverings we use in our designs.
> M　That's great. We're getting busier and busier these days. ⁴²Now we have to make a decision about the best way to find new staff members.
> W　Well, we could post job openings online and see how much interest we get.
> M　Hmm… ⁴³Let's be careful not to spend too much time waiting for people to respond to online posts. Hiring a recruitment firm would be more expensive but a lot more efficient.

中譯
第 41-43 題，請參考下方對話。

女　Marco，**我為我們用於設計中的壁紙和地板材料找到了新的供應商。**
男　太好了。這幾天我們變得越來越忙。**現在我們必須決定尋找新員工的最佳方式。**
女　我們可以在網路上刊登職缺，看看有多少人會關注。
男　嗯… **要注意不要花太多時間等人回覆線上刊登的職缺。**雖然委託人力資源顧問公司比較花錢，但效率高很多。

單字 supplier 供應商　make a decision 決定　post 刊登　respond 回覆　recruitment firm 人力資源顧問公司

41. 說話者最有可能是誰？
(A) 銀行行員
(B) 室內設計師
(C) 送貨司機
(D) 安檢人員

42. 說話者必須做出什麼決定？
(A) 嘗試哪些軟體
(B) 在哪裡廣告產品
(C) 多久要開設新分店
(D) 如何招募新員工

單字 recruit 招募、募集

換句話說 the best way to find new staff members → How to recruit new employees

43. 男子提醒女子注意什麼？
(A) 使用老舊設備
(B) 延後完成專案
(C) 浪費過多時間
(D) 超出預算

單字 outdated 過時的　waste 浪費　exceed 超過

換句話說 spend too much time → Wasting a lot of time

44-46. 🎧 美國女子／澳洲男子／英國女子
Questions 44-46 refer to the following conversation with three speakers.

> W1　⁴⁴Welcome to Benson Institute of Corporate Training. How may I help you?
> M　⁴⁵I'm arranging a workshop for my team on May 8, and I need someone to give a presentation.
> W1　Jillian is one of our staff and can tell you more about it.
> W2　Hi, it just depends on the instructor's schedule. Is there a particular instructor you had in mind?
> M　Yes, Teresa Connelly.
> W2　All right. I can check with her.
> W1　Someone will call you about it later today.
> M　Thank you. ⁴⁶One of my coworkers took Ms. Connelly's class and highly recommended her.

中譯
第 44-46 題，請參考下方三人對話。

女1　歡迎來到Benson企業培訓學院。我能協助您什麼呢？
男　我正在為我的團隊安排5月8日的研討會，我需要有人來演講。
女1　我們的員工Jillian會告訴您更多相關資訊。
女2　您好，這得取決於講師的時間安排。您心中是否有特定的講師人選？
男　有的，Teresa Connelly。
女2　好的，我會跟她確認。
女1　今天稍晚會有人打電話給您。
男　謝謝你。我有位同事參加了Connelly女士的課程後，極力推薦她。

單字 instructor 講師

44. 說話者最有可能在哪裡？
(A) 在圖書館
(B) 在健身俱樂部
(C) 在商業學院
(D) 在藝術中心

換句話說 Institute of Corporate Training → business school

45. 男子想做什麼事？
(A) 聘請講師
(B) 應徵工作
(C) 進行演示
(D) 洽談銷售

單字 negotiate 洽談、協商

46. 男子如何得知Teresa Connelly？
(A) 透過網路搜尋
(B) 閱讀新聞報導
(C) 收到傳單
(D) 與同事談話

單字 flyer 傳單

47-49. 🎧英國女子／美國男子
Questions 47-49 refer to the following conversation.

> W Mr. Abrams, ⁴⁷I've measured all of the rooms in the building except Conference Room B, which is locked. To save time, I can just provide a size estimate so you can order your floor tiles.
>
> M ⁴⁸Actually, we need to know the exact measurements of the room. Because we'll be using a very expensive tile, we cannot afford to buy more than we have to. My colleague has the keys to that room, and he'll be back in twenty minutes. Can you wait for him?
>
> W Well… ⁴⁹I'll need to call my manager to see if it's okay for me to stay here longer. I'm supposed to leave for another job.
>
> M Okay. Please let me know.

中譯
第 47-49 題，請參考下方對話。

女 Abrams先生，我已經量過大樓內所有房間的尺寸，除了上鎖的B會議室。為了節省時間，我可以提供尺寸報價，以便你訂購地磚。

男 事實上，我們需要知道會議室的確切尺寸。我們使用的磁磚非常昂貴，所以沒辦法負擔超出我們所需的量。我同事有那間會議室的鑰匙，二十分鐘後他就會回來，你能等他一下嗎？

女 嗯… 我需打電話給經理，確認我是否在這多待一段時間。我還要去做其他的工作。

男 好的，再麻煩你告訴我。

單字 locked 上鎖　afford 負擔得起　be supposed to 應該要

47. 女子提到什麼問題？
(A) 她弄丟原始報告。
(B) 她無法進入房間。
(C) 部分產品已停產。
(D) 部分地板嚴重損壞。

單字 access 進入　discontinue（生產）中斷

48. 為何男子需要精確的測量？
(A) 材料的成本很高。
(B) 文件會被仔細檢查。
(C) 有助於他節省時間。
(D) 市政府要求的。

換句話說 we'll be using a very expensive tile → The cost of a material is high

49. 女子接下來最有可能做什麼？
(A) 取出一些工具
(B) 下訂快遞
(C) 聯絡主管
(D) 寫下估價

單字 unpack 取出、打開

換句話說 call my manager → contact a supervisor

50-52. 🎧澳洲男子／美國女子
Questions 50-52 refer to the following conversation.

> M ⁵⁰Hello, I have quite a few packages to send today. I've started my own business making handmade leather bags.
>
> W ⁵⁰I can help you with those. But do you plan to come to the post office often?
>
> M Yes, as I need to send items regularly.
>
> W ⁵¹You know, you can print your own postage labels at home if you download our smartphone application. Then just use one of the drop-off points around town.
>
> M Oh, right. ⁵²I saw one at my local supermarket. I'm headed there after this. That would have saved me a lot of time.

中譯
第 50-52 題，請參考下方對話。

男 你好，我今天有好幾個包裹要寄。我開始做手工皮包的生意了。

女 我來為你處理。不過，你打算經常來郵局嗎？

男 是的，因為我需要定期發貨。

女 你知道，如果你用智慧型手機下載我們的應用程式，就能在家列印郵資標籤。然後就可使用市區內任何的寄貨處。

男 啊，沒錯。我在當地一間超市有看到一個。這邊結束後我就要前往那裡。這樣會為我省下很多時間。

單字 package 包裹　regularly 定期地　postage 郵資　drop-off point 寄貨處

102

50. 女子最有可能是誰？
(A) 郵局員工
(B) 財務顧問
(C) 旅行社員工
(D) 工廠工人

51. 為何女子建議下載行動裝置應用程式？
(A) 獲取折扣
(B) 確認營業時間
(C) 推廣一些產品
(D) 在家列印標籤

52. 男子接下來打算去哪裡？
(A) 前往手機店
(B) 前往公車總站
(C) 前往超市
(D) 前往暢貨購物中心

53-55. 🎧 美國男子／美國女子
Question 53-55 refers to the following conversation.

> M　Let's take a look at our upcoming orders to make sure we're on track.
> W　⁵³I've just received a request from Fenton Industries for us to make three hundred office chairs, which they need by June 10. Since the current Valdez Hotel order is so large, ⁵⁴I'm wondering if we could push back their delivery date.
> M　Well, the Valdez Hotel is holding its grand opening at the end of the month.
> W　⁵⁴Oh, so they can't be flexible.
> M　Right. ⁵⁵We could add extra shifts, depending on Kyle's and Ben's availability, as they're the only ones who can operate the fabric-stretching machine.

中譯
第 53-55 題，請參考下方對話。
男　我們來看看即將到來的訂單，以確保我們有在進度上。
女　我剛收到Fenton工業公司的要求，希望我們在6月10日之前生產三百張辦公椅。目前由於Valdez飯店的訂單量過大，我想知道能否延後他們的交貨日期。
男　嗯，Valdez飯店將於本月底盛大開幕。
女　喔，那他們不可能調整時間。
男　沒錯。因為Kyle和Ben是唯一會操作織物拉伸機的人，所以我們可以依照他們的可行時間，增加額外的班。

單字　upcoming 即將到來的　　on track 順利進行中
push back 向後推、延後　　delivery date 交貨日期
flexible 有彈性的、可隨意調整的　　operate 操作

53. 說話者最有可能在哪裡工作？
(A) 在金融機構
(B) 在化學實驗室
(C) 在傢俱製造場
(D) 在美術用品店

54. 為何男子會說：「Valdez飯店將於本月底盛大開幕」？
(A) 拒絕提議
(B) 同意決定
(C) 提供保證
(D) 突顯競爭

單字　reassurance 保證、使放心　　highlight 強調

55. 男子針對Kyle和Ben提到什麼？
(A) 他們已經聯絡Fenton工業公司。
(B) 他們擁有專業技能。
(C) 他們是最新來的員工。
(D) 他們正在維修機器。

單字　specialized 專業的

56-58. 🎧 英國女子／美國男子／澳洲男子
Questions 56-58 refer to the following conversation with three speakers.

> W　All right, ⁵⁶we're here to discuss our online sales of cake-decorating equipment. Daniel?
> M1　Well, we sold about the same number of units last month as in the previous months.
> M2　That's surprising. ⁵⁷Since we lowered the price of the sets in August, I would have expected more sales.
> M1　We need a way to make customers engage with our product.
> M2　⁵⁸How about recording short video clips of different decorating techniques? Then we could post those on our website to inspire people.
> W　⁵⁸Good idea, Takuya. Do you know of any cake decorators who could do that?

中譯
第 56-58 題，請參考下方三人對話。
女　好，我們來討論一下蛋糕裝飾設備的線上銷售。Daniel？
男1　嗯，上個月我們的銷量幾乎與前幾個月一樣。
男2　真令人驚訝。因為我們在八月份調降了套組的價格，所以我預期銷量會增加。
男1　我們需要想辦法讓客戶對我們的產品產生興趣。
男2　錄製不同裝飾技巧的短影片怎麼樣？再把這些內容發布到我們的網站上引起人們關注。
女　好主意，Takuya。你知道有哪些蛋糕裝飾師可以執行這件事嗎？

單字 previous 先前的　lower 調降　technique 技巧、技術　inspire 引起、驅使

56. 會議的目的為何？
(A) 為產業活動做準備
(B) 選出適任人選
(C) 批准預算
(D) 討論產品銷售

換句話說 discuss our online sales of cake-decorating equipment → discuss product sales

57. 公司在八月份做了什麼？
(A) 調降價格。
(B) 更換管理階層。
(C) 推出新網站。
(D) 增加顏色選擇範圍。

單字 management 管理階層

58. 說話者打算做什麼？
(A) 與競爭對手合併
(B) 製作影片
(C) 舉辦比賽
(D) 列印手冊

單字 merge 合併

換句話說 recording short video clips → Create some videos

59-61. 🎧 美國男子／英國女子
Questions 59-61 refer to the following conversation.

> M　Hi, Vanessa. [59] I'm sure you've heard that representatives from the Mumbai branch will be coming to our office for a visit. They've just confirmed that it will be on April 3.
>
> W　Oh, you're in charge of hosting them, right? That must be a lot of work.
>
> M　Yes, there are a lot of things to plan. [60] And I want to make sure I'm respectful of their culture. I know you've spent a lot of time in India.
>
> W　Unfortunately, I have to go right now. [61] A reporter from the *Westbury Times* is about to call to interview me about our environmental initiatives. How about this afternoon? I'd be happy to share some tips.

中譯
第 59-61 題，請參考下方對話。
男　嗨，Vanessa。**相信你已經聽說孟買分公司的代表要來參觀我們的辦公室。他們剛剛確認將於 4 月 3 日來訪。**
女　哦，由你負責接待他們對吧？應該會有很多工作。

男　是的，有許多事需要計畫。**另外，我要確保我有尊重他們的文化。**我知道你在印度待過很長一段時間。
女　遺憾的是，我現在要走了。**有位來自《Westbury時報》的記者正要打電話來採訪我們的環保計畫。**今天下午怎麼樣？我很樂意分享一些祕訣。

單字 representative 代表　in charge of 負責　host 接待　respectful 尊重的、恭敬的　initiative 計劃、主動的行動

59. 4月3日最有可能發生什麼事？
(A) 安全系統會改變。
(B) 召開產業會議。
(C) 一些訪客會造訪公司。
(D) 宣布幾名獲獎者。

60. 為何男人會說：「你在印度待過很長一段時間」？
(A) 解釋延遲的原因
(B) 尋求幫助
(C) 投訴
(D) 表達驚訝

61. 女子接下來會做什麼？
(A) 參與某個訪談
(B) 聯絡旅行社
(C) 確認她會出席
(D) 發送備忘錄

單字 participate in 參與　attendance 出席、參加

62-64. 🎧 澳洲男子／美國女子
Questions 62-64 refer to the following conversation and floor layout.

> M　[62] Caroline, next weekend we will be showing the latest documentary about art trends by director Victor Barbosa. Which room do you think would be best for the event?
>
> W　Well, [63] I think we should set up chairs in the room with the oil paintings. The sound quality will be best in there.
>
> M　Good point. And it doesn't have big displays like the Sculpture Room does.
>
> W　Exactly. Oh, and [64] I spoke to the site manager yesterday. He said he wants to serve complimentary snacks and drinks as people arrive.

中譯
第 62-64 題，請參考下方對話和樓層平面圖。
男　Caroline，**下週末我們將放映由導演Victor Barbosa執導關於藝術趨勢的最新紀錄片**，你認為這項活動最適合在哪個展間舉行？
女　嗯，**我想我們應該在油畫展間內舉行。**那裡的音響效果最好。

104

男　你說的對。而且那裡不像雕塑展間有大型展示品。
女　沒錯。啊，我昨天和場地經理談過。他說他想在人們抵達現場時，提供免費的點心和飲料。

單字　display 展示（品）　complimentary 免費的

1號展間 雕塑	3號展間 油畫
2號展間 水彩畫	入口　4號展間 照片

62. 說話者正在籌備什麼活動？
(A) 志工培訓
(B) 藝術品拍賣
(C) 繪畫展示
(D) 電影放映

單字　auction 拍賣

63. 請查看圖表。女子建議使用哪個展間舉辦活動？
(A) 1號展間
(B) 2號展間
(C) 3號展間
(D) 4號展間

64. 根據女子所述，場地經理想提供什麼？
(A) 音樂娛樂
(B) 一些茶點
(C) 免費停車
(D) 團體照

換句話說　snacks and drinks → some refreshments

65-67. 🎧 英國女子／澳洲男子
Questions 65-67 refer to the following conversation and product catalog.

W　Hi, Curtis. [65] I didn't think anyone would be in the conference room. The employee lounge is full, so I thought I'd have my lunch in here. Do you mind if I sit with you?

M　Go right ahead. I was just browsing this catalog.

W　Oh, are you buying something as a gift?

M　Yes. [66] My sister is receiving an award in Cleveland at the end of the month. I'm going to the ceremony in person and wanted to give her something to congratulate her.

W　Oh, that'll be a nice trip.

M　She already has a lot of necklaces, so [67] I think this bracelet would be perfect.

W　It looks lovely.

中譯
第65-67題，請參考下方對話和產品目錄。
女　嗨，Curtis。我以為會議室裡沒有人。員工休息室滿了，所以我想在這裡吃午餐。你介意我跟你一起坐嗎？
男　請便。我只是在瀏覽這個目錄。
女　哦，你要買什麼禮物？
男　是的。我妹妹這個月底會在Cleveland領獎。我要親自去參加頒獎典禮，並送她一份賀禮。
女　哦，那會是一趟很棒的旅行。
男　她已經有很多項鍊了，所以我覺得這個手環很完美。
女　看起來很不錯。

單字　in person 親自　necklace 項鍊　bracelet 手環、手鍊

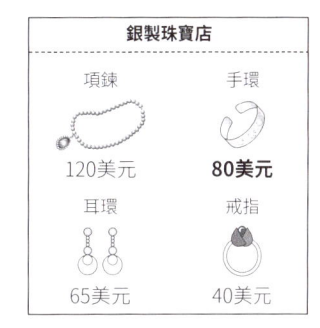

銀製珠寶店

項鍊　　　手環
120美元　　**80美元**
耳環　　　戒指
65美元　　40美元

65. 說話者在哪裡？
(A) 在員工休息室
(B) 在火車站
(C) 在餐廳
(D) 在會議室

66. 男子為何要前往Cleveland？
(A) 出席頒獎典禮
(B) 視察建築物
(C) 演講
(D) 獲頒獎項

單字　inspect 視察

67. 請查看圖表。男子可能會花多少錢？
(A) 120美元
(B) 80美元
(C) 65美元
(D) 40美元

68-70. 🎧 美國男子／美國女子

Questions 68-70 refer to the following conversation and chart.

> **M** Hi, Marta. [68] How are you settling into the new work environment since you transferred to our branch last month?
>
> **W** Well, this shop has a much larger selection, so I'm still learning about some of the merchandise. For example, earlier today, [69] a customer was looking for a cordless vacuum with a removable air filter. I wasn't sure which model would be best.
>
> **M** You can check the product chart to view the features quickly. See?
>
> **W** Oh, that's really helpful. Thanks.
>
> **M** Sure, anytime. By the way, [70] did you hear that the store is going to extend its business hours from next week? We can pick up extra shifts and earn extra money before the holidays. So, I was happy to hear that.

中譯

第 68-70 題，請參考下方對話和圖表。

男　嗨，Marta。**上個月調到我們分店後，你對新工作環境適應得如何？**

女　嗯，這家店商品的選擇多了很多，所以我還在了解某些商品。舉例來說，今天稍早的時候，**有位顧客正在尋找有可拆式濾網的無線吸塵器**。我不確定哪種型號最好。

男　你可以查看產品圖來快速確認功能。有看到嗎？

女　哦，這真的很有幫助。謝謝。

男　不客氣，我隨時樂意幫忙。對了，**你有聽說本店將從下週開始延長營業時間嗎？我們可以在假期前增加排班來賺更多錢，所以我很高興聽到這個消息。**

單字　settle into 適應　　transfer 調職　　removable 可拆式
feature 以…為特色

吸塵器型號	無線	可拆式濾網	除塵刷
Botello	✓		
Activa	✓		✓
Mammoth		✓	✓
Goodwin	✓	✓	

68. 女子上個月做了什麼事？
(A) 她買了一台吸塵器。
(B) 她調到其他分店。
(C) 她獲得升遷。
(D) 她收到了證書。

69. 請查看圖表。哪種型號具備顧客要求的功能？
(A) Botello
(B) Activa
(C) Mammoth
(D) Goodwin

70. 男子對什麼事感到高興？
(A) 年度獎金
(B) 員工優惠
(C) 有薪假
(D) 更改營業時間

71-73. 🎧 英國女子

Questions 71-73 refer to the following tour information.

> **W** [71] Welcome to this virtual tour of Irvine Theater. I am the owner, Lucy Gibbs. It's my pleasure to show you our beautiful site. Since its construction in 1910, this theater has been providing a wide variety of live performances. And [72] we're well known for the unique architectural features of the building, some of which I'll be showing you today. At the end of the tour, [73] please answer a few questions to share your opinions. We'll e-mail you a 20 percent discount coupon as a thank-you.

中譯

第 71-73 題，請參考下方旅遊資訊。

女　**歡迎來到Irvine劇場的虛擬導覽。我是業主Lucy Gibbs**。很高興能向大家展示這個美麗的地方。自1910年建成以來，該劇場舉辦過各式各樣的現場演出。**此建築物以獨特的建築特色而聞名**，今天我將展示其中一部分給大家看。參觀結束後，**請回答幾個問題來分享你的意見。我們會用電子郵件發送給你一張八折折價券作為謝禮。**

單字　a wide variety of 各式各樣的　　architectural features 建築特色

71. 說話者是誰？
(A) 工廠廠長
(B) 建築工人
(C) 劇場業主
(D) 電腦技術員

72. 該設施以什麼聞名？
(A) 募款活動
(B) 知識淵博的工作人員
(C) 獨特的建築物
(D) 現代化的設備

單字　architecture 建築結構、建築物

73. 根據說話者，聽者如何取得優惠券？
(A) 提供一些回饋
(B) 下載一些軟體
(C) 訂閱電子報
(D) 發送電子郵件給說話者

換句話說 answer a few questions to share your opinions → providing some feedback

74-76. 🎧 美國男子
Questions 74-76 refer to the following talk.

> M Thanks for joining the first session of World Tastes, our newly offered four-week course. Each week, ⁷⁴ we'll cover how to create delicious dishes from around the world. You'll learn to make several easy one-pan meals. Some of these recipes come from ⁷⁵ my book, *Henry at Home*. It was published just last week. Now, ⁷⁶ some of you have asked whether you can take any leftover dishes with you at the end of the class. Yes, I have some containers here.

中譯
第 74-76 題，請參考下方談話。

男　感謝各位參加我們新開設為期四周的課程，〈世界味道〉的第一堂課。每週**我們都會介紹如何製作世界各地的美味佳餚**。你將學會如何用一個鍋子製作幾道簡單的餐點。當中有些食譜出自**我的書《Henry在家》。書剛於上週出版**。有些人詢問課程結束後，**能否帶走剩下的食物**。可以，我這邊有一些保鮮盒。

單字　recipe 食譜　leftover 剩下的食物　container 容器、貨櫃

74. 聽者最感興趣的可能是什麼？
(A) 繪畫
(B) 詩詞
(C) 語言學習
(D) 烹飪

75. 說話者最近做了什麼？
(A) 他出國讀書。
(B) 他開設網站。
(C) 他出版書籍。
(D) 他主持網路廣播節目。

單字　host 主持

76. 部分聽者詢問什麼事？
(A) 獲得個人建議
(B) 把食物帶回家
(C) 查看課堂教材
(D) 採買用品

單字　individual 個別的

77-79. 🎧 美國女子
Questions 77-79 refer to the following telephone message.

> W Hi, Adam. It's Isabelle. I'm calling about the work on Mercer Bridge, which your crew has been assigned to. ⁷⁷ The bridge closure is scheduled for Tuesday, so that is the official start of the project. ⁷⁸ Remember that you'll need to meet at the Coleman Building at 6 A.M. and ride to the site together with your coworkers. That's because parking at the site is very limited. ⁷⁹ There are several additional pieces of safety equipment needed for this project. I'll give those to you on Monday when you arrive. See you then.

中譯
第 77-79 題，請參考下方電話留言。

女　嗨，Adam，我是Isabelle。我打電話來跟你說你們員工被分配到Mercer大橋的工作。**橋樑預計於週二關閉，代表該項目正式開始**。**請記得早上6點要在Coleman大樓集合，和你的同事一起搭車前往現場**。這因為現場的停車位非常有限。**該項目還需要一些額外的安全設備**。你週一抵達時我會給你，到時見。

單字　assign 分配　closure 關閉
safety equipment 安全設備

77. 說話者說星期二會發生什麼事？
(A) 公布工作人員名單。
(B) 鋪設停車場。
(C) 完成一項專案。
(D) 將關閉橋樑。

單字　pave 鋪設

78. 說話者提醒聽者要做什麼事？
(A) 共乘前往地點
(B) 出示停車證
(C) 報名參加培訓課程
(D) 穿著保暖衣物

單字　display 出示、表現、顯示

換句話說 ride to the site together with your coworkers → Carpool to a site

79. 將會提供聽者什麼東西？
(A) 安全裝備
(B) 工作時間表
(C) 同事們的聯絡方式
(D) 使用者手冊

換句話說 safety equipment → safety gear

107

80-82. 🎧 美國女子

Questions 80-82 refer to the following talk.

> W [80]Today I'll show you how to use the features of the new application for making customer appointments. You no longer need to be in the salon to make a booking for someone. [81]This may be helpful when you meet a potential new customer in need of a haircut or other styling services. You can help them make an appointment right from your smartphone. Also, [82]one feature that's nice is that this program automatically sends an alert to your phone one hour before you need to see a customer. That'll help you make sure you're here when you need to be.

中譯

第 80-82 題，請參考下方談話。

女 今天我將向大家展示如何使用新應用程式的功能進行顧客預約。你們再也不用到美容院裡幫人預約了。在你們遇到需要剪髮或其他造型服務的潛在新顧客時會有所幫助。可以直接用智慧型手機幫他們預約。另外，**還有一個不錯的功能**。該應用程式會在你要見顧客的一小時前，自動發送提醒通知到你的手機。這將有助於確保有顧客在時，你在現場。

單字 feature 功能、特色　potential 潛在的
in need of 需要…　alert 通知

80. 說話者正在示範什麼？
(A) 經營美容院的方式
(B) 吸引新顧客的方式
(C) 如何使用智慧型手機應用程式
(D) 如何重新啟動安全系統

81. 聽者最有可能是誰？
(A) 醫生
(B) 電腦程式設計師
(C) 藥劑師
(D) 髮型設計師

82. 說話者提到了什麼特色？
(A) 自動通知
(B) 免手動操作
(C) 輕鬆上傳
(D) 每日提醒

83-85. 🎧 英國女子

Questions 83-85 refer to the following excerpt from a meeting.

> W I'd like to start off [83]our monthly library staff meeting with some good news. A member of the community has donated funds so that we can purchase self-checkout machines. The machines are easy to operate. However, [84]we expect you to pay attention to patrons using them in case they need your help. They'll be positioned near the circulation desk for now. [85]After the building expansion project is finished in October, we may move them to another area.

中譯

第 83-85 題，請參考下方會議摘錄。

女 我想以一些好消息來開始**我們圖書館工作人員的月會**。有位社區居民捐款讓我們購買自助借書機。這些機器很容易操作。但是，**希望你們能注意使用機器的常客，他們可能需要各位的協助**。機器會暫時放在圖書借還櫃檯附近。待十月擴建工程結束後，我們可能會把機器搬到其他區域。

單字 donate 捐贈　fund 資金　operate 操作
pay attention 注意、關注　patron 顧客、常客
circulation desk 圖書借還櫃檯　expansion 擴建

83. 聽者最有可能在哪裡工作？
(A) 在銀行
(B) 在超市
(C) 在博物館
(D) 在圖書館

84. 聽者被要求做什麼事？
(A) 參加培訓課程
(B) 比平常提早上班
(C) 注意需要協助的人
(D) 在機器附近張貼一些說明

單字 assistance 幫助、協助

換句話說 pay attention to patrons → watch for people needing assistance

85. 說話者提到十月會發生什麼事？
(A) 將會出現新職缺。
(B) 將舉辦募款活動。
(C) 建築工程將會完工。
(D) 將會公開報告。

單字 make public 公開

換句話說 the building expansion project is finished → A building project will be completed

86-88. 🎧 美國男子

Questions 86-88 refer to the following advertisement.

> M Looking to create a beautiful and relaxing outdoor space at home? Norcross Solutions can help you achieve the look you want. [86] Our experienced designers can create the garden of your dreams. And they'll take into account your lifestyle when it comes to the level of maintenance needed. [87] Have no idea where to start? We have a large photo gallery. Check it out at www.norcrosssolutions.com. [87] We're sure you'll find some inspiration there. Then book your free consultation. Norcross Solutions has been a trusted business for over twenty years, and [88] we are proud to support businesses in the area, purchasing supplies from them whenever possible.

中譯
第 86-88 題，請參考下方廣告。

男 想要在家中打造一個美麗又舒適的戶外空間嗎？Norcross 解決方案公司能幫你達成想要的空間外觀。**我們經驗豐富的設計師可打造出你的夢想花園。**他們會考量你的生活方式，確認所需的維護管理程度。**不知道從何開始嗎？我們擁有龐大的照片庫。請至 www.norcrosssolutions.com 查看。我們相信你會在那裡找到一些靈感。**接下來可以預約免費諮詢。二十多年來，Norcross 解決方案公司一直是間值得信賴的企業。**我們十分自豪能盡可能從當地企業採購用品，藉此來支持他們。**

單字 achieve 達成、獲得　take into account 考量
maintenance 維護、保養　consultation 諮詢　trust 信賴

86. 廣告內容為何？
(A) 線上課程
(B) 不動產仲介公司
(C) 建築檢查服務
(D) 花園設計服務

87. 說話者為何會說：「我們擁有龐大的照片庫」？
(A) 使緩慢的網站速度合理化
(B) 提供保證
(C) 解釋一項決定
(D) 批評競爭對手

單字 criticize 批評

88. 說話者認為企業引以為傲的是什麼？
(A) 支持當地企業
(B) 經濟實惠的價格
(C) 回應速度快
(D) 高評價的客戶服務

單字 rating 等級、排名

89-91. 🎧 澳洲男子

Questions 89-91 refer to the following speech.

> M [89] Good evening, everyone, and thanks for attending our quarterly staff dinner. Before we begin, I'd like to make an announcement. [90] At the moment, our receptionist, Diana Dawson, always has lunch on site so she can answer phones while everyone is away. Well, I'm sure Diana would like a few lunches out. [90] If you have some time, please let me know. And one last thing. You've all made great contributions to the company so far this year, and I'd particularly like to recognize [91] Ahmed Sharma, who came up with a creative solution to our problem with limited storage space.

中譯
第 89-91 題，請參考下方演講。

男 大家晚安，感謝各位參加我們的季度員工晚宴。在我們開始前，我想宣布一個消息。**我們的接待人員 Diana Dawson 總是在公司現場吃午餐，以便於大家不在時，能夠接聽電話。**嗯，我相信 Diana 偶爾也想外出享用午餐。有空的人，麻煩請告訴我。還有最後一件事。今年截至目前為止，大家都為公司做了巨大的貢獻。我特別想表揚 **Ahmed Sharma**，針對我們收納空間有限的問題，他提出了創意的解決方案。

單字 quarterly 季度的　make a contribution 做出貢獻
recognize 表揚　storage space 收納空間

89. 演講在哪裡進行？
(A) 在培訓研討會上
(B) 在員工晚宴上
(C) 在音樂比賽上
(D) 在記者會上

90. 說話者說：「我相信 Diana 偶爾也想外出享用午餐」，意味著什麼？
(A) 他可以推薦餐廳。
(B) 他想歡迎一位新員工。
(C) 他有關於禮物的建議。
(D) 他正在為一項任務尋找自願者。

91. 說話者提到 Ahmed Sharma 什麼？
(A) 他分享一個創新的想法。
(B) 他將要離開公司。
(C) 他擁有很多經驗。
(D) 他很快會發表演說。

單字 innovative 創新的、革新的

換句話說 came up with a creative solution → shared an innovative idea

92-94. 🎧 英國女子

Questions 92-94 refer to the following talk.

> W Since everyone is here, let's get this committee meeting started. ⁹²**The next upcoming project for our department is the cleanup efforts at Grove Park.** This site was badly hit by the recent storm, so there are a lot of tree branches, leaves, and trash all over the ground. ⁹³**I know our group is very small, but we've already started gathering the names of potential volunteers**, and **we have a very long list**. Fortunately, it will be fairly inexpensive to carry out this work. ⁹⁴**I've calculated the approximate expenses on this report, and I'll distribute copies in a moment.**

中譯
第 92-94 題，請參考下方談話。

女　既然大家都到齊了，我們就開始本次的委員會會議。**我們部門即將進行的項目是Grove公園的清潔工作。**該處最近遭受暴風雨的嚴重襲擊，地上遍布大量樹枝、樹葉和垃圾。**我知道我們的團隊規模很小，但我們已開始召集潛在志工，且我們有一長串的名單。**幸運的是，進行這項工作的成本相當低。**我已在這份報告中計算好大致的費用，稍後我會分發影本給大家。**

單字 fairly 相當地、極為　carry out 執行、完成　calculate 計算　approximate 大致的　distribute 分發

92. 談話的重點為何？
(A) 改善回收服務
(B) 清掃公園
(C) 修建運動跑道
(D) 種植更多樹木

93. 說話者說：「我們有一長串的名單」，意味著什麼？
(A) 有些工作分配可能會變動。
(B) 需要延長最後期限。
(C) 聽者將會得到許多支援。
(D) 會議可能比原定時間長。

單字 assignment 分配、指派　extend 延長

94. 說話者將發放什麼東西？
(A) 地圖
(B) 名片
(C) 提議日程表
(D) 成本估算

單字 proposed 提議的　estimate 估價

95-97. 🎧 澳洲男子

Questions 95-97 refer to the following speech and ticket.

> M Good evening everyone. Welcome to this performance by the Lexington Dance Troupe. ⁹⁵**All proceeds from this event will go toward replacing the roof of the outdoor stage at Carrick Park.** ⁹⁶**After the performance, be sure to visit the lobby, where some of the dancers will be signing posters.** Now, we've got the winning number for tonight's prize drawing. Let's see... ⁹⁷**the person sitting in seat H35 has won a $50 gift certificate!** Stop by the box office at intermission to collect your prize.

中譯
第 95-97 題，請參考下方演講和票券。

男　大家晚安。歡迎觀賞Lexington舞蹈團的表演。**此次活動所有收益將用於更換Carrick公園戶外舞台的屋頂。**表演結束後，請務必造訪大廳，有些舞者將在海報上簽名。現在我們拿到了今晚抽獎的中獎號碼。讓我看看…**坐在座位H35的人中了50美元的禮券！**請於中場休息時間前往售票處領取獎品。

單字 proceeds 收益　prize drawing 抽獎　intermission 中場休息時間

1	→	Lexington舞蹈團演出
		五月11日｜晚上8:00
2	→	座位：H35
3	→	價格：15.50美元
4	→	票券號碼：2367

95. 為什麼要舉行表演？
(A) 為社區工程籌措資金
(B) 慶祝劇場週年紀念
(C) 鼓勵人們加入團體
(D) 推廣全國巡演

96. 表演結束後會發生什麼事？
(A) 拍攝一些照片。
(B) 門票可供出售。
(C) 回答一些問題。
(D) 在海報上簽名。

97. 請查看圖表。為得知抽獎結果，聽者應確認哪一行？
(A) 第1行
(B) 第2行
(C) 第3行
(D) 第4行

98-100. 🎧 美國男子

Questions 98-100 refer to the following podcast and instructions.

> M　Welcome to the Gamer's World podcast. Our sponsor today is Dorsey. Enhance your gaming experience online with ⁹⁸ Dorsey's microphones, speakers, and headphones. Visit www.dorseyproducts.com to find out more. Today, I'll be reviewing the board game Igor's Quest. ⁹⁹ This game can be played by two to eight people. It's wonderful to have such a wide range like that. Though the artwork is a bit simplistic, this is a great strategy game. The setup process is easy to understand. However, ¹⁰⁰ placing the resource tokens on the board takes a long time. I think the game designers could have organized that better.

中譯

第 98-100 題，請參考下方廣播節目和說明書。

男　歡迎收聽〈玩家世界〉廣播節目。我們今天的贊助商是 Dorsey。使用 **Dorsey** 的麥克風、喇叭和耳機，提升你的線上遊戲體驗。請至 www.dorseyproducts.com 獲取更多內容。今天我將評論桌遊《Igor的任務》。**這款遊戲可供二至八名玩家一起玩。人數範圍如此之廣真是厲害**。雖然插圖有點過於簡約，但這是一款很棒的戰略遊戲。設定過程很容易理解。但**將資源代幣放到遊戲板上需要很長的時間。我認為遊戲設計者應該可以整理得更好**。

單字　enhance 提升　　artwork 插圖、藝術品　simplistic 簡約的　　organize 安排、組織

Igor的任務—設定過程

步驟1.	展開遊戲板
步驟2.	**把資源代幣放到遊戲板上**
步驟3.	依照顏色排序卡片
步驟4.	選擇玩家角色

98. 根據說話者所述，Dorsey製作什麼樣的產品？
(A) 音響設備
(B) 辦公傢俱
(C) 平板電腦
(D) 軟體程式

99. 說話者喜歡《Igor的任務》哪一個部分？
(A) 人物角色
(B) 使用說明
(C) 插圖
(D) 玩家數量

100. 請查看圖表。說話者認為哪一步驟可以改進？
(A) 步驟1
(B) 步驟2
(C) 步驟3
(D) 步驟4

101. 名詞的位置＋主動詞單複數一致性

解說　空格前方有冠詞，後方為連接詞引導的子句，表示空格要填入名詞。選項中的 (A) receipt 和 (D) receipts 皆為名詞，而空格前方有不定冠詞，表示空格要填入單數可數名詞，因此答案為 (A)。

中譯　如果顧客需要，銷售人員可以重新列印收據。

102. 填入介系詞＋詞彙題

解說　空格前後各連接一個名詞片語，表示要填入介系詞。選項中的 (A) for 和 (B) until 皆為介系詞，而根據文意，表示「請前來參加社區野餐」較為適當，因此答案為 (A)，意思為「為了…」。

中譯　本週六請前來Fairfield公園參加一年一度的社區野餐。

單字　annual 一年一次的　　community 社區、社會　until 直到…

103. 填入副詞

解說　空格位在助動詞 can 和動詞 check 之間，應填入副詞，因此答案為 (C) easily。

中譯　藉由使用銀行的智慧型手機應用程式，客戶可以輕鬆確認帳戶餘額。

單字　balance 餘額、剩餘部分、均衡、協調

104. 名詞詞彙題program

中譯　健身房會員可透過規律的運動計畫，提升體能健康。

單字　fitness（身體上的）健康　　program 計畫　transaction 交易　sequel 續集　response 答覆、回應

105. 主動詞單複數一致性、時態

解說　主詞 it 為單數，表示動詞也要使用單數形態，才符合主動詞單複數的一致性。選項中的 (C) are selecting 和 (D) select 皆為複數動詞，因此並非答案；(B) to select 不適合置於動詞的位置，因此答案要選 (A) will select。

中譯　甜蜜時光烘焙坊的發言人證實，明年將會選址開設新的零售分店。

單字　spokesperson 發言人　　confirm 證實、確認　site 地點、場所　　retail 零售的　　branch 分店、分公司

106. 介系詞詞彙題from

中譯　一年一度的舞蹈比賽包含來自全國各地的20個團體。

單字　competition 比賽、競爭對手　　include 包含　from 來自　　except 除了…　　as 跟…一樣、作為　regarding 關於…

111

107. 人稱代名詞〔主格〕
解說 空格後方連接動詞，表示空格應填入適當的字詞，當作主詞使用，因此答案為人稱代名主格 (D) They。
中譯 他們在包裝前，檢查了所有產品是否有製造上的瑕疵。
單字 product 產品　manufacturing defect 製造上的瑕疵
prior to 在…之前　package 包裝

108. 名詞詞彙題 pillowcase
中譯 飯店的客房清潔部門可應要求更換床單、枕頭套和其他寢具用品。
單字 upon request 應要求　housekeeping 客房清潔、家務
replace 更換、替換　pillowcase 枕頭套
bedding 寢具　curtain 窗簾　carpet 地毯
lighting 燈具

109. 填入介系詞＋詞彙題
解說 空格前方有主詞和動詞，為一個結構完整的子句，空格後方連接名詞，表示空格應填入介系詞。選項中的 (A) after 和 (B) between 為介系詞，而根據文意，表示「春季課程表將於明天早上 9 點後發布」較為適當，因此答案為 (A)，意思為「在…之後」
中譯 Chung商學院的春季課程表將於明天早上9點後發布於網站上。
單字 post 發布　between （兩者）之間

110. 形容詞詞彙題 based
中譯 暢銷作家George Vasquez目前住在加拿大多倫多。
單字 currently 目前、現在　based 有根基的、有基地的
committed 盡心盡力的、堅定的　written 寫下的
moved 受感動的

111. 填入名詞＋詞彙題
解說 空格前方為形容詞，表示空格應填入名詞。選項中的 (B) occupant 和 (C) occupation 皆為名詞，而根據文意，表示「相關職業經驗」較為適當，因此答案為 (C)，意思為「職業」。
中譯 成功申請者必須具備記帳員或相關職業經驗。
單字 successful applicant 成功申請者
bookkeeper 記帳員　related 相關的
occupant 居住者、使用者

112. 形容詞詞彙題 rapid
中譯 Carlyle物流在不犧牲服務品質的情況下快速成長，因而受到讚譽。
單字 admire 欽佩、稱讚　achieve 達成、實現
rapid 快速的　sacrifice 犧牲
enthusiastic 熱情的、熱烈的　frank 坦白的　native 本土的

113. 填入副詞
解說 空格位在助動詞 can 和動詞 accommodate 之間，表示空格應填入副詞，因此答案為 (B) comfortably。
中譯 大舞廳可輕鬆容納多達三百名客人。
單字 accommodate 容納

114. 名詞詞彙題 approval
中譯 所有Tazma公司員工在購買昂貴設備前，都應獲得財務部門的批准。
單字 approval 批准、認可、贊成　finance 財政、財務
purchase 購買　equipment 道具、設備
entry 進入、加入、參加、參展作品
regard 考慮、視為　interest 興趣

115. 填入分詞
解說 空格前方為介系詞，後方連接名詞片語，表示空格應填入適合修飾後方名詞的字詞。選項中只有過去分詞能修飾名詞，因此答案為 (C) extended。
中譯 PJ購物中心希望透過延長營業時間來促進生意。
單字 boost 提高、促進　business 生意
extend 延長、擴大（事業、勢力等）
business hours 營業時間

116. 填入動詞＋時態
解說 空格置於從屬連接詞 while 引導的子句中，且位在動詞的位置。(A) is being 和 (D) has been 皆為動詞，而根據文意，表示「正在接受面試」較適當，因此答案為現在進行式 (A)。
中譯 應徵者接受委員會面試期間，任何人不得進出會議室。
單字 enter 進入、入場、輸入　job candidate 應徵者

117. 填入名詞
解說 空格前方為形容詞，後方連接介系詞片語，表示空格應填入名詞，因此答案為 (B) specification。
中譯 團隊負責人強調，需要反覆檢查專案的每項技術規格。
單字 crew 團隊、小組　emphasize 強調
technical 技術的、專門的、技術性的
specification 規格、明細單　double-check 反覆檢查

118. 副詞詞彙題 directly
中譯 Jacamo公司員工的所有休假申請，應直接交給部門主管。
單字 request 要求、請求　directly 直接、即刻
entirely 完全地、徹底地　hardly 幾乎不
fairly 頗為、相當地、公正地

119. 填入動名詞
解說 空格前方為介系詞，後方連接名詞片語，表示空格要填入適合的字詞，當作介系詞的受詞，同時連接名詞片語當作受詞，因此答案為動名詞 (A) limiting。
中譯 Cayla博物館透過限制在特定時間進入的遊客數量，來保

持舒適的氛圍。

單字 maintain 維持（關係、狀態、程度等）
relaxing 舒適的、令人放鬆的　atmosphere 氛圍

120. 形容詞詞彙題innovative
中譯 PowerVox找出新穎且創新的方法，解決廢棄物處理的成本問題。
單字 innovative 創新的、革新的　disposal 處理、處置
loyal 忠誠的　casual 隨性的、不拘禮節的
appointed 任命的

121. 填入限定詞
解說 空格應填入適當的字詞，修飾後方的名詞片語 job applicant。選項中只有疑問限定詞 (D) which 可以修飾名詞，故為正解。(A) if 和 (B) whenever 為連接詞，若填入空格中，需在 job applicant 前方加冠詞才行。另外，they believe 前方省略 that，引導名詞子句 '------- ~ role'。
中譯 委員會成員將會告訴我們，他們認為哪位應徵者最適合該職位。
單字 be suitable for 適合⋯

122. 連接詞詞彙題although
中譯 儘管Ericson建築公司的薪資高於平均水準，該公司在徵才方面仍面臨困難。
單字 although 儘管　wage 薪資、報酬
have difficulty with 在⋯方面有困難
recruitment 徵才、招聘　because 因為⋯
as if 好像⋯　whether 不管是⋯（或是）

123. 現在分詞vs.過去分詞
解說 空格前方為動詞，後方連接名詞，表示空格要填入適合修飾後方名詞的字詞。選項中，只有過去分詞 (B) rejected 和現在分詞 (C) rejecting 可以修飾名詞。修飾對象為 manuscripts，表示被動關係「被拒絕」較符合文意，因此答案為 (B)。
中譯 Garrison出版社將被拒絕的原稿存檔五年，以備日後市場需要這些作品。
單字 manuscript （書籍的）原稿、手稿
in case 以備不時之需　improve 增進、改善

124. 副詞詞彙題remotely
中譯 在家上班的員工，可遠端存取公司文件，並下載所需的檔案。
單字 work from home 在家上班　access 連接、存取
remotely 遠端地、從遠處　absolutely 絕對地
seriously 嚴重地、認真地　predictably 可預見地

125. 填入介系詞＋詞彙題
解說 空格應填入適當的字詞，連接後方名詞當作受詞。選項中，只有介系詞片語 (A) ahead of 和 (C) along with 可以連接名

詞。根據文意，表示「在入職前」較為適當，因此答案為 (A)，意思為「在⋯之前」。
中譯 人力資源部經理分發員工手冊給新員工，以便他們在入職前幾天閱讀。
單字 dispatch 發送、分發　new hire 新進員工
along with 與⋯一起

126. 介系詞詞彙題rather than
中譯 許多新企業主並非自己設計發票，而是偏好使用模板。
單字 rather than 而不是⋯　prefer 偏好　in light of 考量⋯
among （三者以上）當中　into 在⋯裡面

127. 填入副詞
解說 空格前方為介系詞，後方連接形容詞加上名詞，表示空格要填入適合修飾形容詞的字詞，因此答案為副詞 (C) considerably。
中譯 如果貨物透過海運而非空運，顧客可用相當低廉的價格把包裹寄往海外。
單字 overseas 往海外、在海外　considerably 相當地

128. 片語動詞pour in
中譯 當新平板電腦的折扣碼不小心外洩至網路上後，訂單大量湧入。
單字 accidentally 不小心、偶然地、意外地　leak 洩漏、流出
pour in 大量湧入、大量投入　get along 相處融洽
carry out 執行、實施　settle up 結算

129. 連接詞詞彙題now that
解說 空格後方連接一個結構完整的子句，表示空格應填入連接詞。(D) because of 為介系詞片語，因此不適合作為答案。
中譯 由於繁忙的旅遊季已結束，當地居民遇到的交通延誤減少了。
單字 local resident 當地居民　traffic delay 交通延誤
now that 由於⋯　so that 以便⋯　as though 好像⋯
because of 因為⋯

130. 主動詞單複數一致性＋時態
解說 主詞 an incorrect password 為單數，表示動詞也要用單數形態，才符合主動詞單複數的一致性。選項中的 (B) has been entered 和 (C) was entering 皆為單數形態，而空格後方並未連接受詞，且主詞 an incorrect password 為行為接受者，表示空格要填入被動語態「be ＋過去分詞」較為適當，因此答案選 (B)。
中譯 密碼輸入錯誤三次後，使用者將被系統鎖定。
單字 lock A out of B 鎖住 A 使其無法進入 B
incorrect 不正確的　enter 輸入、進入

113

131-134. 廣告

Romano影院特別優惠！

Romano影院為幫各位開始新的一年，提供超值入場優惠。從1月2日**至**1月19日，所有場次的票券均為買一送一。所有**分店**都適用此優惠，你可以根據需求多次使用。請注意，所有贈送票券均與**購買**票券同一場次。我們還有各種美味零食，供你在觀影期間享用。**請前往販賣處購買。**

單字 admission 入場費、入場許可　screening 放映（電影等）、審查、檢查　take advantage of 使用、利用…
note 關注、提及　a range of 各式各樣的

131. 介系詞詞彙題through
(A) onto 在…之上
(B) toward 朝向…
(C) within 在…範圍內
(D) through 在…期間

解說 through 意思為「在…期間」，如果是 A through B 則強調某種行動從 A 一直到 B 為止。

132. 名詞詞彙題location
(A) statuses 身分、資格、地位
(B) locations 分店、地點、位置
(C) directors 導演、高階主管、負責人
(D) exhibits 展示品

133. 現在分詞vs.過去分詞
解說 空格前方有定冠詞，後方連接名詞，表示空格要填入適合修飾後方名詞的字詞。選項中只有過去分詞 (B) purchased 和現在分詞 (D) purchasing 可修飾名詞。而修飾的名詞為 tickets，為「被人購買的」對象，與空格為被動關係，因此答案要選 (B)。

134. 句子插入題
(A) 近期將公布獎項提名。
(B) 請聯絡我們以應徵該職位。
(C) 請前往販賣處購買。
(D) 電影放映時間可能有所變動。

單字 award nomination 獎項提名　apply for 應徵…
stop by 順路前往　concession stand 販賣處　running time 放映時間　vary 變更、變化

135-138. 文章

Kenwyn海灘度假村計劃於下個月盛大開幕。該地點**將包括**寬敞的套房、三間內部餐廳、室內和室外泳池等設施供客人使用。

目前度假村所在的海灘有部分區域幾十年來一直處於閒置狀態。它以前是歸Capital房地產所有，該公司一直在努力尋找開發資金。**最終公司決定將其出售。**V&G投資公司收購了這片土地來建造一座度假村，並命名為Kenwyn海灘度假村。

建築師Oscar Strope設計了整個設施，充分利用美麗的環境和風景。從該地區其他度假村看來，Kenwyn海灘度假村可能會非常**受歡迎**。

單字 grand opening 盛大開幕、開業　spacious 寬敞的、廣闊的　suite 套房、高級房　on-site 就地的　previously 以前、事前　struggle 努力奮鬥　funding 資金　procure 取得、獲得　property 房地產、建築　architect 建築師　facility 設施　based on 以…為根據

135. 主動語態
解說 空格後方連接受詞，表示空格要填入主動語態，因此答案為 (A) will include。

136. 句子插入題
(A) 其他地點仍可供出售。
(B) 最終公司決定將其出售。
(C) 旅遊旺季持續整個夏天。
(D) 業主在該領域擁有豐富的經驗。

單字 run 持續（特定期間）　throughout 貫穿、遍佈

137. 填入名詞+詞彙題
解說 空格前方為對等連接詞 and，表示空格要填入與 setting 相同的詞性，且當作介系詞 of 的受詞。選項中的名詞為 (A) scenery 和 (D) scenario，根據文意，表示「充分利用美麗的環境和風景設計了度假村設施」較為適當，因此答案為 (A)，意思為「風景、景致」。

單字 scenario 情節、劇本

138. 形容詞詞彙題popular
(A) definite 確實的、明確的
(B) general 一般的、普通的
(C) heavy 沉重的
(D) popular 有名的、受歡迎的

139-142. 電子郵件

收件者：行銷部員工 <marketing@camdensales.com>
寄件者：Richard Hayes <rhayes@camdensales.com>
日期：6月18日
主旨：網站
附件：新配色方案

親愛的行銷部人員，

請參閱附件檔案，當中**簡略說明了**我們網站新配色方案的選擇。更新後的**設計**將展現Camden銷售公司更現代的形象。**此外，還會吸引更多年輕顧客。**

希望你仔細考慮這些選項。請你在星期四下班前，發送電子郵件給我，告知哪種配色方案最好。**否則**，你的意見將不納入考量。

謝謝各位。
Richard Hayes

單字 color scheme 配色　option 選擇（權）
look over （大略）瀏覽
take ~ into consideration 把…納入考量

139. 主動詞單複數一致性＋時態
解說 空格後方連接受詞，表示空格要填入主動語態，答案有可能是 (B) outline 或 (C) outlines。而形容詞子句的動詞與先行詞要符合單複數一致性，因此答案為單數動詞 (C)。

單字 outline （簡略）說明

140. 名詞詞彙題design
(A) schedule 時間表
(B) label 商標、標籤
(C) policy 政策、方針
(D) design 設計

141. 句子插入題
(A) 此外，還會吸引更多年輕顧客。
(B) 大多數人認為該軟體易於使用。
(C) 值得慶幸的是，上個月銷售額有大幅改善。
(D) 未來我會向你推薦類似項目。

單字 attract 吸引　a great number of 大量的
fortunately 值得慶幸的是
significantly 顯著地、有意義地、重要地

142. 連接副詞詞彙題otherwise
(A) To that end 為…起見
(B) Otherwise 否則、除此之外
(C) In contrast 相反、相比之下
(D) Similarly 同樣地、類似地

143-146. 文章

鞋類製造商League Footwears今日證實已**收購**EG Sports。League Footwears代表Nathan Dale表示：「EG Sports以其時尚的運動鞋而聞名，多年來在市場上取得的成功**令人印象深刻**，我們很榮幸能將其帶入League Footwears大家族」。

Dale先生解釋道：「我們知道顧客十分信賴我們高品質的材料，以確保鞋子的舒適度和性能。所有透過我們公司銷售的EG Sports產品，都將遵循同樣的高標準。**因此，顧客可以安心購買**」。

單字 manufacturer 製造商、製造業者　confirm 確認、確定　athletic shoes 運動鞋　demonstrate 證明、展示　representative 代表　ensure 保證、肯定　comfort 舒適、安逸、安慰　performance （機器、車輛等的）性能、表演

143. 動詞詞彙題acquire
(A) advised 建議
(B) acquired 收購、獲得
(C) consented 同意
(D) sustained 持續

144. 填入形容詞＋詞彙題
解說 空格前方為動詞，後方連接名詞片語，表示空格要填入適合修飾名詞的字詞。選項中的形容詞 (C) impressive 和過去分詞 (D) impressed 皆可修飾名詞，而根據文意，表示「展現了令人印象深刻的成功」較為適當，因此答案為 (C)。impressed 的意思為「使人印象深刻的、使人感動的」，主詞需為人，因此不適合作為答案。

145. 片語動詞的介系詞
解說 空格前方為動詞 rely，表示空格要填入適合一起使用的介系詞，因此答案為 (C) on。rely on 的意思為「信賴、相信…」。

146. 句子插入題
(A) 因此，顧客可以安心購買。
(B) 有多種尺寸可供選擇。
(C) 在網路上可找到更多關於比賽的資訊。
(D) 因此，各零售商店的營業時間並不相同。

單字 with confidence 安心地、有自信地　a range of 多樣的
competition 比賽、競爭對手　therefore 因此
retail store 零售商店

147-148. 電子郵件

收件者：Simon Ethridge <sethridge@kessladata.com>
寄件者：Christy Lansing <clansing@kessladata.com>
日期：7月28日
主旨：信函

親愛的Ethridge先生，

此封信為確認我已收到您7月26日的來信。

我已通知所有團隊，您最後的工作日為8月11日。資訊部門將會處理您所擁有的公司設備，因此請在最後工作日前撥打分機號碼25，以進行必要的安排。我們感謝您對Kessla Data的貢獻。

祝一切順利，
Christy Lansing

單字 inform 告知、通知　handle 處理、對待
equipment 設備、道具　extension 分機號碼、延長、擴大
make an arrangement 安排　appreciate 感激、認可、欣賞
contribution 貢獻、捐獻、（報章雜誌的）投稿

147. Lansing女士為何發送電子郵件？
(A) 確認業務結束
(B) 更新銀行記錄
(C) 確認離職
(D) 提供升遷機會

解說 主旨或目的
第一句話顯示該封電子郵件為Lansing女士針對Ethridge先生來信的回覆。而後提到Ethridge先生最後的工作日，表示她接受Ethridge先生提出離職，並告知後續程序，因此答案為(C)。

單字 closure 結束　acknowledge 承認、表達謝意
resignation 離職、辭呈　promotion 升遷、晉級、宣傳、促銷

148. Ethridge先生應在8月11日前做什麼事？
(A) 填寫表格
(B) 與Lansing女士見面
(C) 聯絡資訊部門
(D) 帶走他的個人物品

解說 相關細節
8月11日為Ethridge先生最後的工作日，郵件中告知他須在這天之前打電話聯絡資訊部門，因此答案為(C)。

單字 remove 移除

149-150. 公告

8月22日星期二，Despard自來水公司的作業小組將開始更換該地區的下水道管線。在施工期間，Florence街將會暫時封閉，這意味著在此期間將無法進入Livonia停車場的入口。計畫在8月22日上午8點至8月23日下午4點間開車的居民，應在工程開始前將車輛停放在附近街道上。對於可能造成的任何不便，我們深感抱歉。

單字 crew 團隊、小組　replace 更換、替換
sewer line 下水道管線　temporarily 暫時地、臨時地
carry out 執行、實施　entrance 入口　parking lot 停車場
inaccessible 無法進入的　resident 居民
inconvenience 不便

149. 該公告是針對誰發布的？
(A) 市府官員
(B) 大樓住戶
(C) 建築工人
(D) 房地產開發商

解說 相關細節
因為下水道管線施工，告知施工期間大樓停車場入口會暫時封閉，請有開車的居民把車子停到鄰近道路上，表示該公告針對的對象為大樓住戶，因此答案為(B)。

單字 tenant 住戶、租戶

150. 根據公告，8月23日下午4點會發生什麼事？
(A) 將關閉停車場入口。
(B) 將鋪設街道。
(C) 將重新開放道路通行。
(D) 作業小組將評估專案項目。

解說 相關細節
暫時封閉Florence街的時間為8月22日上午8點至8月23日下午4點之間，表示8月23日下午4點後將會重新開放道路通行，因此答案為(C)。

單字 pave 鋪設（道路）　assess 評估

151-152. 電子郵件

收件者：Rebekah Ingram <ringram@rivendalesales.com>
寄件者：Montoya Fashions <customerservice@montoyafashions.com>
日期：11月18日
主旨：退貨要求

親愛的Ingram女士，
我們已收到您退回的產品，如下所示：

產品描述：Fieldcrest喀什米爾羊毛衣，深灰色，M號
產品編號：748592
購買價格：125美元

我們正在處理您的退款，將於五個工作日內退還至您購買時使用的信用卡。請注意，如果您有獲得任何Montoya時裝店的點數回饋，這些點數將於30天內從您的帳戶中扣除。

另外，不要錯過我們全新的派對禮服系列，現正特價49.99美元，正好可趕上假期！點選此處瀏覽目錄。

Montoya時裝店客戶服務團隊 敬上

單字 return 退還、退貨　request 要求、請求
process 處理、加工　award 回饋（金）　deduct 扣除
just in time for 正好趕上、正好符合…時期　browse 瀏覽

151. 電子郵件的其中一個目的為何？
(A) 宣傳一些新產品
(B) 確認已付款完成
(C) 說明如何登入帳戶
(D) 索取信用卡資訊

解說　**主旨或目的**
電子郵件開頭寫道已收到對方退回的產品，並說明退款流程，後半段宣傳自家新產品，因此答案為 (A)。

單字　promote 宣傳、升遷　confirm 確認、證實
sign into an account 登入帳戶

152. 關於Montoya時裝店，文中提到什麼？
(A) 接受30天內退貨。
(B) 提供顧客回饋計劃。
(C) 退貨時僅退還成商店抵用金。
(D) 銷售家居用品。

解說　**推論或暗示**
郵件中提到如果對方有獲得任何點數回饋，將於30天內從帳戶中扣除，表示在Montoya時裝店購買產品時，會提供點數回饋，因此答案為 (B)。

單字　loyalty program 顧客消費時提供點數或其他回饋的制度
give store credit 提供商店抵用金（代替退款）

153-154. 文字簡訊

> Albert Cotter（上午9點52分）嗨，Ella，你今天有什麼緊急的專案嗎？
>
> Ella Bohn（上午9點53分）沒有。為什麼會這麼問？
>
> Albert Cotter（上午9點54分）**Betsy和我下午四點要開會討論即將到來的實習計劃。既然已經確定錄取人選，我們需要為他們安排第一週的入職研討會。**
>
> Ella Bohn（上午9點55分）我可以幫忙。**我們五點前會結束，對吧？**
>
> Albert Cotter（上午9點56分）正是如此，我不希望有人工作到很晚。

單字　urgent 緊急　upcoming 即將到來、即將來臨的
now that 既然　candidate 應徵者、候選人
finalize 最終確定、結束　wrap up 完成、結束

153. Cotter先生今天為何要參加會議？
(A) 審核實習申請書
(B) 制定培訓計畫
(C) 進行團體面試
(D) 撰寫職務說明

解說　**相關細節**
Cotter 於上午 9 點 54 分表示他和 Betsy 下午四點要開會討論實習計畫。並提到為安排第一週的入職研討會，需要制定培訓計畫，因此答案為 (B)。

換句話說　develop the orientation workshops → create a training program

單字　application 履歷表、申請書、適用
conduct 執行、指揮（特定活動）　job description 職務說明

154. 上午9點56分，Cotter先生寫道：「Precisely」，最有可能是什麼意思？
(A) 會議將於下午5點結束
(B) 會議將有五人參加。
(C) 需要準備五份文件。
(D) 有些員工已經開會第五次了。

解說　**掌握意圖**
Ella Bohn 於上午 9 點 55 分確認會議是否於五點前結束，而後 Cotter 先生回覆：「Precisely」。該句話可用來表示同意對方所說的話。由此可知 Cotter 先生同意 Ella Bohn 所說的話，因此答案為 (A)。

單字　attendee 出席者

155-157 報導

> Carson's自行車店仍在營業
>
> 費城（10月30日）— Carson's自行車店是一間自行車修理店兼自行車零件零售商，目前正在慶祝成立25週年。該公司是由Carson Reese創辦，騎自行車是他的興趣，所以他自學如何修理自行車。他找來他的兄弟David Reese來處理會計方面的事務，生意也穩定成長。
>
> 該公司提供低價維修服務，主要透過銷售自行車零件和配件來賺取收入。經過一段時間，這種方法幫助該店建立了忠實的顧客群。隨著需求的增長，店內增聘了更多自行車技工，並增加了新服務。五年前，它在Willow Grove開設了第二間分店，而位於Trenton的第三間分店則於去年春天開業。Carson's自行車店透過在費城安排自行車比賽，並向體育相關慈善機構捐款，繼續為自行車社群做出貢獻。

單字　part 零件　celebrate 紀念　found 創辦
accounting 會計　steadily 穩定地、逐漸地
make money 賺錢　approach （處理）方法
build up 建立⋯　loyal customer base 忠實的顧客群
demand 需要、需求　mechanic 技工
branch 分店、分公司　contribute to 對⋯貢獻
arrange 安排、籌備　make a donation 捐款
charity 慈善（團體）

155. 這篇文章的主旨是什麼？
(A) 新發明的成功
(B) 自行車產業的發展趨勢
(C) 店鋪搬遷
(D) 一間企業的歷史

解說　**主旨或目的**
本文針對 Carson's 自行車店逐一說明其創辦人、創辦相關背景、公司發展、目前對社會的貢獻等，因此答案為 (D)。

單字　relocation 搬遷

117

156. 第二段第4行中的「approach」一詞意思最接近何者？
(A) 移動、動作
(B) 接近、存取
(C) 到達
(D) 策略、計畫

解說　找出同義詞
approach 所在的句子為「This approach helped the shop build up a loyal customer base」，意思為「這種方法幫助該店建立了忠實的顧客群」。當中的 approach 表示「方式」之意，因此答案為 (D)。(B) access 指的是為了進入而接近，偏向「進入的權限」，因此不適合作為答案。以例句比較兩者有助於理解差異：「have access to the company files（擁有存取公司文件的權限）」和「adopt a new approach to the problem（對該問題採取新的方式處理）」。

157. 關於Carson's自行車店，何者敘述正確？
(A) 設計自行車配件。
(B) 主辦體育比賽。
(C) 最近被出售。
(D) 公司創始於Willow Grove。

解說　事實與否
最後一句話提到 Carson's 自行車店在費城安排自行車比賽，因此答案為 (B)。

換句話說 arranging bicycle races → organizes athletic competitions

單字 organize 準備、整理、組織、構成　athletic 運動的　competition 比賽、競爭

158-160. 電子郵件

收件者：Shirley Amundson <s_amundson@suffolkltd.com>
寄件者：Romulus郵輪公司 <booking@romuluscruiselines.com>
日期：7月11日
主旨：那不勒斯郵輪

親愛的Amundson女士，

感謝您預訂Romulus郵輪公司9月20日從義大利那不勒斯啟程，並於9月27日回程的航線。

您的豪華客艙配有能隨選隨看電影的平面液晶電視、書桌、特大雙人床和私人陽台。郵輪上設有多個用餐區、音樂娛樂休息室和大禮堂。頂層甲板上設有游泳池、熱水浴池和迷你高爾夫球場。

您可以在港口停車場付費停車，但請注意該停車場不隸屬於Romulus郵輪公司。您也可以利用我們提供的免費接駁車，往返那不勒斯國際機場和港口。只需出示您郵輪票的確認電子郵件即可。

當您準備啟程之際，請注意有些物品禁止攜帶上船。欲查看物品清單，請造訪網站www.romuluscruislines.com/boarding。

祝您旅途愉快！

Michael Silva
Romulus郵輪公司

單字 book 預訂　depart 出發
on-demand films 讓消費者隨選隨看的影音服務
feature 以⋯為特色、特別展示　auditorium 禮堂
deck 甲板　hot tub 熱水浴池　for a fee 付費
be affiliated with 隸屬、與⋯相關　confirmation 確認
keep in mind 記住、牢記在心　on board 上船

158. 電子郵件的其中一個目的為何？
(A) 請客戶提供回饋
(B) 解說船上設施
(C) 通知出發日期變更
(D) 提供郵輪客艙升等

解說　主旨或目的
第二段中介紹豪華客艙的配備和船上各類設施，因此答案為 (B)。

單字 amenities 設施　departure 出發

159. Romulus郵輪的乘客享有什麼服務？
(A) 飛往那不勒斯航班的優惠
(B) 港口免費停車
(C) 免費接駁車服務
(D) 當地餐飲折抵券

解說　相關細節
文中提到只要持有郵輪票，便能使用往返那不勒斯國際機場和港口之間的免費接駁車，因此答案為 (C)。

單字 complimentary 免費的、附贈的
voucher 折抵券、禮券　local 當地的、地方的

160. 根據Silva先生所述，Amundson女士可以在網站上找到什麼？
(A) 未來預訂時可使用的優惠券
(B) 限制物品的資訊
(C) 過往旅程的照片
(D) 來自乘客的推薦文

解說　相關細節
最後一段提醒有些物品禁止攜帶上船，並補充可上網確認物品清單，因此答案為 (B)。

單字 restricted 限制的　previous 先前的
testimonial 推薦文、感謝狀

161-163. 信件

5月8日
Wendy Sanford
660 Rosewood Court
Brockport, NY 14420

親愛的Sanford女士，

我們想通知您，您的房屋保險單即將到期。請參閱下方的詳細資訊。重要的是您的房屋任何時候都要投保。您應在當前保單到期前制定新的保單。否則，您的房屋和財務可能會面臨風險。

保單類型：基本型住宅和財產保單
保單號碼：374109
到期日期：6月4日

我們的費用為基本型住宅保單160美元、高級型住宅保單180美元、**基本型住宅和財產保單205美元**、高級型住宅和財產保單225美元。自您去年購買當前保單以來，保費並未變動。

如要更新您的保單，僅需上www.trustedinsuranceinc.com/renew，輸入您的保單號碼，然後按照螢幕上的指示進行操作。整個過程不超過10分鐘。

祝 安好

Manuel Shapiro
客戶服務代理 Trusted保險公司

單字 home insurance policy 房屋保險　expire 到期
property 房產、建築、財產、所有物　insure 投保
at all times 始終　policy 保險單、政策　in place 準備好的
expiration 到期、屆期　current 目前的、現在的
rate 費用、比例　purchase 買、購買、所購之物
renew 更新、延長　instructions 指示、說明

161. 為何要寫這封信？
(A) 確認客戶聯絡方式
(B) 確認房屋價值
(C) 要求支付逾期款項
(D) 說明保單狀態

解說 主旨或目的
第一句便為通知對方的房屋保險單即將到期，提醒對方要更新，因此答案為 (D)。

單字 overdue （付款、歸還等）過期　payment 支付

162. Sanford女士去年最有可能付了多少錢？
(A) 160美元
(B) 180美元
(C) 205美元
(D) 225美元

解說 推論或暗示
Sanford女士投保的是基本型住宅和財產保單，目前保費為205美元，信中提到自Sanford女士去年投保以來，保費並未變動。由此可以推測Sanford女士去年投保時支付相同的費用，為205美元，因此答案為 (C)。

163. [1]、[2]、[3]和[4]當中，何處最適合填入下方句子？
「否則，您的房屋和財務可能會面臨風險。」
(A) [1]
(B) [2]
(C) [3]
(D) [4]

解說 句子插入題
題目提供的句子為「否則，您的房屋和財務可能會面臨風險」，前方應強調房屋保險的重要性或勸說對方投保。[2] 前方便是強調為房屋投保的重要性，並提醒對方應在到期前制定新保單，題目提供的句子置於 [2] 後方最為通順，因此答案為 (B)。

單字 finances 資金、資本　at risk 面臨風險

164-167 線上聊天

Helen Snyder（上午9點24分）嗨，Lee和Aubrey。年終頒獎晚宴的主持人已經確定了嗎？我想確保計劃進展一切順利。

Lee Roth（上午9點25分）是的，**將由Adele Ruiz和Craig Jacobson擔任今年的主持人。**

Helen Snyder（上午9點26分）太好了！晚宴的用餐部分，我們會安排他們坐在舞台附近嗎？

Lee Roth（上午9點27分）是的，主持人會坐在前排。我們很可能會再次使用Glendale大廳，但我還在等Daubert飯店的Tina Vance提供報價。

Aubrey Lujan（上午9點29分）實際上還有一個人。**Bonnie Nelson也會上台。**

Lee Roth（上午9點30分）啊，對。我差點忘了。事情進展得太快了。

Helen Snyder（上午9點31分）**Bonnie Nelson？我以為只有高階主管才會頒獎。**

Aubrey Lujan（上午9點32分）董事會成員今年密切參與了得獎者的評選，所以我們認為他們應該也要派代表參加。

Helen Snyder（上午9點33分）很有道理。**Lee，請聯絡所有上台者，詢問他們何時有空參加電話會議。**

單字 presenter 頒獎者、主持人　awards banquet 頒獎晚宴
be on track 進展順利　portion 部分　quote 報價
take the stage 登上舞台
executive staff member 主管、幹部
give out 分發　board member 董事會
be involved in 和…有關　closely 密切地、緊密地
represent 代表、展示、表示　make sense 合理
conference call 電話會議

164. 將由誰頒發獎項？
(A) Snyder女士
(B) Roth先生
(C) Jacobson先生
(D) Vance女士

解說 相關細節
Lee Roth 於上午 9 點 25 分表示將由 Adele Ruiz 和 Craig Jacobson 擔任今年的主持人，因此答案為 (C)。

165. 上午9點29分，Lujan女士寫道：「實際上還有一個人」最有可能是什麼意思？
(A) 創建了新的獎項。
(B) 活動包含第三位主持人。
(C) 仍可使用另一個場地。
(D) Roth先生被指派了新任務。

解說 掌握意圖
該句話前方討論與主持人有關的話題，而後 Lujan 女士補充「實際上還有一個人」，接著又提到：「Bonnie Nelson 也會上台」，表示主持人不只兩人，而是三個人，因此答案為 (B)。

單字 venue 場地　assign 指派、負責

166. Nelson女士最有可能是誰？
(A) 獎項候選人
(B) 企業主管
(C) 董事會成員
(D) 部門負責人

解說 推論或暗示
Lujan 女士於上午 9 點 29 分表示還有一個人也會上台。而後 Snyder 女士回應她以為只有高階主管才會頒獎。接著 Lujan 女士提到董事會成員今年密切參與了得獎者的評選，所以應要派代表參加。綜合上述，可以得知 Bonnie Nelson 為董事會成員之一，因此答案為 (C)。

167. Snyder女士要求Roth先生做什麼？
(A) 確認上台者是否有空
(B) 盡快確定活動場地
(C) 印出得獎者名單
(D) 轉發邀請函

解說 相關細節
Snyder 女士於上午 9 點 33 分請 Lee（也就是 Roth 先生）聯絡所有需要上台頒獎或主持的人，詢問他們何時有空參加電話會議，因此答案為 (A)。

換句話說 ask when they are free → Find out the presenters' availability

單字 availability 有空的、可利用性　finalize 最後確定　forward 轉發

168-171. 徵才公告

> 誠徵程式設計師
> Lynn能源顧問公司
> 休士頓，德克薩斯州
>
> 為開發一款用於追蹤和報告能源使用情況的智慧型手機應用程式，Lynn能源顧問公司現有多個程式設計師的職缺。
>
> **Lynn能源顧問公司已連續三年被評為業界最值得信賴的顧問公司。無需具備相關經驗，對應屆畢業生來說將是個理想職位。**應徵者應熟悉各種軟體開發工具，並對資料保護程序有深入了解。該職位需每天建立和歸檔報告，**因此必須具備完成任務的能力，同時注重極小的細節。**你將在一個由五人組成的小團隊中工作。
>
> 如欲應徵，請發送求職信和履歷表至 hr@lynnenergyadvisors.com。**我們希望盡快確定上班日期。**然而，我們也願意等待合適的人選。欲了解完整職務說明，請造訪www.lynnenergyadvisors.com。

單字 consecutive 連續的
be familiar with 對…感到熟悉　procedure 程序
involve 有所關聯　daily 每日　complete 完成、結束
demonstrate 展現、證明　cover letter 求職信
résumé 履歷表　job description 職務說明

168. 關於Lynn能源顧問公司，文中提到什麼？
(A) 具有良好的聲響。
(B) 已歸屬新所有權人。
(C) 將搬遷至休士頓。
(D) 提供有競爭力的薪資。

解說 推論或暗示
文中提到 Lynn 能源顧問公司已連續三年被評為業界最值得信賴的顧問公司，因此答案為 (A)。

單字 reputation 名聲、聲響　ownership 所有（權）
relocate 搬遷　competitive 有競爭力的、競爭的

169. 關於職缺，文中指出什麼？
(A) 專門設給初階程式設計師。
(B) 提供很多升遷機會。
(C) 需對應徵者進行背景調查。
(D) 涉及維持能源生產。

解說 事實與否
文中提到該職位無需具備相關經驗，對應屆畢業生來說將是個理想職位，因此答案為 (A)。

單字 be intended for 以…為對象
entry-level 入門的、（公司、組織等）初階的
background check 背景調查　applicant 應徵者
maintain 維持（關係、狀態、程度等）

120

170. 針對工作要求,文中指出什麼?
(A) 管理小型團隊
(B) 注重細節
(C) 回答軟體相關問題
(D) 檢查同事的報告

解說 事實與否
文中提到要具備完成任務的能力,同時注意到極小的細節,因此答案為 (B)。

換句話說 demonstrating care for even the smallest detail → Paying attention to detail

單字 respond 回答、回應

171. [1]、[2]、[3]和[4]當中,何處最適合填入下方句子?
「然而,我們也願意等待合適的人選。」
(A) [1]
(B) [2]
(C) [3]
(D) [4]

解說 句子插入題
題目提供的句子中出現「However(然而)」表示轉折,與前方句子應為相對關係。題目句寫道「然而,我們也願意等待合適的人選」,與其為相對關係的是 [4] 前方的句子:「我們希望盡快確定上班日期」,因此句子適合填入 [4],答案要選 (D)。

單字 be willing to do 願意做⋯　candidate 人選、應徵者

172-175. 公告

> Orland市 提案要求
>
> 摘要
>
> 針對用於整個市中心的數位停車收費儀器,Orland市正在受理來自製造商的提案,提案書應於8月18日前提供。
>
> 目的
>
> 該市老舊的投幣式收費機已不能再滿足社區需求,將被數位停車收費儀器取代。除了使支付過程更加方便外,這些收費儀器接受各種信用卡和手機行動支付應用程式付款,儀器還將省下市府工作人員檢查和清空收費機的成本。對於駕駛人來說,成本也較低,因為收費儀器可以感應車輛何時離開停車位,僅按照實際使用時間收費,而不會多收。已安裝數位停車收費儀器的城市,也獲得來自外地遊客更多的正面評價。這歸功於收費儀器的使用者介面簡單直觀,更易於使用。
>
> 詳細規格
>
> 製造商應提供1800台適合戶外使用的數位停車收費儀器。它們必須能夠全天候監控,並上傳即時數據至交通運輸局辦公室。無論處於任何照明條件下,收費儀器的觸碰螢幕應清楚顯示文字。
>
> 如欲繳交提案,請於2月3日前將您的投標書發送至Jason Bahr的電子信箱 j.bahr@orland.gov。請上網站www.orland.gov/project0894 查詢提交過程中所需的文件清單。

單字 proposal 提案(書)、提議
submission 繳交、提交
manufacturer 製造商、製造業者
parking meter 停車收費儀器　throughout 遍及⋯
outdated 老舊的、過時的　meet one's needs 符合⋯的需求
in addition to 除了⋯之外　regarding 關於
personnel 人員、員工　vacate 空出(建築物、位置)
charge 索取、加值(費用等)　benefit from 得益於⋯
intuitive 直觀的、易於使用、直覺的　specifics 詳細規格
suitable for 適合⋯　be capable of 能夠⋯
round-the-clock 連續24小時的
transportation 交通、運輸、輸送　lighting 照明
bid 投標　no later than 不遲於⋯

172. 公告的目的為何?
(A) 介紹公共停車罰款
(B) 描述城市對於停車的需求
(C) 說明停車費用的變化
(D) 鼓勵企業投標

解說 主旨或目的
本篇公告的標題為「提案要求」,並於摘要中提到 Orland 市正在受理製造商的提案書,因此答案為 (D)。

單字 fine 罰款　encourage 鼓勵

173. 關於停車收費儀器的益處,文中並未提及哪一點?
(A) 駕駛人能更容易找到車位。
(B) 可以使用多種付款方式。
(C) 將會減少人事成本。
(D) 不會向儀器使用者多收取費用。

解說 事實與否
文中並未提到駕駛人能更容易找到車位,因此答案為 (A)。

換句話說 (C) cut costs regarding city personnel → will be a reduction in staffing costs

單字 parking spot 停車位　a variety of 各式各樣的
reduction 減少、削減　staffing costs 人事成本
overcharge 超收費用

174. 其他開始使用數位儀器的城市發生了什麼事?
(A) 他們獲得更多遊客好評。
(B) 他們減少了市中心交通堵塞的情況。
(C) 他們為交通專案籌到更多資金。
(D) 他們增加了該地區主要製造商的數量。

解說 相關細節
文中提到已安裝數位停車收費儀器的城市,從外地遊客那裡獲得更多正面評價,因此答案為 (A)。

換句話說 have benefitted from a greater number of positive reviews from out-of-town visitors → received more favorable reviews from tourists

單字 favorable 有利的、贊同的
traffic congestion 交通堵塞

121

175. 關於提案的儀器有什麼規定？
(A) 它們必須與目前使用的儀器尺寸相同。
(B) 他們應具備電池備份系統。
(C) 他們必須把資訊發送到特定地點。
(D) 它們應在國內製造。

解說 事實與否
文中提到數位停車收費儀器需上傳即時數據至交通運輸局辦公室，因此答案為 (C)。

換句話說 uploading real-time data feeds to the transportation office → must send information to a certain location

單字 backup 備份、備用（品）　location 地點、位置
domestically 在國內

176-180. 網頁與電子郵件

Spark租賃能以價格合理的租借服務幫您省錢—只租不買，僅需支付成本的一小部分！我們所有出租的物品都經仔細檢查，以確保最佳性能。**請注意，我們不再提供送貨選項，因此您必須做好親自取貨和歸還物品的準備。**

搜尋字詞：

地毯清潔設備

兩項結果：

	24小時	週末
Viko 節能地毯清洗機（1.6公升水箱）	29.99英鎊	65.99英鎊
Viko 標準地毯清洗機（3.8公升水箱）	39.99英鎊	85.99英鎊

單字 affordable 價格合理的
a fraction of the cost 小部分費用
thoroughly 仔細地、徹底地　ensure 保障、確保
optimum 最佳的　performance （機器、車輛等）性能
pick up 收取、接送　drop off 放回　in person 親自
search term 搜尋字詞

收件者：Lucas Soltis <lsoltis@duvallinc.co.uk>
寄件者：Isabelle Guthrie <guthrie_i@roxtonfinance.com>
日期：3月4日
主旨：地毯清洗機

嗨，Lucas，

你之前提過將進行一次全面的居家清潔，為親戚來訪做準備。我也有一些清潔工作要做，所以我決定租用一台專業級地毯清洗機。**離我最近，有提供此項服務的公司是Spark租**賃，位於Ancaster，距離約半小時車程。**我打算在這週末租用它，星期五早上取件，星期一早上歸還。我選擇的是水箱較大的設備，但仍放得進我的車內，所以我不需要卡車來運送它。**

你想在週末使用清洗機嗎？我預計在星期六上午稍晚時，完成我家的清掃工作。接著你可以在週末其餘時間使用，**如此我們可以共同分擔費用，減少花費**。我知道這項通知很臨時，所以如果你沒辦法也無妨。請告訴我你的想法，我打算在明天結束前上網預約並付款。

再聯絡，
Isabelle

單字 relative 親戚　professional-grade 專業級的
device 設備、裝置　fit in 對⋯⋯合適　transport 運送、運輸
short notice 臨時通知　work for 對⋯⋯行得通

176. 關於Spark租賃，網頁中提到什麼？
(A) 以前曾配送設備給客戶。
(B) 為企業提供折扣。
(C) 提出特殊要求後可取得新設備。
(D) 部分設備使用後售出。

解說 推論或暗示
網頁中提到不再提供送貨選項，表示以前有提供配送服務，因此答案為 (A)。

單字 acquire 獲得、取得

177. Guthrie女士的電子郵件目的為何？
(A) 更改專案日期
(B) 推薦清潔產品
(C) 提供省錢的機會
(D) 邀請Soltis先生造訪

解說 主旨或目的
郵件中提到自己打算在週末租用地毯清洗機，提議與對方共同分擔費用，減少花費，因此答案為 (C)。

178. 在電子郵件中，第二段第3行「appreciate」一詞的意思最接近何者？
(A) 評估
(B) 明白、理解
(C) 感謝
(D) 享受

解說 找出同義詞
appreciate 所在的句子為「I appreciate that this is short notice」，意思為「我知道這項通知很臨時」，當中 appreciate 表示「知道」之意，因此答案為 (B)。

179. 關於Guthrie女士，電子郵件中提到什麼？
(A) 她將於平日前往Ancaster。
(B) 她每年都會清潔地毯。
(C) 她有一輛卡車。
(D) 她曾使用過Spark租賃的服務。

解說 **推論或暗示**
Guthrie 女士打算使用 Spark 租賃的租借服務，該間公司位於 Ancaster。郵件中她表示預計於星期五早上去取件，因此答案為 (A)。

180. Guthrie女士最有可能在Spark租賃的網站上支付多少錢？
(A) 29.99英鎊
(B) 39.99英鎊
(C) 65.99英鎊
(D) 85.99英鎊

解說 **雙篇文章整合題─推論或暗示**
第二篇文章中，Guthrie 女士表示她打算在週末租用地毯清洗機，選擇租的是水箱較大的設備。回到第一篇文章，週末租用容量較大的清洗機費用為 85.99 英鎊，因此答案為 (D)。

181-185. 報導與招聘公告

Beamont實驗室擴大研發團隊

布里斯本（8月3日）— Beamont實驗室是一家專門為國際品牌生產化妝品的公司，目前正在擴充其研發團隊的規模，以滿足客戶對於護髮產品的需求。**Beamont實驗室成立於18年前**，總部設於布里斯本，一直以來都是創新和環境責任的領導者。尤其在過去五年，促成了穩定成長。**本次是為坎培拉的實驗室進行人力擴充。**墨爾本和紐卡斯爾也有較小規模的研究站點。

新團隊將由Gemma Gabriel帶領，她從公司成立以來就一直都在，從初級研究員開始，逐漸升遷。她負責開發人氣產品Ordell，是一款專為敏感肌設計的洗髮精。Gabriel女士將全程監督招聘過程。

單字 expand 擴大、擴充　specialize in 專門從事⋯
cater to 滿足⋯　headquartered 總部設在⋯　found 成立
innovation 創新　environmental 環境的
responsibility 責任　steady 穩定地、持續地
expansion 擴充　work one's way up ⋯晉升至
be in charge of 負責⋯　sensitive 敏感的、敏銳的
oversee 監督

Beamont實驗室人才招聘
職稱：化妝品資深研究員
刊登日：8月10日
應徵截止日：9月15日

成為我們不斷擴大研發團隊的重要一員。

主要職責：
● 設計各種專案的產品開發計劃
● 開發、分析和測試樣品
● 持續了解實驗室技術的發展
● 採購所有實驗室使用的相關設備和材料
● 為未來的生產製作準確的成本估算

需具備化學或相關專業的學位（碩士學位優先）。**面試時間為10月20日至11月1日**。**到職日為11月22日**。

單字 job opening 招聘公告　senior 資深的　post 刊登
integral 不可或缺的　analyze 分析
advancement 發展、進步　source （從特定的地方）獲取
relevant 相關的、有關的　accurate 準確的、精確的
cost estimate 成本估算

181. 關於Gabriel女士，文中指出什麼？
(A) 她打算搬到布里斯本工作。
(B) 她五年前升遷至目前職位。
(C) 她在Beamont實驗室工作了18年。
(D) 她很快會從Beamont實驗室退休。

解說 **事實與否**
第一篇文章中提到 Gemma Gabriel 從公司成立以來就一直在公司工作，且前方有提到 Beamont 實驗室成立於 18 年前，因此答案為 (C)。

單字 relocate 搬遷　promote 升遷、宣傳

182. 關於Ordell，文中提到了什麼？
(A) 為公司最暢銷的產品。
(B) 由天然成分製成。
(C) 可作為護膚乳液。
(D) 為一種頭髮養護產品。

解說 **事實與否**
第一篇文章最後提到 Ordell 是一款專為敏感肌群眾設計的洗髮精，因此答案為 (D)。文中僅提到 Ordell 為人氣產品，並沒有說是最暢銷產品，因此不能選 (A)。

單字 ingredient 材料、成分

183. 新的化妝品資深研究員最有可能在哪裡工作？
(A) 布里斯本
(B) 坎培拉
(C) 紐卡斯爾
(D) 墨爾本

解說 **雙篇文章整合題─推論或暗示**
第二篇文章為 Beamont 實驗室招募化妝品資深研究員的文章。回到第一篇文章，當中提到本次是為坎培拉的實驗室進行人力擴充，因此答案為 (B)。

184. 大約何時會選出錄取者？
(A) 8月
(B) 9月
(C) 10月
(D) 11月

解說 **推論或暗示**
第二篇文章提到面試時間至 11 月 1 日為止，且到職日為 11 月 22 日，表示會在 11 月選出錄取者，因此答案為 (D)。

185. 該職位的其中一項工作職責為何？
(A) 採購必要用品
(B) 傳授團隊成員技巧
(C) 檢查生產設施
(D) 與潛在客戶會見

123

解說 相關細節
第二篇文章中，主要職責其中一項為採購所有實驗室使用的相關設備和材料，因此答案為 (A)。

換句話說 Sourcing all relevant equipment and materials → Procuring necessary supplies

單字 procure 採購、取得　inspect 檢查、視察
prospective 潛在的、預期的、期待的、有希望的

186-190 電子郵件與課程時間表

收件者：社區藝術中心所有成員
寄件者：社區藝術中心
主旨：暑期藝術講座系列
日期：6月10日
附件：暑期藝術講座系列

親愛的社區藝術中心成員：

暑期藝術講座系列即將到來！請查看附件的時間表。今年我們邀請的都是新講師，**除了一位曾發表過數位時代藝術演講的講師，因應群眾的高需求，我們再次把他請來。**

請上www.commartscenter.org 訂購票券。請注意，我們最大的場館僅接受團體預訂（五人或以上）—**Rivas會議室可容納150人**和Mercier會議室可容納90人。

單字 nearly 幾乎　attached 附加的　except for 除了…
give a talk 演講　demand 需要、需求　venue 場地、場館
accommodate 容納

社區藝術中心 暑期藝術講座系列

講座名稱	講師	日期及時間	地點
光與水彩	Annie Cho	6月29日 下午7-9點	Chester 會議室
環保用品	Samuel Delgado	7月2日 下午1-3點	Barron 會議室
數位時代藝術	**Bianca Fallici**	7月8日 下午3-5點	Rivas 會議室
建築藝術	Hugo Beckham	7月25日 下午3-4點	Chester 會議室
未知的藝術史	Hai Feng	7月31日 下午6-8點	Mercier 會議室
混合繪畫創作	Yolanda Florez	8月4日 下午7-8點	Rivas 會議室

單字 watercolor 水彩畫、水彩顏料　eco-friendly 環保的
supplies 物品　undiscovered 尚未發現的
mixed media 混合繪畫法，綜合多種方法的繪畫技法

收件者：Gerard McCray <gerardmccray@commartscenter.org>
寄件者：Hai Feng <hfeng@hollowayinstitute.com>
日期：8月5日
主旨：謝謝你！

親愛的McCray先生，

感謝您邀請我在暑期藝術講座系列中演講。此次我有了很棒的經歷，希望日後能再次參與。我對本次活動場地印象深刻。儘管會議室看起來相當空曠，但那是因為空間實在太大了。**實際上，參加人數遠超出我的預期，所以我對此感到非常高興。**

此外，我特別想感謝Tony Sheridan，他在講座開始時，立即回應我提出的技術支援請求，並迅速解決了問題。萬幸的是，這表示我們只需晚15分鐘開始，而非取消講座。

致上最溫暖的問候
Hai Feng

單字 participate 參與　attendee 參與者　in addition 此外
grateful 感謝的　promptly 立即地、即時地
assistance 協助、支援　resolve 解決　issue 問題、議題
fortunately 幸運的是

186. 哪間教室可容納超過100人？
(A) The Barron會議室
(B) The Chester會議室
(C) The Mercier會議室
(D) The Rivas會議室

解說 相關細節
第一篇文章中寫道：「Rivas 會議室可容納150人」，因此答案為 (D)。

187. 誰曾在以前的活動中演講過？
(A) Cho女士
(B) Delgado先生
(C) Fallici女士
(D) Beckham先生

解說 雙篇文章整合題—相關細節
第一篇文章中提到今年邀請的都是新講師，除了一位發表過數位時代藝術演講的講師之外。而第二篇文章中，可確認數位時代藝術的講師為 Bianca Fallici，因此答案為 (C)。

188. Sheridan先生最有可能是誰？
(A) 技術人員
(B) 活動策劃者
(C) 研究員
(D) 場地所有者

解說 推論或暗示
第三篇文章提到 Tony Sheridan，感謝他立即回應關於技術支援的請求，並迅速解決問題。由此可知 Sheridan 先生從事與技術相關的工作，因此答案為 (A)。

124

189. 哪個講座的開始時間延遲？
(A) 環保用品
(B) 建築藝術
(C) 未知的藝術史
(D) 混合繪畫創作

解說　雙篇文章整合題—相關細節
第三篇文章為電子郵件，寄件者為 Hai Feng，他提到講座晚了 15 分鐘開始。回到第二篇文章，Hai Feng 主講的講座是「未知的藝術史」，因此答案為 (C)。

190. 關於Feng先生，文中提到什麼？
(A) 他曾和McCray先生一起工作。
(B) 他對出席人數感到滿意。
(C) 他希望有更大的教室。
(D) 他長途旅行來參加活動。

解說　推論或暗示
Feng 先生為第三篇文章（電子郵件）的寄件者，郵件中他表示參加人數遠超出他的預期，對此他感到非常高興，因此答案為 (B)。

換句話說　the number of attendees → the turnout

單字　turnout（活動等）參加人數

191-195. 網頁與電子郵件

樹木護理基金會（TCF）致力於確保林地區域樹木的健康。**我們志工在識別樹木疾病與害蟲方面發揮了重要作用，並查明它們在受影響區域中如何擴散。**這有助於我們採取措施控制疫情，並減少樹木損失。

關於志工服務：
- 透過線上填寫申請表，並進行簡短的電話面談來申請
- 參加培訓課程，學習你所需的技巧
- **在樹木護理基金會從事至少12個月的志工工作**，每月執行 2-3 次調查活動

單字　be dedicated to 致力於、奉獻於…
woodland 林地　volunteer 志工　essential 不可或缺的
identify 識別、確認　pest 害蟲
determine（用明確證據）判斷、查明　affect 影響
take measures 採取措施　outbreak 爆發、暴動
complete 完整填寫（書面資料）　brief 簡短的、（時間）短暫的
session（特定活動）期間　commit to 致力於（工作、活動等）
survey（問卷）調查

收件者：Aida Ferreira, Kevin Murray, Sharad Dhibar, Ruth Bryson
寄件者：Ashley Jackson <jacksona@treecarefoundation.org>
日期：3月5日
主旨：培訓課程

親愛的志工們，

我們很高興大家參與樹木護理基金會（TCF）的工作。多虧有像你們這樣的志工，**自從**七年前 Curtis Baxter 創立以來，我們的基金會已有大幅成長。

下一步是完成密集培訓課程。時間訂於 3 月 20 日星期六，上午 9 點至下午 4 點。地點將在 Aldredge 自然中心舉行，並供應午餐。**該培訓課程將由Baxter先生負責。**

完成初步培訓後，各位將在下一週由經驗豐富的成員監督，執行一次調查活動，如下方表格所示。

姓名	負責區域
Aida Ferreira	Wesley林地
Kevin Murray	Barnbrook森林
Sharad Dhibar	Malham森林
Ruth Bryson	**Denton國家保護區**

如有任何問題，請隨時告訴我
Ashley Jackson

單字　thanks to 多虧…　considerably 相當地
complete 完成、結束　intensive 密集的
take place 發生、舉辦　be in charge of 負責…
initial 初步的、初期的　supervise 監督
experienced 經驗豐富的、老練的　assign 指定、分配

收件者：Stanley Walton <s_walton@victoriamail.com>
寄件者：Ruth Bryson <ruth.bryson@gilbert-enterprises.com>
日期：3月23日
主旨：監督調查

親愛的Walton先生，

我很期待在本週五的監督調查活動上，與您本人見面。感謝您配合我的工作時間表，調整原本的開始時間。我打算開車前往現場，所以我會於下午2點在那裡與您會面。

我會攜帶在初步培訓課程中分發的所有裝備。然而，我想知道是否需要用某種方式包裝以保護它們。我只使用一個普通背包，所以**我不希望損壞任何脆弱的零件。**如有什麼特別需要我做的事，煩請告知。

謝謝您
Ruth Bryson

單字　look forward to 期待…　in person 親自
appreciate 感謝、認可、欣賞　adjust 調整
original 原本的、獨創的　accommodate 通融、給…方便
gear（特定活動所需的）裝備、服裝　distribute 分配、分發
wrap up 打包、包裝　fragile 易碎的、脆弱的
component 零件

191. TCF志工的主要職責為何？
(A) 為樹木專案籌措資金
(B) 在林地種植樹木
(C) 追蹤樹木疾病的傳播
(D) 修剪樹枝

解說 相關細節
第一篇文章中提到志工在識別樹木疾病與害蟲方面發揮了重要作用，並查明它們在受影響區域中如何擴散，因此答案為 (C)。

單字 funds 資金、基金　track 追蹤　spread 傳播、擴散　clear away 修剪、清除

192. 關於第一封電子郵件的收件人，文中提到什麼？
(A) 他們參加了團體面試。
(B) 他們將在TCF工作至少一年。
(C) 他們每週將完成兩到三項調查。
(D) 他們可選擇工作地點。

解說 雙篇文章整合題—推論或暗示
第一封電子郵件的收件者為 TCF 的所有志工。而第一篇文章（網頁）中提到志工需要在 TCF 從事至少 12 個月的志工工作，因此答案為 (B)。

單字 at least 至少

193. 關於3月20日的培訓活動，文中指出什麼？
(A) 由基金會創辦人主導。
(B) 活動持續約三小時。
(C) 在好幾個地點進行。
(D) 從下午開始。

解說 事實與否
第二篇文章提到 Curtis Baxter 創立基金會，後半段提到培訓課程將由 Baxter 先生負責，因此答案為 (A)。

單字 founder 創辦人、創立者　approximately 大約、大略　conduct 執行（特定活動）

194. Walton先生最可能在哪裡進行調查？
(A) 在Wesley林地
(B) 在Barnbrook森林
(C) 在Malham森林
(D) 在Denton國家保護區

解說 雙篇文章整合題—推論或暗示
Walton 先生為第二封電子郵件的收件者。該封郵件的寄件者為 Bryson 女士，她於開頭表示很期待於本週五的監督調查活動上，直接與對方見面。由此可知 Bryson 女士與 Walton 先生會一起進行調查活動。回到第二篇文章，Bryson 女士負責的區域為 Denton 國家保護區，因此答案為 (D)。

195. 在第二封電子郵件中，Bryson女士對什麼表示擔憂？
(A) 損壞部分設備
(B) 停車困難
(C) 尋找偏遠地點
(D) 購買合適設備

解說 相關細節
郵件中提到她會攜帶在初步培訓課程中分發的所有裝備，後方補充並不希望損壞任何脆弱的零件，因此答案為 (A)。

單字 damage 損壞　remote 遙遠的、遠端的

196-200. 電子郵件與網頁

收件者：Jeanette Patterson <jpatterson@charterhotel.com>
寄件者：Mason Emery <mason@emeryltd.com>
日期：4月19日
主旨：灑水系統

親愛的Patterson女士，

我很高興能為貴飯店推薦灑水系統和安裝公司。但為了盡可能滿足您的需求，我需要您回答以下問題：

1. 該系統僅用於草地，還是也包括花圃在內？
2. 該區域的人流量大嗎？固定不會彈起的永久灑水器價格較便宜，但可能有導致行人絆倒的危險。
3. 在接下來幾年，貴飯店是否有任何建築施工計劃？
4. 您需要多快將系統安裝到位？夏季為一年中最繁忙的時期，因為一旦地面結冰，便無法安裝系統。
5. 公司能否在貴飯店平日營業期間施工？部分挖掘設備可能造成干擾。然而，目前於週末工作的需求較高。

先感謝您提供這些額外資訊。
Mason Emery

單字 flower bed 花圃　permanent 永久的、常在的　pop up 彈起來　pose a hazard 造成危險　in place 準備好的、在適當的地方　dig 挖掘（土地）　disruptive 干擾的　in advance 事先、提前　additional 額外的

收件者：Mason Emery <mason@emeryltd.com>
寄件者：Jeanette Patterson <jpatterson@charterhotel.com>
日期：4月20日
主旨：RE:灑水系統

親愛的Emery先生，

Charter飯店Bridgeview分館的腹地完全被柵欄圍住。雖然我們有一些架高的花圃，但我們希望系統能用於我們的草坪區域。我們有一個鋪設的露台，所以多數客人會在那裡過戶外時光。小狗經常在草地上奔跑，但很少有客人使用它。

我們無法停止營業，因此施工人員可在一週中的任一天來訪。請注意，我們願意為高品質系統支付更多費用，並希望由經營較久的公司提供服務。

感謝您的協助
Jeanette Patterson

單字 fence in 用柵欄圍住　raised 比周邊高的、升高的　grassy 長滿草的　pave 鋪設（道路）　patio 露臺　shut down 停止營業　assistance 協助、支援

我們的網站用戶已選出每個地區的最佳灌水系統安裝商。下方為Bridgeview地區的結果。

公司名稱	專業領域	備註
灌溉解決方案公司	戶外灑水器	新開業；最快完成施工
草地醫生公司	戶外灑水器	去年開業；價格最低
Tyler景觀公司	所有類別	在當地經營20年
自來水系統灌水公司	室內消防安全	25年經驗；價格合理

單字 region 地區　specialization 專業領域　outdoor 戶外的　locally 本地、當地　indoor 室內的　reasonably priced 價格合理的

196. Emery先生最有可能在哪裡工作？
(A) 製造工廠
(B) 顧問公司
(C) 房地產開發公司
(D) 行銷公司

解說 推論或暗示
Emery 先生是第一封電子郵件的寄件者。該封郵件表示為滿足顧客需求，在推薦灌水系統和安裝公司前，需要對方回答一些問題。由此可知 Emery 先生從事諮詢業務，因此答案為 (B)。

197. 關於灌水系統，Emery先生提到什麼？
(A) 應由專業人員定期檢查。
(B) 必須在地面足夠溫暖時安裝。
(C) 可以連接城市的供水系統。
(D) 長遠看來，將為用戶省錢。

解說 推論或暗示
第一篇文章中提到一旦地面結冰，便無法安裝系統，因此答案為 (B)。

單字 inspect 檢查、視察　professional 專業人士　regularly 定期地、規律地　hook A up to B 把 A 連接至 B　in the long run 長遠看來

198. Patterson女士沒有回答Emery先生提出的哪個問題？
(A) 問題 1
(B) 問題 2
(C) 問題 3
(D) 問題 5

解說 雙篇文章整合題—相關細節
第二篇文章中，Patterson 女士逐一回答問題 1、問題 2 和問題 5，回答為適用於草坪區域、客人不會進入，以及施工人員可在一週中的任一天來訪。然而，並未回答問題 3：在接下來幾年，是否有任何建築施工計畫，因此答案為 (C)。

單字 address 說話、提及、演說、處理（問題）

199. 根據第二封電子郵件，關於Charter飯店何者敘述正確？
(A) 最近在Bridgeview開設了分館。
(B) 一年中部分時間關閉。
(C) 飯店允許攜帶寵物。
(D) 位於繁忙的道路附近。

解說 推論或暗示
第二封郵件中提到小狗經常在草地上奔跑，表示飯店允許寵物進入，因此答案為 (C)。

200. Emery先生可能會推薦哪家公司？
(A) 灌溉解決方案公司
(B) 草地醫生公司
(C) Tyler景觀公司
(D) 自來水系統灌水公司

解說 雙篇文章整合題—推論或暗示
第二篇文章中，Patterson 女士提出希望是一家經營較久的公司。而第三篇文章中，根據灌水系統安裝公司的清單，符合條件的是 Tyler 景觀公司和自來水系統灌水公司，但後者的專業為室內消防安全，不符合用於草地灌水系統的需求，因此答案選 (C)。

EZ TALK

New TOEIC 一本攻克新制多益聽力＋閱讀700+：
完全比照最新考題趨勢精準命題

| 作　　　者：Eduwill語學研究所
| 譯　　　者：關亭薇
| 主　　　編：潘亭軒
| 責任編輯：鄭雅方
| 封面設計：兒日設計
| 內頁排版：簡單瑛設
| 行銷企劃：張爾芸

發 行 人：洪祺祥
副總經理：洪偉傑
副總編輯：曹仲堯
法律顧問：建大法律事務所
財務顧問：高威會計師事務所

出　　版：日月文化出版股份有限公司
製　　作：EZ 叢書館
地　　址：臺北市信義路三段151號8樓
電　　話：(02)2708-5509
傳　　真：(02)2708-6157
網　　址：www.heliopolis.com.tw
郵撥帳號：19716071日月文化出版股份有限公司

總 經 銷：聯合發行股份有限公司
電　　話：(02)2917-8022
傳　　真：(02)2915-7212
印　　刷：中原造像股份有限公司
初　　版：2024年11月
定　　價：520元
I S B N：978-626-7516-46-1

New TOEIC 一本攻克新制多益聽力＋閱讀700+：完全比照最新考題趨勢精準命題 /Eduwill語學研究所著；關亭薇譯. -- 初版. -- 臺北市：日月文化出版股份有限公司, 2024.11
360 面； 19x25.7 公分. -- (EZ talk)
ISBN 978-626-7516-46-1(平裝)
1.CST: 多益測驗

Copyright © 2023 by Eduwill Language Institute
All rights reserved.
Traditional Chinese Copyright © 2024 by HELIOPOLIS CULTURE GROUP
This Traditional Chinese edition was published by arrangement with Eduwill through Agency Liang

◎版權所有 翻印必究
◎本書如有缺頁、破損、裝訂錯誤，請寄回本公司更換